Savior Complex

Sunset Bay, Book 3

Crissi Langwell

Cover & Interior Design: Crissi Langwell

Inside Images: Canva, Cattallina, vectortatu, MiniDoodle, Maksym Drozd

ISBN: 978-1-961240-05-6

Publisher: North Coast Stories
This book is also available in paperback and ebook.
Please visit the author's website to find out where to purchase this book.

www.crissilangwell.com

NORTH COAST
STORIES

I once had a thousand desires, but in my one desire to know

you, all else melted away.

~ Rumi

Books by Crissi Langwell

ROMANCE

Masquerade Mistake ~ Sunset Bay 1

Naked Coffee Guy ~ Sunset Bay 2

Savior Complex ~ Sunset Bay 3

For the Birds

Numbered

Come Here, Cupcake

OTHER BOOKS BY CRISSI LANGWELL

Loving the Wind: The Story of Tiger Lily & Peter Pan

The Road to Hope ~ Hope Series 1

Hope at the Crossroads ~ Hope Series 2

Hope for the Broken Girl ~ Hope Series 3

A Symphony of Cicadas ~ Forever After 1

Forever Thirteen ~ Forever After 2

www.crissilangwell.com

Sign up for Crissi Langwell's romance newsletter:
mailchi.mp/crissilangwell/romancereads

Dedicated to all my Practical Magic witches
who are ready to fall in love (or not).

Nina's Honky Tonk
Cheating Heart Playlist

Bad Decisions ~ Dylan Schneider

Last Night ~ Morgan Wallen

Truck on Fire ~ Carly Pearce

Big Blue Sky ~ Jackson Dean

Ain't She ~ Adam Doleac

Worst Way ~ Riley Green

A Bar Song (Tipsy) ~ Shaboozey

Wildflowers and Wild Horses ~ Lainey Wilson

She's All I Wanna Be ~ Tate McRae

Guilty as Sin ~ Taylor Swift

Liar ~ Paramore

You Belong to Somebody Else ~ PJ Harding, Noah Cyrus

Hold My Breath ~ Post Malone

Remember That Night? ~ Sara Keys

Think I'm in Love With You ~ Chris Stapleton

Mind on You ~ George Birge

View full playlist at

crissilangwell.com/sunset-bay/savior-complex

Table of Contents

TRIGGER WARNING

Savior Complex is a steamy romance that involves infidelity, references to a past sexual assault, and a toxic family relationship that includes abusive language about body size. If these are deal breakers for you to have a good reading experience, this may not be the book for you. I wish you all the best in your reading journey!

Complete character list located at the back of the book.

Chapter One

Nina

The band left their shit everywhere on their way out. Abandoned coffee cups, used napkins, crumbled muffins. This was a coffee shop, not a goddamn bar, and these guys were slobs.

But Susan had said to treat the band, headed by her nephew Tyler, like guests.

"Nina, this has been Tyler's dream since he was a kid," she'd said when she sprang the idea on me, "and this could be a great opportunity for Insomniacs." I was to keep them happy by offering free refills and pastries. After all, they were bringing paid customers to the shop.

That was one thing they did not do. For the past two hours, not one customer walked through the doors of Insomniacs while Blood Vomit used the coffee shop as their personal garage. Two hours of death metal while Tyler scream-growled and grunted into the microphone.

Either we did a horrible job advertising our new late-night hours featuring live music, or no one cared to hear this fucking band. And judging by the flyers we handed to every customer, plus the way my ears rang despite the wadded-up napkin pieces I'd stuffed in them, I bet it was the latter.

If they'd been any good, I wouldn't have minded staying late. As it was, the perk of this whole new venture Susan thought up meant I could finally sleep in for the first time in years. Today I got to come in at 1 p.m. and planned to leave around nine when the cleanup was done. However, the clock is inching closer to ten, even with an empty shop, because of those pigs.

And cleaning has never been my area of expertise.

Since Maren left, things here really suck. My former coworker and roommate quit a few months ago, but for good reason. She finally figured out how to make money working in music, and now spends her afternoons teaching kids how to play guitar, tutoring them on their band assignments, and giving vocal lessons. In the mornings, she's in the studio recording her first album, which has been her dream forever, and at night, she hangs out with that hunky boyfriend of hers, Mac Dermot—Sunset Bay's Prince Charming of real estate. But thanks to his once early-morning, near naked strolls near my house, I still think of him as Naked Coffee Guy.

Long story. Somebody should write a hot, steamy novel about it. I'd read the hell out of it.

Back when Maren was here, she and I always worked the same shift, and she took on the cleaning. I just wasn't any good at it. But now, six months after Maren left this place for better things, I'm stuck working most of my shifts on my own—which means the cleaning is on me.

At least there are no customers in the evening. Just a sloppy band.

I lock up the shop and head to my car, the lone Cadillac DeVille under a streetlamp in an empty parking lot. The car had been

Nanna Dot's before she died, and somehow I'd managed to keep it running. Sure, it was in the shop every other week, and the replacement parts cost more than the car was worth. But it also held memories of my grandmother at the wheel—old jazz playing on the radio, my cousin and me in the back seat in our Easter bonnets in the middle of June, anticipating the taste of bubblegum ice cream as we pulled up to the parlor.

The car was newer back then and didn't have the musty smell that now mingles with the fresh air as I open the door. There also wasn't the trash I keep in the back seat—used tissues, old food wrappers, a few soda cans. Admittedly, my grandmother would be rolling over in her grave if she saw the way I treat her treasured DeVille. But Nanna Dot also loved me more than anyone else in the world, and I loved her the same. Which means I love this old beauty of a car, even if I know it's on its last leg.

I slide onto the leather seat, slick and scooped from years of ample fannies. My grandmother had never been a slight woman, and despite my best intentions, I'm cursed by her generous genetics. My mother—her daughter—never had this issue, and it has been a source of contention between us for as long as I can remember. I'm always on some weird diet, weighing and measuring my food, and eating celery as snacks while everyone else gets chips or cookies.

But not with Nanna. To her, food was love, both of which she offered freely. Which is probably why my ass fits perfectly into the mold she left behind.

Thanks Nanna.

I turn the key in the ignition, ready to hear the engine cough to life. Instead, I get the radio blaring crackly pop music from the old speakers, but nothing else. I turn off the radio and try again. It clicks, but still nothing.

"Fuck." I open my handbag, rummaging through it for my

phone before remembering that I left it on my kitchen counter before heading to work.

There was always the café phone. But the thought of going back into Insomniacs after this hellish night seems worse than walking a few miles home. Besides, I had two muffins and a mocha for dinner tonight, so walking is probably the best idea.

I look down at what I'm wearing, regretting it immediately; a rainbow tank top that I chose because the blue was the exact shade of my current hue of hair, the black mini skirt that hits at my thigh, fishnet stocking, and my silver platform boots with chunky heels and rainbow trim. I might have more curves than all these skinny bitches in Sunset Bay, but I know how to rock fashion. My motto is the more colorful, the better. With the SoCal weather, there's no need for extra layers.

Except when you have to walk a few miles home because your damn car broke down.

Luckily, I have an overcoat I'd stuffed in the backseat a few weeks ago, and also luckily, I can handle a few miles in these boots.

I slip on the jacket, then start the long journey home.

Sunset Bay at night is not a bad place to be. A total tourist trap, the boulevard along the coastline is full of cute boutiques, surf shops, and other coffee places similar to Insomniacs. Best of all, there are about a dozen trendy restaurants lit up against the star-filled night sky and ocean backdrop, some of the most delicious smells wafting from the kitchens, and full to the brim with crowds of people around my age.

I keep walking, even as my stomach rumbles. Two muffins probably have more calories than a juicy hamburger, which makes my mouth water just thinking about it. Which also makes me want to kick myself for wasting all my calories on stupid muffins. I could have waited and had a real meal instead of those tired gluten bombs.

I pass a group of guys, and immediately feel their eyes rake over me. For a second, my breath catches in my throat, a memory from long ago creeping over me. I shake it off, reminding myself that not every encounter will end up like that.

"Check out that ass," one of them says. "Hey sweetheart."

My stomach curdles, the hamburger forgotten as I feel my heart lurch at the slick voice. I don't look back, quickening my steps.

"I don't think she heard you, Lee. Maybe you should get closer."

They're following me, I realize. I do my best not to panic, trying to be aware of my surroundings and the best route for escape should this escalate beyond catcalls. *This is nothing. It's just nothing. They're drunk tourists having a laugh at my expense. Nothing is going to happen.*

A memory from the past pushes its way into my thoughts, and I fight the urge to vomit. *A hand on my mouth. A hand pushing down my pants. A hand pulling my legs apart.*

A hand grasps my shoulder and I whirl around, backing up out of reach as I face five guys grinning at me like jackals.

"Whoa there, honey. I just want to talk." The first guy towers over me, a smirk on his face, a look in his eyes that says talking is not what he wants. "We're here for the weekend and thought you could show us around."

"I'm not…" I start, almost tripping as my shoulder hits the brick wall of the building beside me. The street is dark, the glow from downtown feeling miles away. "I mean I don't…" *Fuck, Nina. Stop panicking.* "I'm…"

"Emily!"

I hear the call to my right, and I turn to see a man jogging across the street. There are visible sweat stains on his jogging suit, his cheeks are flushed, and his dark hair clings to his forehead. Even more, he's built like a truck. Despite the baggy suit, his muscles are massive, like fucking tree trunks.

And he seems to think I'm someone he knows. Either that, or he's fucking with me too, and I'm about to get murdered by these assholes.

I remember my pepper spray at that moment, and I slip my hand into my purse as he slows to a stop near us. His eyes stay on mine, but he doesn't touch me. My hand finds the spray, and I grasp it tightly.

Then I see something in his expression. It's so subtle, but I see it. A look that says, *play along. I got you. I'll keep you safe.*

I pause for a beat, my eyes remaining locked on his. He gives the slightest tilt of his head. I loosen the spray, but my fingers remain on it.

"Didn't you hear me calling you?" he demands. He moves closer to me, and I realize I've made a step towards him, too. "We were supposed to meet at Mission and College half an hour ago. What the hell have you been doing?" He turns to the guys, and I glance over too. They look uncomfortable, almost sober. "Women, right?"

This stranger, my savior I suppose, turns to me again. "Shall we?" He reaches for my hand slowly, as if asking permission. I have a split second to think about who I trust more—the guys who appear to have second thoughts, or this stranger who is calling me by the wrong name.

"I'm sorry, I got turned around," I say, letting go of the pepper spray and slipping my hand in his. It's warm, slightly sweaty from his run. But safe. He squeezes my hand and guides me away from the men and across the street. They don't follow, and when I look over my shoulder, it's as if they were never there.

Chapter Two

Nina

"Are you okay?" He squeezes my hand before dropping it, and for a moment I forget myself. Because holding his hand felt like the most normal thing that has happened all week. At least, the most comforting. And now that my hand isn't in his, I strangely miss it.

I don't even know him.

I nod in answer, but then shoot him a curious look. "How did you know?" I ask. It had only been a minute or two with those guys, and then this knight in sweaty running clothes came up and saved the day. A fucking hot knight. Now that we're in a better lit area, I can finally get a good view of my rescuer. His face is clean shaven, and he licks his plush lower lip in a way that makes me forget my earlier danger. His shoulders are broad, and I get a much better look at the chiseled definition underneath his clinging, drenched sweatshirt. It feels completely inappropriate to check him out, given the circumstances, and I try to keep my eyes on his. But it's hard to concentrate when my peripheral vision catches his thick as fuck thighs and the undeniable bulge under his grey sweatpants. *Focus, Nina.* "You came running like you knew what was going to happen," I say, hoping he can't see the flush in my cheeks.

He grimaces, and I note the deep dimples in his cheeks, even as his eyes darken.

"I had a feeling," he says, his tone tense and tight. "Are you okay? Did they touch you?"

I put my hand on my shoulder where the one guy grabbed me. My skin grows cold, and I shiver involuntarily. But it's not them, it's what happened before, and it's hard to know what's real and what's just me being triggered whenever any guy get too handsy.

"It was probably nothing," I say, shaking my head. "They were just flirting, and I overreacted."

"They were not flirting," the stranger says. He's angry now, his blue eyes flashing under the glow of the streetlights. "What were you even doing walking alone at night? What if I hadn't been there in time?"

"Hey now." My admiration slips aside, as I feel the heat rise to my cheeks. "What are you, victim shaming? I can walk anywhere I want. It's those guys who need to learn boundaries when it comes to approaching women."

"That's fine. Why don't you tell them that?" He winces as the words leave his mouth, then rubs the back of his neck. "I'm sorry, that's not what I mean." He holds his hand out. "I'm Brayden, Brayden Winters." He waits for me to take it, but I fold my arms in front of me. I don't shake hands with assholes. But I do notice the way his tense expression softens, and the hint of a smile on his lips.

"Nina Chance. Thanks for your help, I got it from here." I pull my pepper spray out and wave it, then turn to go.

"Wait," he says, and damnit, I stop. "I'm really sorry. That was a stupid thing for me to say. I was just scared for you."

"Why? You don't even know me." But my body is starting to

relax, the tension leaving my shoulders.

"I just… Let's just say guys are assholes."

"You got that right," I mutter, and he chuckles. I start to walk, and don't argue when he walks with me.

"You have every right to walk anywhere you want in this town and not be bothered," he continues. "Unfortunately, guys like that don't play by the rules. Add some alcohol, a few friends to egg them on, and you've got yourself the perfect recipe for assault."

I start to protest, but he stops me.

"I am not saying it's your fault. It's not. I'm just saying that because of assholes like those guys, and guys who are even worse than them, you have to be the one to make sure you're safe. And the best way to do that is to not walk around here by yourself."

"You think I don't know that?" I quicken my steps. I'm equal parts annoyed and relieved when he matches my pace.

"Sugar, ten minutes ago, I didn't know you at all," he points out.

"Well, stranger, let me fill you in. I just worked a long shift, and all I wanted to do was get home so I can go to bed and do it all again tomorrow. I didn't plan to walk home alone, but that's what happens when you find out your car won't start. It wasn't my first choice. But you, on the other hand, *did* make that choice. I could drill you on why *you're* choosing to take a run by yourself late at night where any guy could pick a fight with you."

Even as I'm saying it, I know I'm grasping at straws. Brayden is built like a linebacker. There's no chance anyone would mess with him, because it's obvious what the result would be. Even those guys. He didn't even have to lay a hand on any of them, and they still immediately backed off when he approached—even thought he was outnumbered.

Brayden lifts the band of his sweatshirt, and I breathe in sharply at the sight of his perfect abs. I want to trace a manicured nail across them, to feel the valleys of those muscles under my palms, to feel if his skin is as flushed as mine feels right now.

Then I see his own can of pepper spray in his waistband. He's not showing me his Adonis abs, he's showing me his tool of defense. Even though his whole body is a weapon.

"You obviously don't need pepper spray," I say, waving my hand over him. "You're a goddamn tank."

He laughs, and fuck me, his laugh is like a missile to my core. It's deep and throaty, the vibrations giving me heart palpitations. The way his dimples crease as he grins at me has me biting my lip.

"I'm not going to fight if I can help it. I've never even used this. I've found there are better ways to diffuse a situation."

"Like what you did back there," I say, and he nods.

"If I came at those guys, their drunk asses would have welcomed a fight. I'd probably be able to take care of it, but at what cost? I can't afford to get injured. More important, any kind of fight would have put you in more danger. I couldn't defend you and fight them at the same time."

I recall the way he looked when he approached me, frustrated and annoyed, and it suddenly occurred to me how brilliant the whole thing had been. "You pretended to be angry with me instead of getting angry with them."

He shot me an apologetic smile. "It's this trick I once read in a book," he says. "Getting mad at you re-directed their attention and distracted them from whatever they had in mind. But I also was afraid it would backfire, that you'd feel like I was just like those guys. You can't imagine how relieved I was when you took my hand."

"Same," I breathe.

We walk a few minutes in silence. I'm not sure if he'll walk me the whole way home, but I realize how glad I am that he's there. There's a calming presence to him. He has an easy stride to his walk, but I get the sense he's hyper aware of our surroundings. Every time we leave the lights of the street, his hand finds my back, as if to let me know he's here and I'm safe.

It's the first time I've been alone with a man for this long and felt safe.

"I never told you thank you." I look at him, melting just slightly as his hand finds my back again. I wish he'd leave it there. "And I'm sorry I got mad. I was just…" I pause, finding the words. I was scared. But it was more than that. Now that I'm safe, I can feel my whole body letting down, starting with the tears stinging my eyes.

What if Brayden hadn't been there? What if no one saw what was happening? What exactly did they want from me? What if…

"Don't fight this, Nina. You've been asking for this all year."

I shudder as the memory punctures me, and an involuntary sob splinters me in two.

"Hey there, you're safe." Brayden pulls me into him as I try to stop the tears, but I can't stop my moan escaping into the fabric of his sweatshirt. I gulp the air, inhaling the heady scent of his sweat. I cling to him, breathing him in, trying to gain control over my sudden panic.

"I got you, Sugar," he breathes into my hair. He rubs my back, pressing me against him as I clutch his sweatshirt, not stopping as I fight to regain control over my breath. But it's coming too hard, too fast. All I can picture are their faces over mine, their hands holding me down, my clothes ripping away from my body. The pressure, the pain. The hand over my mouth as I screamed, then the complete numbness that took over—as they took over. As I lost myself in the dirt.

I don't think of that day hardly at all anymore. Rather, when I do, I push it away. I push it way down until it feels like it belonged to someone else. Like I was someone else. I have fucked too many guys trying to purge those assholes out of my body. I've protected myself the best way I know how, which is to never let anyone in. I'm the pursuer, and screw anyone who tries to chase me. Because I say what goes, I determine who's coming home with me at night, and I won't be anyone's victim.

Which is why I'm so fucking angry about tonight. I completely froze. If Brayden hadn't shown up… I mean, I had fucking pepper spray, right there! And it wasn't even my first thought.

"I feel like such an idiot," I breathe once my words finally find me. "I didn't even try to fight back."

"Hey, don't be too hard on yourself." He guides me to a nearby bench, and we sit. His arm remains over my back, holding me close to him as I try to contain myself. The feel of his warmth against my body is like an anchor in my despair. "You were terrified, Nina. I could see it all over your body, even from across the street."

But I'm not convinced. I know better. I know! "I could have at least run."

"You could have done a lot of things," he says. "But when your survival instincts kick in, it's really hard to go against them."

I lift my head, wiping away my tears as I look at him. I'm probably a snotty, red mess, and I hate that he's seeing me this way—this guy I don't even know. I hate that I even care, especially when I just cried into his shirt because I can't get over a goddamn assault that happened ten years ago. How can I be so triggered, and also unable to get over how good he smells, especially now that I've had my face buried in his sweat?

"I bet you'd never freeze in the face of danger," I say, laughing to cover up my embarrassment.

He looks down at his lap, his jaw ticking as he stares at his hands. "You'd lose that bet." He looks at me, lifts his hand and brushes a tendril of blue hair from my face before tucking it behind my ear. I hold my breath as he does, my eyes staying with his as he looks at me. "I don't think I've ever known someone with this color of hair," he murmurs, his hand still fingering the lock.

"It's completely natural," I joke, but only to hide how much his touch is affecting me—more than I would have expected.

I can't explain what happens next. All I know is that I feel the electricity. His eyes remain on mine, and it's like our thoughts are connected. Like his body is one I know. Like everything about him is so familiar to me. Had I met him in a past life? Had we been friends in another time? Lovers? Because as I look at him, I can see all the way to his soul, and something inside me is clawing its way out, trying to reach its other half.

He lifts his hand again, his fingers trembling as he touches my skin, his eyes not leaving mine. Even in this dim light, I get lost in the interesting shade of blue and the flecks of gold near the center. I don't move. I don't breathe. I just look into his eyes, then to his lips as they part slightly when he leans forward. But then he jerks back, lowering his hand and breaking the spell.

"Sorry," he says, and I'm left to wonder why he's apologizing. Was it because he touched my face? Because I lowered my guard? Made me question everything I've ever known about men?

Did he just feel what I felt?

I smile, looking down as I hide the way my heart is pounding. What the hell just happened? I want to ask him why he's sorry. "Why would I lose that bet?" I ask instead.

"What?"

"Earlier, when I said you wouldn't freeze in danger. What made you freeze?"

He hesitates for a moment, a flash of pain crossing his face. It's quick enough that I see it, making me regret even asking. I thought I was being cute, making conversation. Instead, I've obviously thrown salt on an old wound.

"You know what, never mind," I say quickly, standing up. "It's getting late, and I'm keeping you from your run, or whatever you're supposed to be doing right now. In fact, you should probably get going. I'm not that far from here."

Lies. I have about two more miles to walk. But I'm out of my comfort zone, and I don't know why. It's not like I've never been attracted to a man before. I'm the one who calls the shots, the one who is ballsy and forward, pursuing the guy who catches my eye. But this feels so different. All the lines I would have used, the quips, the blatant come ons that work best after a few drinks… Right now, I have nothing. I'm completely rocked by this guy, almost nervous, but in a way that makes me feel exhilarated and tongue tied. And if I don't get home now, I'm going to make a complete ass of myself.

"There's nowhere else I want to be," he says.

I am going to have this man's babies. That's it. I will probably be pregnant by the end of our walk. *Fuck, Nina, get a grip. You don't have to fall in love with the first guy who rescues you.*

"Well, then, I guess we better get going."

"Where *do* you live?" he asks, swiping at this hair. It's dry now, unlike the sweaty mess it was before. The dark waves graze his forehead, and I wonder what it would be like to run my hands through his locks, how it would feel to tug the curls between my fingers.

"Holland Heights. Just a bit up the road."

He gives me a sideways glance, and I see the disbelief in his eyes. "Just a bit. Right, nice try." He looks at my shoes, then back at me. "Good thing you wore your walking shoes, right?"

I look down at my funky platform boots, the streetlights reflecting off the silver, making them seem like moons. I grin, lifting a foot behind me with my arms up, and he laughs.

"Can you really walk in those?"

"Walk, dance, run," I say. "Well, maybe not run, because running is for masochists like you. But I've been on my feet in these things all day, and I can walk all the way home in them. Besides, they make me happy."

He looks me up and down, then nods. "You're like the whole entire rainbow," he says without an ounce of judgment. People either love or hate my style, feeling intensely about the loudness of my colors and style choices one way or the other. But the way he's looking at me, it's like he's just figuring out all my layers. Like he's looking past the colors to see the person wearing them.

And I like the way that feels.

The rest of the way home, we play a game of twenty questions. It not only helps me learn more about Brayden, but it's also just distracting enough that I can overlook the blister forming on my heel. Damn platform boots. I realize that while they're great for all day at the café, I've never actually tested them for a multi-mile walk.

As we trade questions, I learn that Brayden's middle name is Walter, he loves country music, and will throw up if he eats peas. He learns that the only country I've listened to is by Taylor Swift, I don't really like most vegetables unless there's dip involved, and I love the color blue.

"So do I," he says, taking a moment to tug at my hair. I laugh, but inside...*fuck.*

Then I find out he lives and works on his family horse ranch—a ranch I know very well.

"The Salt & Sea Ranch?" My mouth hangs open as he nods. "I had horseback riding lessons there when I was seventeen. Were you there then?"

"How many years ago was that?"

"About ten."

A shadow crosses his expression. It's brief, and he flips a quick smile at me as if to pretend like it never happened. But I saw it.

"I left for college in the fall," he says. "We might have been at the ranch at the same time, but I tried to spend as little time there as possible. Between football and school, I only had time for my chores." He relaxes, his smile returning to full beam. "Besides, the girls kept me busy enough."

"Sure they did," I laugh. But inside, I'm wondering what Brayden isn't saying. I know why I was there, and I don't want to discuss it. Is there a reason he had to leave?

"Where did you go to college? And were you studying anything specific?"

"San Francisco State, and just General Ed," he says. "I mostly needed a change of scenery. All I knew was the ranch, and this was my chance to figure out if there was something else I was good at, or even interested in."

"And did you?"

He laughs, then bumps my shoulder. "That's three questions, Sugar."

"You can ask me three more then, but I want to know."

He's quiet for a moment, and I realize that once again I'm asking him about something that's obviously too intimate to share with a stranger. I can't believe I keep tromping on these emotional landmines.

"Sorry, you don't have to answer," I say, but he shakes his head.

"No, it's fine. I really wasn't the college sort. There was literally no reason for me to go. I had a career waiting for me at the ranch. Because it was my family's business, it was pretty much a done deal that I would work there full time." He breathes in sharply, and I can tell he's struggling. In a bold moment, I take his hand. He looks down at our hands, and I feel his grip loosen slightly. I start to let go, but then he tightens, keeping my hand in his. It feels warm. Comforting. Right.

"Something happened that year that really changed things for my family. I don't want to get into it, but it was my fault and being around my family became almost unbearable. I hadn't planned to apply for college, but there I was in my senior year, filling out applications for every college that would accept an average student like me. And college was fine, but my heart wasn't in it. I passed my classes, but barely. I stayed for a few years, but just before my final year, my dad had a heart attack while riding and ended up breaking his back. He's now paralyzed from the waist down, and the ranch was in danger of folding if I didn't come home."

"Oh my God, Brayden. I'm so sorry."

"He survived," he assures me, and I squeeze his hand.

"That's a relief. But I mean, I'm sorry you had to leave school. You didn't really get much choice in the matter, did you?"

He shakes his head, but then laughs. "Look at me, moaning over a great paycheck and a set career. You must think I'm such an entitled asshole."

"No, I think you were laid a hand of cards and told which ones to play without a chance to try your own. I get it."

"You do?"

"Yeah, family is hard. I know mine is. But the difference is that they don't even want me around. I'm such a disappointment to my parents because I'm not who they wanted to be. I'll never be smart enough, pretty enough, or thin enough. They think I'm a spoiled brat who has never had to work for anything, and I guess in some ways they're right. But they don't even try to get to know me so they can see the ways they're wrong. The last time I saw them was Christmas, and my mother spent the whole night telling me…"

I stop myself. My mom ruined my Christmas when she couldn't stop telling me I looked like a sausage in my new dress. I had been fasting for weeks beforehand and had dropped ten pounds. With my Spanx, I felt sexy and slim, even if I was still far from my goal weight.

But the way she spoke to me, I felt like I was thirteen all over again—chubby and stupid.

"Let's just say my mom isn't very complimentary when it comes to me." I wrinkle my nose at him. "Is that how your parents are?"

"No, thankfully. I mean, my dad is a hard ass. Even though he had to give me most of the responsibilities of running the ranch, he still has a way of doing things and wants to make sure I follow them. But he's a good man, and my mom is literally an angel. I couldn't do any of this without her—without both of them, really—and even though I didn't choose this life, I appreciate the ranch so much more now."

I shiver involuntarily, the cold air finally seeping into my bones through my thin jacket.

"Shit, you must be freezing. We're probably close to your house, right?" Is that reluctance in his voice, or am I imaging that too? I reach for my phone to check for the time before realizing I don't have it.

"Just a few more blocks. What time is it?"

He pulls out his own phone and winces. "Almost midnight," he laughs. I laugh too, realizing we made a forty-minute walk last two hours.

We talk the rest of the way, as he tells me about the tours he leads along the beach, and I share about life in a coffee shop. I know my stories are not as interesting as his, but he listens as if they are. By the time we turn onto my street, I know he's a morning person like me, has one younger sister, and has watched every episode of *Six Feet Under*. About me, he knows how much I hate cleaning, how much I loved my Nanna Dot, and the titles of all the books on my nightstand to help feed my nightly reading habit. At the moment, it's *Before She Finds Me* by Heather Chavez, *Iron Flame* by Rebecca Yarros, and *Hello Stranger* by Katherine Center.

"I've never been to college," I admit as we turn on my street. I hate how close we are to home, knowing that the night is about to end. "I don't know what it's like, or even what it's like to be in a new town. So tell me, what was your favorite part about moving away to go to college?

"Not much," he laughed. "The classes were boring, and honestly, I don't even know what I was doing trying to get a business degree. But I did become somewhat of a baseball fanatic. My roommate was this rich kid from Wyoming with a dad who grew up in San Francisco. For Christmas, Freddie scored season tickets at Club level for the San Francisco Giants. Whenever he couldn't impress a girl to go with him, he took me. And I started paying attention." Brayden ducks his head and gives me a side glance before breaking into a Tony Bennett song about leaving his heart in San Francisco. "They play that song every night after the game, when we're crowded like cattle on the winding ramp that leads to the street. It's been a few years, but every time I hear that song, I'm back in the fog, smelling bacon wrapped hot dogs from street vendors, and feeling the cold ocean air on my face, even in summer."

He whistles that Tony Bennett song; one I've heard so many times before. I'm listening as he tells me all this, but a different memory is weaving into the story. My grandmother crooning along with Tony Bennett while washing the dishes, and me at a table writing a list.

The list. Suddenly, I'm anxious to get home, and relieved as we approach the old Victorian. I don't want to leave Brayden, but I have a hunch about something, and it just can't wait.

"Well, this is me," I say, and he groans in protest, but with a smile on his face. He looks up and whistles.

"Wow, you live here? How many of you are in there?"

"Just me," I say, suddenly a little shy. The house is three stories including the walk out basement, plus the tall first floor perfect for a fifteen-foot tree at Christmas—which I get every year in Nanna's memory. This means that the house looms over us, with its dramatic steeple roofline, quaint bay windows, and the stained-glass door that rests at the top of the stairs and expansive porch. With five bedrooms, multiple sitting rooms, and a full library, it's too much house for one person. And ever since Maren moved out, I've never felt more alone.

I'm not sure how to say goodbye to Brayden. Our time together has been incredible, even though we were thrown together by circumstance. He's no longer a stranger, seeming like someone I've known forever. But in reality, we've only known each other for two hours, and in a few moments we may never see each other again.

"Let me get your number," I blurt out. "If you wait a second, I can grab my phone. Maybe we can catch a drink and continue this conversation, or…"

The way his eyes shift, I realize I misread things. No, I was delusional about things.

I shake my head. "Sorry, we can call it a night and you can get back to wherever you need to go. I've already taken up enough of your—"

"No, it's not that." He rubs the back of his neck. "I have a girlfriend."

It's like all the air is sucked from the space around us, then lands with a whomp at my gut. *Of course* he has a girlfriend.

I try to think up a response, something funny to make it seem like being interested in him was the furthest thing from my mind. But all I want to do is disappear, to forget how much of a fool he must think I am.

"It was nice to meet you," I say. "Thanks for saving me and all that. I'll be more careful next time." I turn to go, but he grabs my hand and pulls me to him. My hand flies to his chest, keeping the distance between us. "What are you doing?"

He drops his arms immediately, releasing me. But I can't turn away from the pained expression on his face.

"You felt it, right?" He looks at me with such pleading. Like he's begging me to know what he's talking about.

And I do.

"I felt it," I whisper.

"I haven't felt that in… I've never felt that. Not with anyone. And I'm sorry if this makes me seem as big of a creep as those guys back there—"

"Well, you have a girlfriend." He's never felt that with *anyone*? Not even *her*?

"But I have a girlfriend," he agrees. "Which is why it's completely inappropriate for me to give you my phone number."

"Right," I say. I nod, feeling like a total fool.

"So tell me yours," he murmurs.

I look up at him, trying to see if I heard him right. He raises an eyebrow, then pulls out his phone and waits.

I am not some saint. I've dated guys with girlfriends before and could have given a rat's ass about being the other woman. In fact, it was always the preferable scenario. If they were taken, I didn't have to worry about the drama of a relationship or having to answer to anyone. I didn't even care that I was sharing a guy. I was there for one reason only, and it sure as hell wasn't love.

But this is different. I hardly know this man, and I already know I'd never share him with anyone.

And yet, I can't help giving him my phone number anyways. He types into his phone for a long time, then I hear the unmistakable swoosh. Message sent. He looks up and winks at me. And it's so damn sexy, I have to fight the urge to bite my lip…or lean over to bite his.

"Goodnight Brayden," I say, taking a step toward my stairs. He leans forward and takes my hand again, lifting it to his lips. Holy fuck, why don't guys do this anymore? The way his eyes never leave mine as his mouth presses to my fingers has me quivering inside.

"Goodnight, Nina," he says, then releases me.

Chapter Three

Nina

Inside my house, I lean against the door for a moment, trying to figure out what just happened and why my heart is beating so fast. Then I hear my phone ping in the kitchen.

My phone! I run, tripping over a pile of clothes on the way, then skid across the linoleum I haven't mopped in weeks. There are dishes piled everywhere and open cabinets without a clean dish in them. And there, in the middle of the mess, is my phone.

I unlock it, then click on the text—two of them now—and get to reading.

Brayden: Roses are red, violets are blue, your smile is sweet, and your hair is blue too. I'm not much of a poet, but I do believe in fate, and in beauty and chemistry and all you radiate. See, I'm not much with rhymes or telling you how I feel, but give me a chance to make my appeal—to stay in your life, even as a friend. Because Nina, sweet beauty, I'd hate to see this end.

I smile at his text, then read the one right under it.

Brayden: Please delete that text. Tell me you didn't read it.

I laugh out loud, then text him back.

Nina: Oh, I read it, Tolstoy. And I'm framing this bad boy on my wall in giant font.

He doesn't respond right away, probably because he's still making his way back to wherever he came from before he saved me. But it's fine, because I have work to do.

I race to the bookcase in the living room and kneel to reach the bottom shelf. There, in chronological order, is every single diary I've kept since I was ten years old. Seventeen years of them, to be exact. There were so many times I'd been tempted to throw them away, especially the one from ten years ago. Burn them, even, just so I could forget. But something always stopped me. Maybe it was because these were the true witnesses of my life. The only place I'd ever told the complete truth. The only place where the sins committed against my body were detailed in ways I couldn't even tell my mother. Never even got to tell the police.

I find that journal now and flip it open. It immediately lands on the piece of paper I'd slipped between the pages. My handwriting is rushed, almost like I couldn't get the words down fast enough—as if I was angry and determined.

Because I was.

It had been a weekend at my grandma's house with my cousin, Jordy. She lived out of town, so these rare moments when we could hang out together were very special. It was also full of rituals. The homemade pancakes Nanna Dot placed before us, complete with "magic" syrup. The singing performances for an audience of one, even at seventeen. The late nights talking about fashion, trading gossip about our friends, and swapping stories about boys. So many boys. And snuggling with Nanna on the couch while watching our favorite movie of all time—*Practical Magic*.

But this weekend was different. It was weeks after the incident. Weeks after my mom advised me to keep things to myself.

"You don't want to embarrass yourself, honey," she'd said. I knew what that meant. She didn't want me to embarrass *her*. But some part of that still stuck to me.

So I remained silent at Nanna's house, even when she and Jordy both noticed.

"Sing with me," Jordy begged, handing the karaoke mic to me. I watched the words on the TV roll on by, but my voice wouldn't work.

So there was no singing that weekend. No makeup tutorials or clothing swaps. And definitely no talk about boys.

But there were pancakes, and there was *Practical Magic*. And as we watched the Owens sisters change their cursed witchy fate, I took comfort in the fluffy goodness smothered in spells and syrup.

"I'm manifesting my perfect man," Jordy exclaimed after the movie, leaping up to grab some paper and pens from the kitchen. She gave one to Nanna Dot, who laughed and said she'd settle for someone to rub her feet every night, and that's all.

"Nanna, I'll rub your feet," I said. "You don't need a man."

"Stay right there," Jordy ordered, thrusting a piece of paper at me. "She needs a man, and so do you."

"What about the curse? Won't any man who ends up with us die?" I looked expectantly at Jordy, who only rolled her eyes.

"That's just in the movie, Nina." She pointed at my paper, then got busy on her own, not even giving me an opening to remind her that the lists were make-believe too.

Still, it didn't stop me from playing along, but only to list qualities that were impossible to find in a man, just like Sally Owens.

I was never going to fall in love.

I included a few things that actually mattered to me, just in case something this stupid actually worked. He would make me feel safe. He'd care for animals. He'd listen with his eyes and ears.

But then came the specifics. He'd like country music and have a good singing voice. He'd have deep dimples and hair with curls I could wind my fingers through. He'd have blue eyes with flecks of gold.

I paused, my pen between my lips as I tried to think of a few more things. My grandma was now at the kitchen sink, humming as she washed the syrup from the plates.

"I left my heart, in San Francisco…" she warbled out, singing the same Tony Bennett song she always sang when she was happy. "Sugar, can you pass me that plate," she said, pointing at my dish on the table. I handed it to her, then went back to my list.

He'd have ties to San Francisco where Nanna Dot met Grandpa, he'd like Tony Bennett, and he'd call me Sugar.

Holding the list in my hands now, my mouth drops open. It's Brayden. From the way he saved me to the way he called me Sugar, this list is all about him. I go over each item one by one, just to make sure. Then I go over it again.

1. He'll make me feel safe
2. He'll care for animals
3. He'll listen with his eyes and ears
4. He'll like country music
5. He'll have deep dimples
6. He'll have curly hair
7. And blue eyes with flecks of gold
8. He'll have ties to San Francisco
9. He'll love Tony Bennett
10. He'll call me Sugar

It's him. Ten years ago, I made a list about Brayden, and I didn't even know it. I'd even been to his ranch! And tonight, he walked me home to make sure I was safe—and I let him get away. Even though he was the man I'd conjured up all those years ago. Even though I thought he was an impossibility.

And to just prove how impossible he is...this perfect man I conjured up has a girlfriend.

Fuck my life.

"He has a girlfriend?" Maren steals another one of my fries as I slouch in my seat. She and Claire met me for lunch at Coastal Plate. Actually, I'd only invited Maren. But these days, with the planning of Claire's wedding and all, these two are joined at the hip. I couldn't have Maren without Claire. And Claire? I mean she's all right if you like perfect, thin, and blonde. I find her perky perfection a bit annoying, favoring Maren's moodiness any day. But that's just me.

"Yeah, which is just so fitting for a list of a man I can't have, right?"

"I don't know," Claire pipes in, and I roll my eyes in her direction, waiting for her oh so brilliant, not asked for input. She doesn't even notice—or she's ignoring the bored look on my face. "I mean, this list could be about anyone. It doesn't have to be him."

"Shut your mouth," Maren says, then sticks a French fry in her mouth just to prove a point. Claire doesn't get mad, just laughs as she chews the fry. "This list is not just about anyone." Maren grabs the list from my hands then reads from it. "I mean, Tony Bennett? Blue eyes with gold flecks? Calls her Sugar? Fucking *San Francisco*? She found all these things to be true about Brayden in the matter of an hour. How can that not be some sort of conjuring magic?"

"Don't tell me you believe in this," Claire laughs.

"How can you not? You work with romance authors every day for your job. Have you not read those stories?"

"Those are fiction." Claire leans back in her chair, as if that proves her point.

"And this is fate," Maren replies, crossing her arms in front of her. "Besides, you can't argue against chemistry, and they obviously have it. Right Nina?"

"I guess." I fiddle with a fry, thinking back to last night. We did, right? "He saved me from those guys, so it's possible I might be seeing things that weren't there. Maybe that's why I felt so safe around him. But…" I pause, thinking back to our walk home, how it felt to walk beside him. The moment we almost kissed. "There was something there. I felt it, and I know he did too. Even though he's taken, he still wanted to keep in contact with me. Just as friends, but still. He even sent me this."

I pick my phone up off the table, unlock it and open his text from this morning. I push it across the table for both of them to see.

Brayden: Hey there friend. I have a free afternoon today and wondered if you wanted to go horseback riding, just for old time's sake.

"You didn't respond," Maren pointed out, pushing my phone back to me. "Why didn't you tell him hell yes, you want to come over and ride him."

"Ride the *horse*, Maren," Claire says, laughing.

"Right. The horse." Maren looks at me and winks.

"I can't," I moan, putting the phone back in my purse.

"Because of his girlfriend? That has never stopped you before." Maren arches an eyebrow, then ducks when Claire smacks her on the arm.

"I think that's a healthy boundary," Claire says. "It wouldn't be right."

"It's not about that," I admit. "I have no idea who this girlfriend is, and I don't care. It's never bothered me before because I didn't care about the guy either, but Brayden is different. There's something about him that makes me think I could really fall for him. He's so good and caring, so thoughtful, and I figured all this out in just the time it took for him to walk me home. Also, I'm insanely attracted to him. There's too much at stake if I mess around with him. For one, I could catch deeper feelings and he'll just go back to his girlfriend, or she'll find out and break his heart, and I don't want to see him get hurt."

Maren and Claire are silent for a moment. Then Maren lets out a whoosh of air. "Man, Nina. You really like this guy."

"I know," I moan. "Which is why this is friggen unfair."

"Oh, I meant to send this to you earlier," Claire says, digging through her bag. "This is weird timing, but I don't want to forget or Ethan will never forgive me." She hands me an envelope with my name on it, and I can already tell it's her wedding invitation. Ethan is my cousin, so of course I'm invited to the wedding. But I can't help finding some humor in the way Claire stresses it's *his* idea and not hers. She'd never say that out loud, of course, but I find it funny that we tolerate each other only because we're both friends with Maren and I'm related to her fiancé.

I only have two cousins—Ethan on my dad's side and Jordy on my mom's. Jordy and I no longer speak, and she can kiss my ass. But Ethan? He's like a brother. He lived with us for a while when his dad split, so we grew up close, and we're still cool now.

Claire, on the other hand, is boring and perfect, but fine I guess. Not only that, she and Ethan have a kid together—Finn—who's actually pretty awesome for a seven-year-old. Everyone else will be coupled up at this wedding, so I'll probably end up at the kids table with Finn, who I'm sure will be the best company of all.

"Thanks," I say. I open it just because she's watching me, inwardly groaning when I see the "plus one" next to my name. Nope, no plus one. Just lonely old me on a ship full of couples. Because this wedding is taking place on a nighttime cruise in the bay, which should be ultra-romantic for everyone else and hugely awkward for me.

"Sounds fun," I say, slipping the envelope into my purse.

The afternoon passes and I still haven't texted Brayden back. The truth is, I'm afraid. I can't go on a horseback ride with him. I can't do anything with him. I never even should have given him my phone number, because this man does not belong to me. If I open myself to him in any way, I'm going to get hurt.

But when my phone pings again, I can't help but look. Then

smile. It's a picture of Brayden completely mugging for a selfie with his horse. I can tell he's leaning over awkwardly to get the horse's face in the photo, and I can see the ocean behind him. Oh man, a beach ride. It's something I always wanted to do when I was taking lessons, but never got to.

Brayden: We missed you on the beach today.

It's obvious he's not taking my silent treatment seriously, and I can't help feeling happy about that. I missed him too. I just can't tell him that.

I'm in foreign territory here. In the past, I would have just invited him over, girlfriend or not. Though, looking around, there's no way anyone is coming over. Ever since Maren moved out, I've kind of let things go around here a little bit. Sitting at my kitchen table, my view is of my grandmother's countertops full of all her fancy dishes with some sort of food crusted on them. I have clothes I washed and then hung to dry hanging in the doorway, even though they've been dry for two weeks now. In the living room, the couch has become an extension of my closet, with piles of clothes taking up every inch of space. I haven't mopped the floors in weeks. Even the garbage is overflowing, though I might be nose blind to the smell.

It's embarrassing, and I'm not really sure what to do about it. Sometimes I get a hair up my ass to clean the place top to bottom; sometimes I get stuck in my feelings, consumed by my loneliness and a pit of grief that won't leave.

I miss having a roommate, but more than that, I miss my Nanna Dot.

It's been five years since she passed. Her arms were wrapped around her own body, as if she were giving herself a hug in those final moments. It brought me peace to think of it that way, even as I sobbed into the 9-1-1 call.

I thought I could handle living on my own, but in just a few weeks, the house became dark and cluttered, unlike the bright cheerfulness that existed when Nanna Dot was here. She used to throw open the curtains and sing a welcome to the day. Her voice was shaky and uneven, but angelic to my ears. I loved hearing Nanna Dot sing because it meant she was happy, and her happiness was infectious.

But when she was gone, the curtains remained closed and the house song-free. Silent, except for the occasional settling creak or sound of passing cars. No one visited. No one called, especially not my mother. It had to do with the will, as Nanna Dot left me everything, including this huge house. But they had to have known I would have taken my grandmother over all of it—because without her, I had no one.

My natural impulse was to hide away in this house forever. I had enough money to live the rest of my life without needing to work. The house was paid off, and my bank account had more figures than I thought I'd ever see in a lifetime. But my mental health was plummeting, so I got a job at Insomniacs because it was the best place I could think of where I'd be around people without having to get close to anyone. I started coloring my hair in bright hues, hoping it would help lighten the darkness in my heart. I got a roommate and endured her constant criticism of how I kept house.

That first roommate was just awful. She only stayed because I hardly charged anything for rent. When she moved out, I was more than happy to see her go. I thought I'd see how it felt to live on my own, maybe organize the house and get my act together, but then my coworker Maren asked if she could take over as my roommate, and I agreed.

And it was great while it lasted. Maren hated the mess too, but she cleaned without shaming me. Even more, she hung out with me.

She had her own life and friends, but she still liked my company.

Our living arrangement didn't last long, though. Maren was always slated for bigger and better things. She quit Insomniacs after she started teaching music, got a record deal with a huge producer, and was able to move out. I was happy for her, though selfishly I wanted her to stay here always.

I've been on my own for several months now, and the state of the house is the first sign that I'm slipping back into those dark times. I know I need to do what I can to remain afloat, but it's just so hard. I'm mortified at the way the house looks, but I can't bring myself to do anything about it. Just thinking about someone else walking in here and seeing how I'd singlehandedly ruined the place is more than I can handle.

Brayden: Perhaps my friend here can entice you to join us.

I look at the text Brayden sent, my fingers itching to answer him, even though the best thing I could probably do is block his number. But I wait as the three dots appear under his text. Another photo comes through, this one of the horse he'd been riding on in her stall, and next to her is another horse—a horse I remember.

Meredith.

Nina: That's my horse!

I grin, seeing my old friend on the screen. Every lesson, she was the one I rode. I fell in love with that pumpkin-colored mare. I'd brush her after every lesson, even though there were ranch hands who could unsaddle her and brush her down. But I wanted to spend every moment with that horse, braiding her mane and sticking flowers throughout the weave.

Nina: But how did you know? You weren't at the ranch when I used to ride.

Brayden: I asked the horses, and Meredith whinnied the loudest.

I glare at the way he's messing with me, then touch his name before holding the phone to my ear. He's laughing when he picks up.

"Seriously. How did you know?" I ask.

"I asked my mom," he says, still laughing. "She named off a few of the horses that were used for lessons, and Meredith was one of them. I just had this feeling she was the one, especially since her stall is right next to my horse."

"Sara," I whisper.

"You remember!"

I'm kind of pleased that I remember. It seems like a whole lifetime ago, except that it was the brightest part of my life at a time when everything felt so hard. There is a lot I've blocked out from back then, but the ranch was not one of them. If I close my eyes, I can sometimes remember the way it smelled and how the air felt on my skin there. Different. Healing. Kind of like home.

"I used to sneak both of them cookies from the feed store. Sara was especially fond of them, probably because her owner was too stingy with the sweets."

"Hey, I was away at college. I made up for it plenty every time I came home."

I sensed some regret in his voice. Something unspoken. I remembered the way he looked last night when we talked about that time in our lives.

What happened to you, Brayden?

"I wish I could have met you then," I say, the words slipping out before I can pull them back in. I hear a heavy sigh on his end of the phone, and I close my eyes, just listening to him breathe.

"Me too," he says. "More than you know."

Both of us stay silent after that. I feel like I could crawl out of my skin in this moment, dying to say all the things I wish I could, but mostly just wishing for a chance with him. Wishing I didn't like him so much. Wishing he'd met me first so that he wouldn't be with this other girl.

"So, will you say yes to horseback riding with me, or am I going to have to wear you down?"

Every part of me is screaming yes, except my good sense.

"You know why I can't," I say.

"Because your trainer forgot to teach you how to ride a horse?"

"Hey, I'll have you know I'm an excellent rider. I could probably ride circles around you, even if it's been years since I've been on a horse."

His low laugh vibrates into my ear, and I bite my lip. Fuck, how can a simple sound be so goddamn sexy?

"Guess you're going to have to prove it. Day after tomorrow, meet me at Salt & Sea Ranch. Meredith will be waiting."

I groan into the phone. "You can't do that," I protest. "That's coercion."

"No, that's horseplay."

"Har har." But I'm smiling.

"Come on, Nina," he pleads. "I already told Meredith you were coming, and she got all excited. You don't want to disappoint her, do you?"

I flex my hands, my fingers, my toes—my everything. I am exercising every ounce of control I have, and yet…

"What time?"

"Nine in the morning," he says. "I'll make you breakfast then we'll head out. But we have to be back by noon because I have a tour group coming in.

Then he whoops on his end of the phone, letting loose a wild sound of excitement that leaves me grinning, even if I feel the need to hit the brakes.

"Hold on there, cowboy," I say. "This is strictly for Meredith and has nothing to do with you. Besides, what would your girlfriend say about you going horseback riding with some other woman."

"She'd probably be happy that I found someone who liked riding so I could stop bugging her about coming with me."

The pang of jealousy that rips through me is so unexpected. I have not felt jealousy over a man...ever. I haven't cared about anyone enough to worry about what they do when they're not with me or who they're with. But this...this is different. Knowing that he's asked some other woman to go for horseback rides with him is like death by a thousand cuts. Not just another woman. His *girlfriend.*

But also, what does that say about her that she doesn't go? Knowing how much this horse ranch means to Brayden, how can he be with someone who isn't even remotely interested in horses?

I'm projecting, of course. I don't know anything about this girl. She might love horses, but just not riding. She could be nice and lovely and make Brayden happy.

Nah, she's a bitch. And she doesn't deserve him.

"Day after tomorrow," I agree. "I'll be there at nine."

That evening, I start cleaning. I even sing as I go, blaring Tony Bennett over the sound system I had talked Nanna Dot into buying years ago.

"I left my heart, in San Francisco..." I croon, pushing the pile of clothes off the couch and into a laundry basket so I can transport it upstairs. The doom piles have diminished dramatically and this house is starting to feel like a home again. Even though the sun set hours ago, the house feels brighter somehow. Smells good too, with the lemon essential oil diffusing in the corner and the shine on the just mopped floors.

My phone rings on the coffee table and I glance at it, then groan. My mom's face stares back at me, smiling even though she never smiles at me anymore. I probably should have found a photo of her scowling instead. I pick up the phone, answering it as I switch off the stereo.

"Hello?"

There are only two reasons why my mom calls me nowadays. One is to disguise it as a social call, but then slip in all the ways I fall short as a human. The other is her recent fascination with family dinners. I think one of her friends at the country club mentioned how their family keeps in touch this way, and my mom wanted to pretend that our family was close too. But really, it just became a way for her to tear me down in person.

"Nina, you really need to work on the way you answer the phone. The person on the other end shouldn't be able to tell how tired you are. I don't even know why you're tired, anyway. You don't have a thing to worry about, what with all my mother's money in your bank account."

I pour my coffee while she talks. There's no sense in arguing with her, and honestly, I'm so used to her drivel, I don't even react anymore.

After a few minutes, I finally interject with "Why'd you call?" and then get ready for the lecture on my tone, even as I try to keep my voice light and airy, as she prefers. But she doesn't lecture. No, it's far worse than that.

"Aunt Lil and her family are hosting family dinner tomorrow night, and I'd love if you were here also. It will be a family reunion of sorts, so make sure you're wearing something that fits you and not that godawful skirt you wore the last time."

This is terrible news, and I immediately think of ways to get out of it. I work the early shift tomorrow, so that excuse won't work. But then I remember my car on the other side of town.

"I'd love to, but can't," I say, trying to hide my enthusiasm. "My car broke down last night, so I'm kind of stuck."

"Then buy a new car. Hell, buy ten new cars. Lord knows you can afford it. But I expect you to be here."

"I woke up with a sore throat and a cough this morning," I say, then cough to prove my ailment.

"I'm sure it's just allergies," my mom says. "You'll be fine by tomorrow. We just won't get near you."

Great.

Here's the thing about my Aunt Lil, she is just as bad as my mother. She's different in that she won't say anything to your face, but every comment out of her is this backhanded dig. It might sound kind or thoughtful to the unsuspecting stranger—I know better though.

Uncle Dan is fine, except that he never wants to be there either. He's too busy trying to stay off of Aunt Lil's shit list to actually talk to any of us. I swear he just counts the minutes until they get to leave again. Why, I don't know. Once he leaves, he's alone with Aunt Lil.

And if the whole family is coming, my cousin Jordy is included, and I fucking hate her. We used to be close. We used to spend nearly every weekend together at Nanna Dot's. We were more than cousins. We were like sisters.

But things changed. She stopped coming around. And after Nanna Dot died… It hurts, the way she rejected me. Wouldn't even speak to me. Never even asked for my side of the story as our mothers whispered lies in her ear.

She never even checked on me after the funeral, and that hurts the most.

I hardly see her anymore, but when I do, we barely acknowledge each other. When she looks at me, it's with complete disdain, like she can't believe we have to share the same air space. This from the girl who used to stay up late with me bingeing *Friends* episodes or giving each other makeovers. That girl is gone, and I guess I've changed too, because I don't want to be around her anymore either.

But now I get to drive two hours north when I can think of a million other things I'd like to do tomorrow. I can think up all the excuses I want, but there will be no getting out of this, so I might as well prepare myself for a torturous evening.

"Can I bring anything?"

"No, we got it covered," my mom says. "Besides, I'm still battling heartburn from the last time you brought those acorn squashes stuffed with sausage."

"It was turkey, Mom, from that cookbook you gave me for Christmas." It was actually pretty good, too, even though it was low-cal.

"Oh, are you using that cookbook? It's supposed to help you with that weight issue you're battling."

"I'll see you tomorrow," I say, hanging up before she can answer, knowing I might pay for that later.

I melt onto the couch, a ball of dread already forming in my belly. I have so many hours between now and the time I have to face my family, and I can already feel a stress ache forming in my neck and a dull pain behind my eyes. Every muscle in my body is clenched just in anticipation of the shit show tomorrow night will be. I don't even try to pretend things will be okay. My whole purpose for being there is to be my family's verbal punching bag.

And still, I'll go.

I stand, look at the full laundry basket on the floor next to the couch, then step over it to trudge up the stairs to my room. After undressing, I'm about to throw my clothes into the chair pile I have growing in the corner of my room when I remember the piece of paper in my jeans pocket. I pull it out, unfold it, then read it.

Likes Tony Bennett. Cares for animals.

"Calls me Sugar," I whisper.

After this dinner from hell, I'll get to ride horses with Brayden on the beach. At least I have that to look forward to.

Chapter Four

Nina

I pull up to Aunt Lil and Uncle Dan's house, but don't get out of my car right away. It's already been a full day, and the sun is just starting its descent. This morning's shift was full of issues, starting with Susan forgetting to schedule someone for the afternoon. I had spent every free moment of a very busy morning begging any of my coworkers to give up their day off before one of the guys finally caved. Then I'd Ubered over to the mechanic, who tried to convince me it was time to think about another car. This latest fix cost at least double what the car was worth, which wasn't an easy pill to swallow. But how can you put a price on memories? My grandmother's car was so much more than tin and vinyl. It was a childhood of trips to the ice cream shop or slow drives down country roads. It was my grandmother's off-key singing and windows rolled down. It was my youth, and it was her.

I wasn't giving up the car.

But I still held my breath as I traveled up the Grapevine

highway, or every time I accidentally drove faster than fifty-five. By the time I pull up in front of my aunt and uncle's house, my muscles ache from clenching them and my eyes burn from exhaustion.

The silver Lexus parked out front lets me know my parents are here. Behind them is a huge Dodge Ram, which I guess is Jordy's, even if it seems completely out of character. The cousin I knew would be in a luxury car like her parents', not some huge pickup truck with three-foot tires. But it's been a few years, so anything is possible.

I muster the courage to leave my car, looking down at what I chose to wear. I don't cater too much to my mother's fashion preferences. My hair, much to her dismay, is always jewel-toned. Since I had time this morning, I dyed the fading blue a vibrant shade of turquoise with purple highlights, and I'm wearing fuchsia eyeshadow to match. My skirt is a little looser than the ones I like to wear, simply so my mom won't notice I've put on a few more pounds. I paired it with a baggy sweater that hangs off one shoulder, plus a few necklaces that hang below my chest. On my feet are stiletto booties that show off my calves, which is a feature I'm proud of. I might have too much cushion around my ass and waist, and not enough muscle tone in my arms, but my legs are shapely, especially when I wear heels.

And this outfit is cute enough that even my mom might like it.

I knock on the door, then wait for someone to answer. I can hear them all laughing inside, already starting the party without me. I wonder if I turn around and leave, would they notice? I have half a mind to do so, when Uncle Dan opens the door. He kisses me on the cheek, then steps aside so I can come in.

"How was the drive?" he asks.

"Not bad," I say. This will be the extent of our conversation today. Sure enough, he nods, then heads back toward the dining room where everyone is, leaving me to follow.

"Hey there, Pumpkin. Glad you could make it," my dad says as I pass through the kitchen. He claps me in a hug, then kisses my forehead.

"Hey, Dad. What's new?"

"Not much on the home front. You should stop by sometime, pay your old folks a visit."

Yeah, not going to happen. I love my dad, but the less time I can spend around my mom, the better.

"Can I make you a cocktail or get you a beer?" my dad asks, pulling a beer out of the fridge for himself.

I open my mouth, but my mom calls out from the dining room.

"Lil got her those skinny margaritas in the outside fridge, Steve. Remember?"

My face reddens, and my dad shoots me an apologetic look, then shrugs his shoulders. "I'll go get it for you," he says, and starts to leave.

"No Dad, I got it," I say. I'd rather have a cocktail—a real one—but Skinny Margaritas will have to do. About five of them, please.

I enter the dining room where my mom is with my aunt and cousin, all seated at the dining table. My mom plucks a cheese cube from the appetizer tray in front of them, then glances at me. Her eyes linger on my hair, then sweep over my body, her smile a mask on her face as she does her usual inventory. She catches my aunt's gaze and an unspoken message passes between them. Later, when everyone is gone, my mom will let me know their assessment on my health, complete with a set of instructions on how to fix what I've wrecked. "I made you a special veggie platter with fat free dip, it's in the kitchen." She smiles at her sister, who nods in approval.

"You won't believe the ingredients in some of those full fat dips," Aunt Lil says, taking a swipe at the full fat dip in front of her with her carrot.

I haven't even put my purse down, and I don't even want anything on that tray. But I settle into dutiful family punching bag mode, offering a polite nod to Aunt Lil, then a quick glance at Jordy. In the half second I take to look at her, I am filled with regret—about my outfit, my life choices, everything. Jordy looks incredible. She always has, but I'd forgotten just how beautiful she was, with her white tooth smile and flawless appearance.

She's wearing a low-cut top in silky black, the kind that my mother would never let me wear, but it looks stunning on my cousin. Her skin is golden tan, as if she just got back from the Bahamas. Also gold are the long necklaces resting between her breasts. Her dark hair is sleek and straight, and her brown eyes shine with long lashes and perfectly applied makeup. She excuses herself, and I see the perfect shape of her pear ass in high waisted white pants, accentuating the impossible length of her legs, finished off with a pair of black strappy sandals and a modest French manicure on her toes.

I caught all that in a half second, and I realize that next to her, I'm a goddamn hobbit.

"Did you see the ring on Jordy's finger?" my mom hisses once Jordy is out of the room, but well within earshot of Aunt Lil. I hadn't, didn't even know she was engaged. It's yet one more thing that Jordy has that I don't. Probably never will.

"I missed it," I admit, absentmindedly picking up a prosciutto-wrapped fig with brie and popping it in my mouth.

"Veggies, Nina," my mother hisses. I bite my tongue as I return to the kitchen to retrieve the veggie tray from the fridge, wishing I could stuff about five more of those figs in my mouth because they tasted so damn good, and they might numb this aching feeling that's settling in my stomach.

"I'm just going grab one of those margaritas," I murmur as I slide the veggie tray on the table by the charcuterie.

"Just one," my mom calls out as I escape into the garage. I'm twenty-seven years old, and she's still managing my food. Well, fuck her.

I open the outdoor fridge, note the skinny margaritas, but also the coffee liqueur Aunt Lil keeps chilled in the door. I pull that out, find a red Solo cup and the vodka in my aunt's and uncle's treasure trove cabinet of alcohol—all the ingredients I need to make a proper Black Russian. Filling the cup with ice, I pour a liberal amount of vodka, then top it with the liqueur. I swirl my cup, then take a sip, groaning as the sugary goodness reaches something deep inside me.

I finish the cup, then make myself a second. By the time I head back in the house with a skinny margarita in hand, my steps are uncertain, and I have a perma smile plastered on my face.

"There you are," my mom says, shooting me an annoyed look. The table is already set for dinner, with steaming plates of sliced sirloin, sautéed green beans, and mashed potatoes, plus a large green salad and a basket of rolls. "We thought you got lost out there."

"I was just…" I realize I'm slurring a little, and clear my throat. "I was noticing the backyard. The garden. It's really something."

I have no idea what the garden looks like, but Aunt Lil is all about appearances, including the exterior of her home. She's probably never gotten her hands in that soil, but her gardeners have likely made it lovely.

Aunt Lil takes the bait, mentioning her prize pumpkins and the gorgeous autumn bouquets she put together that are sure to win Best of Show at this year's Harvest Festival. But I barely hear her as I take in everyone at the table; rather, the one new person at the table sitting right next to Jordy, holding her perfectly manicured hand that's home to the biggest diamond ring I've ever seen in person. A man with familiar broad shoulders, a chiseled jawline, and blue eyes that indeed have flecks of gold in them. A man with the same look of surprise on his face as he takes me in.

Brayden Winters.

The man who saved me, who spent two hours talking with me as we walked home last night, who matched every goddamn item on that list of qualities in my manifestation of the perfect man…

The man who I knew was taken, but still agreed to take a fucking romantic horse ride on the beach with, and the whole time he's been engaged to my cousin.

Well played, Universe.

And goddamn, he looks good—even with that shocked look on his face he's trying to hide. I mean, I was distracted by the way he filled out his sweats the other night, but it's nothing compared to how he looks now in his button up shirt, sleeves rolled up to his elbows, thick forearms appearing like he's about to get down to business. Maybe that's just the Black Russian talking, but holy fuck, the man looks delicious. Under proper lighting, I can see exactly how devastatingly handsome he is, with his clean-shaven face and gorgeous dark hair, luscious thick eyebrows, dimples I could get lost in, and eyes that remind me of the deepest part of the ocean.

That's when I realize I'm staring, and I'm a whole lot drunker than I thought. I stumble a little as I take the only seat available, which happens to be right across from Brayden. Uncle Dan sits to my left, which is a relief, because if I reek of coffee liqueur, he won't say anything.

"Pass the rolls," I murmur to Uncle Dan, hoping to sop up some of this alcohol. Everyone at the table is in double, even as I try my hardest to focus.

"Try salad first," my mother says, mid-story, and I glance quickly at Brayden to see if he notices, then away again. It's one thing for my mom to highlight my weight issues among family, but now that we have someone else here, I'm suddenly aware of every word out of my mother's mouth, how fast my heart is racing, and how much I regret slamming two Black Russians despite knowing

I'm a complete lightweight—and I desperately need that bread.

I leap up and snatch the breadbasket, grabbing several rolls and stuffing one in my face. The conversation at the table stops, and I pause my chewing as I remember where I am. Slowly, I replace the basket on the table and perch back in my seat.

My mom gapes at me. "Nina, no one invites the pig to the table."

I flush, knowing everyone heard what she said. "It was a long drive here," I say, waving my hand as if to erase her words, and my behavior.

"I offered you the veg…" my mom starts, but I cut her off.

"Hi, I'm Nina. I don't believe we've met." I stand again, offering a roll-free hand to Brayden across the table. The relief on his face is brief, but unmistakable.

I don't know whether to be amused by this or offended.

"Brayden," he says. He takes my hand, holding my gaze for a beat longer than socially acceptable.

"My fiancé," Jordy adds when he doesn't. I wrinkle my nose and offer her my most patronizing smile. As in, *thanks Dr. Obvious.* Or maybe, *too bad for your fiancé.* Let her figure out the meaning.

"Nina, your mom tells me you work for a law office in Sunset Bay," Aunt Lil says as I find my seat again. "She says they're making you partner."

I snort a little too loudly, then try to cover it with a polite cough. Meanwhile, Aunt Lil is eyeing my ocean-hued hair, probably wondering what kind of law firm I'm working for.

This is my mother's game—making her daughter sound more important as a way of one-upping her sister's kid. Jordy probably has some fabulous job somewhere, spurring my mom to make up stories about me.

"Nope, still a barista," I say, suddenly finding great pleasure in the way my mom's shooting daggers into the side of my head. Maybe it's the Black Russian, maybe it's Brayden sitting across from me, getting ready to marry the wicked witch of SoCal, or maybe I'm just tired of never being enough for this goddamn family. But I seem to have lost all the fucks I had to give. Shit is about to get real. "In fact, I just got promoted to lead barista, which gives me the privilege of staying late while the manager's nephew peels paint off the walls with his scream-o death metal. The last time I closed, his band managed to chase every fucking customer out of the shop, so I not only had to stay late but there were literally zero tips left for me."

"Language, darling," my mother says. "I'd feel sorry for you, except for the fact that you don't even need to work. My mother set you up for life when she wrote my sister and me out of the will. You could spend your days, I don't know, finding a nice husband instead of wasting your time making coffee."

"Poppy," my aunt murmurs, but she's also smothering a laugh.

"A husband?" I snort out loud. "Why settle for one man when I can have them all?" My mom's smile drops, and I can see the pleading in her eyes, but I'm suddenly having way too much fun here. I help myself to the food, bypassing the salad and green beans completely as I plop a huge mound of potatoes on my plate, followed by steak. If this is going to be my last dinner in this house, might as well get my fill. "Hell, just last week, I was with Sebastian, this guy who did a funny little thing with his tongue. What was that?"

"Nina!"

"That's right. He could roll his Rs." I attempt to do it now, but my vodka tongue gets in the way, making me sound like a dying frog. "Whatever, it was just a very, very nice skill to have, if you know what I mean."

I wink at Jordy as if she does, in fact, know what I mean. My cousin looks like she hasn't taken a breath since we sat down. Brayden on the other hand, is doing his absolute best to hold in a laugh, using his napkin to cover his mouth as his eyes meet mine.

"Antonina Dorotea Chance, that is enough." My mother stands. Her tone brings me back to reality, and I immediately sit back in my chair. "You may be a whore on your own time, but in this house, you will act in a civilized manner."

Whore. The word cuts through me. She knows what happened back then. She knows that's what they called me. And the way she's looking at me now, it's obvious she not only *believes* I'm a whore, but also finds satisfaction at my obvious recoil.

"Excuse me?" Brayden looks at my mother like he can't believe what she said.

"I apologize," my mother says, dabbing the corner of her mouth with a napkin. "Nina isn't at many family dinners, so she doesn't often know how to act civilly."

"There's definitely a lack of civility here, but I don't think it's Nina."

"Brayden, please," Jordy murmurs.

"I mean no disrespect," he continues, ignoring Jordy's pleas. "But in my experience, mothers do not call their daughters what you just called yours."

I look at my plate, suddenly wishing I could fall through the floor. I can barely stand up for myself in this house, and it's my family. But Brayden is an outsider—a guest—and when I look up again, he's also the only one who's looking at me.

"Are you okay?" he asks. For a moment, I forget everyone around us as our eyes stay connected. Forget that there's any barriers between this electric connection between us. *Be with me*, I think, and I feel my eyes sting with tears.

"Nina?"

His voice brings me back to reality. Back to the family table where I'm all alone, and he's sitting next to my cousin, his ring on her finger. And yet, he's still making me feel safe, even around my own goddamn family.

"Let's change the subject," Aunt Lil says, sunshine dripping from her voice. "I happen to know of two people getting married soon, and we have plans to make."

"Mother, we've talked about this," Jordy groans, though she places her hand in Brayden's, that giant ring glinting from the chandelier light. I can't take my eyes off it.

"I'm not talking about you two, though I do wish you'd settle on a date so we could start making all the arrangements. I'm talking about Poppy and Steve's nephew Ethan, and his beautiful bride, Claire."

"Oh, that gorgeous girl." My mother sighs, sitting back in her chair. "She's going to be a knockout in that dress. I mean, you can't even tell she's had a child with how slim she is."

Apparently that's what matters most.

"Did you hear it's on a boat?" Aunt Lil gushes. "They're doing one of those evening cruises for their wedding so they can get married at sea."

My mom and aunt continued dreaming up perfect wedding scenarios, from the colors they should choose to the menu. Meanwhile, I make good work of my plate. I've finally stopped seeing double, but I'm ravenous, which always happens when I drink. Or when I'm uncomfortable. Or when I'm absolutely rocked by devastation. Right now, I'm all three, but I'm trying to put on the performance of a lifetime that I'm fine.

No one is paying enough attention to me to care one way or the other, so I grab seconds and go to town.

In between bites, I steal glances at Brayden and Jordy, trying to figure out how the two of them ended up together. At this moment, Brayden is making small talk with my dad as my mom and aunt yammer on. Meanwhile, Jordy seems more interested in pushing food from one side of her plate to the other without actually eating.

She seems just as uncomfortable as I am, and for a moment, I forget that we hate each other. The honest truth is, I miss what we used to have.

She catches me staring at her, and I sense her softening, like she's mulling something over. Maybe she also regrets our rift and misses the bond we used to share. I don't want to make the first move, just in case I'm wrong, but I'm dying to test the waters. Maybe offer a small smile. Or tell her she looks nice. She does look nice. Perfect, in fact. I start to open my mouth to tell her.

"You have something on your face," she says loudly, and the conversation stops around us.

"Excuse me?" I feel my cheeks heating up, and my hand flies to my face where I feel dried mashed potatoes near my mouth—and not just a little bit. The whole table is looking at me, even Brayden, and I feel like I'm going to die.

"Honestly, Nina," my mother sighs.

I grab a napkin and wet it in my glass, then work at finding anything else that has made a home on my face.

"Is it gone?" I whisper to Jordy. She shrugs, barely looking at me as she pretends to be more interested in the table linen. My eyes find Brayden's, and he gives a slight nod, followed by an uptick of the corner of his mouth.

Is he laughing at me? Does he think I'm as big of a joke as the rest of this family. I honestly can't get out of here fast enough.

"So, who will be your plus one?" my aunt asks.

I realize she's talking to me, and once again I find myself at the center of attention. "My what?"

"Your date, sweetie." She glances at my mom and then back to me, as if I can't see their secret messages to each other. Look at Nina, being stupid once again. "To the wedding?" she prompts. "Are you taking Sebastian?"

"Who?" I'm seriously not winning any genius points here. I realize she's talking about my made-up boyfriend. "Oh, him. No, he was just a fun thing to do for the weekend."

Jordy chokes on some water, and I sip mine to hide my smile.

My aunt, however, ignores what I said. "You know we'd love to meet anyone you're seeing. Maybe one day you'll be planning your own wedding, just like Jordy and Brayden."

I mean, it sounded like they were doing everything *but* planning their wedding, but all right. When I look in their direction again, their faces aren't giving anything away.

"Well, the poly throuple I recently joined frowns on institutionalized unions," I say. "Wait, what does that make us now? A quadruouple?"

"Nina, come on."

I ignore my mom and continue. "I mean, Jeff and Sandy might be into it, but David seems to believe it might wreck the balance."

"What's a throuple?" Aunt Lil whispers to Uncle Dan.

"Mom, she's fucking with you." Jordy shoots her mom a look, then glares at me. "She's fucking with all of us. This has been one big giant waste of time, and you all are just playing into her games. Can we either get on with it, or just end the night?"

"What are you talking about?"

"I'm talking about that huge ass house you live in all by yourself. Nanna Dot left you everything and not one cent for the rest of the family, and you sit there on your throne acting like you're better than all of us."

I laugh, tossing my napkin on the table. "That's why I was invited? Just one more night to rub it in my face that Nanna Dot couldn't stand any of you, so she left it to the only person who actually spent time with her?"

"Leeched off her, you mean."

"Jordy." Brayden covers her hand with his, but she yanks it

away.

"It's true," Jordy continues. "She saw an opportunity and went for it." She huffs a laugh, shaking her head. "I got to hand it to you, Nina, you have the patience of a saint. You're definitely smarter than we all gave you credit for. We all thought you moved in with Nanna Dot because you couldn't stand living under your parents' rules. But really you were just worming your way into being Nanna's favorite and turning her against all of us."

I can feel the white-hot rage coursing through my veins as I listen to the horrible words coming out of my cousin's mouth. It doesn't matter what I do, they will always believe I swindled Nanna Dot out of her money, as if her life wasn't as important as the inheritance.

I look at my mom, enraged by the stoic expression on her face. As if she doesn't disagree. As if she thinks I had ulterior motives for moving there.

"You know why I moved in with Nanna Dot," I spit at her, standing and scooting my chair back. "You *know.*"

At least she has the decency to lose her indignant expression. My mom's face falls, and for a moment I see regret. I see the mom I confided in, who held me as I fell apart. Before she forced me to keep this quiet so no one else knew, my mom was who I needed her to be.

And it had been her idea for me to live with Nanna Dot. Not mine.

"Jordy, you're out of line," my mother says, turning her gaze to my cousin.

"Don't talk to my daughter that way." Aunt Lil starts to push her chair back, but my mom stops her with a look. Something in it makes her simmer back down.

"This whole conversation has gotten away from us."

"What conversation?" My jaw can't drop any lower. "This has been a pick on Nina night right from the start. If you all are so mad at me for what Nanna Dot chose to do, why did you even invite me here? Why do you talk to me at all? I don't need any of you, and you obviously don't need me. So if we're done here, I have a long drive to get home."

"We'll take you," Brayden says, placing his napkin on the table and standing up.

"Like hell we will." Jordy stands too, hands on her hips. But Brayden's eyes are on my empty skinny margarita bottle.

"Oh, because I can't handle my alcohol? Because I'm the one causing issues here?" But even as I say it, I know I'm still tipsy. The food helped to dry me out, and my anger helped hide it. But I'd be an idiot to get behind the wheel.

Rule number one when backed into a corner: always have a way out. I fucked that up the moment I decided to drink.

"I've had enough." Then I get up and leave the table, stopping only to grab my purse before I go out the door.

Chapter Five

Brayden

The table is up in arms as soon as Nina leaves, and I'm not sure what to process first; The way this family has formed a united front against the girl, the fact that my fiancé is in on it, or the realization—and not for the first time—that this is the family I'm marrying into.

But above all else, the woman I spent two amazing hours with the other night, a woman I haven't stopped thinking about since we parted ways, is here—and she's my fucking fiancé's cousin.

Well played, Universe.

Today is a whole different level of insanity, and it makes me question what I'm doing here in the first place.

Jordy's mom and aunt are busy in a heated debate, and their husbands seem to be trying to stay out of the line of fire. I take the opportunity to pull Jordy from the table and slip into her parents' garage. It's there that I see the empty coffee liqueur bottle beside an overturned red Solo cup with a smudge of pink lipstick on the rim, plus a large bottle of vodka. So that's what Nina was doing before dinner. I could smell the alcohol on her from across the table, and I'm surprised no one else got drunk off the fumes.

"Looks like a party," Jordy says, nudging the cup with the toe of her stiletto. "Should I make us drinks?"

She's actually laughing, as if her cousin wasn't just raked over the coals by an angry mob.

"What the hell was that?" I gesture back at the house, and she sighs, a look of annoyance on her face.

"God, I know. Nina is just so self-centered and rude, it's hard to be around her sometimes. That was not how things were supposed to go, but of course she had to go ruin everything, as usual."

"That's not what I'm saying." I run my hands through my hair, trying to make sense of how they treated her, and why it bothers me so much. It shouldn't. I barely know her. I shouldn't even be flirting with the idea of getting to know her—you know, like planning a horseback ride with her. But honestly, I'd be bothered by anyone who was backed into a corner by their very own family. The look on her face tonight, multiple times. The way she was treated like a second-class citizen by people who shared her blood. The way her own mother spoke to her, and not one person came to her defense? "It's like you all took turns hitting her with a bat. You all had each other for backup, and she only had herself. And you wonder why she fought back? I just don't get you, any of you."

"Us?" Jordy laughs, her head tilted to the slanted ceiling of the garage. "You don't know how much trouble that girl has caused. Nina moved out of her parents' house when they tried to keep her from getting in trouble. She was constantly out at night, hanging out with guys she shouldn't, and doing God knows what. When Aunt Poppy and Uncle Steve put their foot down, she moved in with Nanna Dot. But that's not even the bad part. She had everyone fooled, even me. We used to hang out at Nanna's all the time, especially when things got hard here. I thought I had an ally in Nina, and we really connected because neither one of us got along with our moms. But the whole time, she was really just grooming Nanna, getting close to her so that she could convince her to change her will. When Nanna died, we found out she left everything to Nina. The money, her house, even her old Cadillac. Millions of dollars, and Nina has all of it."

It all starts to click. The comments at the table. The stories Jordy has told me. The mysterious villain of their family that I've never met in the five years Jordy and I have been together.

It's nothing like the girl I met the other night.

"That's her? Nina is the family member who stole your mom's inheritance?"

"The one and the same," Jordy says, then huffs a laugh. "Damn, she hasn't changed a bit."

"If you all hate her so much, then what was the point of this family dinner? Surely it wasn't to rub all of this in her face."

"Not exactly," she agrees. "It was stupid really, my mom's idea. I'd thought about transferring my senior year to Sunset Bay, because I'm sick and tired of this whole long-distance thing. I just wanted to be closer to you. But the rent is way more than what I'm paying now, and I know your parents would never agree to me living with you on the ranch since we're not yet married."

This is true. My parents are old fashioned enough to believe marriage comes before living together, though they let Jordy stay in a guest cabin on the property when she visits. I know if I insisted, they'd change their mind, but I'll be honest, I'm not ready to take that step—even if my ring is on Jordy's finger.

"What does this have to do with Nina?"

"My mom thought we could talk Nina into letting me live with her while I finish school and hopefully land a paid internship."

"You all have a funny way of asking someone for a favor."

"Okay, I guess we came on strong. And I can see from your side of things that you think we're all the assholes. But I'm telling you, Brayden, that girl is bad news. I mean, she could probably talk your father into giving her the ranch, if given the chance."

That's stretching it, I'm sure. My dad won't trust anyone with his ranch. He won't even put his full trust in me with the ranch, though he doesn't have much choice anymore.

As for Nina, something isn't sitting right with me about all of this. In the short time it took to walk her home, she had been vulnerable, honest…so completely refreshing. I couldn't put my finger on it, but something about her had awakened a part of me I didn't know had been asleep.

But I hardly know her. And the woman I've known and loved for five years is telling me that Nina is bad news.

This shouldn't be complicated. I have a fiancé, and Nina is no one to me. If she's the kind of person who would screw over her family and manipulate her grandmother, she's not to be trusted.

And yet, I can't stop thinking about how she's been run out of her family's house and is possibly too drunk to drive.

"You have to call her," I say, then ignore Jordy's look of shock. "Listen, you may hate her, but I'm sure even you don't want your cousin to do something stupid like drive drunk."

I can tell Jordy wants to argue about it, and I'm ready for the fight. She must sense that, because she finally sighs and digs her phone out of her back pocket.

"She's not answering," she says after a few moments. I don't hesitate, taking the backyard way to the side gate then slam through another gate to the front. I pull my keys out of my pocket, ready to hightail it down the highway when I see Nina in the front seat of a Cadillac across the street, her head in her hands.

"Brayden," Jordy calls after me, but I ignore her as I stalk across the street and open Nina's car door.

"Hey!" She jerks her head up, and I can tell she's been crying. At this moment, I don't care what happened in the past that makes this whole family hate her. I don't even care that Jordy is on my heels, about to witness me getting too familiar with someone who's supposed to be a stranger. There's something carnal inside of me, ready to explode at the sight of Nina's tears. I want to hurt everyone who's ever hurt her.

Jordy arrives at my side and takes my arm. I have to fight the urge to jerk away. I've never wanted to pull away from Jordy's touch, but right now, it feels like the wrong woman is holding on to me. Even more, I can see from the look on Jordy's face that she's gloating at her cousin's tears. I swallow hard, inhaling deeply so I don't do or say anything I'll regret.

"You can't drive." I release my arm from Jordy's grasp and reach across Nina to take the keys from the ignition. She still smells of alcohol, but this close I can also smell the lilac of her ocean hair and the warm honey of her golden skin, igniting a hunger inside me that's white-hot and captivating. I'm going to go out of my mind if I can't touch her.

I yank my head out of her car, then take a few steps back, her keys in my hand. The rage in her eyes tells me she sees this as a violation, but I'm just trying to keep my distance so I don't do something stupid.

"You smell like my father's liquor cabinet," Jordy huffs. "What, you have to steal his booze too?"

"Fuck you, Jordy. And fuck your whole family." She turns to me, too. "And fuck you, give me back my keys so I can get the hell out of here."

"No." I put the keys in my front pocket. Her eyes follow, and my dick twitches to attention, as if she called its name. I close my eyes briefly, willing it to behave. "You're riding with Jordy in the truck, and I'm driving your car home."

"Like hell I'm driving any vehicle with her in it." Jordy glares at me, and I realize she's right. If I put these two girls in the same cab, they're liable to tear each other apart on the two-hour drive home.

"Fine, then drive the Cadillac," I say to Jordy. "I'll follow in the truck with Nina."

"Are you kidding me? Why can't her parents take her home?"

I think of how her mom jabbed at her the whole meal. If this was how she treated her in public, what would it be like for a two-hour car drive?

My inner voice of reason interrupts this thought process though, reminding me that Nina is not my responsibility. Her dysfunctional family dynamic is not my business. The only one I should be concerned about is Jordy, and it would probably do us both good to pack up and leave, letting the rest of them figure it out.

But I can't. Ever since the night I rescued Nina from those assholes, I have not been able to get her out of my mind. Seeing her here is making me question everything. I can't just walk away, and I definitely can't leave her.

"Look, we're going the same way. And you know where she lives." I do, too, but Jordy doesn't need to know that. "We'll just caravan over there and drop Nina and her car off before heading to the ranch. And the sooner we leave, the sooner we can be home."

"Hello, I'm right here." Nina steps out of the car and leans against it. "Don't I get a say in it?"

"No," both Jordy and I say in unison. Despite myself, I quirk a smile at my fiancé. I can see she's softening. I tilt my head in question until she rolls her eyes and holds out her hand. I fish the keys out of my pocket and place them there, holding her hand for just a moment as a way to say thank you. She relaxes, her eyes showing the hint of a smile.

"Let me just grab my purse and tell them we're leaving." She trots back to the house.

"I'm not really drunk, you know," Nina says once she's gone. "I had two drinks and that's all."

"Two strong drinks, if I can still smell it. Come on, let's get in the truck."

"You don't have to save me," she says, unmoving. "You already did that, and I'm grateful, but I'm done being saved. I'd like to just go home and forget I have a family, or that any of this happened."

"You can do that once I drive you home," I say. "Now get your ass in the truck."

Chapter Six

Nina

I keep my gaze plastered out the window as Brayden drives. To look forward is to see Jordy driving my car and getting her perfect ass germs all over my worn-out seat. To look to my left is to see Brayden, who somehow believes my asshole cousin is someone he could spend the rest of his life with.

So I look out the window, glowering as he sings in perfect pitch to the country music blaring over the radio. Of course he sings well. Of course he is everything perfect—except for the person he fell in love with.

And of course, I am still fighting my attraction to him, despite the fact that he's given me no choice on how I'll get home.

If I'm being fair, I know I'm in no condition to drive. I never should have had anything to drink, especially with a long drive ahead of me. If he hadn't stepped in, I probably would have driven around the corner and bunked in my car for the night, just to ensure my parents didn't see. So this is the superior alternative.

Even if I can't get over how good he smells, how his voice is vibrating through me like a just plucked guitar string, and how I have this irresistible urge to scoot under the arm he has draped over the bench seat, just to experience the rise and fall of his chest underneath my head.

Even if that goddamn list is still in my purse, taunting me—because the perfect man is sitting next to me, and he is absolutely hands off.

"So, I guess horseback riding is out of the question," he finally says, breaking the silence. I glare out the window, shaking my head. He laughs slightly, and this sends a bolt of fury through me.

"You think this is funny? Do you make a habit of cheating on your fiancé or something?"

"You and I never cheated," he corrects me. "I think this is ironic, is all. And no, I've never cheated on Jordy in my life. This was the first time I was ever tempted to. It figures you two are related, or maybe it makes sense. Maybe you're my type because I'm with your cousin."

"We are nothing alike," I spit out. But I'm also reeling a bit from his choice of words. *His type.* Am I still his type? Not that it matters. He's with her, and no matter how much I hate Jordy, I can't cross those family lines.

I hate her even more for this.

"Why her?" I finally do ask. "You could have anyone, and you chose someone who is so self-absorbed and the biggest asshole. I mean, you've met my Aunt Lil, right? You're about to end up with a junior version of her."

He takes a deep breath, and I swear, I hear a hint of regret in his exhale. Or maybe I'm just projecting.

"She's not a bad person, Nina."

"Bullshit. She's a two-faced bitch who will stab you in the back at the first sign of weakness. I should know, I trusted her, and look where it got me." I slouch in my seat, daring a glance at the car we're following. It's getting too dark to see her, but just knowing she's there has every muscle in my body clenched with rage.

"Where *did* it get you?" he asks.

"Come on, I'm the big, bad black sheep of this family and not to be trusted. I mean, look at me. I stole my family's inheritance, and then I almost stole my cousin's fiancé. Obviously, everything they say about me is correct."

"Is it though?"

I can feel his eyes on me, and I turn away when the sting of tears hits my eyes. No one who knows this story has ever asked me for my side of it. Not my parents, not my aunt and uncle, and definitely not Jordy. Now that Brayden is there, asking the one question I wished any of them had asked me, I don't know how to answer.

Because of course, it's not true. But what if something I did made it happen? What if I really am to blame for being the sole heir to my grandmother's fortune?

"It doesn't matter," I mutter. "It's what they believe."

"It matters to me," he says, placing a hand on my thigh. I look down at his hand, and he must realize what he's doing because he moves it immediately. "Sorry."

I don't want him to be sorry. I want him to put it back—and that makes me the worst kind of person.

"Here's the thing, I don't think you're responsible for your grandmother's choice. I think you've been made a scapegoat because they're mad, and I think it's placed a heavy burden on you, heavier than any person should have to bear."

I scoff at this, even as his words hit home. "Yeah, poor me with my millions in my giant mansion. My family hates me, I might as well go buy an island because I can afford it now."

"And yet, you work in a coffee shop," he points out.

I bite my lip, unfamiliar with what's happening here.

"It helps me feel less lonely," I admit softly.

"Yet, most people who gain this kind of money would suddenly have tons of new friends, go on a bunch of vacations, and buy everything they set their sights on. Tell me, Nina, how many vacations have you been on since your grandmother died?"

"None," I whisper.

"And how much of that inheritance has slipped through your fingers?"

I exhale a long breath, my heart pounding wildly at these pointed questions. "As little as possible," I say with a shaky breath. "The coffee job isn't enough to make ends meet, and I have to pay the bills. But I don't feel right about it."

"Why not? It's your money."

I turn to him. "I didn't earn that money. I did no work for it, and I don't feel like I deserve it. I don't even want it. What I want is for my Nanna Dot to walk down the stairs and make me breakfast, to sing Tony Bennett in her off key voice, and to tell me that everything is going to be okay. Because you know what, Brayden? No one tells me that anymore. No one has even made me feel like everything is going to be okay since she died. When I lost my Nanna, I lost the last person who actually saw me. So no, I don't spend her money, but I also won't give it to them because she didn't want them to have it, and I don't either."

I'm breathing hard when I finish, my whole body feeling like it's going to explode with the amount of emotion filling this cab. This time when he reaches for me, taking hold of my hand, I don't let go because I need an anchor to keep me grounded. I know it's wrong. But *why* is it wrong? I hate Jordy. I don't care if I hurt her. In fact, I want to hurt her after every way she's twisted the knife in my back.

But I also don't. There's the part of me that doesn't want to flirt with this idea of an affair—if that's even what's happening—because I'll be the one who gets hurt in the end. But there's the other part that feels protective over my cousin, who loves her in spite of our fractured relationship. I miss what we once had, and I think about her way too much for someone who doesn't give a rat's ass about me.

Seeing her today pretty much cinched where I stand in her eyes, and where she stands in mine. The connection we once shared is completely severed. After tonight, I hope I never see her again.

"Have you ever thought about getting a roommate?" Brayden asks, cutting into my thoughts.

I look at him curiously. "That's random."

"It is, isn't it," he laughs. "I was just thinking of the other night, when I walked you home. Your house is so huge, and I can't believe you live there by yourself."

I offer a tight smile, then shrug. "I had roommate a couple months ago, my friend Maren. In fact, we used to work together, but then she got all big and successful with her music and ended up quitting her job and getting her own place. I thought about getting another roommate, but first I wanted to try out how it feels to live on my own since I never really have."

"But you're lonely."

I close my eyes and rest my forehead against the window. "I don't know," I say. "Yes, I miss having someone there to talk to after work, and sometimes being alone makes me feel nervous. But I also like that I don't have to answer to anyone about anything. I can eat what I want for dinner, keep my house any way I want, and walk around naked if I feel like it."

When I look at him, I can see a slight flush to his cheeks. I can't help wondering if he's picturing me naked right now, even as we drive behind his fiancé in my car.

"What about you? What exactly does home life look like to you?"

"Crazy," he answers. "I know you're familiar with the Salt & Sea Ranch, so you know it has lodging there. We have guests staying in the cabins from Thursday to Sunday, so we constantly have a small crowd in the main house and on the grounds. I feel like my mom is always in the kitchen, but she also cares for my dad. He's pretty self-sufficient, but the wheelchair limits him in many ways. You can imagine the strain on my mother's shoulders. I've been trying to find someone to help her, but the right person hasn't shown up yet. It's my family, you know? So whoever I hire needs to be someone who gets along with everyone, as if they're an extended part of our family."

"That makes sense," I say. "Is it just you and your parents?" When I was taking horseback riding lessons, I never had any interaction with the family who owned the ranch. It was just my instructor, and she was only renting the ring we were working in.

"I have…" He pauses a moment, long enough that I realize he's stumbling over his words. I'm about to ask him, but he shakes his head. "I have a sister. Hazel. She's seventeen, a senior in high school."

"Does she work on the ranch too?"

"When she can. But she's also on the track team and has a part time job tutoring a few freshmen, so she's not always available. She's heading to UC Davis in the fall, so I want to rely on her as little as possible." He glances at me. "No use getting used to someone who can't stay, you know?"

It's almost like the words have a double meaning, like he doesn't want to get used to me. But that's silly because we're only on a car ride that will be over in another hour. What will happen then? It shouldn't matter, but I can't help thinking how this could be my last interaction with him.

"Do you like being around so many people, with all the guests who visit the ranch?" I ask.

"Sometimes," he says. "And sometimes, like you, I wonder what it would feel like to own my own space without worrying about anyone around me. But I think it would be short lived. Besides, I'd miss the guys I work with."

"Oh really? Guys? Like single men who look like you?"

Brayden erupts into laughter. "Let's just say our horse tours aren't only popular because of the horses. We get a lot of ladies on our beach rides."

"Damn, I might need to book a tour."

His eyes narrow, and I bite my lip, knowing he's bothered that I'm even pretending to think of other men. Whatever. Maybe I *should* book a tour, meet a cowboy, and ride off into the sunset with some other man. Because Brayden Winters doesn't have the right to be jealous, and I don't have the right to want him to be.

The sky is dark by now, and as the conversation lulls to a close, I stare out at the stars in the sky, mirroring the lights of the towns we're passing through. As relieved as I am to have escaped the family dinner from hell, I'm dreading the loneliness of my empty house. I only touched on it with Brayden, but no one knows how clawing the darkness is, how loud the silence is, how—as much as I love living in my grandmother's home—I also feel like a prisoner, like the walls are closing in. I know I need to find someone else to take Maren's place as my roommate, but I'm also aware of how badly I've let the place go. Even after cleaning all day yesterday, there's still so much to do to make the place presentable. I guess I could hire someone. I mean, what else am I using Nanna's money on? But I can't even bring myself to allow a stranger into my home.

"I suppose I could get a roommate," I whisper, then realize I said it aloud. I peek at Brayden to see if he's listening, but he's just singing softly to the low music.

"It might not be so bad," he says after a few beats. He glances at me, giving me a knowing look.

"What?"

"Nothing," he says, then looks away quickly. So quickly, I know he's hiding something.

"Come on, out with it."

He sighs deeply, his hands running over the steering wheel. "Have you thought about asking your cousin?"

What the hell?

"No way. Are you kidding? I wouldn't let that bitch move in with me if she was on the corner, begging for change. Besides, she doesn't need a place to move into. She lives with Aunt Lil and Uncle Dan."

"Exactly," he says, glancing at me. "But hear me out. You and Jordy have a bond, I know it. She told me about you a long time ago, before your grandmother died. Not by name, but she's actually said nice things about you. Remember the magic syrup on pancakes, or the movie marathons?"

Or the lists that described the perfect man, and now he's driving me home? But I don't say that. I also can't help but soften just hearing that she told him about us. Maybe it still means something to her now.

"She actually told you about that?"

He nods. "I didn't realize the connection until just a few minutes ago though. She told me how the two of you were like sisters, even though you both drifted apart. She loved you, and I think she still loves you. I'm willing to bet you love her too. Am I right?"

"If love means I want her to rot in hell, then yeah, I love her to fucking bits."

He chuckles, then gives me a sideways glance. "Come on. You don't miss her? Not even a little?"

"If she drove my grandmother's car over a cliff right now, I'd mourn the car, but consider it a worthy sacrifice."

"Really?"

I sigh, realizing I'm being over-the-top cold right now. But when I glance at him, the amusement on his face hits a nerve.

"Why is that so hard to believe? I hate Jordy. Whatever connection we had, it's gone."

"Because you are way too affected by your cousin to actually hate her. If you didn't care, she wouldn't have hurt you so bad. If you really hated her, you'd have moved on by now."

I roll my eyes, but my breath feels shallow at the way he's targeting all my fault lines.

"Jordy hurt you," he continues.

"Yeah."

"But what if she apologized? What if she started over, away from your family, and asked you properly if she could move in with you. Would you consider it?"

I slump in my seat, mulling it over. He stays silent, and I know he's waiting for my answer. But I already know the answer, and I hate that I'm this big of a pushover.

"It would have to be a really good apology," I mutter. When he laughs, I glare at him. "I don't get you. The other night, the texts. What gives, Brayden? Are you playing Jordy? Are you playing me? Is this just one giant game?"

The smile evaporates on his face, and he shakes his head. "It's complicated," he finally says.

"It's not, though. You told me you have a girlfriend, which I guess is noble of you because you didn't pretend you were available. But she wasn't just your girlfriend, she's your fiancé. So why would you ask for my phone number? Or to go horseback riding? Or try to do anything that keeps us connected? And why, after all that, are you insisting I move your fiancé into my house? Do you enjoy stringing people along?"

He takes the exit, and we slow to a stop at the red light. Jordy's car made it through already, and we sit alone in the crimson glow.

"I'm not enjoying any of this," he says seriously. "Not one bit."

"So you don't love my cousin."

He sighs. "I didn't say that."

"What *are* you saying?"

The light turns green, but he doesn't move. His eyes remain on me, and I force myself not to look away. At first, I am waiting for him to answer. But then, slowly, I feel it again. That spark of electricity that flows from him to me, and back to him again. That feeling that this is so much more than what's on that paper in my purse. He's the one. Every cell in my body knows it to be true.

"Nina, I—"

The car behind us honks, and we both jump in surprise. He swears under his breath, then turns to the road, driving through the intersection.

"I'm sorry," he says. "I just wish that—" He cuts himself off, and I see the way his jaw is flexing. "If things had been different…" He pauses again, and I groan in frustration.

"Just say it, Brayden. Give me something to understand what's happening here."

"What's happening is there's the right path, and there's the path that makes us happy, and sometimes, they're not the same thing, but they could be with a bit of time. I'm saying, that if our timing had been different, it could have been us. And I know that's so unfair of me to say because there's not an us, and there never will be. So even telling you that is cruel, but I'm engaged to your cousin, and that's not going to change."

"So why are you trying to get me to move her into my house? Is it because my attraction to you isn't enough? You need to torture me too?"

He's quiet for a moment, his eyes focused on the road ahead. Then he clenches that beautiful jaw of his, his eyes narrowing.

"Fuck," he spits out, his hand hitting the wheel. "I shouldn't be asking you at all. The truth is, you shouldn't let Jordy move in, only because it's completely unfair to you. They held this dinner as a way to get you to let her move in. And honestly, Nina, your family doesn't deserve someone like you at all."

This stings, but it makes all the sense in the world. I mean, God forbid this be a happy family dinner. Everything with my family comes with strings.

And now, here's Brayden, pulling one of them.

"So why ask me at all?"

He shoots me a strained look. "Because tonight when I saw the rift between you and your family, I thought maybe this could be a way for you to find peace. I saw the hurt on your face at dinner tonight, and I saw the way you kept stealing glances at Jordy. And you know what? When you weren't looking, she was doing the same thing. So I told myself that maybe the two of you could figure out a way to come back together." He takes a deep breath then glances at me.

"And she's transferring up here for school," I fill in. "So it would make sense."

"And she's preparing for our wedding."

I don't know why the words knock the wind out of me. The wedding. Of course that's what she's doing. She's rocking that huge ass ring, so why wouldn't she want to get going on their wedding plans?

Except that neither of them seemed so keen to talk about the wedding at the dinner table.

"Now?" I ask.

"Well, after she's done with school, which will be at the end of next semester. We've been long distance our whole relationship, and she thought it might be a good idea to move closer before we get married, kind of as a trial before we make things permanent."

I fucking hate this idea. I have no right to feel this strongly about it either. I've known Brayden for all of two days, and I'm feeling crazy possessive over him.

He's not mine.

"And why can't she move in with you?"

"Because my parents won't go for it. I still live at home, since it just makes sense, running the ranch and all. But it is my parents' home, and I have to respect their rules."

I'm so confused by what he's suggesting. My heart is aching for so many reasons, mostly because even with all he's saying, I'm considering it. For one, Jordy and I have a chance to rekindle the bond we once shared—and man, I miss what we had so much. But there's another reason that feels equally as big, and that's knowing I will never be with Brayden, no matter what. What better way to pound that nail in the coffin than by moving his fiancé into my home? Maybe if I see the two of them together more often, it will help me to move beyond this ridiculous obsession that is Brayden Winters.

We take the turn on my street, and I can feel each second like a brick against my head, counting down the final moments of our time together.

"Just forget about it," Brayden says, shaking his head. "Seriously, forget I asked."

But I can't.

We pull up to the house. Jordy is parked across the street, looking at her phone as if she doesn't care that we're here. I reach for the door handle, but then the heat of his hand reaches my shoulder just as I bite back the sob I've been holding. This is so hard, and I never realized how much it hurt. All of this. I never wanted to lose my family. Yet here I am, lonelier than I've ever felt in my life, actually contemplating allowing Jordy to move in, partly because I miss my family.

But mostly because it pretty much guarantees I have to forget anything I've ever felt for her fiancé.

"I'll think about it," I finally say.

Chapter Seven

Brayden

My hand on Nina's shoulder is a brazen move, with Jordy right there across the street. All she has to do is look up and she'll see me touching Nina in a way that is too familiar, too much for someone I should barely know. Part of me wants Jordy to look up. To see my hand on another woman. To realize that I have wants and needs too. That I had a direction for my life once that didn't include the one we're on now.

This isn't Jordy's fault, though. She didn't ask for this anymore than I did. And now we're in this place where she sees the future in my eyes, and I am just getting through a day at a time. I love her. I think I love her. But is it enough? I thought it could be. But that was before I met the girl sitting in front of me now.

A portion of my awareness remains with my fiancé, but most of it is with her cousin, as it's been this whole drive home. On the sweet air she breathes into my car. On the quiet way she hums when she's thinking. On the few times she's laughed, and in the way her eyes blaze when she's angry. On my hand that rests on her shoulder. I'm barely touching her, but fuck, my hand could be inside her with the way she's affecting me right now—for the past two hours, since I saw her at dinner, since I met her two nights ago.

"I'll think about it," Nina says, agreeing to something I had no right to ask in the first place.

I hear the car door across the street slam, and my hand drops from Nina in a heartbeat, and in the next, I see Nina's face fall, just for a moment before her mask is back on. Jordy knocks on my window, and I roll down the window.

"I have to use the bathroom," Jordy says, then pokes her head in. "Nina, please let me use your bathroom."

"There's a gas station a few blocks down the road," Nina says, sliding out of the truck, grabbing her purse behind her. "Thanks for the ride." She doesn't even look at me, pretending like we're perfect strangers—and we are, I suppose. So why does it feel like my heart is folding inside of itself?

"Come on, Nina, it's an emergency. I wouldn't ask otherwise."

Nina shakes her head. "Hell, no. I don't need you poking around so you can report back to the family."

"Come on, Jordy," I say. "We're only about fifteen minutes from home."

"I cannot hold it that long," Jordy hisses, and the panicked look on her face tells me she's serious. I take one look at her white pants, and then the sudden paleness of her usually tan face, and I realize this is a do or die situation.

"Nina," I start, and she sighs.

"Fine, but don't look around. I wasn't expecting anyone, and the place isn't exactly company ready."

Jordy practically sprints up the stairs while I slowly follow behind. She squirms while Nina fishes for her keys, and I'm fairly sure is taking her time on purpose. When she finally finds them, she unlocks the door and pushes against it, but then pauses.

"Not a word," she warns Jordy, then opens the door. Jordy pushes through, and I can hear her footsteps retreating down the hall. I start to follow, but Nina stops me. "Nuh-uh, buddy, you stay out here with me."

"You're not going to watch to make sure she doesn't steal anything?" I'm trying not to laugh, especially as I see the mischievous glint in her eyes. She was fucking with Jordy the whole time, probably hoping she peed her pants.

"I keep all of Nanna's good stuff in the safe," she says. "Alongside my millions of dollars."

"Is this what it will be like if you actually let her move in?"

Too far. I realize it as I see her expression darken, her whole body go rigid. She might be considering letting Jordy move in, but she's definitely not there yet. And I'm sure as shit not saying anything to Jordy about this at all. Let the two of them figure it out.

Besides, if Jordy doesn't move here, maybe we can put the wedding off for a little longer.

Jordy comes out a few minutes later, visibly relieved. Keeping to her word, she says nothing negative to Nina as we say goodbye. I turn back to the house after I help Jordy into the truck—just a glance—and then swallow my disappointment that she's not there.

"You should see what she's done to my Nanna's house," Jordy says as soon as I'm in the driver's seat. "The place is a hoarder's wet dream. There isn't a space in that house that's clean. It's like the rooms threw up and covered every inch of the floor, the furniture, everything."

"Was it unsanitary?"

"Who knows, with Nina," Jordy says, grimacing. "But no, not exactly. I mean, the kitchen looked gross. But the bathroom was usable. It was mostly just her clothes everywhere, or things not put away, and it was like that in every room on the main floor."

"So you snooped." I shoot her a sideways glance, and she shrugs her shoulders.

"I mean, wouldn't you?"

No, I wouldn't. But I don't bother answering her.

"I couldn't help it. I haven't been in that house since Nanna died, and I was just curious. Besides the junk, nothing was different. Nina hasn't even tried to make the house her own, or at least make things more modern. My Nanna kept that house like a historic museum, and it's all still there."

"In the same condition, too?"

"I didn't look that closely. I only had a few minutes. But I think it was. Nothing looked ruined, at least. Just messy."

I don't know Nina well enough to make any snap judgments, but what Jordy is describing makes me concerned. Things obviously changed a lot when her grandmother died, more than just the loss of the family's matriarch, and now that Nina doesn't have a roommate, she admitted she was lonely. I'd sensed something in her voice then, and now the alarm bells are sounding.

It's a lot like that dark place I was in ten years ago, when I ran away to college as an attempt to escape reality. But that darkness hung over me like a cloud, following me no matter where I went. Even now, I feel the cold whisps of fog sinking into my pores, trying to drag me back down.

Is that what Nina feels?

"Are you still thinking about trying to move in with her?" I ask. Jordy huffs a laugh and shakes her head.

"She almost made me pee on the sidewalk. You really think she'll let me live there? It's doubtful. Even if she did, I can't live in a place like that. It's a huge house, but with all the shit that's in there, it doesn't seem to have room for another human."

"You are going to school for stuff like this, though," I point out.

"For interior design, not clutter control."

"Yeah, but you're good at it. Remember when you helped Jake consolidate his grandmother's things before she moved into that senior home, and then helped organize her new apartment? That was a lifetime of things you sorted through, and you did it in no time flat."

Jake works at the ranch, and he'd been worried about his grandma for a while. His parents lived out of state, so it was just him, and the job seemed overwhelming. Jordy had volunteered her weekends to helping out, and she was incredible the way she honored Mrs. Hendley and the sentimental hold she'd had on her belongings. Somehow, Jordy was able to get it done in just a few weeks, two days at a time, and make a home out of that stark, empty room in the facility. I was so proud of her, not just her talent, but her compassion—and it made me a bit more excited about our future together.

"I'm telling you, Mrs. Hendley had less stuff than Nina has in that place. If the main floor looks like that, I can only imagine what the rest of the house is like."

"You know, she's not that bad." It's a weak argument, because Nina is incredible. But I can't say that to Jordy.

Jordy nudges my knee with hers, then gives me a grin. "She got to you, huh?"

"What are you talking about?" I quickly scroll through the last five minutes of our conversation. Was I obvious? Does Jordy know?

"She charmed you, it's what she does. It's how she got to my Nanna, and how she bilked our family out of millions. Now she's doing it to you because you don't know any better."

I've heard Jordy slam Nina dozens of times. In the past, I've just let her vent, but now that I know the person she's referring to, I can feel my whole body tense up.

"You sure figured all that out without even hearing what was said," I say, shooting her a side glance.

"I mean, tell me I'm wrong."

"You're wrong."

Jordy looks shocked that I'd disagree with her, but I continue.

"Nina did not try to charm me. In fact, she was quite angry that we were forcing her to accept the ride home."

"*You* forced her," Jordy says. "And forced me too. I would have let her figure out her own way home."

"Fine, but you didn't hear her talk. I think there are two sides to the story about your Nanna, and you've only heard one of them. And who narrated that story for you? Your mom?"

Jordy doesn't answer, which is confirmation enough.

"It's a shame that you've let family drama ruin the relationship you shared with someone you were extremely close with."

"We weren't that close," Jordy mutters.

"That's not how it sounded whenever you told me about your childhood. You may think you hate her, but I think you might actually miss her."

She snorts, but she doesn't argue.

We pull up to the ranch, and a black and white blur races out of the barn, barking at the truck. I open the door and Cherokee, my favorite ranch worker, dances in front of me until I stoop down to scruff the back of his furry neck.

"I swear that border collie has a tracking device on you. He could be across the field, and he'd still be at your door by the time you park." Jordy reaches down and pets Cherokee too, who licks her hand before going back to saying his hellos to me. "I'll just wash up and see if your mom needs help," she laughs, keeping her soiled hand away from her outfit and pulling her bag out of the bed of the truck with the other.

I take a moment to head to the barns to check on my girls, Cherokee close to my heels. The staff has long since gone home, and the guests are all in their cabins, so I'm quiet as I give each horse a nose rub and a handful of cob. We have eighteen horses in all, enough for two tours at a time along the many trails that border the coastline. Salt and Sea Ranch has been a Sunset Bay destination for horse lovers my whole life, starting the year before I was born. And now, with my dad in a wheelchair, it's up to me to make sure the place continues running for many more years to come. But will I be the one to keep it going? I don't know the answer to that.

Once I get married, everything will change.

I reach the last stall, and Sara nickers at me as my hand brushes against her nose. She's my favorite of all the girls, with her rust-colored fur, the white stripe that centers her head, and the long black mane that's now sectioned into braids with little daisies peeking through the wave. I smile, plucking one flower from the braid and twisting it between my thumb and forefinger. My sister Hazel, most likely. She's always showering Sara with attention, probably because she's my horse.

"That's my girl," I say as Sara takes the rest of the cob from my hand, then laugh as she searches my shirt for more. "You'll get more tomorrow, sweet thing. For now, it's time for bed."

"For you too," my mom says behind me. "And you have someone waiting not so patiently for you to say goodnight." She hands me a napkin with a piece of persimmon cake on it, then nods in the direction of Jordy's cabin. "We already had some, but I brought you a slice so you don't get lost in the house too."

"I'll just say goodnight and then be right behind you," I say, taking the cake from her hands.

"Sure you will." She winks at me. "Your dad is already in bed, and I'm heading there too. I doubt we'll be awake to notice what time you make it to your bed." She pats the side of her thigh. "Come on, Cherokee, it's time for you to go to bed too."

I lean in and kiss her cheek. "I'll be in soon," I promise, because those are my intentions. A curious look crosses her expression. I take a bite of the cake, then hum my appreciation, trying to sidestep whatever question is on her mind. "That's some good cake, Mom."

She smiles, her curiosity disappearing, just like the last of the cake. "Goodnight, Bray." Then she leaves the barn, taking my dog with her.

I leave the barn a few moments later, turning right and heading to Jordy's cabin. I'm not actually sure if she's waiting for me, even if she hasn't been to the ranch for a couple weeks. We've been going through the motions lately, and I haven't let it bother me. I've been busy with work, and she's been overwhelmed by school, so things have been lukewarm between us for a while. It's like we've just been throwing kindling on the fire of our relationship, only to make sure it doesn't go out. But I've noticed the distance I've been feeling hasn't felt very one-sided lately. That said, I know she still loves me and wants to make this work.

Yet, my doubts have escalated the past few weeks, starting with her plan to move closer. Meeting Nina didn't help, but this has been going on for much longer than that. I thought it would pass, that I might actually feel excited to have her closer—instead, there's dread. Am I just too used to the long-distance nature of our relationship? Will she tie up all my time once she's here?

Maybe. But any plans we're making just brings me that much closer to the day we get married and plan a life away from the only home I've ever known. I'm trying my hardest to find something in this to get excited about.

And I'm failing.

I push through Jordy's cabin door. She's already in bed, a book in her lap, but she looks up with a smile as soon as I enter.

"Well, hello there, cowboy," she says, putting her book aside. She makes room for me on the bed, and I join her, wrapping my arms around her as she backs herself into the cove of my body. I inhale the sweet scent of her hair and neck. But all I can think of is the way my body reacted to Nina's scent when I grabbed her car keys, how consumed I was as her natural perfume filled the cab of my truck, how it felt every single time I touched her.

"Long day, huh?" I'm setting the stage for an early exit, but Jordy has different plans in the way she scoots closer. Despite my earlier thoughts, my dick twitches at the invitation.

"We could put a bow on it," she murmurs, arching against me. It's all the coaxing I need as my hands wander over her thin tank top, finding the peaks of her erect nipples, then coasting over the hard smoothness of her curves. Jordy has a smoking body. With her silky tan skin and toned muscles, she's like a Victoria's Secret angel. She works hard on her appearance, spending hours each day in the gym and eating mostly foods that grow out of the ground. It's what turned my head before I knew her. She was turning everyone's head back then—still is—and yet, for some reason, she only has eyes for me.

But as I climb over her, lining my hard cock against her slit, my hand brushing over the firmness of her body, I can't help thinking of someone a little softer. I try to keep my mind with Jordy, staying in the present as my hands weave through her hair, our hips keeping perfect rhythm; but Nina infiltrates my mind with her sweet scent, her luscious curves, and her careful smile. I breathe into Jordy's neck, trying to forget about the softness of Nina's skin under my hand, how I wanted to run my palms over her bare thighs, massage her feet before sucking on her pretty toes, grab the cushion of her hips, and bury myself in her.

I come so hard, muffling my mouth into Jordy's shoulder to keep from saying Nina's name. I lay there for a moment, catching my breath, and willing my guilty heart to slow its beat.

"Wow, that was some pent-up energy," Jordy laughs. I slide off her, then to a sitting position on the bed. She pulls the blankets up to her chin, then looks at me with sleepy eyes and a soft smile.

"I guess it's been a while," I say with a light laugh, then lean forward to kiss her forehead. But inside, I'm dying. She can never know what just happened, and it can never happen again. It's not fair to her that while I'm fucking her, my mind is fucked by her cousin.

Chapter Eight

Nina

I wake up unsure of where I am. I know I'm in my house, but where in my house is unclear. Through groggy eyes, I try to make out my surroundings. Crown molding. A tall ceiling fan covered in dust. Huge curio along the wall beside windows with the curtains drawn. Ah, my living room. I'm buried in a nest of clothes, still wearing the ones I had on last night. Ugh, including my bra.

I make quick work of that, letting the girls fly free as I throw the bra onto the pile. Then I pad to the kitchen to down whatever is left of yesterday's coffee in the pot. It seems a crime, as I sip the cold, burnt brew, especially since I work in a coffee shop. But desperate times and all that.

The phone rings as I wait for the new pot to percolate, and I groan as I see the 805 area code. I deleted Jordy's number from my phone a long time ago, but I still recognize it when she calls, which has been two times in the past five years—yesterday, before she and her fiancé kidnapped me, and now today.

I decline it, then tap my long fingernails on the counter, willing the coffee to hurry up.

I wonder how much shit she talked to Brayden about me once they dropped me off at my house. Not that it matters. Brayden doesn't need to think any good things about me. He's with her, and she'll likely poison him against me. It's probably better that way, anyway.

But during last night's drive, it was easy to pretend. It was easy to imagine he was glancing at me just as much as I was peeking looks at him. The way I studied his jawline, the way his large hands held the steering wheel, how it would feel if he gripped me with the same intensity.

The way he admitted he has feelings for me too.

He's not mine.

By now, Jordy has probably dragged my name through the mud with him, starting with this mess of a house. I already know she's going to blab to the family about what a fuck up I am, how I'm lazy, and most of all, that I'm ruining our grandmother's house I won't let her move into.

And I'm aware of all of that. I *am* a lazy fuck up, and I *am* ruining Nanna Dot's house. Our grandmother always kept this place sparkling. She had help from a housekeeper, but in between cleanings, she still tidied every day. The house always smelled good, with the sunshine beaming through clear windows, plants blooming in every corner, and a welcome feel to the whole house. And her kitchen? It was always spotless, ready for her to come in and whip up something comforting and delicious.

She would be appalled if she came here now and saw the mess I'd created of her home. Even after cleaning the other day, it's like the house reproduced the mess overnight. This is all my fault. The dishes from last night's late-night snack. The overflowing garbage. The tiny ant trail on the counter that's bound to be a bigger issue if

I don't take care of it now.

I did this, and it's time I did something about it.

While the coffee continues brewing, I slip on some gloves and get to work prying dishes and bowls glued to the counter, smushing old food and dirty napkins in the packed garbage bag, then taking the trash to the can outside. I fill the sink with soapy water and let the dishes soak while I retrieve dishes from the other rooms.

The coffee pot beeps at me, and I pause to grab a cup. As soon as I sit down, though, I lose my momentum. It's like my whole body lets down, and I'm suddenly so tired. And so alone. And so sick of this goddamn house that's way too big and way too much work for just me. But I can't leave. I have a whole bank account of money, and I won't even touch it unless absolutely necessary. I could hire someone to help me, but I don't want anyone to see how bad this place looks. I could buy a new house, one that was much smaller. But then what? If I sell the house, it's like I'm abandoning Nanna Dot. And I was all she had left in the end.

Now I'm here, and I have no one. It's almost like the curse of this house—that anyone who lives here will be forgotten and left to die alone.

I'm so fucking alone.

A few hours later I pull into the parking lot at work. A handful of cars are there, including my manager's. I sigh, preparing myself for a day of micromanaging and veiled insults. Oh, Susan thinks she's being nice, but it's like she took a course for managers that uses a transparent method to reframe insults.

Allow me to demonstrate.

"Oh, I wouldn't have thought to do it that way," means "Wow, Nina, I didn't think someone could do that so wrong."

"That's an interesting way to make coffee," means "I'm not sure you could fuck coffee up so horribly."

"I admire your courage with your appearance," means "You look like shit. Did you look in the mirror before you came to work?"

"Looks like you're on Nina time today," means "I'd fire you if you weren't the only one willing to work the shitty shifts I give you."

To be fair, Susan has only been this awful to me since Maren left. It's like all the abuse she handed Maren has now been transferred to me—and Maren never actually deserved it. I've always treated this place like my social club while Maren actually worked. I suppose it's because she needed the paycheck, and I just need the people. But now, there are days when I wonder if I even need the paycheck, because this job stopped being fun the day Maren left the café.

I push through the doors, and Susan looks up quickly, standing by someone new at the register. She shoots me a curious look, then one of knowing.

"Ah, you didn't check the schedule, did you?" She glances up and down at my outfit, then raises an eyebrow. "I read somewhere that unmatched clothes were making a comeback. I thought it was a joke, but look at you."

I chose to wear my loudest pink shirt today, paired with a turquoise skirt and purple striped socks in my black Mary Jane pumps. Yes, it's bright and colorful—and happy—I needed an extra dose of color to fight the darkness I was feeling inside. And honestly, I couldn't care less what Susan thinks.

"I always work Monday," I say, pulling out my phone and tapping the schedule app. Sure enough, my name isn't on there. Not today, and not on any other day either. My jaw drops and I look up. But Susan isn't paying attention to me. I realize now that she's training the girl next to her. She never trains anyone. She never does anything in this café. And yet, here she is, teaching this chick how to use a frothing wand when I'd never seen my manager use one before.

"Why isn't my name on the schedule?" I ask.

Susan looks up, her expression slightly annoyed as if she can't understand why I'm still there.

"I guess we just ran out of spots this week. Wouldn't you like some time off, anyway?"

"No, I want to work my job, like usual."

Susan laughs, glancing at the girl next to her as if she'll understand some inside joke. To her credit, the girl looks as uncomfortable as I feel.

"Nina, honey, you haven't done your job in years. Why start now?"

Is this bitch for real? Is she fucking blind? I think of the number of waking hours I've wasted on this place. And for what? Not money, that's for sure. Not with the pennies we're paid to sling coffee for the caffeinated elite. I'm the only one who shows up consistently, and she has the nerve to tell me I'm not doing my goddamn job?

Fuck her.

"I've been busting my ass around here," I spit at her. "The other day I didn't get out until late because your dumbass nephew and his sucky band ate all our profits and left me the mess to clean up. Every day is a mystery with you, because I don't know which wild idea I'm going to have to scramble for. You think you have to keep coming up with new stuff, but really you need to focus on what we already have going on and improve on that, and you need more than one person on shift, especially for closing."

I'm just getting started, feeling every single resentment well up inside me as I vomit it all at Susan. I know I should stop, that the things I'm saying won't change a thing. But I'm so angry, I can't help myself.

"I've hardly ever called out sick, and trust me there were days

I've wanted to. But I show up because I know if I don't, it's my coworkers who suffer, not you. When was the last time you thought of that? Like when you waited until the last minute to post our schedules, or you hired your nephew's band so that our ears have to bleed while you're cozy at home. Did you think of us? Or even the shop? Because this place ran so much smoother before you became manager and fucked it all up."

"Nina, that's enough. You're not on the schedule because you're f—"

"Fired? Impossible. Because I quit." I throw my crumpled apron on the ground, then turn to the bewildered new hire next to her. "If things get too rough, get out while you can. This place doesn't pay enough for a living wage, and there are plenty of cafés that make better coffee."

Then I storm out of Insomniacs for the last time ever.

I book it to my Cadillac, the rage coursing through me like molten lava in my veins. When I slide onto the seat, I slam the door hard enough that the car creaks at me.

"Sorry, girl," I mutter, patting the dash. Too much of that, and the car will break down for good, just out of spite. I toss my bag in the passenger seat at the same time my phone starts ringing. I manage to dig it out before it goes to voicemail.

"What?" I bark into the phone.

There's silence for a moment, and then, "Don't hang up."

Fuck my life. Fuck fuck fuck. It's Jordy, and damn it all to hell, I *should* hang it up. But I'm so angry, I stay on the phone. In fact, I take the opportunity to tell her exactly what I think of her.

"Go to hell, Jordy. You are the last person I want to speak to, along with either of our mothers. As far as I'm concerned, you all are dead to me. I'm sick and tired of bearing the weight of your blame for a situation I didn't create, and I'm done being labeled the villain of this family over every single lie you three tell about me. Do you understand?"

I breathe hard, waiting for her answer, almost sure she's going to hang up on me.

"I don't," she starts, and I wind up to lay into her some more. She beats me to it. "But I want to. Brayden and I were talking last night, and he mentioned—"

"Brayden," I laugh. "I should have known the two of you were talking shit about me. This is just rich."

"No, we weren't talking shit," Jordy says. "Well, I was. But Brayden mentioned that I've only heard one side of the story, and that it was from my mom. I didn't quite understand it last night, but I've had some time to think." She pauses, and it's the perfect opportunity for me to hang up. But I don't. Some small part of me, the part that must revel in abuse, wants to hear what she has to say. "Nina, can we meet up? I think we need to talk."

"So you can go right back to our mothers and have a good laugh?"

I know that's not it, but I'm not about to bring up her mission of being my roommate. My hope is that she'll forget the whole thing, and maybe if I cut this off now, I can move on from this crazy family and forget they even exit.

"Goodbye, Jordy. Have a good life."

"Wait," she says before I can hang up. "That's not what's happening. Please give me a chance, I'm trying here. You have to understand how it feels from my side. I loved Nanna Dot. Maybe I didn't live with her, but I was close to her. When she died and cut me out of the will, you have to know how awful that felt. It was like she was taking back every kind thing she ever said to me. And because you got everything, it was easy to hate you because I can't get mad at someone who already died. But Nina, I'm so mad, and I'm so hurt. But I'm trying to overcome all of this just so I can hear your side. This isn't easy."

"Easy?" I laugh loudly. "You have no idea. Where were you that last year of her life? It's like you forgot we were even your family. We can pretend our rift happened when Nanna Dot died, but we stopped being close before that."

She's quiet a moment, and I hear her sniff. She's fucking crying. For a moment, my heart twinges at the realization. But then I harden my heart.

"I have to go."

"Nina, you don't owe me anything, but—"

"You're right, Jordy, I owe you nothing." I look up at the roof of my car as my vision turns blurry. "You know the worst part? You *knew* me, you knew what I was going through with my mom because your mom was the same kind of asshole. You abandoned me, and when Nanna died, you took their side. You didn't even talk with me. You just completely forgot about our friendship. You threw all that away the moment you believed your mom, when you knew me better than anyone."

It's quiet on her end, but I can hear her breathing.

"I'm sorry," she finally says. "I want to hear you out. Can we meet? Maybe for coffee or something?"

I look at Insomniacs, tightening the grip on my phone. "Fine," I bite out. "But not coffee, I know somewhere better."

Chapter Nine

Nina

Jordy was waiting at a booth when I arrived at Torches, a Manhattan on the rocks with three black maraschino cherries waiting for me.

Just like Nanna used to make.

I take the seat across from her, then eye the Manhattan. "Did you poison it?"

She stares at me for a second, then rolls her eyes before scooting the drink towards her and taking a small sip. "Mmmm, nothing like poison in a public place." She gives me a pointed look, then nudges the drink back towards me.

"I was joking," I say, though that's only partially true. It's not like I can trust anyone in my family anymore. I take my own sip, and damn if it doesn't bring me back to the old days, when Nanna served up strong cocktails despite us being underage. It was always after we watched *Practical Magic*, but she thought Midnight Margaritas were too basic, so Midnight Manhattans became a thing.

"Don't tell your mothers," she made us promise, then handed us each a fancy cocktail glass full of the syrupy drink, garnished with extra cherries. Nanna Dot had a personal bar that far outmatched Uncle Dan's, and she taught us how to make every drink she knew. According to her, every hostess needed to know the recipe of at least one signature cocktail, so she taught us dozens.

Perhaps my next gig will be in a bar instead of stupid coffee.

"So?" I say, taking another sip of the Manhattan. I'm trying to play it cool, to sip slowly and keep my wits about me. It's not like I need a replay of that family dinner fiasco. But damn, this drink is good.

"So, I guess I want to get to know you better," she says.

"Like, how exactly I talked Nanna Dot into giving me her fortune?" I put my drink down and inspect my nails.

"You're really going to do this?" Jordy hisses, and I look up and grin at her.

"There you are, I was wondering when you were coming out to play."

Jordy takes a deep breath, then lets it out slow. "Look, I know there's more to what Mom and Aunt Poppy are saying. It's why I'm here."

I narrow my eyes at her, finally done with this charade.

"No, you're here because you need a cheap place to live and are hoping I'll forget all the awful things you've said behind my back and invite you to take over my home. Did I miss anything? Or should we have another so-called family dinner to lull me into submission?"

"So, Brayden told you."

"Well, someone had to." I offer a fake pout. "Or did I ruin the surprise?"

Jordy looks down at the table. Even still, I can see the anger blazing in her eyes. "I guess you have it all figured out. Are you just going to continue thinking the worst of me without even hearing me out?" She looks up and glares at me. I, in turn, laugh. Loudly.

"That's rich, coming from you. Let's see, five years ago, our grandmother died and left everything to me. I neither asked for it, nor expected it. In fact, I didn't even think she would die. If giving all that money back meant she could be alive, I'd give it up in a heartbeat, because I loved Nanna Dot."

"And you think I didn't?" Jordy sits up straighter, looking me dead in the eye. "How do you think it felt to know Nanna Dot's last act was to forget all of us?"

Shitty, I know. But then there was the statement she included in her will: "You never cared to visit me when I was alive, so maybe this will help you think of me in my death."

"Like you forgot about her? Where were you that last year?" Even as I say it, I already know. She'd met Brayden that year and was probably too busy fucking her boyfriend to visit, to even pick up the phone.

But just as I'm about to blurt this out, I see her face fall. It's quick, but it's enough to knock the fight out of me. Something happened, something I don't know about. While I want to hurt her, to make her feel everything I've felt since Nanna died, I listen to that small voice inside me telling me to stop.

"It's complicated," she finally says. "I don't have a good excuse. Still, I thought Nanna loved me. It's not so much the money, though it sure would have helped pay for my student loans, it's the way she did it. By giving you everything, she let us know she didn't love us." She looks up at me. "I know you didn't make her do that, I think I've known it the whole time. That's not something you'd do. But I was so hurt. When my mom said you probably talked her into it, well, it just became a way to redirect our anger, I guess. Nanna Dot wasn't there to answer for why she cut us out, but you were."

I feel completely twisted inside. I am still furious, but now there's this ache accompanying it. I look down at my hands, afraid my face will show how I'm feeling now that she's copping to what happened. Honestly, I'm not even sure what I'm feeling. Relief, maybe. Sad. A little defeated, knowing it just took a thought to completely write me out of their lives.

I suppose like Nanna Dot wrote them out of her will.

It doesn't change what happened. But somehow, just hearing Jordy say it smooths the edges of the pain I've experienced ever since Nanna died—and when I lost everyone along with her.

"I wish you would have talked with me." I clench my hands, then unclench them, feeling the tension ebb slightly. "If you would have just asked me about it, or even asked how I was doing. I was left alone in that house after Nanna died, and not one of you came to see if I was okay."

She's quiet. Then she blows out a deep exhale. "I hadn't thought of that."

"Of course you didn't. You all were so absorbed with everything you didn't get, you didn't even see that I'd lost everything. And then I lost—" *All of you.* But I can't get the words out because I'm crying too hard. She reaches across the table, holding her hand out. I look at it, at the open invitation her hand offers.

I don't want to forgive her. I've held on to my anger for so long— especially against her—that I don't know how to be without it.

But it's more than all that, and I know it. I don't want to forgive her because I'm jealous of her. Even admitting that to myself feels embarrassing and icky, but I am. She's tall and gorgeous while I'm short and frumpy. Her clothes are elegantly styled while mine are thrifted and colorful. She has perfect tan skin, and I just discovered a new zit on the side of my nose this morning. She's close with her mom—at least now it seems—and my mom only calls me when she needs something.

And she got the guy.

Fuck. I can't believe I'm being this petty and childish. She got the guy because she met him first. It doesn't matter how I feel about him, or that we experienced this unreal connection. He's not mine.

I look at her outstretched hand, then at the cautious question in her face. The one that seeks forgiveness, to repair our lost friendship, to come back to what we once had.

We aren't there, and it will take so much time to get there; but it has to start somewhere, right?

I take her hand, and she squeezes it. But I pull away.

"Look, I'm not an idiot. I know you're just playing nice because you need a place to stay, and I have the room. So let's not act like this is anything more than it is."

"I really do want to repair this rift between us," she says. I shoot her a narrow-eyed look, and she sighs. "Fine. And I need a place to stay. I know it's a big ask, and honestly, I knew it was too much when we coerced you into that sham of a family dinner. We haven't exactly been on the best of terms lately, and that's hardly the recipe for a good living arrangement. But I'd like to try. For my own selfish reasons, of course, but also to try and mend our broken relationship. I'll even pay rent, whatever you feel is fair, though I do ask that it be kept below market rate because holy fuck the rents are ridiculous here."

I know it, though I've never had to pay rent.

"And you want to move here for college?" I ask.

"Partly," she says. "But also to start planning our wedding."

I fucking hate those words, but I do everything in my power to keep my face neutral.

"Our whole relationship has been somewhat long distance," she continues. "Brayden's parents are old fashioned and super traditional, so I can't move in there, and I won't ask him to leave the farm for me. At least not yet."

"What do you mean not yet? You want him to leave?" The words are out of my mouth before I can pull them back in. I shouldn't care this much, not for someone who's supposed to be a stranger. But if she notices, she doesn't show it.

"Well, yeah. To get my career going, I thought we could try out New York. I considered Los Angeles too, just so we could be near our families. But really, New York is where I need to be if I want to make a name for myself.

She wants him to leave the farm? Alarm bells are ringing inside my head. It's none of my business, of course, but I also know that Brayden is passionate about caring for his family farm. I could tell when he talked about it the night I met him, and even on our ride home. Hell, he won't even hire someone to work there unless they get along with the family.

"We're planning to spend a lifetime together," Jordy continues, "but we hardly spend any time together now. So I thought I could finish my graduate year here in Sunset Bay, and maybe Brayden and I could finally set a date for our wedding and start making plans for our home together."

Oh, my heart. I can't believe how much it aches. Just hearing Jordy talk about all this is like a gut punch.

How will it be if she lives with me? How will I manage it when he comes to visit her, when I see him kiss her, when they disappear behind closed doors?

I have to say no. I have every right to say no. Jordy and I are not reconciled as kin. In fact, it's way too soon for a request like this.

But then there's the loneliness of the house. The walls that are caving in on me. The overwhelming clutter and the amount of cleaning this house requires. The fact that I haven't let anyone in since Maren moved out—and who best to help me but family?

Can I rely on her like others can rely on their family members?

Because the track record is not looking good.

"I'll help you with the house," she says then, as if she's reading my mind. I look at her sharply, but she continues. "I saw it, Nina. You need help, and I can give it. I do this all the time. I recently helped this elderly woman who had decades of stuff in her home, much like you do with Nanna Dot's. While I live with you, I could help you get rid of the things you don't need anymore, and free up some space in that house."

There's a tug-of-war happening inside me. On one hand, I don't want her near any of Nanna's things, and I definitely don't want to get rid of anything. But on the other hand, I'm being edged out by Nanna's belongings. If I don't do something about it, I'll have no room to live.

And I want a relationship with Jordy. I miss her. There was a time when I could trust her with just about anything. Jordy was my confidante, and since her, I've never had anyone come close.

I take a deep breath, then look in her hopeful brown eyes. "I really should say no," I begin, and I hate the way her eyes light up, and how my own heart feels hopeful, "but okay."

Chapter Ten

Nina

I heard the whine of applied brakes outside my house, and I looked through the window to see the moving van slowing to a stop. I wasn't sure how to feel. Excited? More like nervous.

It's been two weeks since I told Jordy she could move in. Since then, I've been working hard to clean the place up and make it somewhat presentable. I'd managed to clear a good portion of the living space, plus clean the kitchen so it didn't look like dumping ground. I also cleared Maren's old room on the main floor, piling everything in mounds around the boxes in the basement. It's kind of like pushing dirt from one corner of the house to the other. Actually, it's exactly like that—not one thing leaves the house, it just finds a new corner to hide.

I open the front doors, and there's Brayden on the sidewalk, looking up at me. He taps his hat in a kind of salute, paired with his lopsided grin, and I feel the breath leave me. But then five other guys show up behind the moving van, piling out of the truck so they can get to work. They're guys from Brayden's ranch, and holy hell, I'm so flustered. I mean, it's like the whole cowboy calendar is in front of my house, lifting heavy furniture up the stairs, and giving me that country nod that would make any girl weak in the knees.

Except, I can't keep my eyes off Brayden. After all this time, I was sure the thought of him would fade into a distant crush, something that could be dismissed as a mere whim. At least, I had hoped. Not so, as I take in the shape of his muscles under a tight fitted t-shirt, the broadness of his shoulders, and the subtle hint of dimples whenever he's hoisting another box in his thick arms. I also note the kind warmth of his blue eyes whenever he looks at me, which are mere glances—as if, like me, he's trying not to linger.

Or maybe he's just trying to let go of our last conversation, when we admitted our feelings, even as he told me it was not going anywhere.

My heart hurts whenever he looks at Jordy. What is he thinking when his eyes catch hers? Has he forgotten everything we said? Is he excited they'll now have more time with each other? Does he picture their future together, looking forward to leaving for New York or Los Angeles, or wherever they land?

Jordy and I have talked several times since I agreed she could move in. There's still a careful edge to our relationship, and sometimes it feels like we're trying on kindness like you'd try on a different style of coat. There are fragments of our old friendship, and every now and then, I relax into our conversations as if there's nothing wrong at all.

But things aren't as they used to be, and I'm not sure how it ever will be. I'm still pissed that she believed such awful things about me, and that she never even came to me to find out the truth. I'm pissed that she went as long as she did without even speaking to me, and wouldn't even take my calls. To go from being best friends to bitter enemies at a time when I needed family the most, it's a hurt I don't know how to get over.

Plus, we're not kids anymore. Both of us have changed. She's no longer this boy crazy teen following makeup tutorials and fashion blogs. Jordy is mellower now, with a calm demeanor and a secret smile for Brayden every time she passes; and I'm no longer the same meek girl who moved into my grandmother's house as an escape, though I do still feel like a kid around her. Especially in the face of her relationship with Brayden.

With so many hands on deck, the move-in portion takes less than an hour. The eye candy cowboys take off soon after, piling into a huge Dodge Ram just like Brayden's. It's like some sort of guy code. If you're ripped and look like you can ride anything like a champ, you drive a huge truck. Despite my annoying infatuation with Jordy's fiancé, I can't help hoping I'll see more of these guys around.

Brayden stays behind, at first to help Jordy unpack her room, but after a while, he joins me in the front room while she stays behind.

"She's particular about where things go," he shrugs, sitting on the couch near the love seat I'm on. There's an awkward silence between us, and I realize that whatever I'd felt before, I'll never feel it from him again. That list I wrote years ago is tucked in the top drawer of the curio just a few feet from him. As stupid as it seems, I want to show it to him—to prove that I actually knew him first, even though we'd never laid eyes on each other. I want to ask if he wasn't meant for me, why is he everything I wanted in a man? Why do I forget that I don't want a relationship when he's near me, and now feel like I can't breathe because I can't have him?

"I'm glad you and Jordy made up," Brayden says, breaking the track of my racing mind.

I let out a breath, gather my wits, then I look at him and smile as if everything is fine.

This is fine. I'm not dying a little every time you mention my cousin's name.

"I think we have a long way to go. I still don't trust her, but I guess it's a start." I realize as I say it that maybe I shouldn't be so forthcoming. He's Jordy's fiancé. It's possible that anything I say to him is just going to get back to her. I should pretend everything is fine, that Jordy moving in feels completely natural.

But there's something about Brayden that makes me want to open up. Especially with the way he listens. His eyes stay on mine, and for a moment I think he gets me. Maybe he understands how hard this is. All of it.

"For what it's worth, Jordy's relieved you both are speaking again," Brayden says. "And she feels bad this didn't happen sooner." He leans closer to me, and I hold my breath. But he just nudges me with his knee. "Thank you for doing this. I know you two had your issues, but I think this could be great for both of you. I know Jordy is itching to get to wedding planning. She's been hitting my mom up for ideas the past couple weeks, so this will definitely speed things along."

And just like that, reality hits. I look at my hands and nod. When I look back up, I peer into his face, searching for something that tells me I'm not a complete idiot. I see nothing.

"Well, that's all of it," Jordy says, emerging from the hallway where her room is. I scoot away from Brayden, even though nothing happened, nor is it going to happen. But she's not even looking at me. Her eyes do a brief sweep over the living room, and I feel my defenses prickling as I also look around, noting everything I missed when I cleaned in anticipation of her arrival. The stack of papers in a messy pile on the curio. The mountain of clothes I forgot in a chair across the room. The layer of dust that still hugs the coffee table.

Jordy turns back to me, a broad smile on her face as if she weren't just judging me. "Should we celebrate by going out? My treat."

"It's okay," I say, settling back into the couch. "You two go on without me. I'll just stay here and straighten up."

Jordy shoots me a pained smile. "Please come with us," she says. "You're letting me live here, and you both helped so much to get me here. Let this be my small way of saying thank you."

Brayden stands and she takes his hand. When he looks at me, he tilts his head toward the door.

"Come on, it will be fun," he says.

This will be the opposite of fun.

I get up, grabbing my purse from the table. "Fine, but I'll pay."

"Like hell you will," Jordy says, opening the door and leading the way out. "You're saving me a shit ton of money. It's the least I can do."

But I got the inheritance. I can't say it out loud though, even though I know it's on her mind too. So I nod, then follow them to Brayden's truck. Jordy moves aside, letting me into the backseat, then she takes the front. The whole way there, I try not to stare as her fingers play in the dark curls of his overgrown hair while he sings to country. Meanwhile, I feel like the loser in the back who can't wait for this day to be over.

At Brayden's suggestion, we end up at the Coastal Plate, this great hamburger place in the touristy part of Sunset Bay. The place is packed, as usual, but I already know what I'll get off the menu. The California burger, which has avocado, bacon, Monterey Jack cheese, and sprouts, all on a brioche bun. It reminds me of times when Nanna didn't feel like cooking and treated me to a dinner out. Nothing fancy. Despite my grandmother's wealth, she was not one to waste money on frivolous things. But she did enjoy a night off from cooking, so at least once a week, we found ourselves on the tourist strip. I've probably tried every one of the restaurants here, but Coastal Plate is my favorite, and the California burger is my go-to with a huge helping of fries I can dip in ranch.

The hostess leads us to a booth, and I sit on one side while Jordy and Brayden take the other. For a moment this feels like the kid hanging out with the parents. Me, the young single girl with no job or direction in life across from the sophisticated engaged couple, one of which is taking courses to excel in her career of choice while the other is running his own business.

Both Jordy and Brayden pick up their menus, and I do too, even though I'm already dreaming of my burger. When the waitress asks for our order, she turns to Jordy first.

"I'll have the garden salad with grilled chicken and a side of balsamic vinaigrette," she says. "Oh, and please hold the croutons. A diet soda to drink."

I bite my lip, taking in the way Jordy's collarbone shows at the top of her blouse, and how dainty her wrists are as they rest on the table. My own wrists look like they belong to a chubby toddler, and my thighs spread thick on the bench seat.

"Miss?"

I look up and the waitress is looking at me. That burger is calling out to me, but I'm suddenly overwhelmed with this feeling of not belonging, seeing Brayden's arm draped over my beautiful, thin cousin.

"I'll have the same," I say, my stomach shriveling in disappointment as I fold my menu and hand it to her.

Brayden orders the California burger with a beer to wash it down, and I nearly collapse with envy. I know I'll have a second lunch once I'm in the privacy of my own home. Then I realize there is no privacy—I have a roommate now.

"I was thinking we could resurrect the Midnight Manhattans tonight," Jordy says once the waitress leaves. "It's totally not on my diet, but don't you think sitting with *Practical Magic*, eating our weight in pancakes, and washing it down with Manhattans sounds like the perfect way to kick off our roommate situation?"

The last thing I want to do is hang out with Jordy. I mean, isn't this enough? But then again, pancakes. And Midnight Manhattans. The thought of both almost makes up for the sad salad I'm about to have.

Fuck the salad.

I flag down the waitress as she passes the table, and tell her to skip the salad and serve me up a California burger instead.

"I just remembered I hate salad," I say, to which Jordy laughs.

"It's not my favorite either," she admits. "But my mom can always tell when I've slipped in my diet, and I don't need the lecture. She's so concerned about how I'll look in my wedding dress, and I haven't even bought the thing. It's just easier to follow a strict diet than to hear her go on and on about what I'm doing to my body." She narrows her eyes as her grin widens. "But she doesn't need to know about Midnight Manhattans."

I nod in agreement, but also can't help wondering what Aunt Lil says about my body. I guess I can just add it to all the other things she says about me.

"So, are dudes invited to Midnight Manhattans?" Brayden asks.

"Absolutely not," Jordy says. "This is for girl witches only, any boys that come within five feet of the house might find themself as fertilizer for the garden."

"Or frog food," I add in.

"Or the victim of house crickets." Jordy claps her hands, her face lighting up. "Oh man, Nina, remember the lists we made that one time?"

My face heats up, as if she can actually read what mine said.

"What lists?" Brayden asks. She turns to him.

"We made these lists that described the perfect man, then cast a spell that night under the full moon so that one day that man would find us. Even Nanna Dot made one."

"Yeah, and look how that turned out," I say.

"Maybe she manifested that old stray cat that showed up on her doorstep. Though I think hers said something about someone who would rub her feet, and all that cat did was hiss at everyone who came close to it."

She named the cat Mr. Whiskers, and it stuck around for about a year, eating the tuna she fed it, along with chicken scraps and a bowl of milk. It never got nicer, though Nanna Dot still cooed at it like it was a baby. Then one day, it took off and never came back. I figured it curled up and died somewhere, but Nanna said it probably moved on to bless a new family. She had a strange idea of what blessing meant.

"So, was I on your list?" Brayden asks. I look up sharply, but see he's looking at Jordy—of course he's looking at her. She shrugs.

"My idea of the perfect guy back then had more to do with how popular he was or if he had a starting position on the football team."

"So, not the guy in Jazz Band or on the debate team who competed in barrel racing on the weekends. Noted," he laughs.

"Hardly." She nudges him with her shoulder, then looks to me. "What about you? Do you remember what yours said?"

I pause, my words suddenly gone. I open my mouth, but nothing comes out. Finally, I shake my head no.

"Not at all," I say, finally spitting out the lie. *Makes me feel safe…* "But I know that every guy I've met hasn't come close to my dream guy." Another lie, since he's sitting right in front of me.

"Ugh, ain't that the truth. Well, except now, that is." Jordy grins at Brayden at the same time I look away. When I look back, I catch Brayden's eyes on me. He shifts them so quickly, I'm unsure if I saw it at all.

"What was on *your* list?" I ask Jordy, only because I can't help myself.

She thinks for a moment, then laughs. "I think I said the guy had to love the *Twilight* movies, know how to do a flip kick, and be super into Fallout Boy. Very aughts."

Brayden gives her a weird look. "Well, that sounds nothing like me. I've never watched *Twilight* or owned a skateboard, and...Fallout Boy?"

"It's a band," Jordy says. "Not country music." She's laughing, but I can't help that this makes me happy. Even though it's just a stupid list that means nothing.

Right?

Our food arrives, and I'm so glad I changed my order in time. Jordy's salad is small and disappointing, but she eats it as if food were no big deal and she isn't worried about dying of hunger. But me, I'm famished. I'd had a protein shake for breakfast, and it seems like that was so long ago with the way my stomach is jumping at the first scent of burger. I take the biggest bite, fully lost as the burger hits my tongue and absorbs all my senses. I wash it down with a sip of diet soda and feel somewhat human again. I realize I'm probably behaving like an animal around food, but neither of them seems to be paying attention to me. In fact, Jordy is stealing fries off Brayden's plate until he finally flags down the waitress and asks for another plate of fries.

"I can't eat that much," she complains, taking another one of his fries. He answers by taking the rest of his fries and piling them next to Jordy's salad on her plate.

"You won't have to," he says, then winks at me. Fuck if it doesn't go through me like a jolt of electricity. "They're for me since you've taken all my fries." His phone buzzes, and he looks at it before picking it up. "Hey, Ma."

"His mom is conducting interviews today on her own since

Brayden was helping me," Jordy whispers as Brayden continues talking. "He didn't want her to, but she insisted because they need help like yesterday."

The plate of fries arrives about the same time Brayden hangs up the phone, and he swears under his breath.

"No good?" she asks.

"Nah. I mean, I guess I'm glad. I don't want my mom to hire anyone without me there to vet them, so this saves me the trouble. But mom is on her own until we get someone in there."

Jordy looks at me, then tilts her head. "Where do you work? That coffee shop? Is it serious?"

"Not really," I say. "I was fired two weeks ago. That day we met at Torches? I came from getting canned."

"Holy shit, Nina! Why didn't you say anything?"

I look at her, then roll my eyes. "You mean, when you still thought I stole Nanna's money? Or when I thought you were poisoning me?"

"Fair," she laughs. "But still, I wish I'd known. I'm so sorry."

I shrug. "It's not like I needed the job. I just…" I sigh. "I liked it, I mean, not the work. But it got me out of the house, gave me a purpose, put me around people. I know it doesn't seem like it, but I actually like being around people. So the past two weeks have felt kind of like hell."

Jordy studies me for a moment, then she nods slowly. "Bray, I think I know the perfect person for you," she says, and I feel my stomach plummet. "This person has hospitality experience, and I happen to know she's super experienced around horses."

Oh no. Please don't.

"Who?" Brayden snatches his plate of fries out of Jordy's reach as she seeks to replenish her empty plate.

"Nina," she grins, turning to me.

"Jordy is messing around," I say. I push my fries toward her, and she happily grabs a handful.

"I am not," she says. "You're highly qualified for what they're looking for. Tell her, Brayden."

"Well, I don't know what Nina is capable of," he says, but his expression makes it seem like he's open to the idea. "But I can tell you about the job."

Then he describes the position. Basically, it's a house manager position, though his mom would be the direct supervisor. The position includes prepping and making meals, kitchen cleanup, and cabin housekeeping, plus filling in on the outdoor ranch jobs like mucking barns and brushing horses. Basically, it sounds completely perfect. I might not be much of a housecleaner in my own home, but the thought of doing it in someone else's home sounds appealing. Plus I'd get to meet different people from all over the world, as Brayden explains.

But most of all, I'd get to be around Brayden every day.

This should be the downfall. This should be why I say I can't do it. Instead, I find myself sharing every reason why I'm qualified for the job, from my experience with horses way back when to the work I did at the coffee shop.

"But you don't need to hire me," I force myself to say. "I'm not desperate for a job, and I know how important it is for you to find the right person."

"Brayden would never hire someone out of obligation," Jordy says. "The guy is picky to a fault, especially when it comes to ranch hires."

He shrugs, confirming that it's the truth. "Want to come out to the ranch tomorrow?" he asks. "You can meet my mom and get a feel of the work involved, and then we can chat if this is a good fit."

"Sounds good," I say, but inside I'm doing backflips. It doesn't help that Jordy catches my eye and grins wide. *You're hired,* she mouths, and I do my best to smother my grin.

Chapter Eleven

Brayden

I wake up the next morning feeling like it's Christmas Day. Like I have a whole pot of coffee racing through my veins. It takes until I'm in the shower to realize why.

Nina is coming to the ranch.

I shouldn't feel this excited. I haven't even hired her yet, and I shouldn't entertain the idea of her working here, even though I can already tell she'll fit in just fine. I can't help thinking of how she'll be around Hazel, and how she'll be around my mom. I can picture the three of them in the kitchen, bringing a new energy to a house that's seen too much tragedy over the past decade.

I believe Nina is the one who can change everything, and that's what makes all of this so wrong.

Because I never thought that of Jordy.

Don't get me wrong, I love Jordy. But she was never one to shoot the shit in the kitchen with my mom, or even want to hang out on the ranch at all. We both blame my dad for the fact that she's never moved in here, but neither one of us fought for it. I'm still not sure how I feel about her moving to be closer to me. But if we're planning a life together, it probably is a good idea to spend more time together.

Which is also why hiring Nina isn't the best idea, because I'm way more excited about Nina working here than my girlfriend living about ten minutes away.

I towel dry, then take my time shaving to ensure a close shave. Cherokee is lying at my feet, patiently waiting for me to leave the room so he can eat, but I take the time to slap on some aftershave, then check my reflection.

"I'm being ridiculous, aren't I?" I say to Cherokee, who only tilts his head in reply. This is high school shit here. It's like I'm getting ready for a date with the prom queen, and each second is five seconds too long.

Wearing my favorite blue flannel and a pair of jeans, I take the stairs two at a time and head to the kitchen, my dog trailing close behind. There are no guests today since it's Wednesday, so my mom is sitting at the table with a piece of toast and her usual cup of coffee, a book in her hand. It's one of those romances she loves to read, and I glance at the title.

"*For the Birds*," I read aloud, and she puts the book down. "Any good?"

"Very," she says, "though it's taking forever for the main characters to realize they're in love, even though they're obviously made for each other."

I give Cherokee his breakfast, he dances in front of me until I place his bowl on the floor. I pour coffee into my favorite mug, the green one Hazel gave me a few years back that says, "I'm kind of a big dill" with a picture of a pickle on it. There's a plate of muffins off to the side of the coffee pot, and I snag one, then take the seat across from my mom.

"I have a possible new hire coming in," I say, then take a bite of the muffin. "Fuck, these are good."

"Thanks. Hopefully this person is better than the last one that came in. She actually told me she didn't do dishes."

"Well, this one is Jordy's cousin."

My mom gives me a wary look, and I know exactly what she's thinking.

"That's not why I'm thinking of hiring her," I assure her. "You know that. This is the family business, not a favor factory. But I have a good feeling about her. She has experience, is easy to get along with, and I think you'll really like her."

"Well, what's her name?"

"Nina Chance," I say. I pull out her application, which I had her fill out before I dropped her and Jordy back off at the house. I happened to have a bunch in my car, and figured we might as well make this official.

My mom looks it over, then zeroes in on her horse experience.

"Oh, she trained under Natalie," she says. Then I see her face fall, knowing she's reading the dates she was here. Ten years ago, when everything went to hell. "I always liked Natalie," is all Mom says, but I know she's thinking of a strawberry blonde girl who is gone, but never forgotten.

"Morning," Hazel says, almost on cue. I turn to my younger sister as she comes in the kitchen and swipes the rest of my muffin right from my hand.

"Stinker," I say, then wrap her up in my arms while she squeals, my stolen muffin falling in crumbs out of her mouth.

"Brayden, you're making a mess." Even as she says it, my mom is starting to get up to grab a rag to clean it up.

"It's not me, it's Hazel," I say, giving her a noogie while she fights to break free, laughing the whole time.

"Bear, my hair!" she cries. She finally escapes, then smooths her hair, peering at her reflection in the window as she does. "Who's that?"

I glance outside, and my heart skips a beat as I see a familiar ocean-haired head emerge from an old Cadillac.

"Wow, I love her hair," Hazel breathed. "Mom, we should do that to my hair."

My mom looks outside too, and I suddenly realize how country bumpkin we all look, staring out the window as if Nina is our first visitor in years.

"Come on, get away from the window," I say, blocking Hazel's view as I stand in front of her. "We don't want to weird her out before she even meets you."

"Is she the new hire?" Hazel asks, pouring coffee in a travel mug. She tops it with a healthy dose of sweet cream before grabbing her backpack from the corner.

"Possibly. It's why I asked her to come so early. I thought it would be nice for her to meet you before you take off for school. Can you hang out for a few minutes?"

"I can blow off the whole day, if necessary," she says, setting her backpack on a chair, then sitting with her coffee.

"No you can't," my mom says, and I wink at Hazel as she groans.

"In just a few short months, you'll be done with high school, and you might even miss it," I say, just as there's a knock on the door. I take a deep breath, willing my heart to stop pounding, trying to appear nonchalant as I go to the door.

"Doubtful," Hazel calls after me.

I open the door, and there she is. If I thought she looked irresistible in her short skirts and heeled boots, it's nothing compared to the way she fills out a pair of jeans. I lean forward to give her a hug, my head feeling lighter as I inhale the perfume of her skin. So womanly and fresh, making me want to grab her around the waist and pull her body into mine. Instead I invite her inside.

"Nina, this is my sister Hazel, and my mom Angela."

"You can call me Ang," my mom says, standing and holding her hand out across the table. Nina shakes it, and I can sense her shyness. *They're going to love you,* I want to tell her. As she does the same with my sister, I realize what this feels like. It's almost as if I'm introducing my new girlfriend to the family.

"I love your hair," Hazel says to Nina, and doesn't even ask before she reaches out and takes a lock of Nina's hair in her hands. "How long does this take you to do?"

"Not long." Nina leans closer to give Hazel a better look. "I mean, my hair is totally ruined now, but that just means it takes color better. It helps that my natural color is blonde, so I don't have to bleach it, and I just use washout color because I get bored of wearing the same color every week."

Soon all three of them are engrossed in hair talk—what it will take to change Hazel's hair. and if my mom's fading strawberry hair should actually be purple. Nina even helps clear the table as they talk, and I'm left off to the side while they forget I'm here. I smile, remaining out of it until Hazel finally breaks away and grabs her bag.

"I like her," she whispers, then slips out the door.

I do too.

The sound of wheels on hardwood makes me turn, and I tilt my head as my dad rolls to the threshold of the kitchen.

"Oh, you need to meet Nina," my mom says, guiding Nina out with her hand at her back like they're already great friends. "Pete, this is Nina, she's the new hire."

I look sharply at my mom, who widens her eyes, but looks amused at the slip. "If she wants to work here, that is," my mom adds, even though I'm the one who's in charge of hiring. But I'm not arguing.

"Really?" Nina looks to me, then back at my mom. Then she looks at my dad and collects herself. "Hi, I'm Nina," she says. She doesn't stare at my dad's wheelchair, or even seems affected by his handicap at all. Instead she crosses the room and offers her hand, just like she did to my mom and sister.

My dad, however, is a hard nut to crack. I realize I should have warned Nina, especially when he grunts in her direction. He can speak, no problem. There's nothing wrong with his mind. But ever since the accident, it's like his manners broke with his spine. At least he shakes Nina's hand, but then he rolls forward, forcing Nina to jump out of the way.

"Don't mind him," I whisper into her ear, and she shivers before grinning at me. Her smile is like a thousand sun rays in our already bright kitchen.

As my dad takes the rest of the coffee, I lead Nina away to show her the parts of the house she'll need to know along with the things that will be under her care, because let's face it, she got the job. My mom will go into more detail when she starts tomorrow, but at least I can give her a tour of the ranch.

The early morning fog still hugs the tree line behind the cabins when I bring her outside. I'm usually caught up in the beauty of these early mornings, but today I can't help noticing the slope of Nina's neck, the small wisps of hair escaping her messy bun, or the way she bites her bottom lip when she's paying attention, her teeth like pearls resting on a plush rose petal. The urge to press my lips to hers—to learn what it feels like if she nips my lips in the same way— is so intense, I feel like I'm white knuckling an addiction.

"It's so darling," she says of the cabin, as I stand in the doorway, watching her survey the room. It's just like a small studio apartment, with everything in it except a kitchen, but all I see is the bed and how good it would feel to lay her down and cover her body with mine.

This is a problem, but I'll learn to move beyond it. The only other option is to let her go, to continue my search for the perfect house manager. But that's not really an option because the thought of not seeing her every day is worse than knowing I'll be fighting my attraction to her on a daily basis.

"Ready to see the horses?" I ask, because I can't be in this room with her much longer. She beams at me, and I can see the younger version of her, the one I wish I knew way back when she was on the ranch, and I didn't even know her because I was away at college, drowning in my grief.

"Can I see Meredith?" she asks, her blue eyes shining with hope.

"I don't know if we'll have time," I say. "There's a lot of work to do and—" I stop when I see the way she's hiding her disappointment, then grin. "Of course we can, I'm teasing."

She smacks my arm. "You can't do that!" she laughs. "I'm extremely gullible and I'm bound to believe everything you say."

"I'll be more careful," I tease, but I also take a mental note, because for her to say she trusts me is a huge deal. Her whole family has let her down, and she still has the ability to trust. Whatever I do, I can't take that away from her.

We reach the barns, and the horses nicker lightly upon hearing our footsteps, noses peeking out from stalls. Nina watches as I hoist a flake of hay into each stall, but soon joins me once she sees how I do it. I'm surprised, as the hay is almost half her body size. But the girl is stronger than I thought, and not afraid to get dirty. I can't help thinking of how Jordy would be in this situation. She wouldn't even be out here, not willing to get her high heels dirty because work boots are not part of her wardrobe. And according to her, hay makes her skin itchy. But here's Nina, hay showering all over her as she miscalculates her aim and hits the top of the stall.

"I thought I had that one," she says as I stoop to help her. Our heads are close together, and when she looks up it takes my breath away. I see the flicker in her eyes, a bridled fire that makes me want to forget the hay as I learn exactly how she tastes. I look down at her lips, which she parts slightly. All I'd have to do is lean a few inches closer, to claim her honey mouth, to show her everything I've been holding back since that first day we met.

She moves back, breaking the spell as she scoops hay into her arms and does her best to fling it into the stall. I pull myself together and help, though we're making more of a mess than a solution. The horse doesn't mind, though, nibbling at the pieces that land on her door, then reaching her long neck out to find the ones in Nina's hair.

"Hey," she laughs, her hand flying to shield her hair. I move closer and pick out the pieces I can. My hand stills at the first touch of her hair, at the lush softness, at the tantalizing urge to tangle her hair between my fingers. This time when our eyes meet, there's a question in hers—a dangerous one. *What will you do with me?*

Everything.

I find the last piece of hay, then drag my hands away, stuffing them in my pockets so I don't cross the boundaries I want to shatter.

"Here they are," I say instead, leading her to the last two stalls in the barn. Meredith pokes her head out, followed by Sara in the stall next to hers. Nina gasps, then cautiously moves forward, her hand finding the top of Meredith's nose.

"Hey girl," she murmurs, pressing her lips to the terracotta mare's soft muzzle and then inhaling. "I forgot how sweet horses smelled," she says to me, and I think I see tears in her eyes.

"Are you okay?" I ask, and she quickly swipes at her eyes.

"I'm fine. I just…" She pauses, offering a shaky smile, then turning back to Meredith. "When I came here, it was because my grandmother thought the horses could be therapeutic for me. She was right, and I guess I didn't realize just how much until I saw Meredith here."

So she came here for healing. I don't ask her about it, because I have my own reasons why this ranch means so much to me. Even though I'll never be fully healed, the ranch saved me. Sara saved me. I'd ride Sara across the white sands of the beach, trying to race faster than my pain. I never could run fast enough. But it's like Sara absorbed everything I couldn't put into words, holding my pain as she carried me down the beach.

The thought of it now inspires a new image in my head—one of Nina riding next to me, her turquoise hair flying in the wind, her face flushed as we run the horses on an empty morning beach.

"Want to go for a ride?"

Chapter Twelve

Nina

"Now?" My heart leaps at the thought, out of excitement, but a little out of fear. I haven't been on a horse for years, and I'm not sure I remember how.

"I owe you a ride, remember?"

As if I've forgotten. "Right. The one you asked me on before I found out you're with my cousin?"

He wipes his hand through the air, as if deleting the facts. "That's neither here nor there. But right now is the perfect time to catch a quick ride. There are no guests and nothing important do right now. Unless you need to be somewhere?"

My day was going to include sitting in my room, eating all the snacks while binge watching *Gilmore Girls*, avoiding Jordy as she settles in, even if we've made peace. I still feel awkward as hell around her, and the idea of riding horses on the beach sounds way better than anything else I could be doing.

"I haven't been on a horse in years," I admit, getting nervous as he places a bridle on Meredith. He opens her stall and hands me the reins.

"Your body will remember," he says, then moves toward Sara as my cheeks burn. Just the mention of my body from his lips, and I'm distracted. I shake myself free as he turns again, and we lead the horses toward the tack. He helps me saddle her, then stands back as I place a boot in the stirrup and swing over. He's right. It's as if I've only taken a few weeks off from riding, because being up there feels like the most natural thing in the world.

He leads the way down the road, then across the highway where we follow a narrow path through the brush to the beach. While getting up on a horse feels natural, riding one reminds me that these muscles haven't moved like this in years. I know I'll be sore later today, but right now the swaying motion is like an old friend.

We get to the clearing, and I inhale sharply at the sight of the beach in the morning. Thin wisps of fog hover over the unblemished sand, which is washed free from the retreating tide. The sky still holds remnants of rosy pink and flush purples, though the light of the rising sun is starting to envelop the colors of dawn. My back soaks in the rays, my skin prickling from the contrast of cool morning air and the succulent warmth from the sun, and I arch as I drink it in. When I glance over at Brayden, he's watching me. Once again, I feel the heat rise in my cheeks, and I duck my head. I can't stop the smile creeping over my lips, and realize I probably look like a fool.

"We can just walk the horses," Brayden says, seeming oblivious to the effect he has on me as the horses sway down the beach, side by side. "Or if you're comfortable, we can trot a little."

"Or we can run," I say, clicking my heels into Meredith's flank. She responds immediately, falling into a gentle trot. I get my bearings, my body jostling awkwardly until my hips become an extension of my horse. Rolling with her as she runs, I click her sides again, and she picks up the pace. My hair loosens from the bun on the top of my head, and I can feel it flying behind me as the breeze whips against my cheeks.

I sense Brayden catch up with me, and I laugh as I try to urge Meredith to go faster.

"You think you're pretty cute, don't you," he calls out, flashing me a wicked grin as he keeps pace with me. Then he's racing ahead. I watch the easy way his body moves with the horse, how natural he looks, his broad shoulders under his thick flannel, the thick strength of his thighs clenching the horse as they run across the sand. For a moment, I lose myself in a vision of what the future could hold. Of us doing this every day, stopping for a picnic lunch, then resting in each other's arms as we watch the waves roll in.

It's so brief, and I brush it aside as soon as it hits me, then nudge Meredith's flanks again to catch up.

Brayden slows as we approach the other side of the beach. There's a post next to the mountain, and we dismount and secure the horses to the hitch. He pulls an apple from his pocket, then breaks it in two with just his hands.

"Showing off, Winters?" I ask him, and he grins as he hands me one half, then holds the other under Sara's nose.

"It depends. Are you impressed?"

He holds my gaze, and I'm overwhelmed by how much I want to just wrap myself up in his arms, press my face against his flannel, and memorize his scent.

"You have to try harder than that," I tease, feeding Meredith my half apple.

We strip off our boots and socks, then roll up our pant legs. I chase him out to the water, laughing as I avoid the kicking splash he sends my way. With the horses tied up, we run through the waves, and it's easy to forget he's my employer, and that he's marrying my cousin. He grabs me around the waist, and I fly through the air in his arms, laughing the whole time. He eventually sets me down, holding me up as I regain my footing.

And he doesn't let go.

The waves rush over our feet, and I look up, my eyes connecting with his. I can't look away. I inhale the musky cologne of his skin over the salt of the sea, and I relax into the solid space within his arms. Our breathing is shallow as we remain frozen, and I see a million questions in his eyes. His eyebrows crinkle on his forehead, and I feel the tension in his body.

You felt it, right?

I'm transported back to that very first night, seeing him in the glow of the streetlights, both of us breathless as we realized this was so much more than a chance encounter.

If our timing had been different, it could have been us.

Damn, I want to kiss him. It's happened so many times today, but now the need is so great I can barely breathe; the way he keeps looking at my lips, I know he's feeling the same way.

But I'm engaged to your cousin, and that's not going to change.

I pull away from him, though it takes all my strength. He swears under his breath, letting go of me completely and turning away. The air feels cold, the waves completely ridiculous and silly—the whole day—and the fact that I'm here with a man I can't have, torturing myself by working for him while my cousin prepares to marry him.

What the fuck am I doing?

"We should go," Brayden says, touching me on the elbow before wading through the water and back up the beach. I nod, even though his back is to me. When I close my eyes, saltwater forms on my lashes, and only the heat of them lets me know the tears are mine and not the ocean's.

We ride at a slow pace, remaining silent the whole way. My mind is a jumbled mess as I replay the moment, trying to get a grip on what happened—what's happened numerous times today. If we keep this up, will we kiss for real? Do I want him to?

Absolutely. But no way in hell can I let this happen again.

We reach the ranch, and there are a few cars in the driveway. Brayden turns to me and grins. "You remember the guys, right?" He hops off his horse, then helps me do the same, his hand resting on my thigh as I swing my leg over. I can do it myself, but I let him help me, then savor the warmth from his palm that lingers on my skin.

Brayden trots over to the house while I follow. I feel a bit shy as I take in the five impossibly hot guys who rise from their spots on the porch, jumping down the stairs to clap him on the back. I'm never shy around guys. In fact, I could probably use a filter most of the time. But right now, everything inside me feels jumbled and weird, and it's all because of Brayden. Meeting his friends and fellow ranch workers, I have this sudden fear they won't like me, or that I won't fit in.

Pull yourself together, I mentally order myself. Then I smile wide as their heads turn to me.

"New hire!" one of the guys shouts, then races in my direction. I brace myself as five guys dogpile me, then wrap me in a bear hug between them.

Seriously, I can die now. I am in a cowboy sandwich, and the rest of life has lost meaning.

They finally let go, and Brayden introduces me to each of them properly. There's Jake, a surfer crossed with a cowboy with his dirty blonde hair peeking out from his hat, sun kissed tan skin with a spray of freckles, and eyes even bluer than Brayden's. Next is Nate, with golden eyes and a warm brown complexion, and smile so wide that I can't help but grin back. Forrest and River are twins, each with curly sun-bleached brown hair they've tied back. There is just enough difference between them to see they're not identical, but I can already tell it's going to take a while to tell them apart. Finally there's Levi, who's tall and lean with eyes darker than midnight, shining out from an even darker complexion and a smile as bright as the sun.

Today's a workday for the guys, so they don't stick around beyond introductions, and soon it's just Brayden and me again. I kick at the ground, scuffing dirt on my boot as I try to think of something witty to say. Something clever. Anything to erase the almost kiss we had before, and how awkward I feel about it now— and frustrated.

"This was—" he says at the same time as I say, "I guess I should…"

We both laugh, then he motions for me to go first.

"I'm going to head out," I say, nodding my head toward me car, as if the car has some say in this.

"This was fun," he says. "But don't think every day is going to be all fun and games." His eyes narrow, and there's a smile in them.

"Right, because you're such a hard ass and will probably work me to the bone." The words are out of my mouth before I can catch the double meaning, the sexual undertones. I bite my lip, looking at his expression to see if he caught that too.

The way his blue eyes darken, hell yes, he caught that. But then he smiles and pulls me into a hug. I inhale his scent, completely aware of how long and inappropriate this hug is, but how much I don't want to let him go. But eventually, he releases me and I step back, trying my damnedest to pretend I'm not affected by him.

"Get some rest, because tomorrow's going to be a long day."

And as I drive away, I can't help but think, *God, I hope so.*

Chapter Thirteen

Brayden

I watch Nina go, realizing the mistake I nearly made. I almost kissed her. It happened multiple times throughout the day, but this time in front of all the guys. It had felt so effortless too, like I could just lean down and taste her. Like her lips were home, and I didn't belong to someone else.

I shake the thought from my head, refusing to go there. I also ignore the side glances from the guys as Nina's car pulls down the gravel road before heading out on the highway.

It's maintenance day, which we hold every week before the guests arrive for the weekend. The guys are here to help repair anything in the cabins, check fence lines, fill holes in the ground, and oversee anything else that needs attention.

"That's Jordy's cousin, right?" Jake asks as we lead the horses to the barn. "The one with that huge Victorian in town?"

I nod, removing Sara's saddle. "I just hired her," I say. "She'll work in the house with my mom. She starts tomorrow, so I thought

I'd give her a tour of the ranch."

"A tour, huh?"

I hear the laugh in Jake's voice, though I act as if I don't hear it.

"Yup." I grab a brush and start on Sara's coat, smoothing the dust from her terracotta fur.

"Does Jordy know?"

"That I hired her cousin?" I shoot him a look. "She lives with her now, of course she knows. It was her idea."

"No, that her cousin is living rent free in your head," Jake says as he brushes down Meredith. "Come on man, I haven't seen you look at a girl like that since…" He pauses is brushing, his head tilted as he thinks. "Naw, I've never seen you like that, not even with Jordy."

"What are you talking about? I'm always good to Jordy."

"It's not about being good," Jake says. "You're good to everyone, to the guests, your mom, all of us, and definitely your girlfriend. But you don't look at Jordy like that, or hug her for that long, or watch her leave when she drives away, even when she was leaving for weeks at a time."

I shake my head, even as Jake's words sink in my belly. "You're reaching," I say, running the brush over Sara's coat. "I love Jordy. We've just been together for so long, things have gotten comfortable. If it looks like I'm treating Nina any different, it's only because I'm grateful she let my fiancé live with her so we could be closer. That's all."

"That's all?" Jake asks. I shoot him a look, and he laughs. "Okay fine. Then can I ask if there's a rule against dating coworkers here? Because that girl is good food."

"What?"

"She's so delicious, I could eat her up."

I grip the horse brush, fighting the urge to throw it at him. "She's not a snack," I say, but through clenched teeth.

"Oh, she's chips and salsa, man. Just one taste, and I know I'd eat the whole bag."

I slam the brush down on the table, and this time I don't even try to hide how badly I want to throw him down too. Even more when I see how funny he apparently thinks this is.

"Fuck dude, you're so smitten. You should see your face." Jake slaps me on the back, even as my fist remains clenched. "I'm not going after her, but you're playing a dangerous game in hiring her."

I lead Sara into her stall, closing the door behind her as she goes straight for the food in the corner—all as my mind races. I want to deny what he's saying, I haven't even been able to admit my feelings to myself. But goddamn, that girl has my heart in a vice, and I still barely know her.

"It's nothing," I finally say. "She's a nice girl who happens to be really pretty. She's also my fiancé's cousin, so whatever you're thinking, it's not happening."

"Which is why you looked like you wanted to take my head off just thinking about me dating her," Jake says as he closes Meredith's stall. I glare at him, and he holds his hands up. "I'm not dating her. I get the message. But do you? You're engaged to Jordy and falling for her cousin. Now you're going to be around her every day. How are you going to manage that?"

"The same way I manage everything," I say. "I'll stick to the plan and wait for my heart to catch up." Then I jog off toward the cabins before Jake can say anything else, or ask what exactly I mean.

My phone vibrates in my pocket, and I fish it out to see who's texting me.

Jordy: Hey stranger, call me when you can.

Fuck. I usually text her first thing in the morning, but it's already closing in on noon and I haven't even thought about her. I immediately hit her number and wait for her to pick up.

"I'm so sorry," I say as soon as she answers.

"For what?"

"For not calling sooner. You just moved here, and I should have called or taken you out to breakfast, but I got so engrossed in work that I completely forgot to—"

"Brayden, it's fine," Jordy cuts me off. "You were busy, and today was Nina's first day. She just got home and hopped in the shower, so I thought I'd check to see how she did."

I have a vision of her riding on the beach, her long hair streaming behind her in the wind. The way she kept looking back at me, her smile brightening the whole goddamn beach and making me want to feel it against my mouth.

"She was fine," I say, shaking myself from the vision of her. "My mom and sister love her, which is probably most important. She officially starts tomorrow morning before the guests arrive in the afternoon."

"That's great! I know your dad will be happy."

No, he won't. But I don't say that.

"So, what are your plans for the day? I can leave the work to the guys here if you want to go grab a bite to eat."

"Nah, do your thing," she says. "I still have lots to unpack, and there's plenty to do around the house. I'll probably be swamped the next few days. But if you want, I could break away this weekend and we can look at venues, maybe?"

"For what?" As soon as the words leave my mouth, I feel stupid. *The wedding.* "I mean, yeah. Venues."

"We don't have to," she says, and I realize how unenthusiastic I just sounded.

"No, I do. But the weekend is never a good time. We have guests until Sunday, and several beach rides. You know, the usual."

"Oh, right. I keep forgetting the tourist gold mine you have there."

The way she says it, it's almost like she thinks this is a hobby, not my family business or my life's work. I've had the same schedule every day since I left college and took over the ranch.

"Yeah, our little corner of the Sunset Bay tourist trap."

"Brayden, that's not how I meant it, and you know it."

But I don't know it. What I do know is that as soon as we get serious about planning this wedding, the more serious we're going to have to be about our future—including my role in the ranch. Because Jordy's plan is to leave for New York, but my whole life is here in Sunset Bay. And I either tell her to give up her dream, or I give up mine, because you can't run a ranch in Southern California if you live on the East Coast.

"So, Monday then?"

I'm snapped back into the conversation. It's just venue shopping, though it's one step closer to the decision I have to make. Stand my ground to stay, or upend my life so she can live hers.

But then I think of five years ago. The hospital bed. The doctor telling her the awful truth as I squeezed her hand. As she sobbed.

I owe her.

"Monday," I say.

That evening, I join my family in the living room while the basketball game is on. Hazel is sprawled out with Cherokee in front of the fireplace, which is burning even though today's temps reached a high of seventy-five. Once October hits, my sister insists on building a fire no matter how warm it is. It's something she's wanted since she was young, and the rest of us sweat it out in favor of her. Like my mom, who's wearing a tank top and fanning herself periodically as she works on the cross-stitch in her lap. Or my dad, who's in a t-shirt and shorts in his favorite recliner.

"Brrr, it's chilly in here," I joke as I remove my sweatshirt and join my mom on the couch. She pats my leg, and I smirk at the thin layer of sweat on her brow.

Hazel ignores me, though, her nose in a book as she uses Cherokee as a pillow.

For a moment, I'm brought back a decade earlier, when there were five of us. Cherokee was only a puppy back then, but she remained still when two strawberry blond heads made him their pillow. Sometimes he'd lick their golden curls, making the two of them squeal before burying their faces into the dog's downy fur. I wonder if Cherokee thought the twins were his puppies. Whatever he thought, he'd do anything to protect them.

And it kills me that I didn't.

I look at Hazel now, wondering if she thinks of her sister. We don't talk about Amber much anymore. In the beginning, she was all we could talk about. But it was like a knife to the gut. Eventually, her name was mentioned less and less, until it was never mentioned at all. Old photos were slowly replaced by new, a family of five disappearing in favor of our changed family of four. Smiles were wan in the beginning, but with the passing of time, they've brightened a little more.

I look at the wall that holds Hazel's senior photo from this year, ones my mother took out in the field behind our home. The lighting is perfect, her hair like a golden halo in the early evening glow. Her smile is wide, as if she's never experienced loss. But of all of us, I know her loss runs the deepest, and while we don't mention her twin, none of us forgets. Especially not her.

And not me, either, because I failed both of them the day I didn't save her.

"How was the new girl?" my dad asks, his eyes still glued to the television. To anyone who doesn't know my father, it would seem like he's just asking a question. But my dad is never casual about anything to do with the farm.

"She's good," I say. "She's Jordy's cousin, who referred her to me." I mean, she did. But this sounds like I never knew Nina at all, which I know is better for this conversation. "She has experience in hospitality, and she used to ride horses here on the ranch a few years back."

"I still don't understand why Jordy can't do the job," my dad grunts.

We've had this conversation so many times, I've lost track. He can't understand why we haven't set a date for the wedding, and forgets that Jordy is in school for something entirely different. Or he's just in denial. In his vision, Jordy would give up school and all her aspirations to join the family business. I've tried to talk sense into him, reminding him that Jordy has her own vision for her life. I've even touched on the possibility of Jordy's dreams taking me away from the ranch. He won't hear it. Won't even acknowledge it, even though he made me promise to marry the girl.

He has no idea that he's the one who sealed all our fates when he made me make that promise.

"Nina will work out fine, Pete," my mom cuts in. "Even though she doesn't start till tomorrow, I have a sense she's perfect for the job. I didn't feel that with any of the other candidates."

"Yeah, and you know mom's intuition," Hazel adds. Her book is resting on her chest now, and she gives me a raised eyebrow. My sister can see right through my dad's stubbornness, and she knows more than anyone how much I struggle with him. Even though there are thirteen years between us, she probably knows me better than anyone in this room. I probably share too much with her, but Hazel is wiser than seventeen, and has always had a good sense of direction. She's had to. Ten years ago she lost her childhood to the sea.

My dad is back to his game, probably sensing he's starting a fight that will end in three against one. I think that's the end of it, so I watch the game in silence until my mom goes to bed. Hazel left a while ago, the fire a glowing ember in the fireplace. The room stays silent, even as the game goes into overtime before our team finally pulls ahead and wins. I turn the TV off then stand.

"Ready?" I ask my dad. I step toward his wheelchair in the corner, but my dad makes a noise in his throat.

"Sit down, Son."

It doesn't matter that I'm thirty years old and running the family business. When my dad gets a tone like that, I feel like I'm eight years old, ready to make excuses for whatever I did wrong this time.

"What's up?" I ask. It can only be one of three things: the ranch, my future, or the latest thing I'm fucking up. I move to the seat near his recliner so we can see eye to eye, noting the tired look on my dad's face. It's late, which is partly to blame. But my dad has aged tremendously since the accident.

"So Jordy's all moved in across town?" he asks, his hand fumbling with the blanket slipping from his legs. I lean forward to help him, but he swats me away. "I got it," he growls, yanking the blanket back toward him.

"She is," I say, sitting back and folding my hands in my lap. When my dad gets like this, it's rarely surface level. I know it kills him that he can't do as much as he used to. I just have to remember that it has more to do with his limitations than with me and try not to take it personal. "The guys and I helped move her in yesterday. She's living with Nina, that girl we just hired."

"Her cousin," my dad says. His mouth rests in a firm line, his eyes laser sharp as he regards me.

"That's correct."

"Did you even ask Jordy if she'd work here?"

"Fuck, Dad—"

"Watch your language," he corrects me, and I stand, finished with the conversation. But he's not. "Sit back down."

"Why? Are you going to listen to me, or talk at me? Because I've told you over and over again that Jordy is not interested in working on the farm. This is your dream, and now mine, but it's not hers."

"She's joining this family. It's about to be hers."

"No Dad, her dream is helping people improve their living spaces. It's what she's going to school for. Soon she'll be interning, and eventually working on her own. That's her dream, not working in a kitchen or making beds, or anything that has to do with running this ranch."

"But your mother…"

"My mother wanted to be a part of this. Jordy doesn't."

My dad breathes in sharply, his nostrils flaring as he grips the arms of his recliner.

"Not at first," he finally says. "Before me, your mom had her whole life mapped out. She was going to travel the world as a flight attendant. But when we fell in love, she joined my life and became a valuable part of running this ranch. If you're going to run this ranch, you need…"

"Dad, I'm already running this ranch," I remind him. " I don't need Jordy to give up her dreams for me to do that. I have staff that can help out. I have Mom, and I have you."

"You won't have us forever." He looks out the window now, away from me, and I sigh heavily.

"I know that, Dad. Believe me, I'm dreading that day more than you know. But it's not because of the ranch. The work here will continue without you and Mom. Hell, it can continue without me."

Dad's head whips to mine, and I let the words sink in, ready for him to question me. *Ask me, old man,* I silently beg him. *Ask me and I'll tell you again.*

"We can talk about this in the morning, I suppose," is all he says, which is his way of ending the conversation until the next time he brings it up. "But I'm concerned about this new hire. Tina?"

"Nina," I correct him. "And she'll be fine, you'll see. Even Mom thinks so, and Hazel is right, Mom is never wrong."

My dad grunts, his attempt at a laugh that got stuck in his throat. "This is true," he says. "But we don't know her. Did you do a background check? Call her references? Do you know anything about her?"

"I know she's Jordy's cousin, which means she'll be my family soon." *And that her hair smells like sunshine and wind, and how her body feels when I hug her. How I want to feel more.* "I know she worked at Insomniacs, that coffee shop on the boulevard, for years now, which proves she commits to her jobs."

"Coffee," he grumbles. "Why does anyone buy $5 coffee when you can make it for pennies at home."

"I know she let her cousin move in with her so that we could be closer together, which says a lot about her dedication to family." Okay, so Jordy and Nina hated each other just a few weeks ago, but my dad doesn't need to know that. "And I know when I told her to show up today, she not only got here early, but wore clothes that were appropriate for a ranch, showing that she's insightful and understands the level of work we do here. Not only that, but she connected immediately with Mom and Hazel, which I'd say is the most important part of all."

"And what about with you?" he asks.

My breath hitches in my throat, and I wonder if he somehow caught on that I have feelings for Nina. But I realize that's not what he's asking.

"Well, I wouldn't have hired her if I didn't have faith in her. You know how choosy I've been about finding someone to take Hazel's place in the house. I believe Nina is a fast learner and will be the perfect addition to the Winters Salt and Sea Ranch."

He doesn't say anything, and I stand there awkwardly, wondering what else he'll grill me on, or if he'll ever trust me to run this ranch completely.

Or if it even matters, since I could be gone in less than a year.

"I'm ready." My dad lowers the recliner, and I position his wheelchair next to it at a ninety-degree angle. We count off, and I lift on three, pivoting before placing him gently in the seat. He grunts his thanks, which is something he always does when we help him. He hates being vulnerable, but he never fails to say thank you. Then he rolls through the doorway, disappearing down the hall where my mom will help him into bed.

I stay where I am, watching the dying embers in the fireplace. Can I really leave this place? I feel like I'm stuck trying to please everyone here, and things are starting to fall apart. And now I'm close to disappointing everyone. Once again, I'm proving what a piece of shit I am, and how I destroy everything I touch. If it weren't for me, none of this would be an issue. Amber would still be here. My dad wouldn't have had a heart attack from the stress or be in a wheelchair now. I never would have gone to college and met Jordy and ruined her life as well.

I wouldn't have to face this predicament of living her dream or mine—stay with the ranch or move to New York.

To Jordy, this decision is made, and I haven't done much to fight the issue because everything I do is to make her happy.

I'm trying my best to make *everyone* happy and failing at every turn.

And in the process, I'm losing myself.

Chapter Fourteen

Nina

Ang is going over the schedule for today, which is a lot, even though we're not expecting guests until this afternoon. I'm trying to pay attention, but goddamn if Brayden isn't outside, washing down the horses with his goddamn shirt missing from his goddamn body. How am I supposed to remember anything when his muscles are rippling like that? Even his back has abs, and I just want to run my hands all over him to feel the dips and curves of his body.

"You can prep the marinade and steaks while I make the potato casserole," Angie says, oblivious that her son is a fucking monument, and he's taking up the whole view with his sexiness.

"Absolutely," I say, tearing my eyes away from the window for the millionth time. But her smile says she caught me.

"He likes the horses to look their best on the day guests arrive," she says, as if that's what I was looking at.

"Makes sense." I study the index card with the marinade recipe—as if it's more interesting than a half-naked man—then collect all the ingredients: red wine vinegar, Worcestershire sauce, olive oil, a clove of garlic, salt and pepper, and a healthy splash of wine. I add the steak, turning it once so that all sides are coated, before placing it back in the fridge. But I can't stop stealing glances outside. This job is torture, and I love it for all the wrong reasons. I mean, where else can I enjoy a view like this while working?

As for the work itself, I feel like I'm actually good at what I'm doing. Rather, I'm good at it here. My own house is overwhelming, even though it appears mostly clean since I stuffed everything in storage before Jordy moved in. Still, I haven't been blind to the side eye she's given each room, as if she's already calculating how much longer she has to live there.

I mean, we're at peace, sure. But I trust her as much as I trust a hornet's nest, and I'm sure she doesn't trust me, either. You don't just erase years of nastiness in a matter of weeks, and as it is, we haven't really talked about any of it.

In fact, we've barely talked at all. It's like a switch went off as soon as Jordy moved in, where I have my corner of the house and she has hers, and we just share the common areas. We didn't even have movie night that first day she moved in, even though we'd talked about it at lunch. She was tired, she'd said, and I wasn't going to argue. When I came home after getting the job yesterday, she was locked in her room. This morning her door was open, but she was gone, and so were her tennis shoes by the door, which made me think she was at the gym or on a run.

I don't really know what's happening here, or how I feel about it. The whole reason I agreed to this was because I was so overwhelmed by being alone. But we're on day three of being roommates, and I might as well still be alone.

After prepping dinner, my job is to freshen up each cabin by remaking the stripped beds, cleaning the bathrooms, and vacuuming and dusting. I finish each room with a fresh bouquet of flowers Ang had picked up at the farmers market, plus a plate of freshly baked cookies we made earlier this morning.

Brayden is waiting outside as I finish the last room, his arm resting against the porch post he's leaning on. There's this space between the post and his body that makes me want to slip my arm through and rest my head against his chest. He's wearing another one of his flannel shirts, much to my relief and disappointment, and I can't stop thinking about how good it would be to bury myself in him and just inhale forever.

"Hey." I try to sound casual, but it comes out as a squeak, so I try again. "Ready for today?"

"I came to ask you the same thing," he laughs. "My mom whipped up some sandwiches for us if you're hungry. We have some time before guests arrive, if you want to take off until dinner." He tilts his head. "Or you could ride along on our pre-dinner horse ride. You don't have to; it's not part of the job. But if you'd like, you're welcome to."

Yesterday's beach ride has been a permanent fixture in my mind since I hopped off that horse and hightailed it out of there. For a moment, nothing else mattered but the wind, the feel of the horse running along the sand, and the way Brayden kept looking at me like this was so much more than a ride. It's all the reasons I should say no, why I shouldn't even be here at all. But the hope in his eyes now mirror exactly how I'm feeling inside.

"I'd love to," I say.

With Hazel at school and Ang scurrying around the kitchen, I'm the only girl at a table of guys, and it's quite something. I keep asking Ang if I can help, but she continually puts me off, insisting that I sit and enjoy. Brayden finally tells me it's what she does, and even if I helped, she'd still be running around like this.

"The best thing you can do right now is relax and enjoy the

pampering," he says, his hand resting on my arm as he leans in. My heart races at the feel of his breath on my ear, and I try not to react even as I inhale the earthiness of his skin.

So I relax, laughing as the guys trade barbs across sandwiches. There are no dainty eaters at this table, and I realize I need to move quick if I want anything to eat. My stomach rumbles at the size of the sandwiches, and I'm pretty sure I can eat two.

But then my mother's voice invades my head. *Nina, no one invites the pig to the table.*

I eye the sandwiches for a moment, knowing exactly how it will feel to eat one. How it will taste. How my eyes will close as I chew and then swallow, enjoying every second of that sandwich.

Instead, I grab a handful of carrots and a half turkey sandwich on whole wheat. I pick at the carrots, unable to even stay in the conversation because my mind is ping-ponging between the food in front of me and my mother's insults, and it makes me want to eat everything on the table.

But I won't. I can have will power, I can make a good first impression. These people don't have to know me as fat Nina who can't control herself around food.

"That's not enough," Brayden hisses at me, then adds a whole sandwich on a French roll to my plate, along with a chocolate chip cookie. "Your mom's not here, and you're not going to last on rabbit food." His voice is low so that only I can hear him. But my cheeks flush just the same at the thought of my mom slamming my body, my eating and everything about me—all in front of him.

"Fuck, I'm sorry," he murmurs. "I shouldn't have said it like that. I just mean that we have a lot of work—"

"It's fine," I tell him, and I mean it. "You were the only one who spoke up for me." I lower my eyes. "Thank you."

"Don't thank me for that," he says, and I look up at the bite in his tone. His eyes flash, but then soften. "The very least anyone could do in that moment was fight for you. I did the bare minimum. They just did less."

I look across the table at the variety of food in front of me. The other guys are eating whatever they want, not even paying attention to what lands on my plate. Even Angie, the only other woman at this table, has a full plate and is laughing along with the guys.

I reach across the table and grab a second cookie. "For fuel," I say, and Brayden laughs as he nabs another cookie for himself too.

The guests start rolling in shortly after lunch is put away. I jump in and help the guys with transporting luggage to the cabins. At first they try to keep me from helping out, but once they understand that I'm capable of a lot more than my 5'3" frame suggests, they stop arguing. Plus, I'm stubborn as hell.

Once everyone is settled, I watch from the Winters' porch as Brayden and the guys show people around the ranch. It brings me back to the days I used to be a regular here. Everything is the same, but different because I didn't know anyone but my trainer. I never even saw the Winters family at all, so focused on riding that ring while Natalie barked out commands. *Back straight. Head up. Relax Nina, just move with the horse.*

Would I have seen something in Brayden if I met him back then? I doubt it. I was in such a terrible space, and all men were the enemy. I didn't trust anyone back then, especially not guys. Not after what happened.

I watch him now, marveling at how easy he talks with guests as he shows them around. At one point he looks directly at the porch, his eyes finding mine as if he knew I was there the whole time. He winks at me, that dimple deepening in his cheek as he shares a smile only meant for me, and it's hard to remember we haven't known each other all our lives. Maybe he actually could have broken through my fears back then.

Would I have been different if we'd met? Would he be with me instead of Jordy?

I can see Ang moving in the kitchen from the window, and I leave my spot on the porch to help her.

"Get out of here," she says, shooing me back out.

"I can help," I insist, but she won't have any of it.

"River and Forrest are already sticking around to start the grill. Besides, I already know you're going on a ride with Bear, and I think you should."

"Bear?"

"Oh, Brayden, I mean," she laughs. "It's just what the girls called him growing up."

I feel like I'm full of questions, but I can't help asking, "Girls?"

She looks up quickly from the lettuce she's chopping, pausing for a moment, then nodding. "Hazel and Amber," she says. "Hazel was a twin. Well, I suppose she's still a twin. That never goes away."

I realize I've stepped on a landmine here. There were two girls in this family, now there's one.

"I'm so sorry," I say. "I didn't know."

"Oh honey, how could you?" Ang shoots me the most compassionate smile, as if I'm the one who lost a daughter. "It was a long time ago, though you never truly get over a loss like that. You just learn new ways to live with it."

I nod, thinking of Nanna Dot. It's been five years now, and that hole still feels as deep and wide as the days after I found her. It will never go away. Yet, I'm still getting up every day. Still going about my day. Still existing even if it seems unfair that life continues after something that should have ended the world.

"I get it," is all I say, and she reaches over and pats my shoulder.

"I had a feeling you would."

"Can I ask how she died?" I ask.

"It was a drowning accident, about ten years ago," she says. Her expression falters, and I know she's recalling that awful moment. "We almost lost both of them," she adds. "We were lucky."

Lucky. The word rolls through my mind long after I've left the kitchen. I feel like a fool for even comparing the loss of my grandma to what they experienced. To tell them "I get it." As if losing my aging grandmother is the same as losing a child, along with the life she had before her.

Lucky, because they only lost one daughter and not both of them. I can only imagine how much this is eating all of them up.

I think back to the earlier conversations Brayden and I shared. He never said anything, but he did allude to something awful that happened to him ten years earlier. This has to be the thing, what made him escape to college around the same time I came to the ranch for healing.

Does the death of his little sister haunt him the way the ghosts of my past do?

"Hey, you ready?" Brayden calls out, and I snap back to the present to see him waving me over. I want to ask him about it, but I also know he hasn't told me for a reason. So I bury my thoughts as I break into a trot to join the small crowd formed around the guys. The horses are already saddled up, tied up to the posts along the fence, and each person is wearing a helmet with the ranch logo on it—a sea horse with "Winters Salt & Sea Ranch" in a sprawling font.

I don't even ask what to do once I see each of the guys helping guests onto their horses. I move toward a family who are waiting their turn, a couple and their young son of about ten years old. His mom is cooing at the horse and trying to get the kids' attention, but the boy ish't having any of it.

"Do you folks need help?" I ask, grabbing one of the steps meant for the shorter guests.

"Oh, yes," the mom says, resting a hand on her son's shoulder. He steps out from under her hand, and she smiles as if to say *kids these days*, but I can sense her frustration too.

"I'm not a baby," the boy says to me, looking directly at the stool.

"Justin Everett," his dad growls, and Justin stands up a little straighter, though the look on his face is full of distrust as he keeps his eyes on the stool.

"I'm sorry," the mother says. "It's been a long car ride, and we probably shouldn't even go on the trail ride." She glances at her husband, and I can sense that car ride was especially long. I also am pretty sure a ride on the beach in the fresh air is exactly what they need.

"Sitting in a car for hours isn't my favorite, either," I say to Justin, placing the stool on the ground near his horse. "Also, this isn't for you. It's for me because I'm a bit too short to get up there on my own." I step one boot on the stool, then place a foot in the stirrup. Then I swing over. "That's all you have to do. Think you can do that?"

He nods, appearing a bit less sullen as I swing back over. The truth is, I don't need the stool. But maybe if he sees me use it, he'll use it too.

Sure enough, after a few tries to reach his foot into the stirrup, he finally gives up.

"Can I use the stool too?" he asks, his eyes on the ground.

"Of course! I'm happy to share it," I say, jumping back down to help. In seconds, he's on top of the horse. I can tell he's trying to play it cool, but his mouth is twisted in a proud smile.

"You're a natural," I tell him, then show him how to hold the reins before I move on to his parents.

"Thank you," his mom whispers. "We took his Nintendo Switch

when we got closer to the ranch, because we made a pact to enjoy a technology free weekend. This might be the longest he's ever been without electronics."

"He'll probably forget all about his Switch by tonight," I say.

"Doubtful," Justin's dad chimes in. "But it looks like his mood has improved." He nods at Justin, who is busy leaning over, patting the horse's neck.

Once everyone is saddled, Jake moves to the front of the group and offers simple instructions.

"Don't fall off," he says, and everyone laughs. But then he shares how a light nudge of the heels will get the horse moving, and tugging slightly on the reins acts just like brakes.

"The horses respond easily," Jake continues. "So keep that in mind when you tap your heels into the horse's side. Too many kicks, and you might find yourself up the coast, halfway to Oregon."

The guests are split into two groups, with Jake and Nate taking one group, and Levi joining me and Brayden. The groups are small, basically just two families in each cluster. I'm pleased to see that Justin and his family are with us, but annoyed that we're joined by four giggling girls who chose the ranch as the setting for their bachelorette party. They're all perfect bottle blondes, which is awfully judgy of me since my hair hasn't been any shade of natural for close to a decade now. They must have scoured H&M for the perfect cowgirl costume, because they're all wearing tight jeans and cropped checkered shirts, tied off just under their boobs. They're also staying close to the front where Brayden is, and are not being quiet about how hot the cowboys are.

"I think we got the cutest ones, though," one of the girls hisses presumably to the bride.

"My goal is to go home with one of their numbers," another Barbie says, not as quietly.

"Well, I plan to go home with a lot more than that," another says, and I finally lose the battle of keeping my mouth shut.

"You're wasting your time on that one," I say, then wrinkle my nose with a fake smile when all their heads whip towards me. "He's taken, and his fiancé is pretty hot."

"You can't go after an almost married man," the bride pipes in.

The girls' eyes go wide. And me? I feel a dagger of guilt pierce my gut. Because isn't that what I want to do?

"What about the guy in back," one of the girls whispers.

"Single," Levi hisses loudly from a few horses back. I can see Brayden's shoulders shaking heavily as he keeps his head forward, and the girls slow their horses to join Levi. I trot up to the front and match Brayden's speed.

"I see why you enjoy this gig," I say, nodding back at the girls now surrounding Levi.

"It definitely has its perks," he says, laughing when I reach out to smack his leg. I'm caught off guard by the solid muscle that meets my hand, and fuck me, I want to grip that thigh before finding other hard places to grip.

"Does stuff like that happen a lot?"

"Like girls on a bachelorette party looking for cowboys to fulfill their every fantasy?"

I groan, tilting my head up to the sky. "Lord, you have an ego the size of Canada."

He just laughs. "They all seem to think this is a ranch rendition of Magic Mike or Girls Night Out."

"You mean, this tour doesn't end with a shirtless dance while you straddle my face," I whisper, then fight a grin when I see his cheeks flush. But there's a wicked glint in his eyes.

"Not this one," he deadpans, his voice hushed as he leans toward me. "But wear face protection if you go on one of our midnight tours."

I burst out laughing, and he grins.

"Fuck, I'm sorry. Too far." He grimaces, biting his lip. I have to fight the urge to lean over and kiss those swollen lips just to see what they taste like.

No. Cousin's fiancé. Off limits.

But I can't help myself.

"Brayden, I have had a really crappy couple of months. Years, to be honest. Talking dirty with you feels like the highlight of my life."

"Happy to be of service," Brayden says, tipping his cowboy hat.

Fuck, this job is going to be both heaven and hell. And I'm here for it.

Chapter Fifteen

Brayden

Tonight's tour is probably the best one I've ever led, and it has everything to do with Nina. Just being around her makes everything better, but especially on this tour, I can see how well she fits in.

First off, she doesn't shy away from helping out. I love that she jumps into working, ready to pitch in wherever an extra pair of hands is needed. Like now, as she rides next to this young boy and talks about her favorite Nintendo Switch games. I didn't even know she played games, but it makes me want to learn just so we have something else we can talk about.

Watching her with him ignites something else inside me. She's a natural with kids. She talks with him like he's an adult, and he's totally feeding into it. I'd noticed him early on, how he was fighting his parents on just about everything. I was ready to wring his neck, but Nina stepped in and somehow diffused the situation.

She also diffused the bachelorette situation. This kind of thing happens almost every weekend, if I'm being honest. But I heard

Nina's tone when she corrected the girls. She was jealous.

Of course, I don't know that for certain. It's possible I'm reading way too much into it because I'm crushing on Nina in completely inappropriate ways. If Jordy knew how I felt about her cousin, she'd straight up murder me. She'd make me fire her, even though hiring Nina was her idea. If she knew the thoughts that go through my head just seeing Nina on a horse, in those tight jeans that show every one of her luscious curves…

I'm leading the pack, but it doesn't stop me from glancing back every few minutes. I say it's to check on the group, but really it's to look at Nina. She's busy making friends with the family, but she never fails to catch my eye every time I look at her. It's as if she knows I'm watching her, like she can feel my eyes on her.

She's a natural at riding. She'd been nervous yesterday, telling me how she hadn't ridden in almost a decade. But seeing her now, it's like she's been riding every day of her life. Nina belongs on a horse. She belongs on a ranch. She belongs here, with…

With me.

I shake the thought from my head. It is not wrong to find other people attractive. I'm sure Jordy has thought other guys are attractive. Hell, I work on a ranch of single guys that gain plenty of attention from the women who visit here. I'd be a fool to believe Jordy didn't think they were good-looking.

But is she obsessing about them? Is she considering what a future with them might look like or how amazingly well they might fit into her life, like I'm thinking about Nina? Is she wondering what would have happened if she'd turned right instead of left?

I can't let my attraction to Nina get in the way of our working relationship. I wanted to find a staff member that would work well with my mom after Hazel went to college, and I needed someone who could fill in as needed around the ranch. Nina is both, and the way she's working now, I know she'll fit in even if I no longer manage the ranch.

We catch up with the other tour at the end of the beach, and I dismount and help the guys tie off the horses. Nina helps the young boy, who I assume has a crush on her by now with the way he's watching her. *Me too, kid.*

"You can use my knee when we get back on the horses," she says as she helps him down. I'd heard him arguing before, but there's no argument now. In fact, he seems to be a huge fan of that idea.

"Looks like you have a new boyfriend," I whisper to her once everyone has dismounted and are gathered around the beach fire Levi lit in a makeshift pit.

"Well, Levi is taken," she says, nodding at the swarm of bachelorettes that have stuck by him since the beginning of the tour. "And you're off the market. I mean, not that I need you on the market. I mean…" She trails off, looking like she wants to sink into the sand.

"You mean, what?" I tease her, pulling her down with me so that we're both sitting in the sand. She leans on my thigh for a moment, regaining her balance, but she lingers for just a few seconds longer than necessary. Rather, it's very necessary. I want to feel the weight of her whole body on mine.

"I mean a platonic gaming buddy who's here with his parents is pretty much my speed right now. Dating is so overrated anyway."

"Wait, aren't you dating someone now?" I ask, even though I know she isn't. But I still can't help teasing her. She tilts her head in confusion, and I bite back a smile.

"You know, Sebastian?" I prompt her. I can't believe I remember the name she said at Jordy's parents' house, when she went on and on about the guy who could do funny things with his tongue. Even joking, I want to murder this imaginary dude.

Nina continues looking confused, but then a light bulb goes off and she bursts out laughing.

"I seem to remember I mentioned several guys that evening. Sebastian. The throuple. Hell, I was getting ready to bring up the whole San Diego Chargers lineup before my mom shut me down."

"That's impressive," I laugh, nudging her. "You're obviously popular."

"It's the only way I can get my mom off my back," she says. "My mother seems to think I'm either one huge project because I can't find a guy, or she thinks I'm a whore. There's no in between. She will never think I'm thin enough, pretty enough, or worth anything until I settle down. But I don't want to settle down, or rather, I don't want to settle. I find guys to be…" She stops, looking out at the ocean, and I can see a shift in her features—a hint of emotion. It's gone in a flash, and she looks back at me with tired resignation. "Guys can be really disappointing," she finally says. "I've learned it's just better not to trust any of them."

You can trust me, I want to tell her. But to what end? I can't be with her, so defending myself against her experience of men would be wasted and inappropriate.

"I'm sorry you've had to deal with such dipshits," I tell her instead. Her eyes widen, and she places her hand on my arm. It's warm on my skin, even as the air is turning cooler.

"Oh, I didn't mean you," she says.

"I know," I say. But I don't laugh. She'd mentioned that her horseback riding lessons all those years ago were like a therapy of sorts. I suddenly need to know, partly so I can understand, but also so I can hunt down whoever hurt her and make them pay. "What happened?" I ask her. "Who hurt you?"

Her face darkens, and she shakes her head quickly. I place my arms on her shoulders and look her in the eyes, now filling with tears.

"You don't have to tell me anything," I say. "But you're safe here. If you ever need to talk about it, I'm a really good listener."

She starts to say something, but shoots me a pained look. *Not here, not now,* she seems to be telling me.

"Let's go see what's happening at the bon fire," she says aloud, and she jumps up and jogs toward the group of people before I have a chance to respond. I stay back for a moment, watching as she keeps her mask on with a huge smile, as if she's been doing this for years. But having even seen just the smallest glimpse of her pain, I can't unsee it. Even more, I think I know.

I think back to the night we met, when she'd been cornered by those guys. Any person would have been scared if they were facing guys that size who were ready to pounce on their prey. But Nina was petrified, completely paralyzed in her fear. I realize now, it's because something like this has happened to her before.

I don't know for sure, but I feel it in my gut, and it makes me want to tear apart any guy that comes near her. At this moment, she's talking with Jake, and I immediately think of our earlier conversation.

"Oh, she's chips and salsa, man. Just one taste, and I know I'd eat the whole bag."

I want to get between them and push him off her. Even though it's fucking Jake, and he wouldn't hurt a fly. Besides, he swore he wouldn't go after her. But is he flirting now? Is she going for it?

Fuck, this girl is messing with my head. I have zero rights when it comes to who's attracted to her, even if it makes me want to tear Jake apart—limb by limb. My only concern should be on my fiancé and doing my job while I still have it.

I push up from the sand and join the crowd. Nina avoids my gaze for the rest of our time at the beach, but once we're all back on our horses, her eyes find mine, and she offers a small, embarrassed smile. I ride over to her, close enough to take her hand, and I do, gently squeezing it before letting go. Then I lead our group back to the trail and the barbecue dinner waiting for us.

After dinner, we light a fire in the pit between the cabins and stables. It's an evening tradition at the ranch, along with all the ingredients to make any flavor of s'mores. There's the traditional graham crackers, chocolate, and marshmallow; but there's also smashed berries, candied bacon, cookie butter, salted caramel, and chocolate covered potato chips.

It's always a treat seeing the guests, especially the kids, exclaim over the different ingredients we offer. But tonight it's a treat seeing the look on Nina's face as she takes in the smorgasbord of sweets. Her earlier discomfort seems forgotten as she catches my eye with an open-mouthed grin, and that's enough to make me jog over to her and squeeze her around the waist, selfishly capturing some of that joy for myself before I let her go.

Let's just sweep stuff under the rug, okay? Because that's what's working for me too.

"This is incredible," Nina says, her plate already loaded with her choices. I make my own plate, then find a space in the group where we can both add our speared marshmallows to the fire. She takes her time, holding hers just high enough to allow for a golden tan. But I stick mine right in the fire.

"Wow Winters, you really lack patience," she says, her marshmallow still hovering above the flames.

I lift my constructed s'more to my mouth, a combination of the chocolate potato chips, bacon, and burnt marshmallow, then crunch down.

"I disagree," I say, my mouth full. "I love a little char with my s'more. But for the things that matter most? I could wait a lifetime."

She keeps her eyes on mine, and the weight of those words settles between us. As if they have meaning. As if they could possibly lead to what I truly want. But they won't, and I break eye contact first, spearing another marshmallow as if that's the most interesting thing here.

"I think I know what happened ten years ago," she says. "Was it about your sister?"

I grow cold at the mention, the wind knocked from my chest. I know she's not talking about Hazel.

"Your mother mentioned Amber," she continues, a note of apology in her expression. "I'm sorry. If you don't want to talk about it, you—"

"No, it's not that," I share with her. "I just…" I pause, unsure what to say because in some ways I could tell Nina every damn thing about me. But this one hurts too much, and with a ranch full of guests, I just can't. "Another time." She starts to argue, but I take her hand. "Please, I can't tonight, and if you can't either, I understand. But if you'd like someone to listen, I'm your man."

She looks at her hand in mine, her dainty fingers entwined with the roughness of mine.

"I want to talk about it," she murmurs. "But I feel stupid because it was so long ago, and I should be over it by now. It's not like I'm the sole stakeholder of trauma." She looks at me then. "It's not like losing someone so young, before their life really started."

"There's no competition on grief," I say, squeezing her hand. "Time doesn't mean it's gone, you just keep learning new ways to live with it."

I keep silent then, but my hand stays with hers, my thumb running over the smooth skin.

"I thought he loved me," she starts, her eyes trained on her lap. Then she shares the most traumatic experience of her life. The date with the football quarterback. The field at their high school where he told her to meet him. Several of his friends appearing when she thought it would just be him.

How they held her down, covered her mouth, laughed while she cried.

"I'm so fucking sorry," I say when she's done. Her face is like stone, though the tears have formed silent trails down her cheeks. I want to scoop her into my arms and make up for everything those assholes did to her. I want to heal the wounds that are obviously still fresh inside her, even ten years later. I want to hunt down each one of those bastards and kick the living shit out of them.

But I can't do anything, and it fucking kills me.

"Is this why you came here?" I ask. "You said it was kind of like therapy."

She nods. "When I came to live with my Nanna, she thought riding lessons would help, and it did in so many ways. At least it kept my mind off it." She looks around, her eyes widening a little as she appears to notice the people around us again. The crowd has dispersed a bit, though a few stragglers remain behind.

"I wondered when I came here today if it would feel the same as it did back then." She looks back at me and smiles. "You know…peaceful. Safe."

"And does it?"

She nods, slipping her hands from mine and clasping them in her lap. I'm struggling so hard to not take her hands back. To kiss them. To pull her closer to me.

"You did not deserve to be hurt like that," I say, and she shakes her head.

"It's fine, I—"

"No, it's not fine."

She swipes at her eyes then gives me a shaky smile. When I don't return it, she sighs, losing the brave look on her face.

"It's not fine," she agrees. "That whole time of my life was really fucked up. My mom didn't know how to deal with me. She never told my dad. She wouldn't let me tell anyone, though I broke down and let Nanna know." She takes a deep, shaky breath before continuing. "At first my mom was so concerned for me, but it's like this switch went off. She made me feel like the whole thing was my fault, and for years I believed her. Even now, I—"

"It wasn't your fault," I say angrily. She gives me a small nod.

"I know it's not," she says. "But you try to stop believing something that's been told to you for years."

I start to argue with her more, but she looks so utterly exhausted, I stop.

"Are you okay?"

She nods. "It was a long time ago," she says. "I'm okay, it's just hard to talk about. Or when something triggering brings me back to that night."

"Like the night we met," I murmur.

She looks up at me then, her eyes shining from tears and firelight. The connection is electric, just like it was that night.

You felt it, right?

"I should go." She shoots me an apologetic look while I do my best to hide my disappointment.

"So soon?" But I get up at the same time she does. "Six in the morning does come quick."

She looks at her phone to check the time, then groans. "Like in six hours." She looks back at her chair, then snatches the plate on the armrest with the half-eaten dessert. "But first, it would be a shame if I didn't finish these s'mores. They're way too good to throw away."

She bites into it, moaning at the taste while her eyes close. "Never in my life would I have thought smashed berries could improve a perfectly delicious s'more," she says. "You have officially ruined basic s'mores for me."

"I sincerely apologize," I say, not sorry at all. She has a little berry at the corner of her lip, and I don't even think as I reach forward and rub it away before licking it off my thumb. I freeze, the pad of my thumb still at my mouth as I taste the combination of berry and the essence of her swollen lips. Her eyes are wide as she bites the place where my thumb had been, her gaze remaining on mine. The flames from the fire are dancing in her eyes, and it's easy to forget there's a crowd of people moving all around us, because all I see is her.

I take one step closer, and her breath catches.

"Nina, I—"

"I should go," she repeats, taking one step back. I look at the ground, feeling like a complete idiot. *What am I thinking?*

"I'm sorry, I—"

"No, it's late." She smiles softly. "I've had the best day today, better than any I can remember, and I honestly wish I could stay all night. But if I don't leave, I'm never going to get any sleep, and I'll be useless tomorrow. Besides, the sooner I fall asleep, the sooner tomorrow will get here."

"Then you better hurry."

She turns to leave, but I can't help myself. I grab her hand, and she turns quickly.

"Thank you," I say.

Her face twists with confusion. "For what?"

"For trusting me. You went through something so hard, and the people who cared about you most weren't there for you in the way you needed them to be. But you need to know that your mom is so wrong about you. I wish I could…" I pause, biting back my words because, no matter how fucked up her mom is, it's still her mom, and it's not my place to say anything against her. "I think you're strong as fuck," I tell her. "You're smart and so fucking incredible. You're devastatingly beautiful, and you've accomplished so much and are capable of so much more than your mom gives you credit for."

She lowers her eyes, but her hand remains in mine. "You shouldn't say things like that to me," she says softly. "I might believe you."

"I wish you believed it without me having to tell you," I say. "Because there are many other reasons why I shouldn't tell you."

And then I let her go.

Chapter Sixteen

Nina

Sunday night comes, and I am ready to call it a week. And it's been a great week. From serving up breakfasts to marshmallows in the moonlight, I have spent the better portion of each day at the ranch—and I love it! Brayden had told me I didn't have to stay for dinner activities and beyond, but he never argued when I did. Besides, what would I do at home? Sit in my room and hide from Jordy?

Because that's what I'm doing tonight.

I still haven't seen much of Jordy since she moved in. It's like we're moving around each other's schedules on purpose. Maybe we are. I haven't made an effort to check in on her, but she hasn't said two words to me. Once she got a copy of the house key, the pleasantries stopped, and I was met every day by her closed bedroom door.

But it's more than that. I have spent the whole week with Brayden, crushing on him, enjoying the way his eyes linger on me, fantasizing about how his hands would feel under my shirt, sliding up my legs, nestling between my thighs… I am so attracted to this man, I can't tell if he's attracted too, or if I just need him to be.

Then there's still the fact that he's engaged to my cousin. I might feel overwhelmed by the idea of him, but at the end of the day, he's telling Jordy he loves her and making her promises about their future.

Thank fuck he hasn't slept over here yet. In fact, I have no idea if they've spent any time together at all. What I do know is that he hasn't set foot in this house since he helped move Jordy in. I also know that the day he does, I will literally die.

Why didn't I think this through before I let her move in, and before I took the job at the Winters ranch? I am setting myself up for a fabulous fall, and it's not going to be pretty when it happens.

I'm full after tonight's barbecue, but I still snack mindlessly on a bag of cheese-dusted chips while scrolling Netflix on my computer, searching for something to watch. I'm interrupted by a knock at the door.

"Nina?"

Her voice is a question I'm not sure I want to answer. But still, I mute my computer, slide off my bed, and drag myself to the door. When I open it, she looks as reluctant as me.

"So, um, how did your first week go?"

"Fine." I start to close the door, but she blocks it with her foot. I open it, looking down at her slipper. Hell, she even wears designer slippers with a label.

"Sorry," she says, pulling her foot back. "I was just thinking we could, I don't know…"

She's stalling, and I'm getting impatient, and all of this is so weird.

"I have a show on," I say, trying to keep the edge out of my voice, but hinting for her to hurry up.

"I was looking through some old photos," she blurts out. "Ones of us when we used to stay at Nanna Dot's, back when we were just kids. It got me thinking about how close we once were, and how much things have changed since then. I don't know you anymore, and you don't know me, and there are so many things I think both of us could do to…" She pauses, then rolls her eyes. "Look, I know things are weird between us still. I feel it, and I know you do too. I've been avoiding you because I don't even know what to say. But we live together now. We used to have some of the best times together. I guess I thought we could try to rekindle some of that."

I sigh. She's trying, I know she is. But I still have so much resentment. I can't stop thinking about how she believed so many of our mothers' lies without talking with me.

Maybe it's because I've spent a week with her fiancé, and it's completely fucking with my head.

Maybe it's because I still love her, and the lingering dregs of our feud is tiresome and old.

"Fine. Whatever." I open the door a little wider. She grins, then gestures toward downstairs.

"I thought we could start with raiding Nanna Dot's liquor cabinet and just talk. No agenda. We don't even need to bring up the past. But I want to get to know you again, and I sure would love for you to get to know me." She crinkles her eyebrows, raising them with an expression of hope. And even though I'd been pretty set to stay in my room for the rest of the night, I relax into something that must look like acceptance. She beams at me, making room for me to join her in the hall.

When I reach downstairs, I realize just how much I've been gone. It seems I haven't noticed all the things she's changed down here. The living room no longer has mountains of laundry on the couch or piles of junk mail and bills on the curio. Instead, the colorful couch has new throw pillows and a fluffy blanket laid over the back, both in stark white. There are new plants in the corners of the room and by the tall floor to ceiling windows. On the curio are three bouquets, all with white pom flowers that send a message of cheerfulness. It used to feel dark in here, but somehow she's made it feel light and airy.

But I'm seeing red. This is not her house, it's mine, and she never even asked if she could do any of this.

"What did you do to my house?" I demand. I don't miss the way the words hit her right in the gut, the way she winces before hiding behind her usual mask of haughty loathing. "Where are all my things?"

She's frozen in place, her mouth hanging open at my outburst—and fuck, I feel bad. I actually feel bad. To be fair, the place looks so much better than before, and I know I'm being a bitch. But then she shakes her head.

"You know what? Never mind. I was stupid for even trying to be civil or do you a favor with this dump." She crosses the room and yanks open a closet. "Here's where all your clothes are, neatly pressed and hanging instead of dying in a mountain on the couch." She points to a shelf on the curio, which is also neatly organized with books and a filing container. She takes the container out and thrusts it at me so that I can see the few bills that are there. "I threw the junk mail away, unless you're really interested in buy three get one free tires. They're still in the recycling if you want to throw it all over the place like you usually do."

She storms into the kitchen while I place the bill file on the curio.

"Put it back where it belongs," she yells over her shoulder.

"You're not my mom," I yell back, but I also pick it up and place it on the shelf next to the books. I honestly wonder how I'll remember to pay any of them now that they're out of sight. She's totally ruining my filing system, which is to leave out anything I don't want to forget about. Well, we'll see how pleased she is when the electricity is shut off from non-payment.

I march into the kitchen to tell her so, but then stop at the threshold and look around. The counters are cleared. The microwave has been moved to a more open spot and out of the way. The kitchen table is completely cleared off and the window has brand new curtains that give the room a fresh look. In fact, the whole room looks fresh as a whole and almost more spacious. On the kitchen island is every single bottle of alcohol Nanna Dot owned, a dust rag next to them. I can see she's been wiping them down, judging by the clean bottles on one side and the still grimy ones on the other.

"So, you not only think you own the place, but you also think you can drink all of Nanna's booze? Well fine, Jordy. Get good and drunk, it always worked for your mom."

"Fuck you, Nina."

I want to be pleased that I got to her, that I broke through her icy exterior. But this time, the wounded expression on her face remains.

I broke the unspoken rule. I hit her in a place I already knew was raw. I took something she confided in me when we were young, and I used it against her. I remember all the times she'd escaped the house after her mom had a few too many, picking me up on the way so we could spend the weekend at Nanna Dot's. It was ironic since Nanna aided and abetted us in underage drinking. "As long as it's in my house, and nowhere else," she'd say, and we'd promise— though I broke that rule at so many high school parties. But on those weekends, Jordy sipped her drinks slowly, then confided in me after the lights went out about the things her mom called her when she was drunk. The way Aunt Lil yelled at Uncle Dan, threatening divorce. The tears, the complete chaos, the way even a pillow over her ears couldn't drown out Aunt Lil's drunken tirades.

I owe her an apology. It doesn't matter that we've been enemies for years, we were friends once, and we told each other things that we never told anyone else. No matter what's happened since, neither one of us has used those confidences as weapons.

Until now.

I lower my gaze to the ground, the apology sticking in my throat. I can't seem to utter the words. So instead, I shuffle over to the island and pick up the bottle of whisky that Nanna Dot always used for Midnight Manhattans. I look at her, but she turns away abruptly, bringing one of the bottles with her to the sink as if she can't be near me. She runs the water while I busy myself with the appropriate ingredients. Nanna always used her favorite whisky glasses, so I retrieve those from the neatly straightened cupboard. It's obvious Jordy worked hard in here, and I never even noticed because I'd been at the ranch during waking hours, and in the kitchen only long enough to get my coffee and go. How long had it been this way? How long did this take her?

"That was shitty of me to say," I finally utter. She stops washing but keeps her back to me. The words are right there, and I can either swallow them forever or be the one with the olive branch. "I'm sorry."

Jordy turns and I hold out a Manhattan. She eyes it, and I see the corner of her mouth twitch.

"Is it poisoned?" she asks softly, then smiles at the joke. I smile back cautiously, still holding it out.

"Guess you'll have to find out."

She takes it, holding it in her hands like she's not sure what to do with it. So I move my glass towards hers, the silvery clink filling the spotless room with the sound of amends. Then, holding her gaze, I take a sip. She does the same.

"You still do that," she says, her eyes crinkling before she takes another sip.

"If you don't hold eye contact, you'll suffer seven years of bad sex. You know that."

At this, she lets go and laughs out loud—and I do too.

Two hours and half a bottle of whisky later, we're huddled over Nanna Dot's old photos and laughing more than I've laughed in years. The past floods into the present as we point out how dorky we were wearing Nanna's smocks and muumuus, as if they were costume pieces and not her everyday clothes. When we were younger, we used to put on these theatrical performances that were mostly made up on the fly, even though we'd whispered ideas beforehand. Our parents would wear these stupid canned smiles that we later realized were their way of humoring two gauche and gawky girls. But Nanna Dot's smile was real, as was the way she clapped her hands and exclaimed. Even when I fell during the dance performance and pretended it was part of the act. Even when Jordy's voice wobbled and cracked during her musical solo.

"We should call that talent agency," I once heard Nanna Dot whisper to my mom and Aunt Lil. "You know, the one that gets kids in commercials or on the Disney Channel. Or maybe dance and acting classes to refine their skills. Agents would fall all over themselves with natural talent like your girls."

"Holy shit, we were awful," Jordy says now, picking up a photo of us in Easter bonnets and long nightgowns. She breaks into a bad imitation of the song we made up for this performance. "I'm like a flower in May, on a bright sunny day, hoping you'll stay if you come my way."

"Oh man," I groan. "Why did we ever think we were any good?" I sip my whisky, then nod at Jordy. "At least you improved with lessons. How did you convince your mom?"

"I didn't," Jordy says. "When my mom said we didn't have time or money for something like that, Nanna Dot signed me up for classes anyway and drove up to Santa Barbara every week to take me."

I'm not sure what to say to this. It's the first I'm hearing of it. Why didn't Nanna Dot do the same for me when she knew I loved performing just as much as Jordy. When I was right here in Sunset Bay?

"Shit, Nina. I'm sorry, I thought you knew."

"It's fine," I say. But it's not fine. This information has chipped the relationship I thought I shared with Nanna Dot, like the first chip in the holiday China. I had always assumed I was Nanna's favorite, though I never said it out loud—but come on, I lived with her. Jordy came over all the time, but I was here every day. Nanna and I had our secrets, our late evening talks. I knew her routine by heart, and she knew mine. I knew the messages behind every expression on her face. I even knew the way she took her coffee every morning—two teaspoons of sugar, a sprinkle of cinnamon, and a drop of vanilla, finished with a splash of cream and stirred exactly three times.

I knew Nanna Dot—or at least I thought I did.

"She got you horseback riding lessons," Jordy continues, making me realize I haven't rearranged the disappointment in my face. She's not even mentioning the inheritance, which is kind of her. I have no right to feel this bitter, but between the whisky dullness in my brain and the suddenness of this new information, I'm vibrating with jealousy.

"That was years later," I say, my jaw aching from how clenched it is. I get that fair is fair and all that shit—but it's not fair. We both wanted to sing and act, but apparently Nanna Dot only saw potential in one of us. "And you know why? Because Nanna Dot thought I needed something to take my mind off being raped by the high school football captain and his friends, not because I had any talent."

The words are out of my mouth before I've even had time to process what I'm saying. Then they freeze between us as reality hits us like shit on a fan.

"What did you say?" Jordy asks, as I say, "Holy fuck," at the same time.

"Holy hell, Nina. You were…" She pauses, and I can see her doing the math. "That's why you moved in with Nanna and started homeschooling," she murmurs. "And why you stopped talking to me about anything. It's why we drifted apart."

"Oh sure, blame me," I spit out. "As if you didn't believe every lie our mothers told you about my relationship with Nanna Dot."

"That's not what I—"

But I wave her words away. I know she didn't mean it, but I feel viperish, ready to strike. I swig at my whisky, relishing the way it rakes over my throat like peroxide on a skinned knee.

"My mom suggested I live here to heal," I continue. "But really it was because she couldn't look at her damaged daughter anymore. When Nanna Dot died and left me everything, my mom had the audacity to tell everyone I'd manipulated an old lady into writing her daughters out of her will, even though she knew why I was here, and why I stayed. But she didn't know anything about the nightmares, or how I couldn't even leave the house. My mom didn't know how my screams woke Nanna every night, keeping both of us up." I take a deep sob of a breath, realizing that I'm crying. With shaky hands, I swipe at my nose, trying to anchor the air I can't catch. "I didn't even want the money," I say. "I wanted Nanna Dot because she was the only one who cared about me. But now I find out that she was paying for you to be something great. She never did that for me."

"Nanna Dot loved you," Jordy says.

I huff out a laugh. "I know," I say. "That's not a doubt. But she saw me as a caged bird while you were a swan. She kept me safe, but she invested in your future."

"Really? You have millions in your bank account and live in one of the biggest homes in Sunset Bay, and you're crying because Nanna Dot didn't send you to acting and singing lessons?"

It really is ridiculous. I sound like a spoiled brat right now, squatting in a mansion with all the money in the world. But it's not about the money, and I tell her as much.

"She saw something in you that she didn't see in me," I finally say. "That's what hurts."

We're quiet for a moment. Jordy plays with her empty glass. I'm feeling drunk enough to know I don't want more. Instead, I go to the sink and pour myself a glass of water, and after a moment, I pour one for her too.

"Thank you," she says when I place it in front of her. She takes a sip, the silence in the room as loud as the silence of the past few years. "It wasn't what you think," she finally says. "Yes, Nanna offered. But I don't think it had anything to do with me. There was always weird energy between Nanna and my mom, as if Nanna could never do enough for us. My mom was constantly crying poor, but we had money. At least, we lived comfortably enough. But whenever Nanna was around, Mom would go on and on about how much we were struggling, and how I was growing out of my clothes so fast. When Nanna mentioned a talent agency, my mom laughed in her face, said she was working too hard to cart me around. Besides, there wasn't enough money for classes or costumes or any beauty treatments I'd likely need for something like that. So Nanna took care of it, and soon she was driving hours every week, sometimes a few times a week, just so I could go to these classes."

She places her glass on the center island and looks me in the eye. "But Nina, I hated it. All of it. There was so much to learn, and I wasn't any good. I was surrounded by professional actors, most of them younger than me, who seemed to be made for the stage. But I would forget my lines, my voice would crack, and I had absolutely no coordination. And once my mom got into it, everything got worse. The pressure I felt in the lessons was now at home since my mom made me practice every free minute of the day. Soon, it wasn't just acting and dancing, but singing and piano too. She saw me as our family's answer to escape poverty, even though we were far from poor. But no matter what I did, I wasn't good enough."

Hearing this, I'm almost glad Nanna didn't choose me. I could almost imagine the strict diets my mom would have forced on me. Well, stricter, at least.

"It doesn't really matter what we do, our moms will never think we're good enough," I muse. Jordy holds her glass out to me, and I tap it with my own in a toast.

"Ain't that the truth," she says. "Imagine what it was like when I got pregnant."

"Wait, what? You were pregnant?"

"You didn't know?" She shakes her head. "Shit, of course you didn't. Your mom knew, but my mom made me keep it a secret from everyone else, especially from Nanna Dot. As if getting pregnant without getting married is some huge sin in this day and age."

"But when? What happened?" I'm crossing and uncrossing my fingers, hoping it was years ago.

"I was pregnant when Nanna Dot died," she says, and I feel the air leave my lungs while the walls cave in. "I lost the baby a few days later, just before the funeral."

The memory of that day exists behind a layer of fog. I was a ghost of a girl, barely able to function in the wake of the loss of my grandmother. I do remember Jordy, standing next to her mother in a shapeless black dress, her face puffy from crying. Or maybe from the baby she'd just lost...

But more than anything is the realization that this was Brayden's baby too. That Jordy and Brayden are not just some casual couple who aren't meant to be together. No, they were going to be parents, to raise a child together. It makes my feelings for him seem immature and childish.

And wrong.

I set my water down and take Jordy's hands in mine. "I'm so sorry," I say.

"I'm sorry to you too. I wish I'd known what you were going through back then. I would have been there for you. I would have helped, or at least listened. When Nanna died, I knew how close you were to her. I was jealous." She closes her eyes, but not before a tear escapes. "And then the baby." She breaks into sobs, and I squeeze her hands tighter.

"I'm sorry," I repeat, my thumb grazing over her hand.

"The funny thing is, I never even wanted kids. Not ever. Brayden did, and a part of me knew that being with him meant one of us would have to give something up. When I got pregnant, I just figured it was meant to be me. He was so happy, he proposed and everything."

My eyes immediately fly to the ring on her finger, that huge carat diamond on her tiny finger. Now that I know the story behind that ring, I just want to crawl inside myself and die.

"I was about seven months along when it happened. Her name was Violet. You know, to continue with Nanna's flower naming ritual."

Violet, like Aunt Lily or my mom, Poppy.

Our mothers had rejected this naming convention when they had us. I never really thought of this before, but now I can't help wondering why. Antonina is a mouthful of a name, and Nina is so unoriginal, it literally means "girl." Jordan would have been Jordy's name whether she was a girl or a boy, and is also nothing like a flower.

If I ever have a kid, I make a vow to find my own flower name. Or maybe nature names, like Olive or Juniper. Anything to make Nanna Dot smile, if she's still looking in on us.

I'm still stuck on the reality that they were going to have a kid. She would have been my niece. If I hadn't met Brayden that very first night, would I have fallen for him with my niece in his arms? Would I dream of kissing him if he were already married to Jordy?

"Is that why your engagement has been so long?" I ask, hating to even ask about it. I don't want to know anything.

Jordy looks at her ring, and a wave of sadness washes over her face.

"I guess I'm not really sure what I want," she says. "And I don't think Brayden does either. He asked me when I was still pregnant, and our plan had been to get married a few months after she was born so that I could wear the wedding dress I wanted. But then we lost her. So we just pushed off the wedding plans, and we never picked them up again." She looks at me then, and winces. "Sometimes it feels like we're no longer in love, just going through the motions."

"What do you mean? I thought you two were crazy about each other?" But even as I say it, I recognize a few things I've overlooked. Like how she's never at the ranch, even though I'm sure she has time, and Brayden has never been in our house.

"I don't know," she says, then waves her hand as if to erase her words. "I guess things cool down when relationships leave the honeymoon phase. I thought it might feel better when I moved here, but maybe my expectations are too high."

There is a war going on inside me. One part of me wants to tell her to break things off now, opening the door for me to swoop in. But the other part—a very small but insistent part—reminds me that even if they broke up, I can't be with Brayden. Not when he was hers first. Even I'm aware of the family line that crosses.

But more than all that, I think of the child they lost. What if Brayden wants to try again with Jordy?

"Well, the two of you just need time," I finally force out. "Maybe take him out on a date or something, or get away on his days off."

"Maybe," she says. She swirls her water, almost like she's swirling whisky. Then she smiles at me. "Yeah, maybe. We've both been so busy, it would probably do us good to get away."

My heart aches at this. Why did I even suggest it? But then again, it would have happened eventually anyway. Them going away, or her staying at the ranch, or heaven forbid, Brayden spending the night here while I slept alone upstairs.

"I guess I just feel bad," she says thoughtfully. "I mean, Brayden was so excited to be a dad. He was ready to dive right in and talked about so many plans."

"Well, you lost the baby too," I point out. "It was both of your loss."

"Yeah, but I never really wanted children. I mean, I would have had one, maybe two, for Brayden. But only for him and now that I can't have any..."

"Wait. Like...ever?" I'm reeling from this. "Oh Jordy, I'm so sorry." My heart hurts for Jordy, but I'm also thinking of Brayden. I don't know how he feels about kids, but now that I know they can't have them, I feel like it doesn't make sense. I can't help thinking he'd make a great father.

"We lost Violet because my uterus can't handle a child," Jordy says. "If I were to get pregnant again, I'd not only lose the child, but I could also die. They tied my tubes to ensure I'll never get pregnant again."

Poor Brayden.

"Poor you," I say. "What about adoption? Or even surrogacy? You could have a kid that's still yours but could just grow in another woman's body. Have you thought about it."

"That's an idea," she says. But her voice tells me she's no longer on that page at all.

I look at the ring on her finger. Brayden gave her that when she was carrying his child. But now?

It's not her fault she can't have kids, but she's not even sure if they're in love anymore…if *she* loves him. So why is she still holding on to him? She's making him upend his life for her dream, dragging him across the country and away from his family. And for what?

I want so badly to tell her to dump Brayden. But I can't. I have so many feelings about this, and all of them point to me. I'm afraid if I say anything, it will reveal how I feel about Brayden, and how much I wish I were the one wearing his ring and having his babies and being a part of his ranch dream.

"I'm sure the two of you will figure this out," I finally say. But inside, I swallow my longing, the insatiable hunger that's growing by the day—and will never be satisfied.

Chapter Seventeen

Brayden

"Brayden, mail," my mom called from the kitchen, her hands elbow deep in a pool of soapy water. I'd gotten her gloves last Christmas because she was always complaining about how weak her nails were, and there they are, hanging on a hook next to the landline phone.

"Should I return those?" I ask, nodding at the gloves. But her eyes are on the mailbox and the departing mail truck, and I know I'm getting nowhere. My mom has this weird obsession with the mail, even though it's mostly junk and bills. It's probably because she spends every day here at the ranch, and the mail is a small outlet to the outside world. She's also one of those sentimental types who still writes snail mail, which means there's sometimes a surprise letter in the box. So I humor my mom by bounding down the porch steps and jogging to the mailbox. When I open it, there's the usual bills, but there's also a large envelope addressed to me from the Horse Ranch Convention—otherwise known as the HRC.

"Anything good?"

I look up from my perusal to see Nina standing there, the sunlight gleaming off her now pink hair like a halo. It takes everything in me to not brush aside the lock across her forehead that's threatening to fall in her eyes.

"Just the usual," I say, "and something from the convention I'm going to in a few weeks. Which reminds me, we're closing down the ranch in three weeks while I'm gone. We do this every year so that the guys and I can get away, and my mom can actually sleep in."

I think I note a hint of disappointment in Nina's face, and I realize she might be jealous that we're all going and she's not.

"I'm sorry," I add. "We booked this last year, and they sell out immediately. But if you want to go next year…"

"And interrupt your stag weekend?" she teases.

"Well, not exactly. Jordy will be there too."

I regret the words as soon as I say them, especially when something I can't quite decipher crosses her expression. And in the moment, I'm more than disappointed that it's Jordy going and not Nina, which really isn't fair to either of them.

"She'll be there mostly for the wine and barbecue," I admit, "and will probably wipe them out of western wear that she'll never put on after the convention." I'm not even sure why I'm still talking. Nina looks like she'd rather be anywhere else than in this conversation.

"What about the horses?" she asks. "Do you need someone to feed and care for them?"

"Hazel can handle it," I assure her. "I also have a crew of FFA members who need the volunteer hours. You should stay home and enjoy having an empty nest."

"Yeah." Her tone is anything but sure, though. "I'm heading back in, want me to take those to the house?" She lifts her chin to the mail, and I put everything except the convention packet in her hands. When she walks away, I swear it's with a loaded weight on her shoulders.

"Oh sweet, is that the schedule?" Jake asks as I enter the barn. The guys are all there, kicking back after an afternoon ride. The horses are brushed and put away, and the guests are on their own until dinnertime. There are a few hours when we're free to do nothing, and yet here they are, shooting the shit. I swear, they'd live on the ranch if I had the housing.

"Yeah, but I haven't even looked at it." Nate snatches it from my hands before I've even finished my sentence and tears into the envelope while the guys crowd around him.

We've been going to this convention for close to a decade now. Some of it is business as usual, with board meetings and discussions with the foundation. I'm the only one allowed at these meetings, since it's members only. My dad had been a part of the leadership before the accident, and after, I naturally took his spot. But going alone isn't that much fun, so I always get tickets for the guys too. There's plenty of good food, and the alcohol is flowing. Plus, five single dudes can find plenty to do at a convention like this, especially when the women are beyond hot in their tight jeans, low-cut tops, boots and a cowboy hat over a low ponytail.

Which is why these guys are amped to go, and I bring my girlfriend.

But this year feels different, and it has everything to do with wishing Jordy weren't coming. It's an awful feeling to have, and I know it's so unfair. But all I can think of is how much she pouted last year, bored out of her mind before the first day was even over. I'd even suggested she leave early, but she said she'd stay to support me. What she didn't know was how miserable she made the whole weekend, from her tireless complaints to her refusal to join in on any of the weekend's fun.

But to be honest, that's not really all I'm thinking of.

I look back toward the house, and Nina is on the deck, watering the plants. There's a kid with her, one of the residents' daughters, chatting her ear off. But Nina is all smiles. She's always like this, especially when there's kids, and something about it makes my heart ache.

"Fuck yes," Nate shouts, and I turn to look at the program I never got to see. "They're bringing back the Cowpokes."

I laugh, knowing he's not talking about other ranch hands. The Cowpokes is this all-girl band; they wear short skirts that make their legs appear miles long, all while playing fiddles and Cajun drums. Every year, Nate disappears with the fiddle player at some point during the conference. And every year, they say goodbye until they meet again at the next convention.

"I think they're pretty much a staple," I point out. But Nate is too busy ogling the flyer with their photo on the front.

"Is Jordy coming?" Levi asks, breaking away from the guys to sit with me. I nod and he claps his hand on my shoulder, as if to say *Tough break*.

"It's fine," I say. "She's been talking more about the wedding, and I think this could be a good chance for her to work on those details while I'm in meetings." When she's not texting me how bored she is, that is.

"Have you two set a date yet?"

It's the most asked question. Her parents. My parents. It's something we should know by now. But I can't bring myself to pull out the calendar, and she hasn't pushed for it either.

"Maybe next fall," I say. "She'll be done with school then, and we'll have more time to make plans."

What I don't tell Levi is that those plans could take me away from here. Which makes this year's convention that much more important. It could be my last.

"You should buy a ticket for Nina next year," Levi says, nodding over to the porch. I don't bother looking, knowing how hard it is to tear my eyes away.

"Maybe," I say. If there is a next year.

Jordy comes over after dinner, when all the guests have gone to bed. Nina left a few hours earlier, opting to skip the barbecue tonight. I couldn't help noticing how quiet she was towards me the rest of her shift. I avoided her most of the night, feeling awkward and ashamed, like I was betraying her or something. Especially when she found out Jordy was coming over.

"Should I expect her home tonight?" she'd asked, her cheeks flushed.

"No," I'd said, and it felt wrong to say it.

But then again, why? Jordy is my fiancé, and we've barely spent time together since she moved here. We haven't even slept together since the night of that God awful dinner at her family's house, which would be weird except sex has played second fiddle for years. Either she's been too busy, or I have. So tonight feels like something we need to do, just to make sure we don't drift further apart.

So why am I thinking of Nina and the way she left early? Why do I feel guilty that Jordy is here and not Nina?

"We haven't seen this in a while," Jordy says now, her head leaning against the crook of my shoulder while she clicks on *The Secret Life of Walter Mitty*. We've watched this movie at least a dozen times, and I know she's watched it at least that many times alone. But here we are, about to watch it again.

"Are you ready for the HRC?" I ask, settling into the couch as she snuggles closer.

"Hmm?" She plays with the button on my shirt, something that used to drive me wild. Now I'm just resisting the urge to bat her hand away. What the fuck is wrong with me?

"The convention," I say. "I got us tickets for the earlier flight so we can check in early and get settled before it gets too crowded. If you want, I can make reservations for that bistro you like—"

"Shit, that's coming up? I completely forgot. What dates?"

I tell her, and she grabs her phone and scrolls through it. "Brayden, I can't. It's finals week, and there's no way to make any of this up."

"I thought all your classes were online."

She unbuttons the middle button of my shirt, and her warm hand slips over my skin. I catch her hand, and she stills. Then she sighs. "Okay, fine. I really, really don't want to go."

The weight lifts off my chest, and suddenly I can breathe easier.

"It's not that I don't want to go away with you," she continues, "I do. In fact, I want to plan something with you as soon as you get back, but not the convention. I felt like I was trapped in one place with nothing to do and no one to talk with. I just can't put myself through that again."

"It's totally fine," I say, and she looks up, her wide eyes smiling.

"You really don't mind?"

"I mean, I'll miss you," I say, "but we've spent much longer times apart. Besides, this way I can focus on the convention and not on whether you're enjoying yourself or not."

I lean down to peck her lips, closing my eyes as I try to remember what it was like when things were new. We barely knew each other, but it fun and exciting…and very not serious. It was so casual, I didn't even tell her I was leaving when my dad had his accident. But then she called to tell me she was pregnant…

"You'll marry her," my father said, his voice wavering only slightly from his hospital bed. There were so many tubes connected to him. His legs remained still beneath the blankets; his skin gray as He leaned heavily against the pillows. He could barely keep his eyes open from the amount of drugs in his system. I was either at his bedside or attached to my phone, afraid he'd have another heart attack and I'd lose him forever.

At that point, I'd promise him the world.

"Yes, I'll marry her," I promised him, reaching for his hand. It remained limp in my grasp, but I squeezed it with reassurance. I'd be a man of my word and care for Jordy and our new family.

It wasn't her fault we lost the baby. It wasn't either of our fault. But I made my father a promise, and then her, and now I'm being a really shitty boyfriend—a shitty *fiancé*.

I deepen the kiss, opening my mouth and touching my tongue to hers in a question. She answers, flicking her own tongue over mine. But then she pulls away. She gives me one last quick kiss, her mouth closed, and then she smiles.

"Maybe later," she says, then turns her head on my chest so she can keep watching the movie.

Later doesn't happen, though. I curl my body up behind hers, and she remains in her tiny shorts and tank top. Neither one of us make the move to seduce the other, and soon her breathing slows. Eventually she pulls away, moving to her side of the bed.

"You should bring Nina," she murmurs, and I almost choke on my surprise.

"Nina? Why?"

"Because she works for you, silly."

I mean, of course that's why. Not for any other reason.

"I didn't book any extra rooms," I say. " I doubt she'll want to stay with any of the guys."

"Just let her bunk with you," Jordy yawns. "She's my cousin, which makes her kind of like your cousin too."

Totally the wrong thing to say. If Jordy even knew how much restraint I had to have around "our" cousin...I can't even think about it, let alone think about Nina as any kind of family—and this inner argument is reason enough to not even consider Nina for this trip.

"I'll consider it," I say anyways, my mouth defying my brain. I reach out to smooth my hand over Jordy's arm, but her eyes are already closed, and I can tell she's fighting sleep. Tomorrow morning, she'll likely still be asleep when I get up to start my workday.

"She'd probably enjoy it more than me," Jordy says. A few minutes later, her breathing turns to light purrs, her body moving with each inhale.

But I stay awake a little while longer, suddenly not tired at all. There's a possibility Nina will be just as bored as Jordy has been. But somehow, I doubt it. The past few weeks, Nina has held her own at the ranch. She's wanted to learn everything, and she's a fast learner. There isn't one job that's too big or too small for her. I swear she'd be there on her days off if she could, if I hadn't insisted she take her time off seriously. But if I were really being serious, I would have told her I wanted her there every day, every hour.

Now, just thinking about five days together at one of my favorite events of the year, I am suddenly way more excited.

But is it wrong to be this excited? Probably. However, Jordy gave me her blessing.

This means nothing. It's a boss taking his employees to the Horse Ranch Convention. Nothing more than that. Maybe she'll have just as much fun as the guys do, though the thought of her bringing home a cowboy is enough to make me want to punch a nail into my fist.

Three weeks can't come soon enough.

Chapter Eighteen

Brayden

The guys abandon us as soon as the bus pulls into the casino hotel, grabbing their bags and booking it through the sliding doors. This year's convention is at the Everglades Casino in Galveston, which means these guys are getting no sleep at all over the next five days.

"Wow, this place is huge," Nina says, standing back while I get both our bags. I'd gone back and forth over whether or not she should come, and only decided to ask her after the hotel confirmed they could move me to a double queen room, thanks to a cancellation.

"You're lucky," the desk clerk had told me over the phone. "We've been booked solid for months."

On the bus, Nina sat with Levi, talking the whole time about who knows what while I tried my best to keep my eyes to myself. I'd hoped she would sit with me, but she chose the seat across the aisle, only glancing at me long enough to offer a quick smile and another thank you for letting her tag along. If she only knew how much I wanted her there, how I wished it were just the two of us on a different kind of trip, not a convention full of people and events.

Now, I can't help smiling at the awe on her face as she looks up at the place we're staying. I know Nina is richer than sin, but the way she's acting, it's like she's never stayed somewhere this fancy in her life—and Everglades isn't even the fanciest place out there. It makes me want to show her more, just to see her eyes light up this way.

"I've got that," she says when I retrieve her bag from the luggage handler. She takes it from me before I can argue. "You have enough stuff to deal with," she nods her head at my bags that are now in a pile. My clothes only fill one of the bags, while two others carry my laptop, binders, and other items I need for a variety of meetings I'll be attending.

If Jordy had been here, she would have handed me her bag too. Instead, Nina is reaching for one of mine, saving me from juggling all the bags at once or having to hunt down a garment cart.

We walk into the casino, and I'm immediately greeted by familiar faces and my name called through the lobby. It took a couple years for me to gain the same respect my dad got here, but now I'm considered one of the old timers—even though it's only been five years. I know my dad hates that he doesn't go anymore, but it was just too hard for him to keep this up. Not just because of his physical limitations, but because it was a reminder of all he'd lost with the accident. Still, every time one of the guys comes up to me and claps a hand on my shoulder, I can't help feeling that a part of it is for my dad too. So I receive each greeting for him, as well as for me.

"And this must be your lovely bride," Mr. Murphy, the chairman of the convention, says as he holds out his hand. I know he's met Jordy, but it's been a whole year, so I cut him some slack.

"No, this is Nina," I say, glancing at her with an embarrassed smile. Her cheeks are flushed, making her blue eyes seem like oceans.

"I work on the ranch," she says, placing her hand in his. "I guess I'm one of the guys." She lets loose a nervous laugh as he raises her hand to his lips.

"Nah, you're nothing like the guys," Mr. Murphy says, his gaze sweeping over her. I narrow my eyes, fighting the urge call him out. I manage to restrain myself. Murphy is one of those old school guys who doesn't understand that girls don't want to be treated like sexual objects. If Nina minds, she doesn't show it. Instead, she beams under his compliment.

"You're going to meet a lot of guys like that," I warn her once we're out of ear shot. "I hope you're ready for the attention."

"Well, any attention I get will probably be because girls like her aren't in the room," she says with a laugh, nodding in front of us. I follow her gaze toward The Cowpokes and laugh when I see Nate already with the fiddle player, holding her bags while she checks in with the front desk. I have a feeling she won't be using her room, though, if Nate gets his way.

"They have nothing on you," I say before I even have time to think about it. I realize how forward that is, and glance at her. There's a small smile on her face, but she says nothing about it.

We check in and take the elevator to the fourteenth floor. I realize there's a mistake when we reach our room. It's the one in the corner, the same one I get every single year, and I know damn well there's only one king bed on the other side of that door. If I'd paid attention at check in, I would have recognized the damn number.

"I'm sorry, I asked them for a different room," I say, unlocking the door. "There's only one bed. I'll call the front desk and see what happened."

"It's fine," Nina says, following me into the room. Her eyes sweep toward the windows offering an incredible, unobstructed view of the ocean. It's why I request this room every year. Even though I know we need to swap, I can't help feeling disappointed we won't wake up with this view every day. "Just request a rollaway and I'll sleep there," she says.

"Like hell you will." I dial the front desk. "If we have to stay here, I'll take the cot."

"Front desk, how can I help you?"

I tell the girl on the other line the situation and am met with a sympathetic click of her tongue.

"I'm sorry, Mr. Winters, but we're fully booked. I don't see a request for a double room anywhere in your notes."

I swear under my breath, then catch Nina's eye. She gives me a pointed look and I lighten my expression. "Okay, that's fine. Can we just get a rollaway bed?"

"We don't have any more available, I'm afraid," the desk clerk says. I huff out a breath, and Nina shrugs her shoulders, then points to the couch.

"I don't suppose you're out of extra blankets too?" I ask through clenched teeth.

"We have plenty of those, Mr. Winters," the clerk says with an overly cheerful voice. "Would you like me to have some delivered."

"Yes please," I confirm, then hang up the phone.

I make my way to the couch and sit on it, testing the cushions. It's fine enough, I suppose, though I can see my feet will hang off the end.

"But just look at that view," Nina says, her wide smile making me forget everything. She's referring to the ocean, but as I watch her, I realize any room would have a great view if she's the one in it.

Once my blankets are delivered and we've unpacked our bags, Nina and I set out to explore. Today's schedule is pretty much one big social event, starting with a crowded conference room and buffet tables loaded with food. I'm happy to see Nina load her plate with some of the best barbecue she'll ever have. It's a major difference from her early days on the ranch, when she'd pretend she only ate like a bird. Weeks later, and she keeps up with all of us and is happier for it.

"So, this is why you like these conventions," she says once we find a table. I nod and start to answer, but we're joined by some other chair members who all remember who I am, but I'm terrible with names.

"This is Nina, one of my ranch hands," I say to the guys, a trick my dad taught me long ago. Sure enough, they lead with their names. Scott. Robert. Ryeson. Bailey. All names I'll forget in a few minutes, though I won't forget the interested way they're looking at Nina. She's hyper aware of it too, with the way she keeps tucking her hair behind her flushed ear, or shifting her eyes even as she smiles. The food goes untouched, and I know she's self-conscious.

"So which of you guys are going to win the calf roping contest tomorrow," I ask, and all eyes are off Nina as the pissing match begins. Immediately she starts eating, and I slip an arm over the back of her chair to comfort her. But as soon as my arm is there, it's all I can think about, even as these guys are one upping each other. Nina's soft hair, a silvery lilac this time, brushes against my skin, sending jolts of electricity up my arm. She leans against the chair, her shoulder pressing against my arm, and she looks at me. Her soft blue eyes catch mine, and I see the smile in them, the way she welcomes my touch. It takes everything in me to tear my eyes away from her face and stay in the conversation.

"Thank you," she says later, when the guys have finished their plates and excuse themselves. Her plate is empty, and she pushes it back with a satisfied sigh.

I don't even have to ask to know that she's talking about my distraction. I'm dying to tell her she doesn't have to be self-conscious, that it's just eating. But then I remember the way her mom treated her that night at Jordy's parents' house. The damage her mom has done so that she can't even eat a fucking bite in front of people—it makes me insane. But I know that lecturing her won't change these deep-seated wounds, so I say nothing, though I vow to be her safe space.

The rest of the evening, I keep Nina at my side. If Jordy had been here, she would have retired long ago, leaving me to the small talk and schmoozing. But Nina is going strong. After a couple drinks, she's even more gregarious, and it's hard to remember that she doesn't know anyone here. I'm soon forgotten as Nina swaps stories about ranch guests and the trouble with manure, making everyone around us laugh with her stories.

And me? I'm mesmerized. She's like a flame and I'm the moth, dancing around her and ready to get burned. Once the stories begin to wane, the bar becomes a landing strip for shot glasses. The bartender lines them up, and Nina leads the charge as we all throw back a smooth shot of Don Julio.

"Again!" Nina laughs, and I catch her as she stumbles. When she looks up at me, it's with a sloppy grin that makes me want to kiss it off her. Fuck, I want to taste that mouth so bad. I keep my hold on her, neither one of us breaking.

The rest of the party disperses, or we just forget about them altogether as she turns in my arms, her eyes never leaving mine.

"Brayden," she whispers, her voice lazy with tequila, but burning a hole within my chest. Holy fuck, the ache is so devastating, I can't let go of her. I can't look away. I can only stare in her eyes, at her mouth—her everything.

"I want to kiss you," I murmur, my heart pounding at the confession, even as the alcohol dulls my morals.

"Then kiss me," she says. It's all I need before my mouth claims her, my fingers twisted with hers as I hold them to her back. And holy fuck, her taste is so sweet. Like the most fragrant flower and the most decadent dessert, all whipped cream and honey and lavender in one. My tongue dances over hers, every part of me hungry for her.

I open my eyes, just to see if she's real, but I'm distracted by Jake just across the bar, looking directly at us. For a moment, I'm sobered into realizing what I'm doing. Looking around, it doesn't seem like anyone's noticed, and when I look back, Jake's gone.

"Let's get out of here," I say, taking her hand and pulling her from the room. She doesn't argue, only clutches my hand tightly as we head for the elevators.

Once inside, we stand next to each other untouching. But once those doors close, I'm on her, my hands in her hair as she meets my mouth with the same urgency. I pray to God no one needs to use the elevator, and will it to hurry the fuck up. The doors open, and we're half falling, half laughing, our mouths still connected as we make our way to the room. I've never felt more alive or more drunk in my life, and fuck it feels like I'm walking on air.

We enter the room and I face her again. This time, the silence is jarring. It's just our breathing as we take each other in. She's wobbling. Or is it my vision? I'm hit with the realization that we're way too drunk right now, and just how far we've crossed the line we've been toeing since the day we met.

I want her. I want her in every way imaginable. But it's not just my life that will be affected if we go through with this—it's hers, and it's most definitely Jordy's.

"We don't have to—"

"Shut up, Winters, and undress me," she slurs, her voice unsteady as a ship at sea. Her eyes dare me to move closer. Beg me.

And when she lifts her arms above her head, I close the space between us. We stumble, but I recover, pulling both of us to standing. Then I clutch her shirt, pulling it over her head, taking a deep inhale when I see the lacy purple bra that matches her hair, and her soft ivory skin that needs my hands all over it. I want to devour her, but I also want to savor every moment.

So I take it slow, cupping her face and stroking her cheek as I taste her lips, her neck, her chest. I slide one strap of her bra over her shoulder, watching with fascination as a trail of goosebumps appear behind my lingering finger. My breath feels shallow when her tiny rosebud nipple emerges over the fabric, and I duck my head to capture it with my tongue and lips. She shudders against me, her hands gripping my shoulders, a tiny gasp escaping her mouth as my teeth graze the tender flesh.

Fuck. What am I doing? I pull back, and she loses her balance without me there to support her.

"Please," she begs, opening her eyes. Those fucking eyes, so blue I could swim in them. Bloodshot from her stupor. Hooded as she paws at me. I take another step back, just out of reach.

"I can't," I say, then shake my head. "I mean, we can't. You're drunk. I'm drunk. We're going to wake up tomorrow and realize what we've done."

She steps closer, her breast still exposed as she presses herself to me. My cock is so fucking hard I'm seeing double. Or maybe that's the tequila.

"Brayden," she murmurs, her hand making lazy circles on my chest, "I won't regret this, I promise."

I look at her, so captivated by her. I could take her right now. I could kiss every fucking inch of her, taste the honey of her essence. I could bury myself in her and remain there all night.

I capture her hands, and she lifts her sweet face to mine.

"I can't," I repeat. She closes her eyes, takes a deep breath, and steps back. As she adjusts her bra, I feel the air in the room grow thick. I may have ruined everything, and it's not even my relationship with Jordy I'm concerned about. All I can think about is this beautiful girl in front of me, and how I'd give anything to be tangled up inside her. She's the perfect storm, and I'm just a vessel on her waves. I'm ready to drown in her.

"Brayden, I want this," she says softly, even as she puts her shirt back on. "I want you. I'll wait, but this is happening."

"You don't know what you're saying."

"I do know," she insists. "And tomorrow morning, when we're sober, I will still want you."

I close my eyes, the room wavering as I rub my forehead. There are so many thoughts in my head right now. How carnal my need is for this woman in front of me. How I could give a shit about the consequences. How my whole entire life has been about taking care of everyone else, but being here with Nina, I'm finally free—and yet, my hands are tied.

Nina steps toward me. She takes my hands, presses them to her chest. To her heart.

"Come on," she says, pulling slightly. "Let's sleep this off." She turns to the bed, and I let my hand slip from hers.

"My bed is over there," I rasp, my voice hoarse from the tequila, or from the sheer effort to not cross any more lines.

"You and I both know you're not sleeping there," she says, flipping back the covers, then turning to me. "I'll stay on my side, and you can stay on yours. But that couch is about a foot too small for you, and this bed is big enough to sleep sideways. So get undressed and get your ass in bed."

I hesitate for a moment. I know I should stand my ground, especially when she slips off her shirt and pants in front of me, trading her clothes for an oversized t-shirt. Sexiest lingerie I've ever seen.

This is the worst idea, and yet, I strip off my clothes. I usually sleep naked, but for her I keep my boxer briefs on. I feel her eyes on me as I slip under the covers, then feel the weight of her body settle next to me.

"There's a line, Winters," she says huskily. I turn my body, our heads resting on our own pillows as we face each other. She traces a line between us with one painted pink fingernail, and I'm a goner for that evil glint in her eyes. "Cross it, and your ass is grass."

Chapter Nineteen

Nina

He crossed the line. I realize it when I wake up to Brayden's bare chest against my cheek, his arms resting protectively around my shoulders, and his … Oh my … his rather large cock pressing against my stomach.

I should move. I know I should. But I don't. Instead, I relish how hard he is as I inhale his musky scent. Fucking hell, he smells good. There are the remnants of last night, a hint of tequila emanating from both our pores. But there's also the earthy scent of him, a smell that's like wind-rustled trees and rain on pavement, mixed with sweat and the sweet tang of his body odor, which gives me a heady feeling every time I inhale. I could bottle him up, make him my air, and dissolve into his chest.

His body rises and falls against mine with each breath, and I remain as still as possible so I don't break the spell. It occurs to me that this is the first time I've ever done this. I've never slept with a man—like, physically fallen asleep. I've fucked them, and they've fucked me; but this is a level of intimacy I've never experienced in my life.

But he's my cousin's fiancé.

This is wrong. I know this is wrong. In five days, we'll leave this place. He'll go back to her, and I'll go home alone, and it's likely we'll never speak of this again. If he stays with her, there's a chance he'll fire me from the ranch. I mean, why would he let me stay when my presence could ruin everything?

But in this moment, I can't care. I won't. Whatever is happening between Brayden and me, it's been brewing for a while. Since that night he saved me from those assholes. Since I was a broken girl and wrote a list of qualities that belong to him.

Brayden inhales quickly, shifting in a way that lets me know he's waking up. I hold my breath, unsure what he'll do when he realizes how close we are, how his cock is still pressing against my belly.

His breathing slows, but his arms move slightly. I feel his head move, and I lift my eyes to meet his. He blinks slow, licks his lips. Then a small smile tugs at his mouth.

"Good morning," he says. There's a slight twitch against my belly, and I try not to laugh as I see the realization cross his expression. He pulls away, and I already miss his warmth. "Guess I'm glad to see you," he laughs. He pulls back the covers and sits on the edge, groaning as gravity catches up with him. "Fuck, how much did we drink last night?"

I actually feel fine this morning. Even last night when we kissed, I'd been sloshed, but completely aware of what was happening. Still, I'm glad he didn't follow through. Not while we were drinking. If he kisses me again, I want to be sober as fuck so I can remember everything.

Brayden goes to the bathroom while I remain in bed. It's weird listening to him pee. No, not weird. It's like we've done this a million times, like I wake up with him every morning and go to bed with him every night. Like we could blow off this whole day and just stay in bed, watching the ocean from our corner room.

He re-emerges but hesitates at the threshold. "We have a full plate today," he finally says, crossing the room and sitting gingerly on the edge of the bed. I know what he's doing—completely pretending like this heat between us doesn't exist. I have a choice; I could play along, shifting back into this game of platonic pretend we've been playing, or I could stall and see where this leads.

"How many hours until we need to be out of here?" I ask. He raises an eyebrow, but looks over my shoulder at the clock on the nightstand.

"We have a few hours," he says.

"Good." I swing my legs over the edge of the bed and get up. I can feel his eyes on my ass while I move to the coffee pot. "Then we have time to enjoy a slow cup of coffee before we start talking schedules and shit."

He chuckles, settling back into bed as I set up the coffee before I relieve myself in the bathroom. After, with two steaming cups in hand, I head back to the bed and hand him his.

"Coffee in bed," he murmurs. "Do you make house calls?"

"I won't even answer that," I tease, letting the insinuation rest between us. Because I'd give him coffee in bed every morning just for the pleasure of waking up to him.

We sip in the quiet of the room, the golden rays of sunlight casting a hazy glow over the room.

"About last night," he finally says.

I take a deep breath, then another sip of coffee as scenes from last night unfold in my mind. His tongue in my mouth. His lips on my breast. His hands everywhere, everywhere, everywhere. The sheer intoxication of him, so much more than a dozen shots of tequila. How I could get drunk on him all night long, and never grow tired.

"What about it?" I ask. I shift my gaze to him and suddenly feel the heat from his stare—the way his eyes search me, the unasked question resting on his lips. "You mean, now that it's morning, do I feel any regret?"

He sets his cup down and turns to face me. I put my cup down too, shifting my body so I'm looking at him.

"Brayden, when it comes to you, I only have one regret. And it's not about kissing you last night."

He breathes in, closes his eyes, and I can see the war going on inside him. But I'm too selfish to help him make the right decision. The proper one. The only one we should make.

"What's your regret?"

"I think you know," I say. He says nothing, and I know he wants the words aloud. "That I didn't meet you first," I whisper. My heartbeat rushes to full crescendo in my ears, and I swallow my panic at finally admitting how I feel. "Do you have any regrets?" I ask.

He looks at me for the longest time. I can feel the electricity pulsing in my veins, the magnetic pull I'm losing a battle against.

"I should," he says. "Especially about what I want to do to you, but I don't." Then he pushes forward. I don't move, letting his lips find mine. He kisses me. Tentatively. Seeking. Verifying if the door is open. I part my lips, let him inside, melt into the groan that vibrates from his chest.

"Fuck Nina, you make me feel…" He kisses me again, shifting his body so that he's on top of me. His hand finds my ass, and I lift my hips so that my groin brushes against the cloth covering his cock. He groans again. "So out of control. Just completely blitzed," he says. "We shouldn't…"

"Not now." If he so much as mentions her name, or even refers to her at all, I'll die. I'll realize what we're doing, and right now, I just want to pretend we're on the right side of any moral line, that there are no consequences to our actions. So I kiss him, meeting the urgency of his mouth as my hands claw at his skin. "It's just you and me, okay?"

His kiss deepens, and he presses himself to me in a way that makes me breathless. The intoxication of last night is nothing compared to the way my body is spinning now.

"Just you and me," he agrees, then lifts my shirt above my head. The feel of my naked skin against his is exquisite, like slipping into a warm bath. He's warm and hard and soft all at once. I can't stop touching him, feeling every way his body dips and folds, the way his muscles ripple while he straddles me, the way his mouth tastes like something I could live on.

As much as I want this to last all morning, I feel the urgency of impatience. It's a relief when he reaches over to his side, pulling out a foil packet.

"This wasn't planned," he says, even as he rips the condom wrapper open. "But I'm sure glad I have this anyway."

As am I, especially as he lowers his boxers and I get a look at the full length of him. Fuck, he's beautiful. Long and thick, his swollen head just there for the taking. I lick my lips, aching to taste him. He must see my intentions, because he places a gentle but firm hand on my shoulder.

"I'd love nothing more than your lips wrapped around my cock. But if I don't feel myself inside you, I'm going to explode."

I watch him roll the condom on, the need inside me so strong just to see his hand stroke over his beautiful cock. Then he lifts my hips, his fingers tugging the hem of my panties. With an excrutiatingly slow movement, he eases them down, his breath catching as his eyes land on my sex. He starts to dip his head, and this time I'm the one to catch him.

"Fuck me, Brayden."

The way his eyes turn up, his mouth twisting into a wicked grin, I completely melt. Then he defies me, ducking between my legs.

"Holy hell," I breathe as his mouth lands on me, his tongue spreading me apart before licking my center. He finds my clit and traces circles around the hood, and the whole entire room disappears as I lose myself to the magic of his mouth. The pressure gradually mounts, and I claw at the sheets for something to hang on to. He clamps his mouth around my clit, and I erupt. My cries fill the room as I writhe under him. He expertly hangs on, flicking his gentle tongue while he sucks me into oblivion, and just when I think I can't handle anymore, he releases me. I'm still coming down as he climbs over my body, pulling my legs up and apart so that they rest on his shoulders.

"Is this okay?" he asks, lining himself up to me. I nod, words escaping me as my breath comes out in pants. I need him inside me like my lungs need air. "I'll be gentle," he murmurs, nudging at my entrance.

"Don't be," I moan, then cry out as he pushes in. He fills me completely, stretching me to the hilt as his hips still over mine.

"Still okay?" he asks.

"Fuck yes," I breathe.

Then he moves, spearing me over and over with long strokes as his mouth claims my screams. He's deliberate in the way he grinds me, lifting my hips so that I completely receive the fullness of him. I come undone, unable to make sense of time or place or anything else but his cock sliding in and out of me with precision.

But he isn't even close to done. Once my heart slows to normal, I open my eyes, and there he is, looking at me with the softest of smiles.

"You're so beautiful," he murmurs, brushing a sweaty strand of hair off my forehead. His hand smooths over my face before caressing my neck. His mouth follows, leaving a trail of kisses across my damp skin. "I could taste you forever," he whispers against me, his hands continuing their worship as I soak up the pleasure of his touch. But I want more. I want him.

"My turn."

He doesn't argue, just licks his lips as I maneuver myself on top of him, then take a moment to take him in. His tan skin is smooth, save for the small splay of hair that covers his chest and travels down to his beautiful dick. I let my fingers explore the gorgeous trail, winding curls between my fingers as I feel his hard abs underneath. I trace the V of his muscles just above his hips, followed by slowly unrolling the condom from his cock, and tossing it in the garbage. I lower myself to taste the delicious line, lifting my eyes to meet his as I drag my tongue over the length of his shaft.

"Jesus, Nina." He throws his head back as I take him in my mouth, savoring the smells and taste of our combined juices. This is us. This is perfection. This is everything it's supposed to be.

I tease him with gentle strokes, relishing in the way he submits to me as I work him with my mouth. His hands are tangled in my hair, but the movement is all me. There's no forcing, only giving—and I'm ready to give him everything.

"I need you," he finally rasps out. I run my tongue along the underside of his shaft, but then continue up the ridges of his belly, between the soft fur of his chest. He hands me another condom and I take my time rolling it on, stroking him as I do while he groans into the stillness of the room. Finally I straddle him, his cock straining at my entrance.

"Then have me," I say, then push down. He groans, capturing my hips as I roll over him. My thighs clench as I ride him, his hands helping me grind even harder. I feel the waves of passion wash over me, the friction rubbing against my clit while my core throbs around him. I can't get enough of this man. I capture his mouth, our taste still on my tongue. He lets go of my hips, cradling my head as he deepens our kiss. He rolls me on my back, still connected inside me.

"I could stay inside you all morning," he says against my mouth. "But I don't think I can hold out that long."

"Then come inside me," I beg. "I want to feel every part of you."

It's all I need to say. He pushes inside me, quickening his pace as he grips my ass to keep me close. I feel the way he swells, and I cry out when he bites down on my neck. Then he's exploding, grunting against me as I come with him. My whole body is drenched in sweat—my sweat, his sweat. My thighs are slick with my essence. He remains inside me while we recover, his rapid breathing eventually slowing as he sinks on to my body. Then he slides out, slipping off the condom as we keep our eyes locked on each other.

It's the closest I've ever felt to love, at least the romantic kind. I know it's not. It can't be. But I've never felt so connected to anyone in all my life more than I do now, staring into his beautiful coffee eyes while his fingers explore the features of my face.

"That was…" He laughs, shaking his head. "I don't even have words for what that was," he finally gets out.

"It was a long time coming," I say. He chuckles again, then nods.

"It truly was."

Chapter Twenty

Brayden

My phone rings while Nina's in the shower, and my breathing grows shallow because I know exactly who it is.

"Hey," I say, once the phone is at my ear.

"Hey," Jordy says. I can hear the smile in her voice. She's likely already been to the gym, eaten breakfast, and has her whole day planned. I, meanwhile, haven't showered or shaved, won't have time for breakfast, and just got done fucking her cousin.

I'm absolute scum.

"I know I said I wouldn't call while you were at the convention, but I just wanted to hear your voice," she says. "I'd ask you how the whole thing is going, but you know I don't care." It's a running joke between us, but this time it hits a little harder. "So, I'll just ask if you two are having fun."

Yeah, I'm having fun. But not the kind of fun you'd want me to have.

"It's been good," I say.

"Good," she repeats. "Wow, way to go wild there, Brayden."

"We're having fun," I assure her. *Pull it together, asshole.* "Last night was the big welcome party, and today is chock full of meetings."

She gives an audible yawn, and I laugh even though it annoys me so much. Why can't she even try to be interested in the things I do?

"Point made," I say.

"Is Nina into it? You're not going to drag her to all those meetings, are you? Shit, she'll probably gouge her ears out with the way those guys drone on."

As if she hears her name, Nina comes out of the bathroom wearing nothing but a towel, a wall of steam behind her. She drops the towel and does a little shimmy, all while Jordy keeps going on about how horribly boring this conference is.

"Actually, she's having a great time," I cut in. Nina's eyes widen, and I can tell she just realized who I'm talking to. As if Jordy can see us, she puts the towel back on. I want to tell her to drop it again. Maybe bend over. Maybe sit before me so I can taste that clean, wet pussy.

"Good to hear it," Jordy says, reminding me how much of an asshole I am. "But if she looks ready to die from boredom, tell her to call me and I'll share every spa I recommend within a ten-mile radius."

It's still weird to me that they're getting along, especially when Jordy has spent years talking smack about Nina. But I don't argue.

"In fact, put her on the phone."

No, this is weird.

"Hold on."

I hold the phone out to Nina, who shakes her head no.

"I can't talk to her," she mouths to me.

"Take it," I mouth back. She glares at me, then snatches the phone out of my hand.

"Hi Jordy," she says, turning her back to me.

I want to hear what they're saying, but I also don't. So I leave the room for the shower to wash my sins off while my fiancé talks with … fuck, my mistress? A fling? What the fuck was this? And what the fuck was I thinking?

I wasn't thinking, that's what. It never should have gotten this far, starting with my decision to bring Nina here and let her stay in my room. I didn't need to bring her at all. I definitely did not need to sleep with her.

Nina's shape appears through the fogged glass of the shower. I turn off the water, grab the towel, and wrap it around me before I open the door. It's not like she hasn't already seen me naked, that I haven't wrapped my body around hers all morning long. But hearing Jordy's voice adds some clarity to the situation.

"We can't do this," Nina says, hugging her arms around herself and staring at the tile.

"I know." I close my eyes, rub the back of my neck. This whole thing is so goddamn unfair. "I made a mistake," I mutter.

She looks up at me, a look of hurt crossing her face. Then a flash of anger before she turns to leave. I grab her by the hand and hold tight.

"Let go," she says, pulling when I won't. "Fuck off, Brayden. Let me go so you don't make any more mistakes."

"You're not the mistake," I growl, pulling her towards me. She crashes into my bare chest, and wraps her arms around my waist, burying her head into my skin. I feel her shudder, completely let go, but then she pushes against me. This time I release her.

"Yes I am, and you know it. Everyone thinks it. I've been a goddamn fool to think I could even come here and not end up in your bed, because that's what I do. I ruin everything."

"The only thing you ruined is my belief that I could live happily ever after without you," I tell her. "You're not the mistake. The mistake was making a promise I never should have made. I never should have…" I close my eyes, clenching my fists. "I never should have asked Jordy to marry me. But it felt like the right thing to do."

"Because of the baby," she whispers. My eyes dart to hers, surprise quickening my heart.

"You know?"

"Not for long," she admits. "Jordy told me a few weeks ago. How you proposed when you found out. Then you lost the baby, and she can't have kids." She reaches for my hand when I don't speak. I hesitate for a moment before I take it. She guides me into the bedroom, and we both take a seat on that hard-as-rocks couch that I almost slept on last night. That I *should* have slept on.

"It's my fault," I say, looking down at my hands in my lap.

"How could it have been?" she asks. "These things happen all the time."

"But I should have been more careful. We weren't even that serious. It was a fling we were flirting with, and I didn't use protection. It was stupid, and I knew it. But then my dad had the accident, and I came home. Then Jordy called and said she was pregnant."

I take a deep breath, thinking back to that day. We were on again, off again. We didn't even have a name for what we were for each other. Convenient, I guess. When I came back home, we both called it off, knowing that I wasn't coming back to college. But then she called.

"I'd wanted to be a dad my whole life," I tell Nina now, looking over at her. The way she's looking back at me, I want to bury myself in her arms, ask her to take away all the mistakes I've made. "I asked her to marry me because it was the right thing to do, but also because it was everything I wanted. A wife who loved me and was the mother of my children. A kid I could raise with the same values I was raised with, that a Winters lives by their words. So I bought the biggest diamond I could find, drove all the way to her dorm room, and asked Jordy to be my wife."

That was my second mistake, something I've never fully admitted out loud to anyone until now. Telling Nina this feels so wrong, but I do it anyways. How we never fully connected. How her mom wanted us to have this shotgun wedding before Jordy started showing, but we stuck to our guns to wait until after our daughter was born. How we had to keep everything secret because of this supposed family scandal, when all I wanted to do was shout to the world that I was going to be a dad.

"But then she lost the baby, and we were told she'd never have kids. She was upset, but I was devastated." I shake my head at the way the words come out, knowing they sound selfish. "I mean, of course she was upset, we'd just lost our daughter. She's just been told she couldn't have kids. But…" I pause. The loss had been hard for her. But learning she'd never be a mother seemed almost a relief to her, even though it was like my world was ending. She knew my dream of being a father, and while this wasn't her fault, and we could have children other ways, it was obvious there would be no kids in our future. I'd never been sure about the future we were planning, but her obvious relief to never have kids made me regret it. But with that ring on her finger, and my dad's voice in my ear, I couldn't take it back. "Anyway," I continue, swiping at the moisture in my eyes. "We buried our child; it was so incredibly…" I take a deep breath, daring a look at Nina. Her eyes are shining, her hands folded around mine. "She would have been five this year, and Jordy would have been a great mother. We both had so many dreams for our daughter that were all buried with her when she was lowered into the ground. But for Jordy, that was the end of it. Once our daughter was buried, she was done grieving. Her biggest worry was whether I still wanted to be with her, and what the fuck am I supposed to say to that? Because we were never in love. Not when we got pregnant, not when I put that ring on her finger, and not when I renewed my commitment to be with her forever. But a Winters man keeps his promise. It's what my father said, and it's what I live and die by. Which is why I wish I had never promised anything, because now, I'll never know what it feels like to be a dad. But more than that, my promise to Jordy will keep me from the woman I was supposed to be with when she finally came into my life." I squeeze her hand, then bring her fingers to my lips. "I'm sorry I didn't wait."

Her own eyes are filled with tears, but she says nothing. She doesn't have to. It's all right there between us, laid out before us, made up of the path I created when I didn't turn right.

What's done is done, and we can never go back. I'm with Jordy, and that's the end of it.

"I'll bunk with one of the other guys," she finally says, breaking the silence.

"Like hell you will," I growl.

"Come on, Brayden. You and I both know I can't stay in here. We're just asking for trouble."

I know she's right, but I can't stomach the thought of her in another man's room. Even if I know nothing will happen.

But what if it does? What if whoever she stays with pulls a move on her and she goes for it? Either because what happened this morning meant nothing, or because she needs someone else to help her forget? It's unfair that I'm even bothered. I'm going home to Jordy, and she's going home alone.

"Stay," I ask her. I offer nothing else but the word, though I'm sure my hope is all over my face. She looks at me for the longest time, then nods.

"Fine. But I get the couch."

Chapter Twenty-One
Nina

As soon as we leave the room, Brayden and I go our separate directions. I'd originally planned to attend all his meetings and seminars with him, which I'd been looking forward to. But under the circumstances, we thought it best that he go alone, and I'd be free to do what I want.

What I want is to curl up in a tight ball and cry.

Instead, I leave the casino and start walking. I haven't had breakfast yet, and I should be starving. But the morning left me feeling raw and shallow; a feeling that can only be compared to what it felt like losing my Nanna. Which is ridiculous, because that was losing someone who had been my sky since the day I was born.

I've known Brayden all of a couple of months, and I never had him. But losing him is like watching the stars go out, one by one, knowing they're never coming back.

My mind drifts to that wish list I created all those years ago. Was it him? Did I really conjure him up? Or did I know him before I'd met him?

"Stop being so stupid," I mutter to myself. It was just a list. A game. An idea created from a fictional story, and I believed it like a fucking child. Now, look where it got me—alone, which feels like forever, all because of some idiotic list.

I end up at the ocean, stopping at a café on the way for a cup of coffee and a croissant. I'm still not hungry, but no man is going to make me starve. So I eat the bread that feels like sawdust in my mouth, washing it down with a tasteless latte, watching the waves roll in through blurry eyes as my heart breaks all over the sand.

My whole life has led me here, and I shouldn't have been surprised. My mom taught me I was nothing more than my body, and that wasn't even good enough. Every pound I gained increased the contempt with which she looked at me. When boys started noticing, she called me a whore.

When I was raped, she acted like it was my fault.

This family is one big lie, and I'm just a part of it. Jordy and I had just made peace, and I go and take the one thing that's sacred to her. Even now, I'm trying to excuse what happened. She pretty much told me they're having issues. He confessed he doesn't love her. But he's still with her, and that's what makes this so wrong. Even if he broke up with her, I couldn't be with him.

Because then every lie my family has believed about me would be true, and their reasons for hating me will be justified.

So, I'll live this new lie—that I'm not in love with Brayden Winters, and I don't wish his ring were on my finger or his children in my future.

I stay at the beach for a few hours, even though the autumn chill keeps me from soaking up the sun rays. Even though my coffee has grown cold and a few seagulls are fighting over my breakfast scraps, I stay long enough that when I hear footsteps behind me, I know it's him.

"How did you find me?" I ask when Brayden sits down beside me.

"I smelled your perfume on the wind and followed it here," he says, placing a wrapped-up sandwich in my hands.

"You can't say things like that to me." I turn to him, hating how even now, I am so utterly attracted to him. His blue eyes consume me, and I want to crawl into his arms and soak up his body heat while inhaling his rich smell.

"I know. I'm sorry." He looks out at the ocean, and I keep the sandwich unopened in my lap. By the smell, I can tell it's barbecue. It reminds me that I actually do love food, especially barbecue. But who can eat at a time like this? "What are you doing out here?" he asks, his eyes remaining on the waves.

"Avoiding people," I say. He gives a light laugh, then nods in agreement. "And seeking answers."

"Did you find any?"

I shake my head no. "Just confirmation that once again, my destiny is to lose."

He turns to me, his hand finding my leg. I want to pull away, to tell him that doesn't belong to him. But who am I kidding? He owns every part of me.

"That's not—"

"True? Yes it is, Brayden. It's the only way I can explain how I could fall for an impossible man, knowing damn well I'm going to get burned in the end."

"You fell for me?"

For just a moment, amidst all these impossibilities, I let his question open me to hope—that he will make *me* a promise he won't back out of. That he'll choose me, consequences be damned, because we were meant to be with each other.

I nod. Our eyes connect, and I can feel the electricity in my every pore, feel it coursing red hot through my veins. I search him, pleading silently for him to say the words, and we could run away together. Maybe stay in Texas and escape all our issues, or go back to Sunset Bay and face the truth—because the connection between us is stronger than a Texas tornado or a California wildfire.

"I can't be with you," he finally says, and I look back to the ocean. He turns my head to him again. "But I'm not ready to let you go, and I know that's so fucking selfish of me. I have no right to even ask something like this of you. But I'm asking anyways."

"Asking something completely unfair," I say, my eyes brimming with tears. And fuck if I don't lean into his hand when his thumb brushes the tears across my cheek.

"Completely unfair," he agrees. "And if you say no, I'll respect your wishes and never ask it again."

I close my eyes, bracing myself for the disappointment, even though there's only one answer bursting inside me.

"Stay with me this weekend," he says, "not as my employee, and not as my friend. Stay with me as my lover. Let me make up for all the things I'll never be able to give you in this lifetime. Let me try to give them to you now, while we have time. We could even go away, leave all of this behind so we don't miss a single moment."

"But the conference," I say.

"Fuck the conference."

I shake my head. "You've been planning for this all year long. You use this for your business."

"By next year, there might not even be a business," he says, his eyes flashing as he pounds the sand.

"Because of her," I mutter. He doesn't respond. I want to ask him why. If he leaves, he's giving up his family's legacy—all for a woman I know he doesn't love. It's all so fucked up, the way he's trading one promise for another. It's infuriating how fucking blind he is, and it makes me question whether this is really a man I'd give up my morals for when I can't make sense of his logic.

But when I look back at him, I see the man I met so many months ago. The one who is bent on saving everyone around him, even while he's the one drowning. The one who, just this once, is asking for something he can hold on to. Something I want to give to him because I need this anchor too. Even if I'm the one who will lose in the end.

"Stay with me," he whispers, his voice shaking with hope.

"I will."

His mouth crashes on mine, and I breathe him in, my hands combing through his hair as he lays me back on the sand.

"Fuck, I wish I could take you right here," he growls against my mouth, and I laugh, pushing against him.

"I'm fairly certain there are laws against that," I say. " I also think we're breaking enough rules as it is."

Fuck the rules. Fuck the consequences. Fuck every way I'm going to die when this is over. Because right now, Brayden is all I need. And if I can't have him forever, I will take him for now.

Chapter Twenty-Two

Brayden

Within two hours, Nina and I are in the back of an Uber headed toward an Airbnb I found down the coast. It's expensive as hell since it's last minute, but I'd pay ten times this amount for this weekend with Nina.

I told Jake that a friend of mine in Louisiana had a ranch emergency and I was heading out to help, and taking Nina with me since she didn't know many people.

"She knows all of us," Jake countered, and I'd heard the disbelief in his voice. I hated lying to him, even more so because I knew he wasn't fooled.

"We're just going to shoot down there and back," I said anyway. "We'll be back in time to catch the bus back home together."

Lying is apparently becoming my forte. But as I lace my fingers with Nina's, I push aside any guilt I have in favor of enjoying every remaining second I have with her.

As we pull in front of the house, Nina gasps before turning to me with a huge smile.

"It's literally on the ocean," she squeals. "How much was this? You have to let me pay half."

I shake my head because I want to treat her. To spoil her. To make everything I can of this weekend, because we both know we have a time limit. So no, I will not have her help me pay for our weekend together.

Once inside, Nina looks around the house, exclaiming over the beach theme of each room, and the massive view of the ocean right outside the wall of windows. It's not as private as I would have liked, but you either get the beach or privacy in a house in Galveston, and I figure curtains are created for a reason. Besides, just watching her eyes light up as she opens the sliding doors and breathes in the ocean air, it's enough for me to find new reasons to love her.

Because I have completely fallen for her—body and soul—and it's going to tear me apart to let her go. But goddamn, I'm going to enjoy every second of her until the moment we have to say goodbye.

There's a knock at the door, and I excuse myself to answer it.

"Expecting company already?" Nina laughs, turning to shoot me a curious smile.

"Something like that."

I open the door, and the delivery guy on the other side is there just long enough to check my ID for the wine before he leaves me with my groceries.

"You deserve a night out," I say as I carry grocery bags into the house. "But tonight we're staying in, and I'm cooking for you."

"You cook?" She starts to unpack the bags, but I swat at her ass and order her to sit down. She raises an eyebrow at me as I pour her a glass of Cabernet Sauvignon, then one for myself.

"Yes, I cook," I say. "You're not a child of Angie Winters without learning your way around the kitchen. Prepare to be impressed." I clink my glass with hers, then go back to unloading the groceries.

It's not a baseless brag. The truth is, cooking is my second love behind horses. By the time I was twelve, I had a few dozen signature dishes I would make for my family when I could talk my mom into letting me make dinner. My favorite was pan-seared gnocchi with sausage, broccoli leaves, and blistered cherry tomatoes. And I didn't just get store-bought gnocchi. No. Even at twelve I knew the art of folding flour and egg with potatoes and shaping it. How do you purchase gnocchi in a package when you've experienced the real thing?

"Tell me about your childhood," she says, twirling her wine in her glass while I work on dinner.

"That's random," I laugh. "What do you want to know?"

"Everything," she says. "I want to know who you were and what you did and all the things that made you who you are today."

I mull it over as I roll the potato dough into a long snake under my hands. "There's not much to tell," I finally say. "I rode horses, helped my dad on the ranch, and took care of my sisters so that my mom could catch a break."

"Sisters," she repeats, then shoots me a sympathetic smile. "Can you tell me about her?"

I pause, unsure of what to say because I've spent ten years actively not talking about her. But where has that gotten me? The hurt is such a chasm in my heart, I'm unsure how I'll ever fill it again.

"Her name was Amber," I say. "She was the funniest, sweetest little girl I've ever known. A lot like Hazel, but even more strong willed. You could not tell that girl no, and lord knows my mom tried."

There's a lump in my throat, but I push through it as I tell Nina about the time Amber snuck a kitten into the house, hiding it in her closet for a whole week before my mom caught on. "She'd been sneaking tuna into the room for the cat, and my mom kept mentioning how awful the twins' room smelled."

Nina's covers her mouth, her shoulders shaking as I describe the moment my mom broke into the room while the girls were in school, ready to clean it top to bottom. "My dad told us later how livid she'd been beforehand, ready to take the cat to the pound. But you know my mom. The woman has a heart full of love for every living creature, including tiny orange kittens. When my sisters came home, my mom had the cat on the kitchen counter, rubbing its belly full of real cat food."

"So Amber learned a real lesson in how to get what she wants," Nina says, laughing.

"Yup. Act first, apologize later. That was pretty much her motto."

"What happened to her?"

Nina's voice is soft, and she rests her hand on mine. When I look into her eyes, I want to tell her everything.

So I do.

I tell her about the day I wanted to go to the beach with my friends, but my mom wanted me to watch the twins so she and dad could get some time together. I took the girls with me, even though the last thing I wanted was to have them tag along. I had planned to ask this girl out that day, and the twins were the perfect cock block. So I told them to get lost once we got there so I could hang out with Shayna and they wouldn't mess everything up. But then Amber ran to me screaming that Hazel had been swept away.

There was no lifeguard on duty, and everyone on that goddamn beach was just watching the water instead of doing something. I ran faster than I've ever run in my life, crashing into the waves even though I had no idea where she was. Somehow I found her body as it was churned helplessly in the waves, and I managed to drag her back to the beach. She looked so blue as I pumped at her chest, and the water poured out of her once she stated coughing.

But I was so consumed with saving Hazel, I never noticed Amber was missing.

"She'd followed me into the water," I say now, my vision blurry from the tears I can't stop. She reaches forward and brushes them away, the same way I've done for her. "My parents came to the beach, the police were there, dozens of volunteers, and a diving team. We stayed all night, watching the spotlights as they searched the water. But they didn't find her body until a week later when it washed ashore a few miles down the road."

I don't tell Nina about the condition of her body. How there was so little left of her, they had to use Hazel's DNA to prove this unidentifiable mass was her sister.

"It was my fault," I whisper. Nina shakes her head, but I stop her before she can speak. "I never should have brought them there. They were only seven, not old enough to watch themselves."

"You were a kid yourself," Nina says.

"I was old enough to know better," I insist.

She continues stroking my hand. Behind her, the sky outside is darkening with the setting sun. The gnocchi lie in perfect mounds in front of me, ready for water. But I'm stuck in the past, remembering how Hazel became a shell of human and I couldn't look at her for close to a year.

"You have to forgive yourself," Nina whispers. I look away, but she lights a soft hand on my cheek and coaxes me back to looking at her. "It all makes so much sense now," she says.

"What does?"

"You," she says. "You're going around saving everyone in this world, trying in your own way to bring back your sister. Meanwhile, you're drowning with her. When are you going to come up for air? When are you going to let your sister go so that you can finally live?"

If anyone else suggested something like this to me, I'd punch them. Let her go? I haven't stopped thinking of Amber since the day she died. I don't speak of her, but she haunts me.

But dammit, she's right. From my father, to Jordy, to every way I've lived my life, it's been to save others while my needs are forgotten. I've done it so long, I don't know how to stop it.

"When will you take care of your needs, Bray?" Nina asks.

"Isn't that what this weekend is about?" I ask, offering a light chuckle even as I feel dark inside. "I sure know how to ruin the mood, don't I?"

"You didn't ruin anything," she says. "I want to know you. All of you. Even the hard parts. We have so little time…"

"Don't," I say, capturing her hand and pulling her to me. "Let's not talk as if there's a time limit. Let's just be."

"Then let me take care of you." She rests her hands on my chest, her eyes filled with compassion, along with a hint of heat. I glance at the dinner I'd started, at the gnocchi that just needs to boil and the sauce that's simmering on the stove. Her stomach rumbles as if to answer, and I shake my head at her.

"No, let's eat first," I say.

The conversation never ends over dinner. I'm beginning to think we'll never run out of things to say. She tells me all the adventures of living in an old house, from the old pipes to the weird storage cupboards she keeps finding all over the house.

"It's like they're reproducing," she says after telling me about the one she found in the stairs.

"In the literal stairs?"

"Yeah, right there. I lifted one of them by chance, and there's another cupboard. So far, they only hold junk or old papers. But I'm hoping one day I'll find something juicy in one of them."

I tell her what it's like to run a ranch, which most of the time is incredible. But also about the tension of working under my father's watchful eye and never feeling like I'm getting it right.

"They don't know you might be leaving, do they?" she asks.

I'd mentioned it earlier, and she hadn't been surprised. There's only one person who would have told her that, and we promised not to speak about her this weekend. So I shake my head, clicking my tongue. But inside, I'm dying a bit more, because I don't want to leave the ranch or my family.

And now I don't want to leave her.

After dinner, she helps me clear the table and put the food away. I wash the dishes and she dries them, and I swear it feels like we've done this before. For a moment, I picture us years down the road, doing this exact same thing, but with a couple of kids running through the kitchen, and her belly swollen with another.

It will never be, but God she'd be so beautiful carrying my baby.

While I finish putting the dishes away, she disappears into the other room, instructing me not to leave the kitchen. I do as I'm told, though the sounds of clanging and moving furniture make me wonder what she has up her sleeve. Finally she comes back into the kitchen, and I swear to fuck, I'm about to nut myself just from her outfit alone. She's wearing nothing but panties and a tank top, and fuck me, it's the sexiest thing I've ever seen.

"Get your ass over here," I growl, grabbing her and pulling her close while she squeals.

"Brayden, no," she laughs, pushing against me. "You're ruining it."

"Ruining what? Your hair? Your makeup? Because Sugar, I'm about to ruin a whole lot more than that."

She bites her lip, but still presses her hand to my chest until I finally let her go.

"Come on," she says, taking my hand and leading me to the

living room. Once we get there, I see a fire burning bright in the fireplace. I laugh, thinking of home where my sister is probably also in front of the fire. But on this cool Texas evening, the fire breathes a warm, welcome air to the room.

"You built a fire?"

"You're surprised?" She grins. "When you live in a drafty house like mine, you better know how to build a fire or your heating bill will suck you dry." She points to my clothes, moving her finger up and down, "All right, Winters. Strip."

I raise an eyebrow, then start to sway my hips as I unbutton my shirt. She laughs, then pushes at me before working my buttons for me. "I'm not fucking you," she says, taking my shirt off. Her eyes linger on my chest, and she licks her lips. "Well, not yet," she murmurs. Then her cheeks turn rosy, and she ducks her head. "I meant what I said earlier. I want to take care of you. All you need to do is get undressed, get your ass on the floor, and let me straddle you."

"That's what I'm talking about," I say, grabbing for her again. She laughs, scooting out of reach.

"I'm massaging you, pervy."

I'm not going to lie, I'm a little disappointed. I want nothing more than to bury my face between her legs and breathe her in.

"You're going to have your hands all over my body and I can't even touch you? That hardly seems fair."

She unbuckles my belt and whips it out of the loops in one swift movement. "Tough shit," she says as she unbuttons my pants. They drop to my ankles, and I step out of them. I'm no longer helping her undress me, enjoying this moment way too much.

Soon I'm completely naked. She lays a blanket on the floor and instructs me to lie face down.

I've never had a massage in my life. That seems weird, but I just haven't. I've given them to Jordy, and to other girlfriends I've had; but being on the receiving end always felt self-indulgent. But once Nina's hands start kneading my muscles, I can't stop the groan that comes from somewhere deep in my chest.

"Fuck, that feels good," I say. She laughs lightly but keeps working. Between the wine at dinner, my full belly, and her healing hands, my whole body feels like it's unclenching, completely relaxing into her touch. Her hands are strong as she kneads my muscles. I want to say it surprises me, but I've seen her on the ranch. The girl is a beast, keeping up with the guys like she's been working there all her life, and looking like a fine piece of ass while she's doing it.

Right now her ass rests on mine, her hot pussy like an oven against my skin. I'm both completely relaxed and achingly erect. Her hands move from my shoulders to my lower back, and she presses in while I moan into the blanket. It's not only working my sore back, but also my cock into the floor. She reaches my ass, her hands squeezing my muscles, but not before she grazes one finger against my balls.

"You keep doing that, and I'm going to have you on your back," I warn her. She laughs, and then fuck if she doesn't do it again. I take my legs and wind them with hers, flipping her over so fast she only has a moment to take a breath in before she's laughing.

"I'm not done!" she insists.

"Oh, you're done all right." I hold her hands above her head with one hand, tight enough that she can't move, then I lift that tiny little tank top and groan at her exposed breast. "You look so fucking delicious, Nina." Then I clamp down on her nipple, taking that tiny bud between my lips and teasing her with my tongue. She writhes under me, her thin panties the only barrier between her and my rock-hard cock. I make quick work of that, though. I pull the flimsy fabric over her hips, moaning as her scent fills my nostrils. I could breathe her in all day long, get intoxicated off her. I dip my head, and she tilts her head back as I find her sweet honey and savor it on my tongue. She's dripping wet, and I bury my nose in her folds, wanting to consume her. My tongue spears her core, and she cries out, her hands tangled in my hair as if she's holding on to keep from flying away. And holy hell, I want to suck her dry, to consume her, to crawl inside her and never leave. This woman is everything to me, sexy as all get out and so soft and vulnerable. I don't know if I'll ever get my fill.

"Please," she breathes, and I take her clit into my mouth and suck her in. Her legs writhe under me as I lift her ass to give me better leverage. I can feel her pulsing against my face, her wetness drowning me as she comes. I lap up every drop, eating her like she's my favorite meal. "Please," she says again, but this time she's pushing me away, trying to regain her breath. I grin against her but release my hold so I can look at her face. She's fucking radiant. The flames from the fireplace cast an orange glow on her skin, but it's more than that. She's glistening with sweat, and a wide grin is cast on her exhausted face. She looks up at me, her eyes narrowing.

"My turn," she says, sitting up and pushing me back. I fall but keep my eyes on her as her gaze lands on my cock. She licks her lips—those sensual, swollen lips—her blue eyes running the length of me before her hand does the same. She finds my balls and lightly runs her long fingernails over the most sensitive parts. I arch my back as she does it again, this time tracing a line down my cock.

"You like that?" she asks.

"Jesus, Nina."

The corner of her mouth lifts, and she leans down, her tongue tracing the same line her finger did. Then I'm in her hot little mouth, feeling every nerve in my body ignite as she glides her lips and tongue over my cock.

"You're killing me," I breathe, and she looks up at me, still holding me in her mouth. Her baby blue eyes are full of fire and ice, of innocence and lust—of everything that makes me wish I could run away with her forever, just forget the whole world. She looks at me like I own her, but really, she owns me. I am completely hers, and I cannot stand another moment not tangled up with her. It's so fucking beautiful, seeing her mouth around me this way. I almost come right then, except she pulls off and gives me a wicked grin.

"Are you waiting for something?" she asks, and the glint in her eyes makes me want to do dirty things to her. She's being slow and deliberate, and I'm a raging animal, ready to pounce.

"I am exercising all my restraint right now," I tell her. "But if you keep teasing me, I might lose all control."

She grins around my cock. And fuck, that look … the sheer wickedness in her eyes as she continues to taste me, to devour me, to thoroughly undo me. "Nina, baby, I'm not going to last if you keep going," I groan.

Her mouth leaves my cock, and I mourn the loss. But to bury myself in her will be nothing short of divine.

"Let yourself go," she says, then her mouth is back on my cock. And holy hell, it's a delicious undoing. I close my eyes, one hand finding and gripping her hair as she fucks me with her mouth. I don't push, though. I just want to feel her movements, to have something to anchor me as I completely drown in ecstasy. I feel the small tendrils of completion radiating from the crown of my head, through my veins, until my whole body is a tingling mass leading toward a fiery eruption. I cry out as I come, my hot ejaculate shooting into her soft mouth. She doesn't stop, continuing to devour me as I lose control. I am wholly gone, my eyes closed, head tilted back as I moan into the void, her mouth working me until there's nothing left to give. Just as I shudder back to reality, she lightens her touch, her mouth opening as her tongue laps up any remaining juices. When I finally open my eyes, she grins up at me, her mouth glistening with my essence.

If I had anything left, I'd take her just for that look.

"You naughty girl," I say, laughing as I regain my senses. She stands and brushes a kiss on my lips, and I don't even care that my juices are all over her. I grip the back of her head and she opens, letting me in as I taste myself combined with her sweet honey mouth. Her body presses against mine, and damn I just want to lick every inch of her curves.

We finish the night with a sinfully rich chocolate cake, each of us taking a humongous slice along with a scoop of ice cream. It's delicious, but nothing compared to Nina. I want to take this cake and smother it all over her body, and lick her until every inch of her is clean. Then I want to do it again. But the way her eyes are drooping, her body slumping against the counter as I take her plate away, I know she's exhausted. As soon as the kitchen is sparkling, I carry her to the bedroom. I'd only planned to sleep, but just looking at the curves of her body, the sleepy look on her face, and I feel like the greediest man alive. Luckily she doesn't argue as I sheath myself with a condom, then slip inside her.

"I got you," I whisper as she molds around me. It's a sensual dance, my eyes locked with hers, sweat glistening on her brow as we grind against each other. When she comes, I taste the salty skin of her neck, inhaling her sweet scent until I pour every ounce of myself into her.

Only then, with our scents mingling as I stroke her back, her head resting against my chest, do I finally fall into sleep—and what a sweet surrender it is.

Chapter Twenty-Three

Nina

The weekend is over in a heartbeat. One moment we were wrapped in each other, interrupting naked tangles between the sheets with sustenance to keep our energy up and occasional toe dips in the freezing ocean just to cool ourselves off from our passion. The next we're in the back of an Uber on our way to the bus terminal, the coastline whipping beside us as I wonder what the fuck we're going to do.

The whole weekend was like a dream. Brayden ravished me in every room of that house, and my body is a new kind of sore that I know will stay with me longer than the time we spent here.

I hope I feel it forever.

But it was so much more than that. We savored long evenings talking about life and our hopes and dreams. We avoided the obvious, refusing to taint our time together with things we can't change. Instead, our discussions were filled with philosophies and ideals, what would make for our idea of utopia, and which was more important—the journey or the destination.

To be fair, I was always after the destination. I just wanted to get there already. To reach the end of the meal. To experience true love. To finally see my goal weight on the scale. I even peek at the endings of books, just to make sure there's a happy ending.

"You're missing the point, though," Brayden had told me. "If you're so consumed by the end, you'll completely miss out on everything that gets you there."

Now that we're reaching our end, I would give anything to stay within the journey forever.

I glance at Brayden. We've avoided talk of this moment the entire weekend, as if not mentioning the inevitable will keep it from happening. Yet, here we are, driving towards a future that doesn't include the two of us together. I want to tell him to choose me. To forget my cousin and break every promise he's made to her. I want him to make *me* a promise of forever, one he refuses to break.

But then I think of Jordy, who has no idea what's happened this weekend. Whose child was taken from her. Who can never have kids of her own.

Who has Brayden's ring on her finger and a promise in her heart.

I think of the girl I grew up with, who was my best friend in so many ways. Jordy was raised the same way I was, with a mom who would never think she's good enough, and who forced her to keep secrets she never should have been made to keep. Both our moms made us sweep our blemishes under the carpet, when what we really needed was a friend.

How would things have been different if Jordy knew I'd been raped in high school, that this was why I was living at Nanna Dot's in the first place? Would Jordy have healed better if she could have shared her pregnancy loss? Would she have shared it with me?

Of course she would have. The fact that she opened up about it now, when our relationship is so fragile, says a lot about where she is with me. How she trusted me with her heart. And how do I repay her? By sleeping with her fiancé.

So how can I even consider begging him to choose me?

How could I fall in love with him when he's not mine to fall in love with?

He looks my way now, and I immediately avert my eyes. His hand takes mine, and tears spring to my eyes, making a trail down my cheeks.

"Hey," he says, tugging on my hand. I wipe my eyes and look back at him, offering a weak smile that he matches with his own tear-filled eyes.

"I know," he whispers.

He doesn't tell me he'll change things. Even after all this, amidst all my guilt, I still want him to choose me. But he doesn't say it. Even though I know both of us will lose so much if he chooses me, I am so disappointed that he won't make it happen.

"How do we go on from here?" I ask him. I genuinely need the answer, because I don't know. How will I not die every time he's with Jordy? How do I breathe when I go to the ranch and can't touch him? How will I survive without his body pressed to mine, our lives intertwined?

"I'm not sure," he admits. "I didn't realize how painful this would be. I just…" He pauses, wiping at his eyes. When he lowers his hand, his face has a look of fury. "I feel torn," he bites out. "This whole thing is fucking unfair. To me, to you, and to Jordy. I know what I want to do, and I know what I need to do. But both are going to make me hurt the people I love, no matter which way I turn." He looks away, slipping his hand from mine. I feel the chill in the car immediately. The silence is deafening; the sound of my heart pounding in my ears is all I can hear.

He won't choose me.

The Uber driver takes the offramp toward the terminal, and I can feel the countdown as if it's clicking to completion in front of me. *One one-thousand. Two one-thousand. Your time is almost up.*

"I don't regret it," he whispers.

I bite back a sob, because I'm not sure I can say the same. If I'd never experienced what it was like to open up to him, to love him, to feel what it was like for him to love me back, then I wouldn't hurt this badly.

I loved every minute of being with him, but I wish I'd been able to see the ending before we got here. I should have at least predicted it. Because now I'm filled with more regret than I've ever had in my life.

So I say nothing, and when we pull in front of the bus stop, I exit the car without so much as looking at him.

On the bus, I find a seat near the front and immediately put my headphones on. Brayden has no idea, walking in front of the guys as he leads the way to the middle of the bus where we were last time. I think I'm in the clear, except Levi slips into the seat next to me, much to my disappointment. I keep my headphones on, my head turned toward the window, hoping that Levi will get the message that this will be a silent ride home if he stays next to me.

I like Levi, though. Over the past month, I've gotten to know all the guys fairly well. At least, I've gotten to know them as well as any coworker gets to know the people they work with. I know enough that I like all of them, but Levi is probably my favorite outside of Brayden. He's the most down to earth and levelheaded of the crew. Whenever I didn't know how to do something, which was often, Levi was always there to help me see it through.

"You missed a great conference," he says, ignoring my headphones and my turned away head. For a moment, I think I'll pretend I can't hear him. But it feels so completely rude to a guy who doesn't deserve it. So I remove the headphones and give him a nod and a tight smile.

"It's not like I know enough to be there," I point out. "I'm not even sure why I came. It seems silly when I'm just a barista without a coffee job who happens to work on a ranch."

"You belonged there," Levi says. "I know Brayden wanted you there."

Just the mention of Brayden's name has me turned towards the window again, just so Levi can't see the tears in my eyes.

"Did you guys get whatever Brayden's friend needed sorted out at his ranch?"

I nod, unable to say any words that will be a lie. I let the silence linger long enough that I consider putting my headphones back on.

"Let's play a game," Levi says, ruining my plan. I can't help the loud sigh that escapes my lips, but it makes him laugh. "Come on, it will help pass the time."

"Fine," I say, packing my headphones in my travel bag, but keeping them within reach. "What game?"

"Story time," he says. He peeks over me through the window at the people still waiting in line to get on the bus. "See that man there holding the green suitcase?"

I scan the line until I find him. He's clutching the suitcase like it's precious, even though it's larger than anything we're allowed to bring on the bus. There's a high probability he'll be forced to give it to the attendant once he reaches the front, and yet, the determined look on his face says he'll take the gamble.

"He's a crocodile smuggler," Levi whispers as we watch the man inch forward in line. "In that suitcase is a rare baby albino crocodile that he's keeping alive by feeding small fish that he keeps in his suit pocket."

"Oh wow, I bet that smells heavenly," I say, my mouth turning up even though my insides feel like lead.

"It's pretty rank," Levi says. "But he covers up the smell with mashed bananas."

I can't help but laugh, my face twisted in a grimace. "Apparently he doesn't know the cardinal rules of travel. No smelly foods in the vehicle, especially fish or bananas."

"Or crocodiles," Levi points out. "Though I read somewhere crocodiles don't smell all that bad."

"So, what is he going to do with this crocodile?" I ask.

"Well, his intention is to impress a lady," he says, a smirk on his face.

"Isn't that the start of every good story?" I'm beginning to enjoy Levi's distractions, almost forgetting my own ill-fated love story.

"So true," Levi agrees. "He's offering it to a woman who raises crocodiles to make coats out of them."

"How awful!" I exclaim, but I'm laughing as we watch the man arguing with the baggage person as he holds tightly to this suitcase.

"Indeed. But there's a good ending." Levi raises an eyebrow for dramatic effect. "The lady receives the crocodile, and she is definitely impressed by the man's thoughtfulness. She invites the man to move in with her so they can raise crocodiles together. On the day they decide the albino crocodile is fully grown, they approach the backyard moat, ready to hunt him down. But instead of being the hunters, the man and lady become the hunted. The albino crocodile sneaks up behind them and swallows them whole."

"Wow, that's quite a story," I laugh. "Where does this crocodile end up?"

"No one knows," Levi says. "It disappears after his very delicious meal and hasn't been seen since. But ever since it disappeared, the neighborhood has an influx of missing cats and dogs. Related? Maybe."

We both fall silent as the man enters the bus, walking past us without a suitcase in hand.

"Hopefully they lose his luggage," I laugh.

The bus pulls away from the curb, and Levi and I continue the game with the cars we pass. There's the astronaut on a family vacation, with an alien in the back seat that looks an awful lot like a golden retriever. There's the pregnant assassin on her way to her next job, a beauty case of poisons next to her. There's the pretty blonde baker who magically infuses her desserts with emotions.

By the time we hit the first state line, my mood has shifted dramatically. Yes, the heavy weight of loss is still there, but it's cushioned by the knowledge that I can get through this, no matter what happens.

"So, how were James and Olivia?" Levi asks, and I tilt my head in confusion.

"Who?"

He gives me a knowing look, but I have no clue what he's talking about.

"Brayden's friends with the ranch in Mississippi," he prompts.

"Oh, James and Olivia." I rack my brain. Did he mention names? Is that right? "They were nice," I say. "Very appreciative of our help."

"And how did you like Mississippi?"

"It was nice," I lie. "Super cute state." *What the heck is in Mississippi?*

"Did he take you to that Elvis museum?" Levi asked.

"There wasn't time," I say, feeling my tongue dry out with each lie. Damnit, why didn't I put my headphones on? "We didn't really see much of anything there."

"Probably because you were in Louisiana," he says, and my stomach plummets.

"Right," I say, then flash him a smile. "I wasn't really paying attention. We practically flew there and back."

"Or you never left Texas."

I realize he knows exactly what happened, and he's totally fucking with me. I fidget with my hands, trying to come up with the next lie, whatever will absolve us of our sins.

"It's fine," Levi continues. "But the next time Brayden comes up with his own story, he should turn his location services off." He holds up his phone. "We all know each other's location, just in case something happens on a ride. Apparently there's never been a good reason to stop sharing our location until now."

"Who knows," I whisper.

"All of us."

Fuck.

"What are you guys doing?" he asks me.

I feel totally on the spot. I don't even know what to say. I have the strongest urge to look behind me at Brayden, but I'm not exactly speaking to him right now.

"I don't know," I whisper. I look at him. "Are you going to tell Jordy?"

"No," he says, and I breathe a sigh of relief. Then it hits me how lame it is that I'm relieved. If Jordy doesn't know, she wins. But it's not like I win in either scenario.

"Look, I'm not trying to get in the middle of anything. What Brayden or you do on your own time is your business. But it's not like Brayden to leave a commitment midstream, especially the HRC. He spends all year preparing for that, and just as much time anticipating it. It would take a lot to take him away from it." He appraises me for a moment, then nods. "Or someone special."

I look down at my hands. He's right, of course. But it's not like I'm the one who came up with this wild idea.

"I guess my biggest concern is that whatever this is between the two of you, it's going to mess with Brayden's head. I don't want to see him do something he regrets."

"Like be with me?" I ask.

"No, like leave the ranch."

At this, I grit my teeth. I'm not the one that would take him away from the ranch, but Jordy is. If he marries my cousin, he'll be on the next plane for New York, leaving the ranch and everyone on it in his dust.

"I wouldn't make him do that," I say.

"You might think that," Levi counters, "but I've seen the way that guy looks at you. He's ready to throw it all away for you, if you just say the word."

It's not true, though. If it were, he would have already said it to me. He'd make me a promise to break things off with Jordy and find a way for us to be together. He'd burn bridges just to be with me.

"He doesn't love me like that," I say. "He's with Jordy. We were just messing around, but it's over now."

I grab my headphones from my bag and slip them over my ears. But Levi puts a hand on my arm to stop me.

"Nina, I'm sorry. I know I'm being hard on you. But I'm just looking out for my boy, and I'm looking out for his family. The ranch is like my second home, and we've all been a part of the Winters family for years now. I don't want to see anything mess that up."

Or anyone. Noted.

I slide my headphones on and stare out the window. This is going to be a long bus ride.

Chapter Twenty-Four

Brayden

We cross the New Mexico border, but my heart is still in Texas with Nina. The guys have just finished grilling me about my time with her. Apparently they were all on to us, and this is some kind of coup. I can see Levi sitting next to Nina, and no amount of daggers I'm shooting his way will make him get up and move. I can just imagine what he said to her, because the rest of the guys were on me as soon as my guard was down.

Am I fucking moron?

Did I even think about how this would affect the ranch?

Did I only hire Nina because of her great ass?

Am I aware of how many corporate laws I'm breaking if she decides to press charges?

They don't understand, of course. How could they? But I should have seen this whole intervention coming, starting from the moment Jake saw us kissing that night in the bar.

Did I really think we'd get away with it? Or that they guys

wouldn't say anything about it?

Of course they would. We're family, it's what we do. But in this moment, I want to kick the living shit out of all of them, starting with Jake for alerting the masses. Especially since he knows that things with Jordy aren't exactly that great.

I keep my eyes on the back of Nina's head. She has her headphones on and she's looking out the window, and I can practically feel the chill from her icy demeanor all the way back here.

I hope Levi is getting frost bite.

I pull my phone out, giving a side glance to the guys just to see if they're watching. It's stupid, really. It's not like they own me. They even said they're not telling Jordy, and what I do in my time is my own business, as long as it doesn't affect the ranch. But I'm pretty sure fucking my employee is not on their approval list. Neither is texting her, but I'm going to do that anyways.

Brayden: Are you okay?

I wait a few beats, and finally see the read receipt show under my text. But that's all. I could tell she was looking at her phone, but now her head is turned back to the window.

So what do I do but try again.

Brayden: I'm sorry about Levi. They got to me back here too. Apparently we weren't as secretive as we thought.

This time, my message stays unread.

Correction. My text turns from blue to green, meaning she's turned her phone to airplane mode, no doubt to avoid me.

But she's got to read them sometime, right? So I text her one last time.

Brayden: The only regret I have about this weekend is that it had to end. The more I think about it, the more I don't want it to end. You and me, we just make sense. Things are easy with you. Waking up to you every morning was like coming home after a long day. I would just open my eyes, and there you were in all your radiant beauty. This morning, I woke up extra early just so I could watch you sleep, and it made me realize how utterly, devastatingly, wonderfully in love with you I am. I've been a fool to think otherwise, or that I could even go back to my old life after being with you all weekend. The truth of the matter is that I want all of you always and forever, and nothing less. I'm ready to make those sacrifices. Damn the consequences, because the only thing I'm scared of is what will happen if I let you go. Nina, I'm not letting you go. Let's make this work.

I take a moment to read through the text one more time before I send it, my heart pounding the whole time. Once I press the button, there's no turning back. I'm ready, I know I am. So why am I so scared to just pull the trigger?

Fuck it. Let's do this.

I lift my finger, but then the screen changes and there's Jordy's face, beaming back at me. And damn it all to hell, my finger hits the button and answers the fucking call.

I say nothing for a beat, paralyzed in this moment where I'm literally holding two paths in my hand.

"Brayden? Are you there?"

"Yeah, I'm here. Hey." My heart is pounding, the words I need to say stuck somewhere in my throat. *It's over.*

"Oh, good. I thought I caught you in a tunnel or something.

How was the conference? I bet you're exhausted!"

"It was good. Yeah, I'm pretty tired."

More silence as I drum up the courage to say what I need to say. But is this a phone conversation? Or do I wait for an in-person conversation? What's the proper way to break the heart of the woman who gave birth to our dead daughter?

"Well, obviously you're already napping on this conversation," she laughs. "So I'll just talk, you listen, okay?"

"Sorry, baby, it's just that—"

"I got us a venue!" she squeals, and I pull the phone away from my ringing eardrum.

"A what?" I say.

"A venue. And a date. I'm sorry I didn't confirm with you. But I told you I wouldn't bother you during the conference, and there were decisions that had to be made, and I figured you would probably go with what I wanted anyways, so I just went for it."

"What are you talking about?" My head feels like a jumbled mess, made up of Nina, breaking up, long texts, our weekend. The wedding.

"The wedding, silly," she says.

Fuck.

"I just kept looking at the invitation to Ethan and Claire's wedding on the fridge, and how it's coming up so fast. The more I looked at it, the more I wanted to start planning our own wedding. I mean, we've been engaged for five years! And I know I told you we'd start planning when you got back, but I just thought I'd get the ball rolling by booking a place. Oh Brayden, it's just so perfect."

She keeps gushing, going on about the country club it will be at, the banquet room full of plants, and the variety on their menu. But I feel like I've been punched in the gut. Because of course she's planning our wedding, we're engaged to be married. And while she's planning our life together, I'm off fucking her cousin.

What the fuck am I doing?

"I booked us a tasting for the day after tomorrow," she continues. "I know you'll still be tired from the trip, but I just thought since the wedding is in three months, we have to—"

"Three months?"

"I said that, Brayden. Aren't you listening?"

No, I'm drowning.

"Jordy, I can't—"

"It will be fine, Bray. I promise. I'll take care of everything. Even the tasting. I'll just call you if I'm not sure about anything, but I know you'll like anything I choose. You always do."

I close my eyes. She would think that. I haven't given her any reason to believe otherwise, always being so fucking agreeable without an opinion of my own.

Maybe that's been my problem the whole time. It's been easy with Nina because the decisions we've made truly felt like ours. But with Jordy, I always bowed to her whims, and it's not even fair to refer to it this way because she's never required it. But it's been this way since she lost our child. I just felt so horrible for her, it became my life's mission to make her happy. But in the process, I lost myself.

Maybe I never gave us a fair chance.

"No, I'll go with you," I say. Something deflates inside me, but I brush the feeling aside.

"Oh that's so great!" she cries, and I smile in spite of myself.

"But when I get home, we need to talk, okay?"

She doesn't answer right away, then, "You're making me nervous. Is everything okay?"

I'm not going to tell her about Nina. I can't. It would absolutely kill her. But it's time I addressed the ranch situation. She thinks we're moving away after the wedding, but I'm not leaving.

"Everything's fine," I say, because it will be. "But we're planning a future together, and I want us to be on the same page from this point on."

"Absolutely," she agrees. Then she laughs. "I am so damn excited, I can't stand it. Can you please hurry up and get home?"

I note the trail of red brake lights on the freeway in front of us. "Sure thing," I say.

"I love you, Bray."

I close my eyes, then nod my head. "You too."

When she hangs up, I start to move my phone back to my pocket, but the text I was about to send Nina faces me once again.

The only regret I have about this weekend is that it had to end.

I look ahead where she's sitting. Her head is resting against the window, and I think she might be sleeping. My whole body aches because I'm not the one she's leaning against.

It has to end.

I delete the text completely, one letter at a time, then I stash my phone in my pocket before resting my own head against the window. The guys are all already napping, no doubt making up for lost time after a wild weekend. It's not like I got much sleep either. But right now, sleep is the last thing my body wants. It wants Nina, to hold her against me, to find a way for us to be together.

But if I do that, too many people will be hurt. Too many lives ruined.

So I'll stay with Jordy—she's a good woman, and she'll be a good wife—and the only lives ruined will be mine and Nina's.

Chapter Twenty-Five

Nina

It's nearly nine in the morning when we get to Sunset Bay. I barely got any sleep overnight, even though I tried. Every time I closed my eyes, I was overwhelmed by memories of the weekend, broken up by Levi's words, and my heart aching about what needed to happen. Worst of all, I have no idea how Brayden feels.

That's my fault, I know. He texted me almost immediately after Levi was done raking me through the coals, and I blocked his calls to keep anymore texts from coming through. It was juvenile, I know. But I couldn't think of anything else that would keep me from begging him to choose me, and everyone else be damned.

I'm pissed. Levi didn't come out and say it, but it sure seemed like he thinks I'm the problem. But to be fair, I *am* the intruder. I've only known Brayden for a few months. Jordy has been with him for years, and it doesn't matter how I feel about Brayden, or how I think he feels about me. He's engaged to her, and that's the final answer.

"Can I help you with your bags?" Levi asks as the bus stops at the transit station. I know he's just being nice. He probably feels terrible he had to say anything at all. I shake my head no, then scoot around him and down the steps before anyone else. I stand at the far end of the bus, waiting for the driver to start unloading the bags, hoping mine is one of the first so I can just leave. While I wait, I open my phone and order an Uber, sighing when it says it's fifteen minutes away.

"You all made great time."

I turn around and there's Jordy, grinning at me. And like dark magic, I feel the weight of what I did this weekend. How wrong it was.

She wraps her arms around me in a hug, and it takes everything in me to hug her back. When she pulls away, she frowns.

"What's wrong?"

"Nothing," I say quickly. I flash her a smile of apology. "I'm just tired. I didn't get a lot of sleep."

"I can never sleep when I'm traveling," she agrees, reaching forward to grab my bag before I do.

"Oh, I got that," I say, trying to reach it.

"Nonsense. You've had a long drive."

"It's just that I have an Uber coming—"

"An Uber? Why? You knew I was coming to get you."

I'm scrambling for excuses, anything that will get her to release my bag and let me escape.

"I just figured it's been a long weekend, and you and Brayden probably want to catch up at his place."

She laughs, shaking her head.

"Trying to get rid of me already," she teases.

Yes, I am. "Of course not, I just know how much he's missed you." *Fuck, why did I say that?*

She smiles, as if this is absolute news to her. "I missed him too. There he is!"

She releases my bag when he reaches us, throwing her arms around his neck and ambushing him with a kiss. His eyes catch mine, lingering for a moment too long. Long enough. Then he closes them and wraps his arms around her waist while he returns her kiss.

I snatch up my bag before she can take it back. I'm about to walk away, but she whirls around.

"Cancel that Uber," she commands, and I deflate. There's no getting around this. I pull my phone out and hit the cancel button. "I have the biggest surprise for you," she continues. "I want to be with you when you see it."

I want to look at Brayden. It's crazy how natural it feels to seek him out anytime I feel anything. But I refrain, instead following the happy couple back to the car. Brayden offers me the front seat, but I slide into the back without saying a word, using my luggage to take the seat next to me. As if he'd sit next to me in his fiancé's car.

Admittedly, this whole silent treatment is weird after the weekend we had. In so many ways, I feel like he belongs to me and I belong to him. But the fact that he never even tried to make a way for us to be together, that he's continuing to go along with this sham of a relationship after the intense connection we shared this weekend…it says novels about where I stand with him. I don't belong to him, and he is definitely not mine. I realize I fell for Brayden's charm like I was the fish and he was the lure. This whole infatuation is completely one-sided.

"Did Brayden tell you?" Jordy asks once we're on the road. Her eyes find mine in the rear-view mirror, and I shake my head.

"Tell me what?"

"You rat, you're going to make me spill the news?" She swats Brayden's arm, and he gives an embarrassed laugh.

"We weren't sitting together on the bus," he says, then he looks at me over his shoulder. There's something apologetic in his eyes, and my heart plummets.

"We set a date!" Jordy exclaims. "Well, I set the date. You know that country club Nanna always took us to? That hoity-toity one with all the ice sculptures and tiny food plates? I thought, why not throw the wedding there? I mean, it's expensive as hell, they needed the date to book it, and the non-refundable deposit is practically a house payment. But you only get married once, right?"

I want to throw up. It feels like all the air in the car has been sucked dry.

"You didn't tell me it was non-refundable," Brayden says, his jaw ticking.

"Why, you already looking to back out?" She laughs. The sound is like daggers in my heart. "It's fine, Brayden. When you see it, you'll understand. We'll be making payments on it for years, but it's totally worth it."

I stare out my window, trying to mentally escape the prison of this car. It's like a bad dream I can't escape, except this is my life on repeat. I want to kick myself over how delusional I was. I mean, I knew they were engaged, of course they're going to get married. Why the hell would Brayden choose me over Jordy, when she's tall, lean, and so glamorous, and I'm … me? The fact that I'm surprised at all just shows how utterly stupid I am. I actually believed Brayden was in love with me…

My eyes blur as the scenery whips by. Jordy is still talking, but it's to Brayden, so it's safe to tune out. I wipe away angry tears as I sit forgotten in the backseat while they plan their future together. All I want to do is go home and wrap myself up in the quilt Nanna Dot made, sink into her cozy couch, and watch some lame movie on Netflix while I cry into my popcorn. I want to shut all the curtains, as if the outside world doesn't exist, and dissolve into the house until the world forgets me too. I hope Jordy is staying with Brayden tonight, even if it kills me to think of him with her, just so I can lose myself in takeout and sappy movies and all my tears. I hope they get married and move far away so I never have to see either of them ever again.

We pull up in front of the house, and the way it calls to me is like a siren to a sailor. I can't believe how much I missed being home, though it was only on the drive I realized this. I unbuckle my seatbelt and grab my bag before throwing open my door.

"Wait," Jordy calls after me, but I'm already up the steps, my keys in my hand. I unlock the door, then breathe in the familiar scent of hardwood, decades of home cooked meals, and moth balls.

Instead, I'm met with cedar and citrus, fresh paint, and several other aromas I can't decipher—the scents of a stranger's home.

"You're going to flip," Jordy says behind me, her voice full of smiles. I can't even look at her as I make my way down the hall, my hand on the wall for support. Gray walls. When I left, they were wallpapered with lemons and yellow striping.

I reach the kitchen first, and my heart nearly falls from my chest. From the threshold, I take in the room with just my eyes. The cabinets are painted black with gold fixtures. The weathered wooden table where we used to sit with Nanna is gone, replaced with a smaller bistro table—black, to match the cabinets—and three tiny stools. Nanna Dot's towels, her quirky art, her millions of magnets— all gone—replaced with more modern art and towels, and the refrigerator remains naked.

"If I had more time and money, I'd have replaced everything," Jordy says. "I even found this mystery cabinet in the stairs, though I just nailed it shut so no one would trip over it." She grins, looking at me with bright eyes. "It's great, isn't it?"

I don't say a word, so in shock I can barely breathe. I leave the kitchen door and head to the living room, my heart aching in my chest.

"My design class needed a real-life project," I hear Jordy explaining to Brayden. Or maybe she's telling me, I'm not sure. All I know is that when I reach the living room, I want to fall through the floor.

The couch is gone. The curio, her quilts, the rocking chair—all of it, gone. Even the curtains, which are replaced with filmy pieces of cloth that do nothing to block the light or the outside world. The furniture is all modern and boxy, hardly the place to curl into and disappear. A new couch is the centerpiece of the room, a lemon-yellow leather sofa full of angles. The softest thing on it is a throw pillow with daisies on it. The rest of the room remains stark and cold.

"I never realized how big this room was until I got rid of all the clutter," Jordy says.

"Where are the teacups," I ask, my voice cracking. She looks at me with surprise.

"I sold them on Facebook Marketplace," she said. "I was able to get rid of a lot of things that way, really quickly in fact. It helped fund so much of the work I did. I didn't have a chance to get to the basement, but I bet…"

"Where's the couch?"

Jordy's eyes widen.

"Where's the chest of her crafts? And the potholders? And her candy dish?" My mind reels from all the things that were once in this one room. "Where are the pictures that were on the walls? Did you get rid of everything?"

"Not everything, Nina. Her quilts are in the closet, so are the pictures. Her crafts are in a box for us to go through. I just got rid of the unimportant stuff."

"It was all important!" I scream the words, and they feel like fire in my lungs.

"Nina, she was just trying to help," Brayden says, and I whirl on him, my eyes narrowing.

"Fuck you, Brayden." There is so much more I want to say, but I won't. I'll keep his secrets, but only because they're mine too. I was a fool to ever let him touch my body. I turn back to Jordy. "And fuck you, Jordy. This is my house, not yours. Nanna Dot gave me everything here, and you had no right to get rid of any of it. You had no right to change anything without my permission."

"We talked about this, though!" Her eyes are flashing, but I could give a fuck about her anger.

"We *never* talked about this. The last time you pulled this shit, I obviously hated it. So what makes you think I wanted you to do more?" I look around, searching for anything left of Nanna. Instead, all I see is fucking Jordy. "This was my home, and you've ruined it!"

"You're never going to move on if you keep living like this." Jordy waves her hand over the room. "You kept every goddamn thing she owned. It's like this place was a museum for the dead, straight out of the eighties. I could even smell Nanna Dot in the furniture."

"And that's such a bad thing?"

"It is when she's been dead for over five years!" Jordy yells. "She wouldn't want this for you, and you know it. You've had years to make this place your own, but it's like Nanna Dot will walk into the room at any moment. There's nothing that's you here."

"You don't even know me," I point out. "So how can you say that?"

"I know you aren't an eighty-year-old woman," she scoffs. "And that this house has gotten out of control because you can't let go of a goddamn thing." She takes a deep breath, then offers a pleading look. "You're drowning, Nina. This house is consuming you. Nanna Dot is gone, and it's time you moved on. I just wanted to help you let go of some of the emotional baggage."

"You had no right to get rid of anything! You have no idea how much I loved her because you obviously didn't feel the same."

"How dare you. I loved her plenty," Jordy says. "We all loved her. You don't own the exclusive rights to a relationship with her, regardless of who she kept in her will and who she left out. Maybe you're the only one who got anything because she knew you'd never amount to anything in your life."

The words hit a space in me that has always been there, a fear I've been ignoring for years. Now fed, the fear grows into a dark and wild beast inside me, transforming into something that feels an awful lot like truth.

"Get out of my house," I whisper, my eyes boring a hole into hers. I look at Brayden one last time, carving the shape of his face into my memory, along with the way he once held me and how I felt in his arms. Then I burn it all to hell. "Both of you. I don't want to see either of you ever again."

"Nina, I—"

"Get out!" I scream.

She looks like she'll argue again, but then her shoulders fall. "Can I at least get my things?" she asks.

I want to tell her no. Tell her to use her earnings from my things to buy new stuff, since she's so good at it. Maybe I'll set her room on fire, set the whole house on fire, because this place doesn't feel like mine anymore. But something tugs inside me when I see the remorse on her face. I fucking hate her. I won't feel sorry for her. But I can at least let her get her shit before she leaves. So I nod, stepping aside as she runs toward her room.

"Are you okay?" Brayden asks quietly. I glare at him.

"No, I'm not okay," I growl, then regret it immediately. I don't want him to know how badly he's affected me, or how hurt I am that he's now standing by her instead of me. "I'll be fine. I just need both of you out of here before I really lose my shit."

"I'm so sorry," he murmurs. "I didn't know she was going to…"

He shakes his head. "I just didn't know, okay?"

"It doesn't matter," I say quickly.

"And about this weekend—"

"We both knew what this weekend was," I interrupt. I can't stand the way he's looking at me now, so I avert my eyes to the drab gray wall behind him. "It's done. There's no need to talk about it anymore."

He starts to say something, but the footsteps behind me shut him up.

"Come on, let's go," Jordy says. She doesn't acknowledge me as she slides past both of us and heads to the door.

"Take the weekend off," Brayden says once she's gone. "We can talk at the ranch after this week."

"I'm not coming back," I say quietly. I look at my feet. This one hurts, but I know there's no other choice. How the hell am I supposed to act like nothing happened? Every guy on the team knows what we did. But more than that, *we* know what we did. And if I'm around Brayden again, I'm going to forget why we're a bad idea.

"Please don't do this."

I look up at him, and I hate that I can't stop the tears that fill my eyes. I search his, looking for something to hold on to. Something that will tell me that this weekend wasn't a lie.

I find nothing but sadness and regret. It's not enough.

"I'm not coming back," I repeat. "I quit, and I'm not coming to your wedding, so don't bother sending me an invitation. Lose my number, your future wife needs your attention."

Chapter Twenty-Six

Brayden

"Can you believe her?" Jordy says. It's the third time she's said it in the twenty minutes it takes me to drive her car from Nina's house to the ranch. And frankly, I can. Jordy had no right to touch any of Nina's things, and it's insanity that she doesn't understand what an intrusion this is.

It's right up there with picking a wedding date and venue without any input from the person you're supposedly marrying.

"Now you know why I can't stand her. She's always been a selfish bitch, and I can't believe I was lulled into actually believing she's a decent human being."

"What part, exactly, is selfish about her reaction?" I've been refraining from saying anything during Jordy's tirade, but I've had enough. "Was it the part where you sold off all her belongings? Or the part where you took away the things that mattered to her most?"

"Whose side are you on?" Jordy asks. "That house belonged to both of our grandmother."

"But now it belongs to Nina. Don't you think you should have included her in any decisions regarding the house?"

"Brayden, you saw that place. It was a pit. She didn't change a thing. If Nanna Dot gave that house to me, the first thing I would have done was to hire an estate planner and get rid of all that old crap."

"But she didn't give it to you. She gave it to Nina."

"Yeah, but—"

"Not only that, but that house has been Nina's home for years before your grandmother died. Did you even consider the emotional ties she has to that place and the things in it?"

"That's beside the point."

"That's the whole point!"

We pull into the ranch, and I haven't even put the car into park before Jordy's door is open and she's leaping out. I stomp my foot on the brake and throw it into park before hauling myself out after her.

"Are you trying to get yourself killed?" I slam my door shut and stride over to where she is.

"That would probably solve all your problems, wouldn't it?"

"What the fuck is that supposed to mean?" I ask. I'm fuming hot from her words, just knowing she's aware of how they'll hit. "You mean like my problems were solved when my sister was killed?" I ask. She flinches, but I'm not done. "How about when our child died. All my problems were solved then too?"

"It got me to marry you, didn't it?" She glares at me.

"Like I said," I mutter.

She looks closely at me, and I regret my words immediately. I see a flash of hurt cross her eyes, then it's gone.

"Jesus, Brayden, you were going five miles an hour. I wasn't going to die."

"No, you're just being reckless because you don't like when I disagree with you. But Jordy, we're not always going to be on the same page."

"I know that," she huffs. "But this is my family, not yours."

I flex my hand, gritting my teeth against the statement, saying nothing. I made my choice—rather, the choice was made for me. Jordy has more of a claim over a relationship with Nina than I do, even though she still feels like mine.

"I'm not staying here tonight," Jordy says, snatching her keys from my hands. "I need time to think, and I can't do it here."

"Don't be stupid," I say. "The cabins are open for another night, and you're more than welcome to stay. I'll even leave you alone."

"It would be stupid to stay when no one even wants me here."

This is so typical Jordy. Going to extremes so I can beg her to stay. I always know what she's doing, and yet I fall into this trap every time. But not this time.

"Fine." I open the trunk and grab my suitcase. "Drive safe."

She makes a noise of surprise, but I am already walking toward the house. I hear her slam the door and then the gravel flying under the tires as she peels down the dirt road.

I take the steps two at a time, then burst through the door, flinging my suitcase against the wall. It leaves a scuff mark in its wake, one I know I'll be buffing out once I've cooled down.

"Brayden, what's gotten into you?"

My mother stands in the doorway, her hand on her hip as her eyes sweep over the damage.

"Sorry," I mutter. She shakes her head, then motions for me to follow her into the kitchen. All I want to do is go to my room and close the door—maybe punch a few things.

No, all I want to do is call Nina and see if she's okay. To tell her I'm sorry. To try to undo all the damage I've done to her heart.

I trail behind my mom instead.

"Sit," my mom orders, pointing at the bench seat like I'm five instead of thirty. I do as I'm told, and she places a bowl of tomato soup and a grilled cheese sandwich in front of me.

"Thank you," I say. Food was the furthest thing from my mind, but now that I smell the buttery richness of the sandwich, my stomach growls eagerly. I dip a triangle in the creamy soup and take a bite. My eyes immediately close, and comfort envelopes me like a hug.

"Doug Murphy called this morning," my mom says, and I almost choke on the soup. Doug Murphy is the head of the convention, and while I can't be sure, he may have noticed my absence throughout the weekend.

"Oh yeah? Did he tell you how good the convention went?"

"I'm sure he did," she answers. "He talked to your dad, so I'm not really sure what he said. I'm sure you're aware of how proud he is of that convention, just like your father was when he was chair."

I nod, but my ears feel hot, especially with the hawkish way she's watching me.

"He figured you'd be taking on the chair role in the next year or so, you know, for the sake of tradition."

"I hadn't really thought of it," I lie. I'd always figured I would too—if I were staying in Sunset Bay.

"Which is why he was so disappointed you had to leave early with Nina."

I keep my eyes on my soup, no longer tasting it as I spoon it into my mouth.

"Where were you?"

"A buddy of mine needed ranch help," I say, not meeting her eyes. "I'd hoped to be back before the end, but it wasn't in the cards."

"Brayden. Look at me."

What is it with moms? How do they master that tone that strikes fear in the bravest heart? When I'm seventy years old and she's in her nineties, she'll still get me to fess up just by using that tone.

I look at her.

"Tell me what happened."

The truth is in my throat. If I so much as cough, I'll spill everything. I shake my head at her. Her mouth sets in a firm line, and I see the disappointment on her face. It makes me want to crumble into ash and blow away.

"Your father wants to speak with you," she finally says. "I suggest you get your story straight before you see him." With that, she exits the room, leaving me alone at the table with my soup and enough shame to bury myself in.

Like I'm fucking five years old.

I toss the rest of the soup in the sink and feed my sandwich to Cherokee, who's been waiting for this moment all his life. Then I head for the study, knowing it's better to face the music now than to wait any longer.

My dad is sitting at his desk, making notes in the ledger. He's so old school it hurts. I have a program on the computer that can handle all our bookkeeping, and he still insists on writing it down by hand.

"Have a seat," he says, not even turning around. I take my place in the cool leather chair behind him and wait. My dad continues with the books, as if I'm not even there. The air in the room is thick with judgment.

What's the worst he's going to do, even if he knows the truth? Take the farm away? Fine. My fiancé will be thrilled with that one. Lecture me? I've survived quite a few of those. Believe that I'm worthless? Been there, felt that.

"Did I ever tell you about the time I got cold feet before I married your mom?"

Shit. He's going the moral of this story route.

"No," I say, fighting the urge to crawl out of my skin.

"Her name was Betty Sherman."

"Dad, please don't."

"No, you need to hear this. Betty was my high school flame before I met your mom. Everyone thought we'd end up together. But the summer before our senior year, she broke up with me for a college guy. That girl shattered me, and I was certain I'd never meet someone like her. I was right, because when I met your mom, she was very different from Betty and much better suited for me. I was so sure about your mom that I asked her to marry me before I graduated high school, and we planned our wedding for the following spring. But somewhere between fall and winter, I got scared. It was all too much, too fast, and I started second guessing the whole relationship. It didn't help that Betty and that guy broke up, and she started calling me on the side."

"Dad, I don't want to—"

"I'm not done. I finally agreed to meet Betty one night, and one thing led to another. I realized it was a mistake while it was happening, but I couldn't stop what was already in motion. I figured it would be a secret that would go with me to the grave, but people talk. Betty talked. The week wasn't even over before your mom was throwing her ring at me and calling the wedding off."

"You cheated on mom?" I ask. I did not want to know this. My dad nods.

"It was the worst mistake of my life, and your mom didn't deserve it. She didn't deserve me."

"So how did you convince her to take you back."

"A lot of groveling," he says. "I not only had to make it up to her, but also to her parents. You remember your grandfather, right?"

It's been years since Grandpa Cordy has been alive, but even at his frailest, his voice was strong and abrupt.

"Let's just say, I'm glad your grandfather is not the gun toting type, because he'd have shoved that barrel up my ass." He chuckles now, but I can also sense the deep remorse he has. "The point is, you're ruining a good thing all because you think you're not ready for this next step."

I take deep breath. He doesn't know me at all. Has he forgotten the role he played in this whole sham of an engagement? The promise I made him from his hospital bed, and then later when she lost the baby?

"I'm not scared to get married." I watch the floor, unable to meet his eyes. "I'm scared of marrying the wrong girl."

"What are you talking about? The two of you have been planning this wedding for five years now."

"No, Dad." This time, I do look at him. "We've been engaged for five years. There's been no planning." I scoff. "Well, until this weekend when Jordy decided to speed things along."

"I know," he says.

"You what?"

"She had us put the date on the calendar."

"And no one even thought to tell me about it?"

"She asked us to keep it secret. She wanted to surprise you."

"This is just rich." I get up from the chair and pace the floor before I plant my feet and face my dad. "My whole life has been planned for me, and I don't even get a say in it."

"This is the date of your wedding, not your whole life."

"It's absolutely been my whole life!" I repeat. "From taking on the ranch to asking Jordy to marry me, none of it was my decision."

"If you don't want this ranch, I can find someone else that would be more than happy to take your place."

"I want the ranch, Dad, but I never got the choice. With Jordy,

I fulfilled whatever obligation you said I had to fill. Why, because I got her pregnant?"

Then the math hits me. The reason my dad was so insistent that we get married.

My parents weren't married in spring like he said they'd planned, but in winter—and I was born eight months later.

It suddenly makes all the sense in the world.

"Was Mom pregnant with me when you two got married?"

My dad looks out the window, and my mouth drops.

"You only married her because she was pregnant. Otherwise, you'd probably still be with Betty."

"I would not be with Betty. I loved your mother. But you're right, the wedding would have been called off if your mom wasn't already pregnant, all because I made a mistake."

"Fuck me." I run my hands through my hair. My whole life feels like a lie. I realize just how orchestrated my life has been, and how obviously spineless I've been to not make my own decision. How my mom probably didn't even love my dad when they got married, not after what he did to her. She's had to live with this decision her whole life, and if that's not bad enough, now he expects me to do the same.

I pick up his damn ledger and throw it across the room. Papers scatter through the air like leaves in the wind, twirling in their descent while I breathe fire.

"Control yourself, Son."

"Why, so you can tell me how you stepped up and were a man by forcing mom to marry you, so I should too? News flash, Dad, I'm not you. I should have never agreed to marry someone I wasn't in love with."

I slam through the door before he can say anything else, almost running into my mom on the other side. For a moment, I stand frozen, realizing she's heard every word we said. I feel terrible that this is the way she finds out her marriage is based on obligation rather than love. But I can't burden myself with this, so I push past her, but not before she grasps my arm in an effort to make me stop. It would take nothing to brush her off and keep going, but this is my mom, and I'm not going to do that to her.

"Let me go," I say.

"No. Come back in the office and have a talk with us."

I look at her, and I see the conviction in her eyes, the sheer strength of her—and I fold.

She leads the way, and I take my place on the leather couch while she perches herself on my dad's desk, ignoring the papers all over the ground. Her hand rests on his shoulder, and I want to pull her away from him, to protect her from his lies.

"I love your father very much," she says, "and he loves me."

"But—"

"He loves me," she repeats, firmer this time. "Yes, it's true that when we got married, it was not the ideal situation." She shakes her head. "Rather, it grew into the ideal situation. But on that day, it wasn't what we thought it would be. I was still upset that he'd gone back to Betty. He was still battling unresolved feelings from that relationship and if we were doing the right thing. We weren't sure we loved each other enough to get married. But there were greater forces at work, and we knew for the sake of you, we had to at least try."

"You don't owe me anything," I mutter.

"No, we don't. If our marriage was based solely on you, it never would have worked. But we grew to love each other. Your dad is my best friend, the person I can go to about anything. I trust him with my life."

"And I trust her with mine," my father says. "Together, we've made this beautiful life, and it's all because we chose to make it work."

"But I'm not you," I point out. "I never should have listened to you. Did you know that Jordy and I barely knew each other when we got engaged? We weren't even boyfriend and girlfriend. We'd only been messing around when you got in the accident and I had to move home. We'd agreed to end things before I found out she was pregnant."

"And your father talked you into marrying her," my mom confirms, looking down on my dad with new understanding. "Oh Pete, really?"

"It's the right thing to do," my father grunts. "Especially now."

"Why, because she can no longer have kids?" My mom shakes her head. "Pete, the only reason two people should get married is because they're in love."

"But look at us." My dad tilts his head up at her. "We never would have discovered how good we are together if we hadn't gotten married."

"Not everyone is us," my mom points out. She waves her hand in my direction. "You should have never told Brayden to marry Jordy."

My mind is reeling from all of this. Five years of pretending, hoping my heart would catch up only to realize it likely never will. I look at my parents and realize I will never have this with Jordy. Even now, knowing what they went through in the beginning, I can see how deeply they care for each other. I think of the home I was raised in, the love that surrounded me and my sisters as we grew up, and how tight we all became after Amber was gone.

I think of the separate lives Jordy and I lead now, and how I just can't imagine either of us molding into the other's dreams. We don't fit, and one of us will lose if we keep trying.

Then there's Nina. I don't know where things will lead for us, I don't even know if she'll speak to me again. All I know is that in all the time I've known her, it's been the closest to forever I've ever felt. This weekend sealed those feelings, but it's my time with her that has helped me know what it's like to fall in love with your best friend.

"I can't stay with Jordy," I whisper.

"Is it because you're in love with Nina?"

I dart my eyes to my mother's, and she rolls her eyes. "Come on, anyone can see the way you two are with each other. I just wish you hadn't acted on that while you were still involved with someone else."

"Did someone tell you?"

She and my father exchange a glance.

"We're not dumb, Son," my father says. "As soon as Doug Murphy said the two of you had left for the weekend, we knew exactly what you were up to."

"I've never loved Jordy. At least, not the way she deserves. But meeting Nina made me realize I can't keep up this charade." I hang my head. "I've really made a mess of things," I say. "I should have let Jordy go ages ago. She never deserved any of this."

"No, she didn't," my mom agrees.

I get up then and look at my parents. "For what it's worth, I'm glad you two stuck it out."

My mom looks at my dad and smiles, "We are, too."

Chapter Twenty-Seven

Brayden

I sit in my truck in the Sandpiper Inn parking lot, next to Jordy's car. I knew she'd come here First, it's where she always stays when she doesn't stay at the ranch. Second, I can see her on my location services. Which means she could have seen me when I was with Nina, and I should be grateful she didn't.

I still don't know what I'm going to say to her.

Brayden: Can I come up?

I wait a few moments, then see the three dots light up before her text comes through.

Jordy: Rm 324

I smile in spite of myself. I might have been playing a game of pretend for the past five years, but it doesn't mean we don't know each other. She's probably been waiting for me to show up, which is both cute and annoying, since it's also part of her game. She runs, I chase after her, she puts me through hell, then finally forgives me—even if it was all her fault.

This one was on her. But what I'm about to do to her is completely on me.

I take the stairs to the third floor, racking my brain for a way to break things easily to her. *Easy.* That's a misnomer. Nothing about this is going to be easy, and now that I'm nearing her door, I can feel the knots forming in my stomach and a sense of nervousness I haven't felt in a very long time.

I reach her room and knock three times. I can hear her footsteps on the other side before she answers. There's an annoyed look on her face, but her makeup is freshly done and she's wearing a tiny black dress that just barely covers her assets.

"Going somewhere?" I ask as she moves aside, letting me in.

"I could only grab what was within reach." She shrugs and gestures to the duffel bag on the bed. It's true, there's a mishmash of stuff falling out of it. But Jordy isn't accidental when it comes to fashion. This outfit is for me and me alone.

But as I look around, I realize I'm being too quick to judge. The truth is, there isn't much here for daily comforts. Most of her stuff is at Nina's house, and for Jordy, this is a bit like hell. She won't even go camping with me because roughing it is not her cup of tea. It hits me how out of place she is. Sure, it was her choice to refuse to stay at the ranch, but she'd been unprepared to get kicked out of Nina's place. I know Jordy's intentions were pure—even if skewed—and suddenly I wonder if my timing is completely callous and insensitive.

"Do you need anything?" I ask. "More clothes? Toiletries? Some dinner?"

She rolls her eyes. "I still have my key. I'll get my shit tomorrow somehow. She can't keep all of it, right?"

I don't know and choose to play dumb. Nina was pretty pissed when we left, and I wouldn't be surprised if she throws a giant bonfire in our wake, burning everything Jordy owns.

"Look, I'm sorry," Jordy begins, catching me off guard. Jordy never apologizes. "I know I should have included you in the wedding plans. It's just that neither of us were doing anything, and it felt like if we waited any longer, it wouldn't happen."

I look at my hands, all the words I want to say to her just sitting there, waiting for me to let them loose.

"I guess I missed you while you were gone," she continues. "I thought I could do some mental planning, you know? See a few places and take notes, and then go back with you once I'd found some that both of us would like. But then the country club looked so beautiful, and I kept remembering the times when Nanna brought both me and Nina there as little girls. You know that we used to have matching Easter bonnets and gloves we wore all year long?" She laughs, and I see the faraway look in her eyes. "We were close once," she murmurs, "almost like sisters." She shakes her head, and the look disappears. "I asked the manager a few questions and found out he only had one Saturday left on the books, and the next open date isn't for another year. I guess I got swept away in the moment, because all of a sudden, I was signing paperwork and forking over my savings. Then it was done."

She looks at me, her eyes big and wide, brimmed with tears. "I know I should have waited, and in hindsight, I wish I had. I didn't even give you a chance to choose a place with me. You should have been able to."

"It definitely surprised me," I say carefully, "and it's too soon."

"It's been five years, Bray." She wipes at her eyes, then takes my hand in hers. The diamond on her finger flashes in the low lights of the room. "It was starting to feel like you didn't want to get married at all."

"I didn't," I say. I remove my hand from hers. "I don't."

A flash of surprise crosses her face. Her brow wrinkles, and I can see she's fighting tears. But she composes herself.

"You're just getting cold feet," she says, offering a small laugh. It reminds me of my conversation with my dad—how he dealt with his cold feet—and what I did this weekend that had nothing to do with cold feet, but it was unfair all the same.

"I'm not. The truth is, I don't think we're supposed to be together. You want to see the world, to live in a big city and make a name for yourself. But my life is here on the ranch. All this time, you've made plans that include me leaving the family business. But Jordy, you never once asked me what my plans were, or how you could fit into them."

"We can make it work." Her eyes plead with mine. "I can stay here in Sunset Bay. I know I can find work, even travel to San Diego or Santa Barbara and work at some higher end offices."

"Jordy, listen to yourself. You don't want this. You'd be miserable here."

"You don't know anything about me," she spits out. "Besides, the deposit is already paid. My mother is working on the invitations. I have a registry started and everything. People are going to talk if we cancel."

"I can give you the money for the deposit, it's just money. As for people, who cares what they say? This is our lives we're talking about."

"Exactly! This is our life!"

"You've worked your ass off for yours," I point out. "Your dream was to always go to New York. Are you really willing to give that up? For me?"

Her lip trembles. "Maybe we could split our time," she eventually says. "I can get a place in New York while you stay here on the ranch. We can see each other on weekends. We've already been doing it for years, so why not just do it for a few more?"

"Is that really a marriage?" I ask. Her tears are falling freely now, and I feel like the biggest ass. "Jordy, we've been living apart for years and surviving because we are completely okay apart. Even since you've moved here, we barely make time for each other. I don't want a marriage where we're fine with being apart. I want to be with someone I can't wait to wake up next to, who is excited about the things I'm excited about, who wants to be on the same journey as me. And I think you deserve the same thing."

"We can have that," she whispers.

"We'd already have it if it were possible."

"But Bray—"

"Jordy, I slept with someone else."

The words tumble out of my mouth before I can think too hard about what I'm saying. Her expression freezes, and I watch as she absorbs the words. I feel terrible, I really do. But I also feel some relief because I know this is the only way she's going to let our relationship end.

"When?" There's devastation on her face, but then it turns to anger. "With who?"

"No one," I say. She throws one of her shoes at me, and I duck in time to miss it. "Jordy, it was no one important." Because I'm sure as hell not telling her about Nina.

"What, are you going to leave me for her now? Is that why you're calling this off?"

"No," I say, because what the hell do I say? I realize there's no coming back from this at all.

"You fucking asshole, how could you? Do you have any idea how much time I've wasted on you? I could have had anyone, but I stayed with you! I never strayed. What the fuck were you thinking?"

She sinks on to the bed, twisting her ring on her finger. "Oh God, what is my mother going to say? Our whole family thinks we're getting married. What do I say?"

"I'm so sorry." I really am. She doesn't deserve any of this. I'm the biggest asshole there is.

"I'm serious," she says, wiping at her face. "What the fuck do I say?"

"You say I was a cheating bastard." Because I am. "It's my fault, and I'm so sorry."

"She told me this would happen." Jordy gets up and starts pacing the floor. "She said no man would ever stay with me."

"First of all, your mom is a bitch."

"Don't talk about my mother that way!" Her eyes flash, and her other shoe is in her hand.

"Don't throw that at me," I warn her. "But she is. There is nothing you can do to make that woman happy, and you know it. We could have the most perfect wedding, and she will still find flaws in it."

But I can tell Jordy has checked out completely.

"We can move past this," she says, turning to me. "Couples do this all the time. Someone cheats, and it sucks. But then you come back stronger than ever."

"This isn't one of your romance novels, Jordy."

"No, but we cannot break things off right now. Not yet, not until we've given this a chance." Her eyes light up. "We could get married this weekend. Just run away and do it, and I'll move to the ranch. I'll quit school and everything."

"Do you even hear yourself? This isn't you."

"And this isn't you!" she screams. "The Brayden I know and love doesn't sleep with other women. He's kind and generous and thoughtful and…" She breaks into a sob, falling to the floor. I kneel beside her, but don't touch her. I lost that right long before I told her what I did.

"Please don't do this," she begs. "Can we just wait before calling it off? Just take a breather? We don't have to talk about the wedding anymore. I'll cancel it, and just forget about the deposit. But please don't break up with me. Not now. Can we at least get past Ethan and Claire's wedding before we do anything drastic?"

I close my eyes. I feel like the biggest dick, because now that the truth is out, all I can think about is going straight to Nina's and letting her know that Jordy and I are over. But what the fuck will that solve? Nina doesn't even want to see me, and judging by the way she threw both of us out of her house, I don't think this is going to fix anything. But more importantly, I cannot go from Jordy straight into her cousin's arms.

This is a fucking mess.

"Bray?"

I look at her, then nod. "We can wait," I say. "But don't think this is going to change my mind. Taking this time should give you some clarity. You deserve better, Jordy."

"Oh, I know I do," she says, her voice steadier as she wipes her face with the heel of her hand. "But the thing is, I love you. And I think you love me too." She scootches over to me, her hand traveling my thigh until it lands on my cock. The traitor springs to attention under her touch, and she gives a light laugh.

"Jordy, come on." I brush her hand away. But she scoots a little closer. "I'm serious."

"So am I." She starts to kiss my neck, and I have to restrain myself to not push her off me.

"Jordy."

"Please make love to me, Bray."

"You can't mean that," I say, moving away from her and standing up. "I just told you I cheated on you. You should be throwing me out of here."

She stays on the floor. Something about her just looks so defeated, and it kills me that I'm the one who did this to her. Even more, that I can't fix it for her.

But I'm done fixing things for her. That's all I've been doing this whole entire time, and look where it got me.

"I need to feel wanted," she whispers, "even if it's a lie." She looks at me, her wet eyes piercing my soul. "Please."

The old Brayden would have caved. Would have done everything he could to make her stop crying, to take away the hurt. He would have fucked her just to save her from this pain.

But I can't, because my heart is no longer hers. Arguably, it hasn't been hers this whole relationship. But now, there's no other woman for me but Nina. Even if Nina never speaks to me again—and God, she has every reason to forget me—I can't. Nina is the last woman who warmed my bed, who touched me, who owns me completely. I won't have another. Not Jordy, and not any other woman.

It's Nina, or no one.

"No," I say firmly.

Jordy looks shocked for a moment. Then angry. She scrambles from the floor and starts throwing more shit at me. Her clothes, the pillows, her duffel bag. I block each of them, trying to get close to her to make her stop. Then she grabs her remaining shoe and yanks her hand back to throw it, but I catch her, locking her in my arms so she can't move.

"Fuck you!" she screams, pounding at my chest. "Fuck you to hell. I fucking hate you. I fucking—" She pitches into a sob, her fists falling against my chest as she crumples. I hold her shaking body up, my heart breaking, knowing I'm the one who did this to her.

"I'm sorry," I whisper, smoothing her hair. I cautiously move my hand to her face, daring to wipe her tears, and she lets me. "I'm so sorry."

"Please don't leave," she whispers.

"Jordy, I—"

"Not to sleep with me." She pushes off me, wipes her face. "I know that's dumb. I don't even want your stupid, soiled cock. But I don't want to be alone. Please stay with me, just tonight, just so I can sleep."

I look at her, seeing the pain all over her face, like her heart has completely shattered.

She wore the same look on her face in the hospital when they told her our baby had died. I knew she hadn't been excited about getting pregnant, neither of us were in the beginning. But as the months passed, we both had dreams about the future. Especially when she started to show, and when we felt our daughter's little kicks.

Then she was taken from us, and Jordy's face looked as it does now, like the world would end. On that day, with my ring on her finger, I swore I'd never let her hurt like that again.

Yet, here I am ending her whole entire world in a cold, empty hotel room.

"I'll stay," I agree.

I help her clean the room and put the bed together. She undresses in the bathroom, then comes out in a pair of thick sweats. I stay in my clothes and take the space beside her. She curls into me for a moment, her head on my chest, her hand resting on my abdomen. I don't move to envelop her. I just lay there, waiting for her to fall asleep. Eventually she rolls away from me, facing the wall in a fetal position. I remain still, aware of her quiet sniffling and shuddering breaths as she cries into the night. But then her breathing slows, the shuddering making way for deep exhales into the quiet of night.

I slide from the bed and out the door, silently saying my final goodbye.

Chapter Twenty-Eight

Nina

I sit alone at the tiny bistro table in my kitchen. The sunlight streams through the windows, no curtains to keep the light from blinding me. My coffee sits untouched in front of me, likely cold. Like my heart. The house is silent, save for the clicking clock on the kitchen wall, keeping time with the passing of the day.

I haven't changed my clothes in a week, haven't visited a store in two, and I should probably invest in DoorDash stock with the amount of to-go bags piling up in the corner. I haven't talked to anyone in three weeks, since I kicked both Brayden and Jordy out of the house. Not even when she swung by the next day to retrieve her things. I remained in my room the whole time, not even caring if she took anything of mine. There was nothing left to take, anyways. I don't give a fuck about any of it.

I've avoided the outside world as much as possible, except to check the mail every few days. Bills. Junk mail. And my final check from the ranch.

I haven't opened that last one. I can tell it's Angie's handwriting on the front, and it brings another wave of shame over me. What if she knows too? What is she thinking?

Are they all laughing at me, about what a fool I've been?

I abandon my coffee on the table, my eyes sweeping over the crusty coffee cups that have accumulated on the counters alongside forks and plates, dirty napkins, and more containers. In the corner, my trash can is overflowing. I haven't even taken the trash cans to the curb, and I'm sure my neighbors will complain to the city any day now.

I don't care. Nothing matters. I just exist to wake up, force myself to eat, then go back to sleep. Repeat.

If anyone is checking on me, I wouldn't know. I've put my phone on do-not-disturb to avoid talking to anyone. Besides, who would call? Not my mother, unless she needs something. Maybe Brayden, but his number is still blocked. Definitely not Jordy, who would probably prefer to nail my heart to a stake than talk to me ever again.

So it's just me, existing in a house that doesn't feel like mine anymore.

Which is why, when my doorbell rings, I instinctively freeze. I turn slightly toward the door, as if whoever is on the other side can see me. But through the etched stain glass, no one can. So I sit on the couch, waiting for my unwanted guest to leave. They knock and I hear my name.

It's Maren, and the sound of her voice makes me crave the presence of a human being. I place my hands on the arm of the couch, ready to stand. But then I look down at what I'm wearing, becoming aware of my unbrushed teeth and rat's nest hair. I realize how awful I look and how I can't let anyone, not even Mare, see me in this condition.

With horror, I hear a key applied to the lock, and the door opening. I dive onto the couch and hold my breath.

"Nina? Are you—what the fuck is that smell?"

I grimace but stay hidden on this horribly uncomfortable couch. Seriously, how could any store sell this as something to sit on?

"Wow, things have changed since I lived here." I hear Maren's boots clod down the hall and approach the couch. "Come on, get up."

"No." The sound of my voice is almost shocking to me. Slightly raspy. I guess that's what happens when you haven't said a word in three weeks.

"Get up and help me clean this place now, or I'll take photos of you and post them all over Instagram."

"Bitch," I mutter, sitting up. My hand flies to my hair, noting the greasy mess under the fading lavender tangles. Maren looks me up and down.

"Okay, plan B. Claire and I will start cleaning while you go take a shower."

"You brought your annoying friend here?"

"Present!" Claire sings out, and I groan, sinking back against the couch. "And I brought sustenance!"

I glance in her direction, and my stomach rumbles when I see the label on the bag—Sunset Sourdough, home of the best deli sandwiches in the world.

"We got you the Brooklyn Bridge," Maren says with a smile, and I nearly pass out with need. The Brooklyn Bridge is basically every Italian meat there is, with buffalo mozzarella, roasted red pepper, pepperoncinis, and Italian dressing on a crunchy sourdough roll. It is literally the best sandwich in the world, and this might be the first time I've felt any sense of craving in three weeks.

"But you can't eat until you've showered," Maren says as I eye the bag.

"Yes, Mom," I mutter, then drag myself to my room while Claire and Maren get to work cleaning.

The shower feels incredible—more incredible than it has any right to feel. It's like every part of my body has been craving the feel of soap and water, from the dry skin on my face to the wiggles in my toes. Even though my belly is crying out for that sandwich, I take my time in the shower, washing my sorrow down the drain. Afterwards, I brush my teeth—and wow—who knew brushing your teeth could feel like self-care?

When I look in the mirror, I see a slightly fresher me staring back. My roots are starting to show, and the purple color of my hair is practically grey. My cheeks are flushed, but my skin is pale. My cheeks appear gaunt, and when I weigh myself, I see I've accidentally lost ten pounds. That's on top of the other ten I've lost since I started working at the ranch. But I've never lost weight accidentally, and now my sweats are hanging off my hips.

When I pad down the stairs, I'm greeted by the smell of lemon cleaner and candles. Then I see the house and realize just how long I've been in there. Maren and Claire have made quick work of cleaning. Everything is sparkling from the weird modern furniture in the living room to the counters in the kitchen. Even the garbage is gone, and when I peek out the kitchen windows, I see the cans are at the curb.

"You guys," I say, and there's a catch in my throat. Maren comes over and gives me a side hug. She's not a hugging person, so I immediately realize something is up.

"Ethan said we should check on you," Claire explained. Which reminds me of the invitation on the fridge. A wedding between my cousin and Claire that's happening in two weeks, where I not only have to leave the house, but likely face Brayden since Jordy is invited with a plus one.

"Are you two ready for the wedding?" I ask, because that's the polite thing to ask. She waves her hand in dismissal.

"Never mind about us, how are you? What's going on?"

"I'm fine, obviously," I say, then grimace because I'm obviously not okay. "How would Ethan even have known?" I ask. But as soon as the words leave my mouth, I know. "My mother."

Claire nods her head in confirmation.

"She's been trying to reach you for weeks. When she couldn't get a hold of you, she tried Jordy, who basically said you could rot in hell."

"Sounds about right."

"So your mom called Ethan, and here we are."

"When you didn't take my calls either, I figured something big was going on." Maren looks at me carefully. "Is something big going on?"

I look at the ground, then nod. "I mean, it's not what Jordy thinks," I say. "I kicked her out because she decided to make my house her personal design project while I was gone." I gesture to the living room. "She took out all of Nanna Dot's things and brought in a bunch of modern furniture and art. She even painted the walls, and she took down all the curtains."

"It looks nice," Claire says, and Maren and I both glare at her. At least Maren remembers whose side to be on.

"It doesn't look like my house," I say. "She didn't even ask. I mean, how would you feel if someone decided to redesign your whole living space without even talking with you."

"You have a point," Claire says.

"It's the only point." Damn, she can be so clueless.

"Not the only point. What is the big thing Jordy doesn't know."

"I slept with Brayden." I pull the Band Aid off quick, then brace myself for the reaction?

"What?" Claire says at the same time Maren laughs, "You slut!"

Claire gives Maren a look that clearly shows they're on separate sides about this too. And honestly—surprisingly—I'm siding with Claire.

"It shouldn't have gotten this far," I admit, sinking onto the couch.

"Hold up. I'm starving, and by the amount of to-go bags we just threw away, I know you need some quality food. Let's sit in the kitchen and talk about this over sandwiches."

I think of the impracticality of the tiny bistro table in the kitchen.

"Better idea. Let's huddle around this ugly ass living room table and talk here."

"Just don't make a mess," Maren warns, setting the sandwiches and some napkins on the table. I knock the napkins to the floor, just because I can.

Over sandwiches, I tell them everything. About the horseback rides, the weeks of flirting, and then the convention with only one bed that led to a weekend away on the coast.

"One bed, huh? That's how it always starts," Claire says with a smirk. Fair. She's read enough romance novels to know.

"But this isn't a romance novel," I say. "It's my life, and his, and my cousin's. Now I've done something unforgivable to her, but still kicked her out of my house just for redecorating."

"She shouldn't have touched your things," Maren says.

"And I shouldn't have touched hers."

She tilts her head, agreeing ... but not.

"When I saw everything Jordy had done, I lost it. But honestly, the place isn't that bad. I mean, I would have liked to have had a say in this, and maybe picked some more comfortable furniture. But it was time to let go of the past. It's just that when I saw the house, it's like all my guilt, plus how badly it hurt to see Brayden just re-enter his old life like none of it mattered... I had to put my anger in something. So I kicked her out and told both of them they couldn't come back. I quit the ranch too."

Maren places her hand on mine. "Oh sweetie," she says, and her sympathy spills tears onto my cheek. Damn it, I was trying so hard not to cry.

"So, what will you do now?" Claire asks.

"I'm doing it," I say, wiping my tears and then sweeping my hand over the place. "I'm existing until I wither away and die."

"You could work for me," Maren says. "Between recording and lessons, I hardly have time for the administrative stuff. You could help me keep track of my calendar and bookkeeping."

"Obviously my organizational skills have impressed you," I laugh, wiping away my tears. But really, I can't bear the thought of my friends playing charity. Besides, I don't need the money, I just need something to do besides look at these four walls.

"Point taken," Maren says. "Well, have you considered Insomniacs? I heard the owner canned Susan after she ran that place into the ground, and hired a new manager who's now running a respectable coffee shop, free of garage bands."

"Tempting. But I don't know. I think that chapter has passed, especially since you don't work there anymore."

"I haven't been back since I quit," Maren confessed.

"Same," I say. "That place could catch fire and I'd fan the flames."

"Face it," Claire says. "They lost their soul when they gave you your last paychecks." Then she looks at me. "Have you thought about investing in a business?"

I tilt my head for a moment. I usually dismiss Claire as some ditzy blonde, but time and time again she proves me wrong. I'd never tell her as much, but the girl has brains, and right now, her idea is interesting.

"I know you inherited a lot of money a while back," she continues, then wrinkles her nose in apology. "Ethan told me. But it's also kind of obvious, with this big house on a coffee shop paycheck."

"Yeah, so? I don't use that money if I can help it."

"But what if you could make that money work for you? Like, invest in a business or some other financial opportunity that lines up with your interests. What are some things you like to do or that you're good at?"

"Fashion," Maren says without hesitation.

"Wait, what?" I look down at my clothes now—purple sweats with a lime green crewneck sweatshirt, and some hot pink socks decorated with scenes of goat yoga. "Excuse me while I laugh, because this is the first outfit I changed into in a week, and this is what I chose."

"A bold, colorful statement," Maren says. "Point is, you have a unique style that makes people happy. What if you were to start a clothing boutique that specialized in colorful clothes that inspire joy?"

"You mean, I'd be the Marie Kondo of the fashion industry, sparking joy everywhere."

"Well, kind of," Maren says.

"It's brilliant!" Claire exclaims. "We can work on consignment for now, pulling pieces from small designers who are looking to make a name for themselves. I see them all the time on Etsy, and I'm sure they'd be thrilled to have a storefront." She turns to Maren. "Can you talk to Mac, see if he knows any businesses for sale?"

"Wait, hold up. I haven't even said yes."

Both Maren and Claire turn to me. "Well?" Maren asks.

I breathe out a sigh, my heart racing as I consider the possibilities. Honestly, with Claire's business sense, Maren's boldness, and my crazy fashion style, this could actually become something.

But do I dare? I've only ever known what it's like to work for someone. I've never been the kind of person who tries new things or even leaves the comfort zone. Risk is foreign to me.

I look around the house, at the rooms that no longer feel like Nanna Dot—that still have a sense of home, but maybe not mine. Then I look at my friends. I have an opportunity most people don't have, and maybe I'm ready for a change.

"Let's make this happen."

Chapter Twenty-Nine

Nina

I sit in my car at Insomniacs, the last place I want to be for the last reason I want to be here. I'm a few minutes late, but not in any hurry.

I look at my phone, which I'd finally charged a few days ago after Maren and Claire left the house. When it powered up, I had a voicemail from my mom, a few spam texts, and a curt message from Jordy.

Jordy: Meet me at Insomniacs on Wednesday at 1 p.m. I need to talk with you.

She knows. That's the only thing I can think of. While I want so badly to ignore it, just like I've ignored everyone else, I just can't. If she's coming for the truth, I need to put my big girl pants on and fess up.

I mean, it's not like I can ruin a relationship that's already burned to a crisp.

I take a few more moments, waiting just long enough to be late, but not so late she thinks I'm not coming. Then I trudge my way to the café.

The place hasn't changed much from when Maren and I worked here. The layout is still the same, with blonde tables and matching chairs spaced generously from each other, and high ceilings with exposed pipes. The minimalist industrial look gives it a trendy vibe. Folk indie music plays low throughout the shop, a mix of Novo Amor, Bon Iver, the Nationals, and other similar bands that are a lot like ones we used to play. I don't know anyone behind the counter, but that's cool. I do notice how the manager is ringing people up during this rush hour, something Susan never did for us. She'd rather watch while we drowned, or just pretend it wasn't happening.

I scan the shop until I finally find Jordy sitting at a table with Brayden beside her. I freeze where I am, the air in the shop feeling shallow as I run through scenarios of what's about to happen, and I come to only one conclusion...

She wants to save the effort by killing us both at the same time.

I consider turning around and booking it to my car, but she looks up at the same time I start to turn and raises a hand in greeting. Brayden looks up too, and the expression on his face is grim, like he doesn't want to be there either. But Jordy looks almost relieved I'm here, which is a bit confusing.

I approach the table, and she points to a morning bun and a cup of something at the space in front of an empty chair.

"The dirty chai might be lukewarm," she apologizes. "I ordered it fifteen minutes ago."

But you were late, I read in her unspoken words. I take the seat and sip the latte. It's just warm, but still good. "Thank you. I love dirty chais," I say.

"I remember," she says, followed by a nervous laugh. "You used to get them all the time when Nanna took us out."

"At Jaya Java," I say, the memory dislodging from a hidden corner of my mind. Nanna used to take us there every Sunday after church because she loved their samosas. But I loved their chai, which was so different from the sugary chai lattes you find at corporate coffee shops. At Jaya Java, they made their chai teas with spices like ginger, cardamon, and vanilla, cut with oat milk and lightly sweetened with honey. I always asked for a shot of espresso with mine, inspired by some of the girls at school who giggled about ordering dirty chais at Starbucks. At Jaya Java, they laughed too, but it soon made its way to the menu.

Drinking this one, I realize I inspired it as well. When I'd arrived at Insomniacs, their version of a dirty chai was that sugary crap in a container mixed with steam milk. The manager before Susan used to listen to our suggestions, though, and liked my idea of an authentic chai drink on the menu. As I sip it now, I taste the same ginger and cardamon, creamy oat milk, and a touch of honey, all enhanced with a bold shot of espresso. Even cold, it's delicious.

Meanwhile, Jordy is fumbling with her napkin. Beside her, Brayden keeps averting his eyes every time I look in his direction. I'm sitting here drinking a chai latte as if this is social hour, still not quite sure why I'm here, and still kind of nervous that this has to do with Brayden.

"So…" I say, now picking at my morning bun.

"Uh, yeah. I wanted to apologize." She glances at Brayden, as if he's going to help her out here, but he's busy looking everywhere but at her.

"About the house," I say, because *of course* it's about the house. I'm relieved it's about the house.

"Yeah, I overstepped," she says.

"You did," I agree. But now that I've spent weeks in this house, thinking about what I did to her, I am having the hardest time being mad at her. "It's fine, I'm over it." I dismiss it with a wave of my hand, while her eyes widen.

"No, I'm serious. I mean, it does look amazing though, you have to admit."

"Jordy."

The one word from Brayden, and Jordy's smile evaporates. She glares at him, but then seems to compose herself quickly.

"No, really, it's fine," I insist. "I mean, it's not even close to my style. But it did need a complete makeover, something that didn't look so…Nanna Dot."

Jordy snorts. "You did still have that crocheted doily blanket on the back of the couch, both straight out of the seventies. It's like she thought muted paisley and neon flowers went together."

I look at the table, trying not to fume. I have no right to fume. I fucked her fiancé, and she just got rid of a dusty old blanket, among a couple other things.

"I liked the blanket," I say, "and neon is kind of my thing." I wave my hand over my outfit of the day as an example. Today it's lime-green leggings and an oversized purple sweatshirt. My hair is now a beautiful shade of fuchsia.

"I love your style," Jordy says. "I should have kept that in mind when I decided to do something nice."

"No, you should have talked with Nina first," Brayden cuts in. Jordy looks at him again, and there seems to be some kind of unspoken message being passed between the two of them. Brayden's jaw pulses, and I can see he's irritated. More than he should be. The look increases when she takes his hand in hers. She flashes a smile at me, but his face lets me know he wants to be anywhere but here.

I am just trying not to look at his mouth, remembering all the ways he dragged those lips across my body, tasting every inch of me as if I were his personal snack. The corner of his mouth upticks, and I avert my eyes quickly, looking back at Jordy.

"I should have talked with you first," she agrees, completely ignorant of the eye fucking that just happened. Fuck, that was close.

I should just call it fine and move on, get out of here as soon as I can and leave these two to enjoy their stupid happy lives together. But something makes me stay. Part of it is that I actually miss Jordy, in spite of all the things about her that piss me off. I miss what we used to have, and I miss what we could have had if I hadn't kicked her out.

And I miss the fuck out of Brayden.

I don't dare look at him as I pretend to be engrossed in my pastry and latte. But I'm so aware of him. The way he smells. The sound of each breath he takes. The way his fingers touch the table, reminding me of how he touched me. How, after weeks of feeling completely rejected, my body still wants him.

I don't know how to reconcile the two. How can I crave the close relationship I once had with my cousin while also craving everything about her fiancé? Because I can't have both.

But I do get to choose. I look at both of them, really take them in. I focus on the relationship they have, and even though my heart hurts so horribly, I make the conscious effort to accept that he belongs to her.

Not to me. Never to me. What we did was wrong, and it can never happen again.

"We could make it right," I say, shifting my focus to her. She lights up, her face erupting in a grin.

"Fuck yes! When do we start? How about now?"

"We could, but I also have an idea I need your help with." I tell her about the clothing boutique idea, how Claire has already contacted interested designers, and Mac found some leads on prime locations.

"I know the styles of clothes I want, but I'm having a hard time envisioning what the shop will look like. I don't have your design sense when it comes to my home or shop. So, if you're up for it, I'd like to hire you to design the shop, and also to help me figure out a style for the house that's a lot more like me."

"Are you serious?" She looks at Brayden, then back at me. "You want to hire me?"

There are actual tears in her eyes, which feels like such an extreme reaction. "Jordy, it's nothing. I just trust you more than some stranger working on this new venture."

Trust. What an ironic sentiment.

"No, it's not that. It's just..." She pauses, then she takes Brayden's hand back in hers. "We've been having some serious conversations about where to live after the wedding. It's actually been a place of contention, because Brayden's home is here, but my dream has always been to move to New York so I can do more high-end jobs. But what if I stay local? Your shop could be a new direction for my business. I could expand beyond designing homes by also partnering with businesses by refreshing their layout." She squeezes Brayden's hand, which I notice because my eyes keep drifting there. "We won't need to make any hard choices because my business would be here while Brayden continues running the ranch."

I look at Brayden then, risking a quick glance. His eyes are on mine, but this time there's rage there. I look away, unsure what the deal is. Is he mad I'm hiring her? Does he hate that I'm even here? Maybe all this was a huge mistake.

Or maybe it's a great way to pay him back for playing with my heart, then crawling right back in Jordy's arms.

"That's great!" I say, even though I realize this means I'll never escape the two of them. Not if they stay in Sunset Bay, and definitely

284 — CRISSI LANGWELL

not if I hire Jordy as my personal interior designer. I glance back at Brayden, and this time I flash him a winning smile, like there's not one thing wrong in the world. Not one fucking thing.

"Let's start making plans tomorrow. Swing by the house around ten." I finish my chai and stand up, taking one last glance at Brayden. "It'll be fun, just us girls." I say, making it clear who is *not* invited.

Chapter Thirty

Brayden

"What the fuck was that?" I ask, once Jordy and I are in the truck. She rolls her eyes and gives me a withering stare.

"That was coffee with my cousin, and I have a job now. Stop being so dramatic. Can we just go home now?"

Every time she refers to the ranch as home, I cringe. For the past few weeks, she's been staying in one of the cabins—which was my mother's idea. Both of my parents are well aware that Jordy and I are no longer together. After I came back from Jordy's room at the Sandpiper Inn, I let them know we broke up, but that she didn't want to announce it yet. Of course, Jordy had a fit when she learned I'd told my parents. But I could give a fuck. I just can't wait for this nightmare to be over, and if that means dragging this out for a few more weeks, then fine.

But hearing Jordy tell Nina about her plans to stay here with me? It made me realize just how toxic this whole arrangement is.

"No, that was you pretending like we're the happy couple, as if we're going to live some married life on the ranch. Jordy, we're not getting married."

She glares at me. "We agreed to give it time," she says.

"No, we agreed not to announce our split until after Ethan and Claire's wedding," I remind her. "I already know what I want and don't want, and that is not going to change."

She stares at me for a moment. I can tell she's fighting back tears, even as her eyes narrow with irritation. I won't cave though. I can't.

"Right. Well, this is us not announcing our split," she finally says, forcing out the words like she doesn't believe them. I am starting to wonder if she does. "Nina doesn't know, and I'd prefer to keep it that way for now. If this got back to my mother in any way, my life would become a living hell."

"After the wedding, she'll know," I remind her. Jordy sighs but says nothing.

What Jordy doesn't know is that I already texted all of this to Nina. Or at least I tried to. I told her everything, including how Jordy knows I cheated on her. I wrote my heart out in that text, telling her how I felt about her, and how—if she just gave me some time—I'd make all of this up to her.

Seeing her today, it's obvious she never read the text, or any text after that. I even tried calling her in a moment of weakness, and it went straight to voicemail. Now I realize my number is still blocked.

Meanwhile, living with the enemy has been one giant game of dodgeball. She's been super sweet with me, actually asking about my day and taking an interest in what I have to say. But I'm not saying much. The truth is, her presence makes me furious. The fact that I'm even playing this stupid game makes me furious. I've spent years as her puppet, doing everything I could to make her happy just because I thought that was what I was supposed to do. Because of our loss. Because of the promise I made. Now that I'm starting to put my needs first, I'm fucking pissed, and she's the easiest to be pissed at.

But it's not her fault. Not entirely, at least. The bulk of the blame is on my shoulders. She didn't ask me to do any of that stuff. It's me who set the precedent. I just hate that it took this many years for me to wake up and see the light.

We never should have stayed together. Even if she was going to have my kid, we could have figured something out. We knew back then we weren't right for each other, and we've both wasted so many years by staying together.

Because of this, I may have ruined my one shot at true happiness. I love Nina. I fucking love her. Not being able to tell her that is tearing me up inside. The fact that Jordy roped me into one last game of pretend is just the icing on this shit cake.

Ethan and Claire's wedding cannot come soon enough. Once it's done, I will do everything in my power to win Nina back, regardless of the backlash both of us will face.

Except, I had really counted on Jordy moving away. Even if she hasn't mentioned this plan since our breakup, I figured it was still in the works. The fact that Nina inspired Jordy's shift in plans is just so ironic, and really complicates things.

I'm not a callous bastard. I'm mad as hell, but I know how much it's going to hurt Jordy once she realizes my heart is for her cousin. I'm not sure how to soften that, though the move was going to help. Now that she's planning to stick around…

I won't let it ruin my plans. I will be with Nina, and that's final.

As soon as I put the truck in park, Jordy is out of the cab, stomping back to the cabin she's staying in. I sigh, grabbing my jacket before opening the door. Cherokee is waiting for me, and I scruff the top of his head while he bounces all around me.

He's not the only one waiting. All five guys exit the barn upon my arrival, and by the look on their faces, I'm pretty sure I'm up for an ambush.

"We need to talk," Jake says, looking at the other guys in confirmation. Then he glances at Jordy's cabin, then back to me. "In private."

There's only one thing that means. I nod and follow them back to the barn where the horses are already saddled up. I place my jacket on a hook, then head to Sara, tied up outside her stall. Meredith is still inside hers, and I can see she's offended she won't be part of this ride. It's hard not to think of Nina when I see her, recalling the times we rode out on the beach together. I close my eyes as Meredith presses her nose into my hand, as if she's also waiting for Nina.

"Soon," I whisper to her. "I hope."

We ride out of the barn like bats out of hell, and for a moment it's easy to forget the dark mood I've been in the past few weeks. I've treated each day as a job to get through, from feeding the horses to leading tours—even telling the same jokes to different tours just so I don't have to expel extra energy being funny or clever. I just don't have it in me these days.

But with the guys, it's different. We haven't had much fun lately, ever since the conference. I'm still sore at them for the way they ambushed both me and Nina, so much so that when Jordy and I broke up, I threw the information at them. I never told them they couldn't tell her about Nina, but I know these guys. They have my back, even when I think they're assholes about it.

Right now, as we ride out, I can sense the change in the energy. Jake races beside me on one of the black mares, laughing as he edges in front of me, then gritting his teeth as Sara pulls ahead. The other guys are behind us, hooting above the sound of pounding hooves and the rhythm of hard breaths in open air. The smell of ocean mingles with the sweet hay smell drifting off Sara's coat, and I close my eyes so I can take it all in. I feel alive—more alive than I have in a while.

And still, all I see is her. Nina's face exists in my mind at all times, and right now I can almost smell her. The sweet honey of her skin, the lilac in her hair, the earthy scent of her sweat just before she climaxes.

I wish she were here. I wish she were with me always.

We reach the beach and the horses take off, running even faster than they were on the trail.

"Fuck yes!" I shout, then grin over at Jake as we continue leading the pack. I turn my baseball cap backwards to keep it from flying off in the wind, then crouch down as Sara gives it everything she has. She loves this more than I do, she practically flies through the air, the shadow of her feet barely keeping up with us. The waves crash beside us, and occasionally the mist from the water reaches my face. I lick the salt from my lips. I'd almost forgotten what it was like to have fun, or that I actually love what I do for work.

We reach the end of the beach and tie off the horses. No instructions are needed as we form a circle in the sand, facing each other. The last time we did this was with Jake when he was obviously struggling, back when his grandmother's memory was failing and it was on his shoulders to get her set up in a facility.

Now the guys face me, the same look of concern on their face that we had for Jake back then. Ironically, it's Jake who speaks up.

"What's going on, man?" he asks. The look on his face lets me know he won't expect anything that resembles bullshit, and yet I shrug, because I can't bring myself to talk about it. Not after they all made themselves clear about how they felt about Nina and me.

"You know," Levi says. "It's time for this to stop."

"How?" I force out. "How, when my whole entire life feels like it's falling apart without her. I get that you all hated her, but—"

"Nina? We never hated her."

"But you said—"

"We said we didn't want drama," Forrest pipes in. "Didn't need two women tearing you down. You've already had enough issues with the first one, and lord knows you weren't happy. But to stick it out with her while being with someone new? Man, Bray, you know better than that. You were stoking a wildfire and didn't even know you were burning alive."

"Not to mention Nina was still working with us at that point," River adds. "We liked her a lot, still like her. But you two getting involved was bad news for the ranch. If anything went wrong, we would all go down."

"All right guys, back off," Nate says, before turning to me. "The guys and I are just concerned. You've spent half your time stuck in a dark cloud, and the rest of it working your ass off to avoid Jordy, and that stupid charade she has you playing. You're miserable, man. It's obvious you're going through it alone. But we're family, Bray. We got your back. If there's something we can help you with, we want to hear it."

"I don't know how you can help." I slide my hands through my hair. "I thought I'd feel better once I told Jordy the truth, but it's like she has blinders on. I can't believe I even agreed to this, or that she's even still there at the ranch. Fuck!"

The horses nicker behind us, and I refrain from yelling more so I don't spook them. But the rage is always simmering, just waiting for me to explode.

"You don't have to do any of this," Jake says. I look at him, and he nods. "You could tell her to leave today. Do you not get that you're still doing it?"

"Doing what?"

"Saving her. Saving everybody."

"I cheated on her," I point out.

"Yeah, and it was fucked up. You also ended the relationship, and she's still got you on the short leash."

"Still?"

"Dude, that woman called all the shots. It's like you were boss in every area but with her. It all started when she got pregnant, and then lost the baby. She'd come here, and you became a different person, always making sure she was comfortable and taken care of. Jordy was a nice girl, but man, she was an awful girlfriend. She couldn't even see all the things you were doing for her. It's like nothing was ever good enough, and you just kept working to make her happy. You never even relaxed until she left for home."

"But with Nina," Levi laughs. "Hoo boy, we saw it right from the start. The way you smiled when you were around her. How she looked at you. The way you relaxed whenever she was near."

"Do you love her?" River asks. The question knocks me off guard. I know I do, but I've never told anyone else. It feels like Nina should hear it from me first, but I can't even reach her.

But these guys are family, and they know me better than anyone in this world. So there's only one answer to give them.

I take a deep breath, then nod. "I've never felt this way about anyone," I admit. "I didn't even know you could feel this way about someone, and I still feel like I barely know her. It's just so easy with her, you know? It's like, all the puzzle pieces fit. I can't stop thinking about her when I'm not with her. When I am... Well, it's been a while. But it's like I can see my past, present, and future with her. It's like no other woman exists. All I see is her, and without her, everything is so fucking stale. Today, when Jordy and I had coffee with her, she barely even looked at me. All I wanted to do was grab her hand and get out of there, to just escape somewhere where there's no barriers to us being together. I just wanted to tell her everything I felt, even with Jordy sitting right there. But like a coward, I just sat there and pretended nothing had changed. But *everything* has changed."

"We know," Nate says. "If it wasn't apparent then, it definitely is now. Bray, we're so sick of seeing you walk around with your tail between your legs. It's time for this to stop, which is why we're calling this meeting." He looks at the other guys, and I furrow my brows trying to understand what they're saying.

"Get your girl, Bray," Jake says.

I stare at him for a moment, then look at all of them.

"Dude, get your girl," Levi says, nudging me.

"*Dude*, she blocked my calls," I counter. Levi groans, rolling back in the sand.

"Brayden, get your fucking ass up off the sand, get on that horse, and don't stop until you're back at the ranch," Jake says. "Then drive your ass over to that house and tell her how you feel about her."

My heart lurches at this. What if I did? What if I threw caution to the wind and just said *fuck it*?

"What if Jordy finds out," I say. "She doesn't know it's Nina. If this gets back to her..."

"What if it did," Levi says quietly. "What's the worst that will happen?"

"She'll be pissed," I say. "She'll never speak to Nina again."

"She's already pissed," Levi points out. "And if you and Nina are truly meant to be together, she's going to find out eventually."

"She's going to be so hurt." I look down at my feet.

Jake gets up and crouches next to me. "This will be messy," he says. "Whether she finds out now or she finds out later, there's really no way around it. The question is, are you willing to sacrifice a chance with Nina just to prolong the inevitable with Jordy?"

I look out at the ocean, at the quiet waves rolling in under the late afternoon sun. A pelican is off in the distance, diving into the waves and then pulling out. Completely fearless. I think of myself these past few weeks. Months. Years. How I have lost so much of myself trying to please everyone around me. Trying to please Jordy.

"What's done is done," Jake murmurs. I look at him. He nods back up the beach toward the ranch. I scramble to my feet as the guys cheer me on. As Sara carries me back home, I let the wind strip away any lingering doubts.

I'm getting my girl.

Chapter Thirty-One

Nina

The doorbell rings, and I sigh, knowing I specifically requested a contactless delivery from DoorDash. Since Claire and Maren cleaned up my depression disaster, I've been working really hard to keep the place just as clean, along with taking care of myself by eating better foods. But after today's visit with Jordy and Brayden, I knew nothing would make me feel better than something hot and greasy and completely horrible for my health.

Just this once.

I tell myself as I trudge to the door, not really keen on seeing anyone, even a delivery guy. But when I open the door, there's Brayden, holding my food bag with a sheepish look on his face.

I grab the bag and go to close the door before he can make a move. I'm not quick enough, though. His foot catches in the jam, and he swears as I continue trying to close it.

"Move," I say, pressing against it with more force.

"Nina, please hear me out." Both of us know that he could force his way in, that my strength is no match for his. But he doesn't push on the door, the only intrusion is his foot that I'm working to sever with my weak strength, and I guess this is why I finally give in, stepping back from the door and letting it open.

Lord help me, the man looks like something I could wrap myself around. His cheeks are flushed, as if he ran the whole way here. His baseball cap is on backwards, which is a whole look in itself. He looks like he hasn't shaved in a week, making me ache with need to run my hands over his stubble. His lips are so plush, ready for the taking. He's wearing that flannel jacket I've always loved, one that smells of hay and wind, even from my safe distance away. I want to bury my face in his chest and just breathe, breathe, breathe, and never exhale.

But he's not mine. He's hers—and I'm done playing this game where I'll be the only loser.

I scowl, turning away from him and entering the kitchen. I hear the door close gently behind me, and his footsteps follow me. I sit at that damn uncomfortable bistro table, and kick the other stool to the floor, leaving me on the only upright seat. It was supposed to be aggressive and angry, but his chuckle as he rights it has me fighting a smile as I dig into the bag for my burger. He sits, and I properly ignore him, not even worrying how I look as I sink my teeth into the ciabatta roll and half pound patty in between, barbecue sauce and cheese oozing out as I do. It's a fucking mess, and I'm delighted— both at the taste and knowing this might knock me completely out of the running in the battle for Brayden's heart.

He's said nothing so far, so after a few more bites, I finally clear my mouth with some soda and ask him why he's here.

"I don't know where to start," he says.

"How about the part where we have a magical weekend together, and you end it by riding off into the sunset with your fiancé?" I say, batting my eyelashes at him. Then I glare and go back to my burger.

"I suppose you'd see it like that since you haven't read any of my texts."

"My phone must be broken," I say dismissively. "It doesn't accept messages from assholes."

He chuckles again, which is both so aggravating, and also drives me crazy. Something about him being here makes me want to stop being mad at him, to curl up in his arms and let him take the pain away. But what good will that do? Once he leaves, I'll be right back where I started, nursing a broken heart while he goes home to fuck my cousin.

He fishes his phone out, and I shake my head.

"No," I say, "I don't want to read it. I can't do this anymore. We never should have done anything to begin with."

He continues, unlocking it.

"Are you even listening to me?" I push it away when he holds it out to me.

"Please just read it. If you still hate me afterwards, I'll go. I'll never contact you again. But please, just give me this one thing and read it."

"I owe you nothing," I say, narrowing my eyes at him.

"You don't," he agrees.

I stare at the phone. My hands are a mess, and I have half a mind to pick up his phone just so I can get barbecue sauce and grease all over it. But I have a smidge of decency left.

I get up and wash my hands, then sit back down and hold my hand out. He places the phone in my hands.

Brayden: I told her tonight. I didn't name you, but I let her know that I cheated on her. Then I told her it was over. And

Nina, it's over. She wants to wait until after Claire and Ethan's wedding to say anything, and against my better judgment, I agreed. Only because I feel like I owe her this one last thing. But say the word, and I'll end it all. I'll do anything to be with you, to live every day like we did this weekend. Just to wake up to you is everything my soul has been crying out for. Just to taste your smile, to breathe in your breath, to hold your body against mine, skin to skin. I don't want us to end. But the look in your eyes when I left you this morning tells me that you think it's over. Is it, though? Have I fucked things up that badly? Will you find it in your heart to forgive me for not fighting right from the beginning? Because that first day I saw you was the day I fell in love with you. The first day I kissed you was the day I knew you'd forever be under my skin. And whether you take me back or not, I will be yours forever. There is no one else for me, Nina. There's only you.

My eyes sting, the tears threatening to fall as I read the last line of his text. I won't show him emotion, though. I should just hand the phone back now after reading the first text. But my eyes won't let me, and my finger disobeys as it scrolls down the phone, revealing the next text, then the next, and the next.

Brayden: You're killing me, Nina. I deserve this, I know. But I can't let you go, and in the slim chance that you're actually reading this, I'll continue to tell you every day. I love you. I love you. I love you.

Brayden: This morning I was thinking about the first time

I woke up to you in my bed. You were still asleep, and I just watched you breathe. You have the most beautiful lips, and it was the hardest thing not to touch mine to yours just to remember what they felt like. But I refrained, and I'll always remember. I remember now, how soft you are to me, how you feel like home. How I could kiss you for hours, nothing more, and feel complete.

Brayden: Today, the guys and I took a tour out to the beach, and there was one family with a reluctant son who wanted nothing more than to stay in the cabin and play video games. None of the guys could get this kid to enjoy himself, not even Levi, who's usually a hit with the kids. All I kept thinking about was that day you helped out on a tour and got that one kid to put down his devices and have a good time. If you'd been on today's tour, there's no doubt in my mind that you could've gotten this kid to smile, maybe even have a great time.

I think about you every day. How you were on the ranch. How you were with my family. How much they love you. I think about what it would be like to have you here all the time, with my ring on your finger, and our futures combined. I think about that a lot, actually. Nina Winters. It kind of has a nice ring to it, doesn't it? Or maybe you'd want to stay Nina Chance. I don't care either way. I just want you, any way I can have you.

Brayden: I should tell you that Jordy is living here on the ranch. Not in the house, and definitely not in my bed. My mom heard she was staying in a hotel, and even though I told her we weren't together, she still invited her to stay. You know my mom. I know what you're thinking, because I'm thinking it too. This is fucking stupid. Nina, this whole thing is fucking stupid. The fact that I'm here and you're there is fucking stupid. The fact that I haven't just driven to your house to tell you how I feel is fucking stupid. But you're not taking my calls. I don't blame you. I'd ignore me too. You placed a boundary, and as much as I want to plow through it, I'll respect it. But only because there's a time limit here. As soon as I'm free, I'll be on your doorstep, boundary or not, begging you to take me back. And Nina, I'm not sure I know how to take no for an answer. So...don't say no, okay?

Brayden: Do you ever think of me? I had this horrible thought today that you've completely forgotten all about us, and I can barely think of anything else but you.

Brayden: I'm sitting outside your house, and I'm so damn nervous, I can barely breathe. The guys pulled me aside today when I came home from seeing you. Told me to stop moping around like a bitch and get my girl. It's like they could see the heartbreak all over my body. Who am I fooling? I've been like this since the conference. But today, after being in that coffee shop and not able to tell you how I feel, I was torn up inside. The way she kept grabbing my hand in front of you... Nina, I saw your face. I saw the way it made you feel to see her with me. While I never want to hurt you again, it did give me a sliver of hope that you won't turn me away tonight, that maybe you miss me as much as I miss you.

And Nina? You're my girl. I'm so fucking crazy about you, I haven't been able to sleep. I've barely been able to eat. If we have to burn every bridge just to be together, I'm ready to light this whole damn world on fire.

So here I am, about to approach your door for the first time in forever, praying that you'll let me in.

Because I'm so in love with you, and I hope you love me too.

I can barely read the last text because my vision is too blurry. I swipe at my eyes, then look up at Brayden. He's watching me with tears in his eyes too. I push my soggy French fries at him.

"Here," I say. He looks down at the fries, then back at me, his brow furrowed.

"What is this for?"

"You said you've barely been able to eat," I say, and his face breaks into a grin. "I just thought I'd—hey!" I laugh as he catches me around the waist and swings me off the stool. I don't fight him. I was done fighting him before those texts. But now?

His mouth lands on mine and it's a full on claiming. Without words he tells me that we're never going through this again, that he's mine and I'm completely, head over heels his.

But the thing is, falling into bed with him is not going to undo all the things we need to talk about. I push against his chest, and he reluctantly releases me.

"There's too much to say right now," I tell him, and he wrinkles his brow but nods. "And I'm still mad, even if I get it."

I sit down, folding my hands in front of me. He does the same. I could speak. I could tell him all the ways he affected me these past few weeks. How much I missed him, and how much it hurt to see him this morning. But I need words from him; I need to hear in his own voice every way he's feeling, and what he plans to do now.

I need to know that I'm not going to get my hopes up only to play second fiddle. Because I'm done with this shit.

"First, Jordy and I are done. I broke up with her the night we came back."

"Yeah, about that. She's living with you?" I tilt my head at him.

"I know," he groans. "It's my mom. She'd take in every stray if she could, humans included. I told her this was like taking Jordy's side over her own son's, but she wouldn't listen. She said Jordy had been too important of a person to me to just toss in a hotel, especially now that Jordy was recovering from a breakup."

I feel a little guilty at this. Angie insisted on taking Jordy in like she was family. But I'm Jordy's actual family, and I'm the one who kicked her out.

"Your mom probably thinks I'm trash." I grimace, absolutely gutted by the thought. I really love Brayden's mom. Just as much as I miss Brayden, I miss working in the kitchen with Angie. She talked to me like we'd known each other for years, and it made me feel like I meant something to her. But now?

"No, Nina. She actually understands. I told her how Jordy swept in and got rid of all your grandmother's things, and my mom was shocked but not surprised. Jordy doesn't have a sentimental bone in her body. She doesn't place meaning on things the way most people do, which is great if you want to live a minimalist life. But it's not so great when you have family heirlooms. She sees the price tag, not the history that goes along with them." He takes my hand in his, running his thumb over my skin with reassurance. "Besides, she figures it's probably best under the circumstances that you and Jordy don't live together.

"Oh fuck, she knows?" I hide my face in my hands, unsure how I'm ever going to face his mom again. He takes my hands in his, laughing at me.

"Yes, she knows. My dad does too. They figured it out when the chairman called and repeated my bullshit story. While they're not thrilled about what I did to Jordy, my parents are happy to know it's you I've fallen for. They love you."

I laugh even as I narrow my eyes in disbelief. "Your dad said that?"

He cocks his head, as if to ask, *are you serious?* "I don't think my dad has ever expressed a positive emotion in his life, but I know he likes you. If he didn't, he wouldn't even pay attention to you. When he's gruff with you, that's when you know you're on his good side."

"So your parents are all keen on us being together, right?"

He squeezes my hand. "They're just sitting back and letting me figure out my own life. They want me to be happy, and I'm happy with you."

It's not exactly an answer, but there's hope in it. If his parents feel any reservations about us, I can't blame them. They've spent the last five years getting close to Jordy, imagining their son's future with her. Now we've gone and switched the narrative. A change like this wouldn't be easy on anyone.

"So, you're still going to the wedding as Jordy's date."

He winces, his expression clearly pained. "I can get out of it," he says. "It was stupid to even agree. I should—"

"No, I get it," I say, even though my insides are completely twisted at the thought of seeing them together even for just one more day. "If you knew our family…well, you do know them. Her mom is just—I mean, my mom is a complete bitch, but Aunt Lil puts so much pressure on Jordy to be perfect. If my aunt finds out you guys broke up…" I realize what I'm saying, that there's so much more at stake here. "If they find out I'm the one that broke you two up—"

"You didn't, though. I mean, yeah, meeting you sped things along. But you saved me from an expensive divorce, because that marriage was not going to last. It was never meant to be. So it wasn't you, it was my decision to end things."

"They'll never see it that way, though. I'm the whore of the family, the one who was handed everything, thanks to my grandmother, and still manages to ruin everything. They will only see this as another way spoiled Nina inserts herself into a situation and takes what she wants."

"And is that true?" Brayden asks.

I look at him, my eyes narrowing. "What the fuck?"

"*I* don't think it's true," he says. "But do *you?*"

I shake my head. I've believed a lot of things about myself, but not this—at least not now. "I've asked myself so many times if I did anything to deserve what happened to me." I don't mention the rape by name, but the sympathy in his eyes lets me know he understands. "I know now that it was not my fault. But back then, it was more confusing. Especially when my mom turned on me, calling me a whore." I shake my head. "That's really where all of this started. She was embarrassed by me, her broken daughter. She's the one who suggested I move in with Nanna for a fresh start. But when she saw how much her mother cared for me…" I sigh out a breath, feeling shaky as tears spring to my eyes. I swipe them away. "Whatever it was, her treatment of me spread like wildfire. She claimed I was difficult, and it didn't take much for the family to believe that of me. So when Nanna Dot left me everything—" I pause, clenching my fists at my side. "Let's just say the groundwork was laid to completely write me out of the family." I look at Bray, nearly breaking at the way he's looking back at me with so much compassion, so much concern. "I guess I shouldn't care. They already think so little of me."

"It's okay to care," Brayden says. He takes my hands, unfolding them both before lacing his fingers with mine. "Of course you care. We'll do whatever makes you feel comfortable. I'll stand by you in everything."

"Well, first you'll go to the wedding with Jordy. I don't think I could handle unleashing the drama that day, either. I don't want to ruin Ethan and Claire's day, even though they already know."

This time it's his turn to balk. "They know? You told people about us?"

"Was I not supposed to?" It does seem like our little secret is becoming less of a secret every moment. How many people know already? The five guys, Brayden's parents, Maren, Claire, and probably Ethan. And soon…

"God, soon the whole world will know." My voice shakes a little, realizing the implications. Once my mom knows? What will she say?

"I *want* the whole world to know," he laughs. "I love that you've told people. I want you to tell everyone."

"Even Jordy?" I ask, a teasing glint in my eyes.

"At this point, I'd be fine if you told her too. She's going to find out anyways, because I'm not letting you go."

"Oh really? Don't I get some say in this?" I push against him teasingly, but he wraps his arms around me.

"You get all the say," he murmurs, his lips coming closer. "Anything you want, I'll do it for you."

"No," I say firmly, backing away while still safe in his embrace. "That was your last relationship. In this one, we're partners. We work together. Sometimes I'll be happier, sometimes you will. But hopefully—most times—we'll fall in the middle." I run my hands over his chest, my fingers grazing against his bare skin just above the button line. "But we can't tell Jordy yet. I agree, she'll know, and it's not going to be pretty." I bury my head in his chest. "Ugh, especially since I already hired her."

"I wanted to kick you under the table for that one," Brayden laughs. "What the fuck were you thinking? If you're looking for ways to make this more awkward and painful, you've done it."

"I know." I look up in his eyes. "But it has to be done. Once this wedding is over, no more secrets. No more hiding who we are or what we want. We live the truest lives we can, and whoever sticks around can be our family."

He leans down and kisses me. Tenderly. As if we have all the time in the world—and for a moment, we do. For a moment, I forget the outside world and all the consequences and everyone who is bound to hate us by the end of next week. Right now, there's only us standing in my kitchen, wrapped in each other's arms.

And I want more.

I deepen my kiss, gripping his neck as if I'm going to fall through the earth without him to anchor me. In response, he sweeps me off my feet, lifting me into his arms as if I weigh nothing. I break our kiss, gasping in shock.

"I got you," he says, kissing me again. "But if I don't get you naked now, I'm going to go out of my mind."

"Then what are you waiting for?"

The words are barely out of my mouth before his mouth claims me again. His tongue brushes over mine in a way that leaves me lightheaded and needing more—so much more. We're moving, but I don't know where until he's laid me on the hard couch. Making quick work of my clothes, I lie naked before him, and he takes a moment to drink me in.

"You are so damn beautiful," he breathes, his eyes running over my body. Just his gaze alone feels like his hands are already on me. I arch my back, closing my eyes as I feel heat bloom in my core. He groans in response, and then his mouth clamps down on me. It's so sudden, I cry out, then moan as his tongue finds my most sensitive parts. He stops suddenly., and I open my eyes, looking at him like *what the hell.*

"This couch is hella uncomfortable," he says, a grimace of

apology on his face.

"Right?" I grin, feeling vindicated even if I also feel like there's been a disturbance in the force. "My room is a pit, but it's a hell of a lot more comfortable than this seat coffin."

He needs no further prompting. He gets up, looks at me and grins. His clothes are off before I can even stand, and I have half a mind to find out what he tastes like. But when I stand, he smacks my ass.

"Get upstairs," he growls. I don't need to be told twice. I lead the way up the stairs, only a little self-conscious that he has a full view of my jiggling ass on the journey there. I open the door, relieved that I actually cleaned my room this week, save for a few outfits that didn't quite make it in the hamper. I retrieve them quickly and stuff them in with the rest of the dirty clothes, and start to look around for anything else that needs to be hidden. But he catches me off guard, spinning me around so that I land on the bed. It's so smooth, the way he has me on my back, my legs propped up with him kneeling before me.

"I'm not turned off by your mess," he says. "Nothing about you turns me off. I want all of you, even the things you think are imperfect. To me, every part of you is perfect, from your beautiful mind, your caring heart, and your perfect," he leans down and kisses my waiting pussy, "delicious," he kisses it again, followed by a swipe of his tongue—and a squeal from me—"hot as fuck body." This time he stays, clamping down while I squirm beneath him—rather, squirm as best as I can. He has a firm grip on my hips, and he anchors me in place while his tongue bathes me, alternating between hardened strokes and silky-soft glides. The guessing leaves me lightheaded, and soon I feel myself open, the ember inside me igniting into a flame, then a firestorm, then a blazing inferno as I let myself go under his touch. He plucks my erect bud between his lips, sucking lightly in a way that has me screaming his name, the waves rolling over me like the waves on our beach in Texas. I ride the current, and he lets up only when I can't handle anymore. He stands, licking my moisture from his lips before crawling over the top of me and kissing my mouth. I taste myself on him, and it's so utterly erotic.

For years, I've hated my body, been embarrassed by every part of it. My smell. My shape. Anything that made me feel vulnerable and unattractive. But tasting myself on him ... It's like I can see myself through his eyes. I like the way he smells when he smells like me. I like tasting him when he tastes like me. I feel beautiful when he looks at me, and I want to be seen by him.

I lean over to my side table and retrieve a condom from the nightstand and hand it to him. He rises from the bed, and I watch as he slips it on, noting the ripple in his solid abs, the peaks of his broad chest. I take in the length of him, marveling at how I can look at his cock and think it's as beautiful as any art piece in a gallery.

"What are you thinking?" he asks, kissing my lips as he straddles me. He doesn't rush to enter me, which is both sweet and aggravating. I want him in me. I want him to fuck me hard. But I also don't want it to ever end. And this—the pillow talk, the way he's just enjoying my company without needing to be inside me—it means more to me than he knows.

"I was just thinking how I will never grow tired of this," I murmur, running a finger along his cheek. "Of you. I've never had someone treat me this way, or love…" I pause on the word.

"Love you like this," he finishes. He places a hand over mine on his cheek. "I love you, Nina."

"I love you, Brayden."

He kisses me again, his lips soft on mine, his hand gently resting at my throat, his body pressed against me as his cock nudges at my entrance. Then he pushes in slowly—so slowly—as if he, too, wants to make this last forever. I weave my hands into his hair, tasting him with lingering kisses, and he whispers sweet words in between.

"You feel so damn good."

"I want to drink you in."

"I can't get enough of you."

"Look at me."

At those last words, I do, my eyes finding the blue of his. I feel the last puzzle piece click into place, the distance between our souls diminishing as our bond locks together. We keep eye contact the whole time he moves inside me, as I arch into him, as he cups my face, as I grip his ass. The intensity of it all washes over me, running straight through me, and I come for the second time this hour, all while he continues to insist I look at him. Only after I'm completely sated does he allow himself to finish, exploding inside me as I lock my lips with his.

Chapter Thirty-Two

Nina

The day of the wedding arrives, and I wake up with a start, the butterflies already churning tornadoes in my belly.

Brayden has been at my house almost every night this week. I know he and Jordy broke up, but I can't help feeling like we're playing with fire, like she'll somehow catch on. At this point, though, would it matter? Because after today, the secret will be out.

It's why I'm nervous. Don't get me wrong, I'm excited too. Knowing we won't have to sneak around is an exhilarating thought, and a reality I can't wait to experience. But this could be the end of me being a part of my family forever. Sure, the bridge has been burned time and time again, but this final act could incinerate it.

As much as my family drives me crazy, I don't know if I can handle complete exile.

Still, if these nightly visits are just a taste of what's to come, I'll take anything life throws at me. My mind drifts to just last night, my body still aching from all the ways he wore me out and put me to sleep before he slipped out. Now that he has his own key, his comings and goings are on a whim, and I find myself watching the door constantly.

Like now, though I know he's working the ranch before it's time to get ready, and finalizing the charade he and Jordy are playing. Aunt Lil and Uncle Dan showed up last night, bunking with Jordy in her cabin. While I know this is all part of the plan, my veins are flowing with pure jealousy. I have to keep reminding myself that we're at the finish line.

I also have to remind myself that we're about to tromp on the heart of someone I care about very much.

I've done a great job this past week of glossing over the morality of this situation, but I can't ignore the fact that Jordy will be crushed when she finds out what happens. Having our moms hate me is one thing, I'm used to that by now. But Jordy? That's been a relationship I've missed for years, and now that we're cautiously friends again, I'm about to drive the stake in her heart.

She never should have trusted me.

I spend the next two hours getting ready. Maren is busy doing Maid of Honor duties with Claire, which means I'm on my own to apply makeup with shaky fingers and keep the heater on high as my nerves add ice to my veins. I have this strange thought to call my mom, as if my mom will offer calming words of encouragement. When has she ever done that, though? How could I tell her any of this? It's more likely that she'd tell me what a whore I am, and all the ways I'm an embarrassment to our family.

She wasn't always like this, though. I mean, she was never that great in her mothering. There was always this edge to her where I needed softness, and she was constantly on me about my weight. But sometimes, she knew the right words to say at the exact right moments. Like when Stacy Kendrick told me my hair looked like yarn, and my mom told me it reminded her of spun gold, like the kind in Rumpelstiltskin, that everyone wanted hair like that. Or when David Emery snapped my bra in front of the whole class, and my mother reminded me of how warped boys were that they had no clue how to tell a girl they liked her. "They don't change much with age," my mom told me. "Boys would rather show off than bare their feelings. Just ask your father."

"It's ingrained in us," my father confirmed. "Just look at how birds flaunt around hens." And with that, he strutted around the kitchen with his arms as wings, then planted a kiss on my mom's lips. She just rolled her eyes.

When was the last time I'd laughed with my parents, or even enjoyed their company? When have they enjoyed mine? After the news of my home wrecking goes on blast, will they ever speak to me again?

My phone rings just then, and when I look at the name on the screen, my heart leaps. A small smile tugs at my lips as I answer.

"Hey, you," I say.

"Hey, Sugar," Brayden says. His voice is like honey, soothing my ruminations with just one word. "How are you feeling?"

I sigh, spinning my chair away from my makeup table. "Let's see, my makeup looks like shit, my hair is sticking out weird no matter what I do, my undergarments feel tight, and my skin is all blotchy because I keep going from hot to cold to hot. But, I'm good."

His laugh is a low rumble on the other side of the phone, and it makes me wish he were here.

"Do we have to do this?" I ask.

He's silent for a moment. But then, "You don't want to be with me?"

"No! I mean the whole wedding thing. Telling everyone. Shining a spotlight on any of this. Can't we just run away together and not let anyone know?'"

"Sugar, just say the word, and I'm there. I'm more than willing to blow all of this off. I just want you."

I take a deep breath in, willing my racing heart to slow its roll. "We have to," I groan. "My parents will be there. My aunt and uncle. Jordy would absolutely murder you."

"I'm not worried about Jordy," he says.

"Well, I am. We're about to completely blow up her whole world. The least you can do is hold up your end of the bargain."

"You mean lie to everyone."

"Exactly."

There's silence again, but I can hear him breathing. I close my eyes, lulling myself by the sound of his breath, wishing I could be his air.

"I miss you," he says quietly.

"I miss you too," I say. "Only a few more hours to go." As we say our goodbyes, I can't help feeling like time passed so quickly only for these next few hours to feel like an eternity.

The wedding is on a small dinner cruise ship that will sail into the heart of Sunset Bay. I stand at the back of the line on my own as everyone files onto the vessel. For the occasion, I chose to strip the color from my hair and leave it platinum, which to me, sometimes feels more dramatic than dyeing it pink or mermaid—more vulnerable because I'm showing the world the real me. I'm wearing a pale-yellow strapless dress with a faux fur wrap, strappy stiletto heels, and a simple gold chain with a small hoop in the center. I feel elegant in this dress, though I haven't compared myself to Jordy yet. Knowing her, she'll show everyone up—including the bride—without even trying.

I can see my parents near the front, my mom wearing a ridiculous purple hat with netting on it, which matches her purple dress and jacket. She's leaning toward my dad, either gossiping about someone or nagging him on something he isn't doing right.

Aunt Lil and Uncle Dan are in front of them. My aunt looks back, gauging the line behind her, and I duck behind the person in front of me. When I look back up, it's Brayden's eyes that catch mine. He and Jordy are in front of my aunt and uncle, but all I see is him. For a moment, time slows down and it's just us. His mouth quirks into a smile, and I feel so utterly calm in his presence.

But it's all interrupted when Jordy plants a big kiss on his cheek, then laughs at something her mom says. I can't see what she's wearing from back here but can tell she looks perfect. Her face is expertly contoured, highlighting her already chiseled cheekbones. Her lips are a rusty shade of red, accentuated by her glowing white smile. Her hair is piled into the perfect twist, with a few tendrils escaping, as if on accident. I look away sharply, my heart suffering a sudden pain at just knowing Brayden's there with her, and she looks so beautiful. He's not mine, but he is. Even knowing I only have a short while left to endure this, I can't help thinking I might not survive.

"Well, hey there sexy," Maren's raspy voice says beside me. I turn to her, relieved at the distraction, only to find my friend looking like a goddamn vixen. Usually Maren wears black, but somehow Claire talked her into wearing jade green, and it looks incredible against her fair skin. Even though Maren is super slender, the dress finds all her curves and accentuates them. It dips low in the front, and she is wearing a drop necklace that rests daringly between her breasts. "Damn, Maren. You look fucking hot!"

"I almost didn't let her leave the house," a low voice says, and I turn to see Mac with his luscious beard, filling out his grey suit in ways that should be illegal. I no longer lust after him, now that Maren's snagged him as her own, but I can't help thinking of those days when he was my neighbor, teasing every housewife in the area with his near naked strolls.

Now he's just my hot as hell Realtor.

"Naked Coff… Mac! Great to see you, you look well," I say, then widen my eyes at Maren, as if Mac can't see. He's fighting a smile when I look back at him.

"Don't inflate his ego," Maren says. "He already has a hard time fitting through the door with that big head of his."

"That's not my head," he murmurs in her ear. I bite back a laugh as Maren gives him a mock glare at his audacity.

The line moves quicker now, especially with Maren keeping me company. She gabs about all the ways Claire choreographed this whole wedding, and how perfectly imperfect it's been, starting with the photographer calling in sick this morning.

"Luckily she knows a bunch of talented people," Maren says. "She ended up hiring this college student who makes extra cash photographing her book crafts. He's never done people, but what the hey."

"Damn," I breathe. I can only imagine how much Claire is freaking out. But when I say so, Maren shakes her head.

"Last I saw her, she was finishing her second glass of brut. She's such a lightweight, she's nothing but smiles."

"And you're not there with her?" I ask, realizing that this is probably when Claire needs her most.

"She's fine," Maren says. "But we both know how hard today will be." She gives me a sympathetic look. "How are you holding up?" she asks, then tilts her head in Brayden's direction. They've just boarded, and he takes one last look at me. It's brief, as Jordy drags him off into the crowd.

"I'm okay," I tell Maren. But I feel like an ass. I haven't told her or Claire that Brayden and I reconciled, or even what our plans are after today. I don't want anything to overshadow Ethan and Claire's wedding. But looking at my friend now, I'm dying to tell her everything.

We board the ship, the last in line to do so, and I turn to Maren.

"Listen, I—" It's then that I notice my mom staring in my direction. She says something to my father, then starts heading our way.

Fuck. It's not the time. Just a few more hours, and I'm free.

"Thank you for staying with me," I say to Maren. "But you should be with Claire."

She shoots me a grateful smile. "Mac can stay with you," she says, but I shake my head. I hardly know her boyfriend. Even though he's working to find me a place for my new shop, almost all our business dealings have been handled through emails and texts. With my mom just seconds away, I can't bear the idea of him overhearing anything she has to say to me. Because it won't be nice.

"I'll just check out what's happening at the bar," Mac says, then offers me a sideways hug. "Hang in there, kid."

They both leave just as my mom reaches me. "So typical that you're late," my mom says. I turn to see her appraising me, stopping at my midsection. "Did you forget to wear your Spanx?"

I didn't forget, and now I feel like a cow. But what's new?

"Nice to see you, Mother," I say coolly. "I think you were shaming me publicly the last time we spoke. Good to see times haven't changed."

Her face takes on a look of shock, then she catches herself. "Yes, well, if you'd call once in a while, we'd have plenty of pleasant conversations too."

"Oh, right. All those mother-daughter heart-to-hearts we always have." I tilt my head and pout in mockery. "I miss those."

She seems at a loss of words, which is rare. Then she glances around to see who's witnessing this exchange. Leave it to my mother to worry more about the opinions of strangers than that of her own daughter's.

"Since you don't have a date, your father is saving a seat for you next to us."

I groan, thinking of what it will be like to sit with my mother for a whole ceremony. But before I can answer, an arm slides around my waist.

"She's with us, Aunt Poppy," Jordy says. I look to her and feel both relief at the quick save, and total dread at sitting next to the fake fiancé of the man I love. But at this moment, she feels like the safer option. I grin at her, then look at my mom.

"Sorry, guess I'm taken." Then I let Jordy lead the way. She laughs once we're out of earshot, and I can't help but join in.

"I could see the venom in your stance a mile away. I did this purely to save Aunt Poppy from getting her eyes scratched out." Jordy grins at me, then gestures at the row we're in.

"Trust me, I'm not ruining this paint job on that sow," I say, showing my gorgeous French manicure with glittery tips. I laugh, but my laugh falters when I see Brayden sitting in the row I'm about to enter. Our eyes meet, but I'm the first to look away, aware of Jordy standing so close to me. I look at her, checking to see if she noticed anything.

"You first," I prompt, making way for her. I take a moment to study what she's wearing, and yup, flawless. It's simple and black, but completely form hugging—and Jordy has curves in all the right ways. Her tan skin is practically glowing, and despite the slight chill in the air, she wears nothing to cover herself up, nor shows any sign of being cold. Her jewelry is silver and diamonds, adding the perfect amount of sparkle to her outfit. She easily outshines everyone here, especially me. I thought I looked very Andie Anderson in this dress. Now I feel like Big Bird. Especially as her perfect ass sways down the aisle before she sits next to Brayden, and I waddle after her.

The seats fill quickly as soon as the orchestra begins playing. I wrap my shawl around me, feeling alone as Jordy steals most of Brayden's attention. My parents are in the seats in front of us, and my dad turns around and squeezes my hand.

"You look beautiful, Antonina," he says. When my mom uses my full name, it's because I'm in trouble. But when my dad uses it, it's because he's proud of me. It's been a while since he's said it, and I glow under the compliment.

My mom doesn't even acknowledge me.

"You really do," Jordy whispers once my dad has turned back around. I blush under her compliment.

"Thanks, but nothing compared to you. You look so elegant."

"I forgot I even had this dress," Jordy says. "It's very last season, but it works."

It's not last season. It's timeless, and I know she knows this. But I still kind of appreciate her humbleness, which feels genuine—which makes me feel like an absolute ogre.

The orchestra finishes their song, and then allows for a moment's pause. When they play again, I recognize it as an acoustic version of "Fever Dream," by Iron & Wine, not readily known but a surprisingly perfect song for the wedding party to walk down the aisle. I turn with everyone else, and see Ethan walk first.

As long as I've been alive, there's been Ethan. My dad and his brother are very close, which means we spent a lot of time with Ethan's family. But when Ethan's dad, Uncle Tom, split for another woman, my dad cut ties with his brother. He didn't cut ties with my aunt, though. We took them in, and they lived with us for a few years before Aunt Stacy could make it on her own.

So in a way, Ethan feels like a brother to me, even if we aren't as close in our adult years.

While we've become distant, I still recognize that smile on his face, the one that says he's about to get something he's always dreamed of having. Back then, it was a new video game, or a double-double from In-N-Out, or his favorite sports team was about to win it all.

Today, he's getting the girl.

I watch as Ethan approaches my row, and I'm so proud of the man he's turned out to be, and also that he's marrying the woman he loves. His eyes catch mine, and his expression turns to one of *Can you believe this is happening?* I grin and give him a thumbs up before he passes my row and reaches the front of the church.

Next are the mothers of the bride and groom, who chose to walk down the aisle together, arm in arm. Even though I don't know Claire well, I do know that she's had a difficult relationship with her mother, who finally decided to get clean last year.

Maren is next, and every eye is on my friend as she classes up the place in her green gown. I take the moment to find Mac a few rows over. His eyes are on her, and when she glances his way, he mouths *I love you.*

The rest of the wedding party makes their way down the aisle, but we're all impatient to see the bride. I know I am. It wasn't long ago that I thought Claire was the most annoying person on the planet. But over the past few weeks, I've realized she wasn't half bad. In fact, maybe she's pretty cool.

The music shifts, and I recognize it as another Iron & Wine song—"Love and Some Verses." Everyone rises, which is the worst practice for people who are short like me. I can barely see over the tall people surrounding me, but when Claire appears, she takes my breath away. She's literally the loveliest person I've ever seen, wearing a dress entirely made of lace that cascades behind her as she walks. On her head is a beautiful tiara instead of a veil, making her look both mystical and royal. Her makeup is beautifully understated, showing off her natural beauty, and her golden hair is in waves, brushing against her bare back.

The ceremony is more romantic than I anticipated. I never considered myself a sappy person, but being here, I can't help but wipe at the moisture collecting in my eyes. I take a moment to look in Brayden's direction, and I regret doing so, because at that moment, Jordy moves her hand to his leg. He promptly removes it, and Jordy quickly looks at me. There's no denying that I saw the whole thing, but I move my eyes to the ceremony as if that's taking all of my attention. When I dare to glance back at Brayden, my eyes fall on Jordy instead, seeing the fallen look on her face. She's not watching the ceremony at all.

I think about how she saved me with my mom. How she was so excited to help out with the new shop I'm planning. How close we were as kids—close enough that it was clear nothing and no one should ever come between us.

What the fuck am I doing? How can I do this to her? Do I really want to be the kind of person who lets a man come between me and my closest friend and confidante? Because in everything that's happened in our lives, Jordy and I were each other's first friends, and I want more than anything to recapture what we once had.

I can't have Brayden and also remain close to Jordy. And I can't be close to Jordy and remain in Brayden's life.

What's more important to me?

At that moment, I feel something brush against my bare shoulder. I look over, and there's Brayden's arm, draped over Jordy's chair, his fingers grazing against my shoulder. I realize at this moment that anyone could see, and we're making Jordy out to be a fool. It's wrong, and I can't do this anymore.

I scoot closer to my neighbor on the left side of me, effectively out of Brayden's reach. I don't dare look at him, but his hand eventually finds its way back into his lap. A glance at Jordy's face

320 — CRISSI LANGWELL

shows she's not devastated like before, oblivious of the reason why Brayden's arm was around her to begin with.

Once the ceremony ends, and Claire and Ethan make their way down the aisle, I murmur a goodbye to Jordy then leap up. I scramble over the rest of the row, mumbling apologies until I'm finally free. I book it away from the wedding party, trying to find a place to regain my composure. We're stuck on this godforsaken ship, and my breath comes out in labored spurts as I fight claustrophobia. There are too many people, too little places to hide, and not enough air on this floating prison.

I finally find a corner of the ship that's not taken and immediately take cover, catching my breath as I try to make sense of my life, what I'm actually doing.

I love Brayden. I love him so goddamn much, it hurts. I have never known someone to be so perfectly suited to me, to know me inside and out without having known me for long. Brayden and I have a lot to learn about each other, and yet I already know I can't live without him. Every vision of my future includes him.

But how can I be with the love of my life if it means the people closest to me will reject me forever? How can I do this to Jordy, when we were once each other's closest allies? Have I really sunk this low?

A warm hand touches the back of my neck, but I don't flinch. I know it's him, knowing he'd find me.

"Nina, please talk to me."

Chapter Thirty-Three

Brayden

I watch her run off, and I know exactly what's going on in her mind, because I'm grappling with this too. The past few weeks, I have been so annoyed with Jordy, I can barely breathe. I'm angry at this fucking charade. I'm mad that she's trampled all over my comforts as I maintain hers. I'm mad that she's staying on the ranch, and that her parents are here this weekend, as if we never broke up at all.

Yet, I don't want to hurt her. It's one thing to have told her I cheated, but once she finds out it's Nina…

I'm both looking forward to moving on with Nina and feeling completely gutted about telling Jordy the truth.

It had surprised me that Nina still sat with us, but her presence brought me peace. My mistake was touching her shoulder. I shouldn't have done that. It was irresponsible and completely disrespectful to Jordy. I don't even know why I did it, except that it was hard to be that close to her and not touch her. But when she jerked out of my reach, I was instantly brought back to reality. Even worse, Jordy thought I was being affectionate with her, which will only confuse things when the truth finally comes out.

Then Nina ran. I knew if I didn't check in with her, she was going to tell herself all kind of stories that would make her believe we shouldn't happen.

I care that we're about to hurt a lot of people, but I love Nina more—and I won't lose her again.

"Go find your parents. I'm going to use the restroom really quick," I tell Jordy. She nods, not even bothering to question me.

As soon as her back is turned, I'm off and running, watching Nina weave in and out of the crowd, frantically looking around. Finally she dips behind a pillar next to the ship railing. If I hadn't seen her disappear, I wouldn't know where to find her.

I look behind me to make sure no one is following me, then I slip toward the same place Nina is. Her back is to me, her shoulders heaving under her wrap as she looks out at the ocean. I hesitate, knowing she's processing some heavy feelings right now. Even in her grief, she's easily the most beautiful person on this ship. Her hair is like silk, cascading down her back in soft waves. I've never seen it this color, and it's mesmerizing. Her curves are celebrated in the dress she's wearing, the way it tapers at her waist and skims over her hips. I want to run my hand over the pale-yellow satin, to feel the smoothness of it over the warmth of her body.

I can't hold back any longer. I reach out, my hand brushing her hair aside to find the warmth of her neck. She doesn't jump or try to move away. She just breathes, her shoulders relaxing slightly as she leans into my touch.

"Nina, please talk to me."

She turns, her eyes red and filled with tears, and she shakes her head. "I can't do this, Bray. I can't hurt her like this."

"I know this is hard, Sweetheart," I murmur. "There are no winners here. Either she gets hurt, or we do, and Nina, sometimes you need to choose you."

"Yeah, but this is such a fucked up way to do it. Every time I think about what we've done, what we're going to do, I just want to crawl into a hole and die. I feel like the worst person in the world."

"But you're not," I tell her, cupping her face in my hand. She closes her eyes, running her cheek against my palm. A fresh tear escapes her eyes. "Sugar, neither one of us wanted to hurt anyone. But don't you think we fell into each other's lives for a reason? Don't you think fate had a hand in bringing us together? Because I do."

"The list," she whispers.

"What list?"

She opens her eyes, then takes a step away from me, wiping her eyes. "Nothing. Something stupid and childish. It doesn't matter because we can't do this."

"Nina, please. Don't do this." I reach for her, but she turns her head. My hand drops at my side. "I can't live without you."

"Yes, you can," she says. Her mouth forms a firm line, and I can almost see the tears she's holding back. "You have, and you will. We need to stop before we're in too deep."

"We're already in too deep." God, the desperation I feel. The sheer panic that's racing through my veins. I'm watching her slip through my fingers, right in front of me, and it feels like death calling me.

"I can't," she says, but it comes out like a whimper. I see her lower lip tremble, the tears now cascading down her cheeks as she looks at me. Her eyes are so damn blue I could lose myself in them. My heart shatters for her. This time when I reach for her, she doesn't break away. She leans into my chest, wrapping her arms around me.

"I love you so goddamn much," she says. "And I'm fucking mad at our timing. Why couldn't we meet all those years ago when I was at the ranch? Why couldn't you come home from college and see me and let me see you? We could have bypassed all of this mess."

"I wasn't ready for you," I tell her, then kiss the top of her head. "And you weren't ready either. We both had so much healing to do that we wouldn't even have recognized each other if we'd met." I lean back, and she looks up into my eyes. "I know it's messy, but I think we met at the perfect time. Because Nina, I see you. I can see all the way to your soul, and there is no one I'd rather be with than you."

She looks to the side, sighing out a shaky breath. "I'm so torn."

"I know." I smooth the hair from her face, run my finger along her eyebrow, her cheekbone, her perfect little earlobes.

"I'm sick and tired of constantly worrying about what my family will think," she forces out, then huffs a laugh. "I mean, they already think I'm shit. They think I've done all these terrible things, but this time they'll be right." She looks at me. "Except, things with Jordy are different. We were once so close. She was the only person I could tell everything to, and when we lost that, I felt like I'd lost a piece of my soul. To have her back in my life…" Nina wipes at her eyes. "I can't do this to her. I can't even believe I did."

"We're over though," I say, the panic welling up in me again. This feels an awful lot like goodbye.

"It doesn't matter," Nina says. Her face crumples briefly, but she then regains her composure. "You're off limits. Once you became hers, you were never supposed to be mine."

"Nina." The tears fall from my eyes before I know they're there. She looks up, then places a gentle hand on my face. With the lightest of touches, she smooths away the tears, but more keep coming. "Please don't do this," I whisper. "It was supposed to be you. It was always supposed to be you."

"You'll survive this," she whispers. "So will I."

I watch her face, searching for something to hold on to, anything that tells me she doesn't mean what she's saying. It's not there. I can see her sadness, but I also see her resolve.

It's over.

I hang my head, my arms dropping slightly. She falls into me, and I immediately wrap my arms around her, not letting go. Once I let go, I'll lose her forever. As if she understands this, she remains in my embrace. I feel the shudder of her body, the sobs coursing their way through her, my own body shaking as I lose the woman I love. I close my eyes, breathing in the lilac scent of her hair, the sweet perfume of her skin, feel the weight of her body against mine for the very last time.

"You fucking whore."

We let go of each other at the same time, whipping around to face Jordy standing there with rage in her eyes, her lip upturned at the sight of us, tension racking her whole body.

"It was you? You're the bitch who's been fucking my fiancé?"

"I'm not your fiancé," I remind her, and she lands a glare on me.

"But you were, Brayden. And she," Jordy jerks her head in Nina's direction, "she's just been biding her time to steal the one thing that means anything to me. It wasn't enough to steal all our grandmother's money, she had to have my man too. Well, are you happy, bitch? Have you gotten everything you wanted? Or can I offer you anything else of mine to take from me?"

I grip Nina's shoulders as Jordy's blows land exactly where she wanted them to. I can feel it in the way Nina tenses, in the frozen air around us.

"That's enough, Jordy," I say through clenched teeth. "Those are lies, and you know it."

"Really Brayden? You want to talk to me about lies? How about telling me you love me while you're fucking my cousin?"

"You're causing a scene," I hiss at her, aware of the eyes that have pivoted in our direction. "We can all talk about this, but don't ruin Ethan and Claire's wedding over this."

She looks around, as if noticing for the first time the spotlight we have on us. She looks at Nina again.

"As far as I'm concerned, you can go to fucking hell," she hisses. "I never want to see your face or hear your name again."

At this, Nina wrenches from my grasp and runs through the forming crowd, disappearing from sight. Jordy spins on her heel and walks away in the opposite direction. I move to take off in Nina's direction, but I feel a firm hand on my bicep, giving me enough pause to look at who's holding me.

Dan Gallo, Jordy's dad. *Fuck.*

"Sir, with all due respect, let me go."

"Son, you lost my respect about five minutes ago."

This stops me, and I stay where I am, even when he drops my arm.

"You owe my daughter," he says.

"Sir, I've been owing your daughter our whole relationship, and I can't do it anymore. I know what I did was wrong, but I was drowning with Jordy. We both want different things, and we're still trying to make it work. But Sir, there's not enough there to hold the pieces together. She knows it, and I do too."

"I know."

I narrow my eyes at him, caught off guard. "You *know?*"

"It doesn't take a genius to see that you two were polar opposites. Hell, Lil and I have had so many discussions trying to figure out the puzzle of you two. I quickly realized it was because of the baby."

I look away. "I never meant to get your daughter pregnant."

"We didn't mean it either when Jordy was on the way. Luckily it worked out for us. Lil drives me crazy, and that woman has an opinion for everything. But she also comes from a deep place of hurt and at the end of the day, she needs to know someone is on her side." Dan gives me a meaningful look. "I'm afraid my daughter is a lot like her mother. Neither one of them had the kind of mother they needed, and they've looked for it in the men they love. Jordy needed that from you."

I close my eyes, feeling every ounce of my regret in a deep sigh. "I couldn't be that for her," I say softly.

"Then you never should have promised it." He looks in the direction where Jordy left. "You may not love her, but I know you care about her, and Brayden, you owe my daughter a conversation. It might not fix anything, but it will at least give her a chance to be heard, and maybe find some closure."

"But Nina…" I trail off, knowing that his niece is hardly his concern. That she hasn't been the concern of anyone in her family. But I'm surprised by the compassion I see in his eyes.

"Her mom is taking care of it."

"Are you sure? Because Poppy seems to make everything worse when it comes to Nina."

"I know," Dan admits. "I think there are a lot of conversations that need to be had for any kind of healing to take place."

I pause, then nod. This is probably the most Dan has ever said to me—or to anyone, that I can recall. But at this moment, I realize he probably knows more about the family than any of us.

"Thank you, Sir," I say. I start to reach out my hand to shake his, but falter when his hand remains at his side. "I'm sorry."

"I'm not the one who needs those words," he says.

I find Jordy in another corner of the ship, sitting on a chair and desperately trying to hide that she's crying. Curious glances turn her way, but not one person has offered to help. I want to ask what their problem is, if they find the tears of a grieving woman that entertaining. But I'm the asshole who made her cry.

This is my fault.

I take the seat closest to her, then scoot it even closer. She doesn't move away, but the way her crying stills lets me know she's aware of my presence. I reach for her hand, but she jerks it away.

"You don't get to touch me," she hisses. But she doesn't leave, either. I wait, staying at her side while she stares out at the ocean from where we sit. "You could have picked…" She stops herself, shaking her head with a sardonic laugh. "No, I guess it doesn't matter who you picked. It never should have happened."

"You're right," I say. "I should have done a lot of things differently."

"I just … I had plans," she says, her eyes filling with tears as she meets mine. "Before we met, I had all these damn plans for my life. I was going to go places, see the world, figure myself out before I settled into a career. College was just a pitstop while I summoned my courage to leave. Then we had that one night…" She looks up at the sky, as if cursing the heavens. "It wasn't supposed to be like this. I wasn't supposed to get pregnant. Not then, and not ever. I didn't even want to be a mother. But I fell in love with her, or at least the idea of her, only to have her yanked away. It shouldn't have been like this. What the fuck did I do to deserve this?"

"You didn't do anything," I tell her. I dare to lean forward to take her hand again. This time she lets me, clutching my hand as if I'm going to keep her from drowning. But I can't save her anymore. "And you would have been a wonderful mother."

"That's the thing, Brayden, I wouldn't have. Is it unfair to say I was relieved when it happened? I was devastated. But a small part of me felt like a huge amount of pressure had just left my shoulders. When they told me I couldn't have kids, well…" She looks at me now, her forehead furrowed in grief. "I was so sad for you. I loved how excited you were to become a father, and how sweet you took care of me." She squeezes my hand while I remain silent. There's so much I want to say, but right now, I know my role is to listen. "That's the thing about you, Bray. You were always so good to me. The way you visited so often, or sent me care packages to let me know you were thinking of me. How you'd rub my belly and talk to our little bean."

I smile at this, even if I feel the hole that's been torn in my heart since the day we lost our daughter.

"Then you asked me to marry you, and…" She looks away, a sob choking in her throat. I hold her hand tight, and she doesn't let go, even as her shoulders shake. My heart breaks for her in this moment, and for me too. Amidst the hard parts of our relationship, there were also a lot of good parts. I know I loved her, at least in some sense of the word. I could have even married her, had I not met a woman who showed me what I needed.

"I never should have asked you," I say softly. "Neither one of us was ready. We barely knew each other. We weren't even in love."

"I know," she says, looking at me a bit sadly. "But I was glad you did, and for a while, it was easy to believe you really loved me, and that I loved you." She takes her hand back and then folds herself into the chair. She always does this when she's uncomfortable—makes herself as small as possible like she can't take up space. I know damn well it has to do with how she was raised, how her mother made her believe that she had to be perfect to be worthy. Now we're having this conversation, admitting all the things our relationship lacked, and she's here making herself small.

"You deserve someone who believes you are the brightest part of their world," I tell her. She laughs, rolling her eyes at this.

"I don't think there's anyone in the world who has that kind of patience."

"You're not impossible to love," I say forcefully. "I know because I loved you. Maybe not the way I should have, but there are a lot of things about you that are easy to love, and it's time you actually believed that."

"If I were so easy to love, why is it hard for you now? If you hadn't found..." She stumbles over the words, then catches herself. "If you hadn't found her, could you have stayed with me?"

"I probably would have," I admit. "But not for the reasons you want me to. It would be to fulfill a duty, to keep the promise I made to you." I look her in the eyes, searching her dark iris for some truth. "Would you have been happy if I did?"

She's silent for a moment, breathing in and out as she doesn't break eye contact. Then her mouth forms a small smile.

"No," she says softly. She drops her head in her hands for a moment, then brushes her hair off her face. "Isn't that so odd? We were strangers when we found out I was pregnant. I didn't even know your last name. When you asked me to marry you, and then kept our engagement after we lost the baby, I knew you weren't the right person for me, and that I wasn't right for you. You're a family man, through and through. Me, I can't wait to escape my hometown, to see new places and try new things. Being with you tied me down. Even when you agreed to entertain the idea of New York, I knew it wasn't for you. I knew, and I held you to it anyway, because I wanted at least a portion of my dream, even if it meant making you give up yours." She sighs then, and starts to hug herself into a tighter ball. But it's like she sees herself, and she cautiously unfolds, sitting on the chair with her arms draped over each arm rest. She looks up at the ceiling and lets out a deep, audible breath—like she's releasing every single bit of grief from her soul.

"Damn, we needed this conversation," she says. She looks at me then, and her mouth twists slightly. "Don't get me wrong, you're a fucking asshole." She's grinning now, and I laugh out loud.

"Jordy, I never deserved you," I say.

She appraises me for a moment. "No. No, you didn't." She inhales, then lets it out. "But God, we had some fun, didn't we?"

"We did, and we grew a lot too."

She nods slowly. Then she gives me a hard look. "But of all people, why Nina? If you had to stray, which was such an asshole move, why did it have to be her?"

I don't have an easy answer for her, even though I know it.

You know when you walk outside and the air just feels right, the sun shining on your skin in a way that penetrates your soul and leaves you with goosebumps? How you'll inhale, and you're aware of every millimeter of expansion and how your whole body is taking in breath? How every person who crosses your path meets you with a smile, how the smallest gesture of witnessed kindness brings tears to your eyes? How it feels to wrap someone you care about in an all-engulfing hug, only to receive one in return?

This is how it felt when I first laid eyes on Nina, and how I knew I'd spend every day of my life saving her, because it felt like she was saving me.

"I can't explain it," I tell Jordy. "It was like everything inside me was calling out to her, without regard of timing or who it could hurt. I couldn't help but fall for her. I'm just sorry I didn't treat your heart with more care."

She looks away, and I know my words have scraped her tender heart. But I can't take them back, nor do I want to. I can't live a lie any longer.

"Do you love her?" she asks. She turns back to me, peering into my face for the answer. I nod, and she takes a sharp inhale. "Are you going to marry her?"

"Come on Jordy, you don't want to know this."

Because yes, I love her, and if she'll have me, I'd marry the fuck out of her. But the way she ran off, I'm not sure she's coming back.

"I'll understand if you hate me," I continue. "What I did to you is unforgivable, and you didn't deserve it. But Jordy, Nina loves you.

When you saw us together, she was telling me she couldn't be with me because she loves you too much."

Jordy huffs a laugh. "So much that she slept with you behind my back." She shakes her head, then glares at her hands. I watch as the anger falters, fading into sadness. "She was really breaking up with you?"

I nod. "She said you were the only person she could tell everything to, and that losing you was like losing a piece of her soul."

"She said that?" Jordy's face crumples. "Why was she with you then?"

"She didn't know at first. Neither of us knew about our mutual connection to you, and we fought it, especially after that family dinner."

"What the hell? It's been going on since then?"

"No. Yes. Not exactly." I shake my head. "We never acted on it until…" But I stop. She doesn't need the details, and she's not asking for them. "We couldn't have helped it if we tried, and lord, Jordy, we tried." I look at the ground. "But I guess it doesn't matter now, does it." I can't believe my whole life changed in an instant, and we're still stuck on this damn ship. We've missed most of the after party, but I could care less. I'm ready to go home and sleep this off.

I look at Jordy. "Can you find it in your heart to forgive her?"

She shakes her head no, but then falters. "I mean, I don't know. I loved her. I still love her. She was my first friend, and when we reconnected, it felt like old times. It's hard not to feel like she played me for a fool, or if I can even trust her when all she told me were lies."

"She's not a bad person," I say. Jordy starts to protest, but I stop her. "You have no idea what that girl's been through. Your whole family has pegged her as the villain, starting with a time when she needed all of you the most. She's been living with that weight ever since." I shake my head. "What we did was so wrong, but we also fell in love. As much as I want her back, I want the two of you to find your way back to each other. You're family."

She stands just as the ship reaches the dock. Everyone is starting to move toward the side of the boat. I stand too, and we face each other. If we'd stayed together, in a few short months, we'd be standing this way again, but with her in white. I can see the defeat in her eyes. The knowledge that what we had was over. The heartache of betrayal.

We did this to her. *I* did this to her.

"I'll think about it," she says. "Right now, I just need to be mad."

Chapter Thirty-Four

Nina

It's been weeks since the wedding. Weeks since I last saw Brayden, since I've re-blocked all his calls.

Weeks where I have spent every minute since craving his connection, yearning for his touch, wishing I could hear his voice tell me this will all work out in the end.

It's been weeks since Jordy's last words to me, even though I've texted her numerous times to express how sorry I am. I know no amount of apologies will ever get her to forgive me, because *I* wouldn't forgive me. Still, I keep trying. I even found out the amount of her non-refundable deposit she put on the wedding venue and sent her a check in the exact amount. The check was cashed. The letter of apology plus a plea to talk was sent back, "return to sender" in huge red letters on the re-sealed envelope.

I'm stuck in a shame spiral, but I refuse to dip into darkness or resort to isolation. During Claire's and Ethan's honeymoon to the Caribbean, Maren brought their son Finn over to help paint the walls of my house in vibrant colors. I even reserved one wall for free paint, and we all took turns making messy art with only our fingers and happy, gloppy hues of paint. When the happy couple returned, the three of us girls held cooking parties with wine for Claire and me, and sparkling water with a splash of tonic for Maren. We watched all the cult classics on my grandma's old DVD player, though I hid the one of *Practical Magic*.

I'm not sure I'll ever be able to watch that movie again.

The brightest spot of the past few weeks is the perfect building Mac found for my new shop. I purchased it in a hurry, and the business license is currently in process. I named it Polka Dots after Nanna Dot, because it's her money that's made this possible. Now I get to improve the space on my own, since Jordy is no longer speaking to me.

Which is why I'm here past 10 p.m., with a bottle of wine, a Bluetooth speaker playing my favorite music, and a paint roller. I went with yellow since it makes me so happy. Never mind that it was the color of the dress I was wearing the night my life went to hell; I'm taking it back and painting the walls around me with it.

Painting is kind of like meditation, and I lose myself in the broad strokes and careful edging. I'm so lost in the project, I nearly leap out of my skin when I hear the light knocking on the glass door. Fumbling with the paint roller, I look toward the door to see my mom standing there, a bag of food in her hand.

The only reason I'm letting her in is because I'm starving.

"What do you want?" I ask as I open the door. "How did you know I was here?"

"I'm not supposed to tell you," she says, which I understand to mean that Jordy told her. She's the only one in the family I've told through my unanswered texts. At least she's reading them.

"How is Jordy?" I ask, and my mom shakes her head as if she

won't tell me. But then she leans forward, as if to keep what she's about to say secret from the hundreds of people around us in this empty space.

"Not so high and mighty anymore," she says, almost gleefully.

My mom is an awful gossip. Both she and Aunt Lil are. So it's not surprising she finds amusement in this situation. In the past, I've glommed onto this, feeling a sense of connection when she shares gossip with me. But this time, I recognize the sickness in it, the way it's a source of power for her—an ugly one at that.

"Mom, she just found out her whole relationship is a lie. That's hardly something to feel happy about."

My mom looks shocked for a moment, then narrows her eyes. "That's rich, coming from you. You're actually correcting my behavior when you're the harlot who stole her fiancé?"

I pause for a moment, taking in the words she's spitting at me. They just don't have the same impact. I've beat myself up over this for weeks. For months! I'm so damn tired. I can't take back what I did, and I know it was wrong, but my mom has been calling me these names since long before they were true, and frankly, it's just getting tiresome.

I tilt my head at her, offering a look of confusion on my face. "Harlot? Is that one of those old-timey words?"

She bites her lip, and I think she's going to be mad. But then I realize she's fighting a laugh. Finally she loses it, and all I can do is watch with bewilderment as she is practically crying from laughing so hard.

"Oh honey, I needed that." She wipes at her eyes, still laughing. "That's what your grandmother used to call me. I hated that word because of the way it made me feel. I can't even believe I used it now. God, I sound just like her." She sighs out a breath. "I'm sorry, I came over here to find out how you're doing after all that drama."

"Drama. That's what we're calling it?" I ask. "Mom, I slept with

Jordy's fiancé. We were getting ready to make it official. But Jordy found out before we were ready, and now I've lost everyone. So how am I doing? I'm doing pretty awful. I'm alone in that old house, I've lost the last person in this family who cared about me, and I have no one to blame but myself. So, things aren't that great right now."

"Jordy and Brayden weren't going to last," my mom breezes out. "Those two were night and day. They couldn't have been more different."

"That's not the point, Mom." Then I pause. "Wait, why are you even defending me? Just a second ago, you were calling me a harlot. Now you're acting like she deserved it."

"I guess, I…" She trails off. "I just realized…" She stops again. "Look, your Uncle Dan had some words for both Lil and me after the whole wedding. We all saw what happened, and how it affected both of you. When he found out that I didn't talk to you after Jordy found out … well, you know … he told me I was an awful mother. I tried to argue with him, but I've had some time to think, and I realized that I could have done a few things better."

"That's an understatement," I mutter.

"The point is," she says, ignoring me, "you're right that you shouldn't have slept with Jordy's fiancé, but you're hardly the worst person in the world because of it. Hell, how do you think I got your father?"

"You stole Dad from another woman?" This is the first time I'm hearing this story, and I'm floored.

"Well, he was with Kitty Majors, who was seriously the most annoying person in our class. I did him a favor by dodging that bullet."

"Mom, that's terrible," I say, but I'm also laughing. It's not quite as bad as carrying on a relationship with my cousin's fiancé, but it does soften my shame about it. Then I recall the earlier part of our conversation. "Nanna Dot called you a harlot?"

"Oh lord, she called me worse. Honestly, that woman's sole purpose was to make my sister's and my life miserable. She couldn't be happy, so she made sure we weren't either. Oh, here," she remembers the bag she brought and pushes it toward me. "I picked up some burgers on the way because that's all that's open right now."

I peer in the bag and see two greasy burgers and two orders of French fries from Sonic. I know they serve salads too, so the fact that she ordered the burgers instead is a shock.

"Who are you, and what have you done with my mother?"

"I know," she groans. "But I've been meaning to check on you since Dan read both Lil and me the riot act, and figured these made a better peace offering than health food."

"This is not like you," I say, but I dig in anyways. One thing these past couple weeks have taught me is that I am my own best advocate, and I know what's best for me. Including food. I will never be good enough in my mother's eyes, so why am I trying so hard? Why try with any of them? I can eat what I want, especially if it makes me happy.

That said, this burger is the first junk food I've had in weeks. In my efforts to avoid slipping into that deep dark place, I've been reaching for healthier meals, and even taking walks and practicing yoga. I figured I could fight the doldrums by taking care of my body. I have no idea what I weigh, though, nor do I care. I threw my scale out last week, and I'll be damned if I bring another into my house.

But right now, after weeks of balanced meals, this burger tastes like heaven. "Damn," I say after another mouthful.

My mom, with her own burger, nods in agreement. "I get why you eat this crap all the time."

"About that," I say, setting my burger down and grabbing a napkin. "I need you to stop commenting on my food."

"But I—"

"No, Mom. I'm twenty-seven years old, and I've been affected by your comments for almost all of them. It needs to stop. You don't get to say anything if I eat junk food, and you don't get to comment if I'm eating healthy. You also don't get to talk about my body, good or bad. It's none of your business what I eat, or how much space I take up. So please stop."

My mom is quiet for a moment, then closes her eyes and sighs. "Damn it," she mutters, then she looks at me. "I don't know why I didn't see this before. I am so sorry." There's a look on her face that seems both faraway and ashamed, and I realize something I never saw before, either.

"Did Nanna Dot tell you that you were fat?"

"Fat, lazy, stupid. You name it. There was one summer that I ate only one meal a day and got down to eighty-nine pounds. I was practically bones, but she pinched the loose skin at my hips and told me she'd never marry me off since I was so fat."

My mouth drops at this. I try to reconcile my mom's description with the Nanna Dot I knew. My grandmother was plump and matronly, full of smiles and always ready with warm cookies. She listened to me for hours when I cried about boys, or friends, and especially about my mom. She was always on my side, and would tell me that my mother had no clue how to raise a daughter the right way.

I thought I was lucky to have her, someone who listened and understood how cruel my mother was—and my mother *was* cruel. But never once did my grandmother defend her, or say anything nice about my mom at all.

The pieces start shifting into place.

"Mom, tell me about your childhood."

So she does. What she describes is so eerily similar to mine, but so much worse because she didn't have a father who evened things out, and her mother seemed to have no warmth for her daughters at all. They'd been left a lot of money to survive when my grandfather died, but it was at a time when women didn't have the same rights as men. My mom spoke of Nanna Dot with some compassion, recognizing how hard it must have been to raise two girls when she couldn't even get a credit card in her name. But also, my grandmother rode my mom and Aunt Lil hard, making them feel like they were never good enough. In return, they had daughters they raised with the lessons they learned.

The cycle continued.

"The nail in the coffin was my mother's inheritance," my mom says, and I feel something strange in my chest.

"Mom, I never told Nanna Dot to make me her sole heir. I didn't even know I was named in her will. I never thought she would die, so I didn't think of her inheritance. But I assumed everything was going to you and Aunt Lil. When I was named heir of her estate and fortune, it was just as much of a surprise as it was to you."

"I know," my mom says.

"Wait, you knew?" I'm suddenly filled with so much heat, so much anger. "You ran my name through the mud. You told everyone that I stole our family money by manipulating an old woman. But you knew why I was there and wouldn't even acknowledge your part in that!" I clench my fists, the rage coursing through me as years of unnecessary hurt roll through my mind. "I moved in with Nanna at your suggestion because you didn't know how to handle a rape victim." My mom flinches at the word. "That's right, Mom. Rape. I was raped. I did not spread my legs for those guys, they forced them open. Then, one by one, they forced themselves on me. I was not a whore for what happened. I was a victim."

"Nina, please." She reaches forward and clutches my hands. I try to wrench them free, but she holds tight.

"You made me feel like I was worthless," I scream, but now I'm crying. "Then you shipped me off to Nanna Dot's like I was ruined goods, like you couldn't even look at me anymore. You made me keep it a secret from everyone else, as if what happened to me was catching. I felt ashamed and rejected, and ever since then, you have rubbed my face in it. You've told me I'm worthless. You've made me feel disgustingly huge and incredibly small. You... You... You..." I sob and she pulls me forward into her arms. I resist for just a moment. But it's almost like Nanna Dot is there, her plump arms wrapping around me, smoothing my hair, telling me I'm perfect the way I am. Except it's my mother's slim arms around me. It's her hand that smooths my hair, and her voice that tells me I'm perfect, that she's sorry she ever said anything less, and that she promises to be a better mother.

I cry, letting my mother comfort me, the conflict swinging through me like a goddamn pendulum. I'm comforted by her. I'm so angry with her. I don't know how to feel.

Eventually my sobs ebb, and I pull away to wipe my face.

"There's no excuse," my mother says. "I didn't have the tools, and I was so angry about what happened, and I just... I handled it in the worst way possible. I'm so sorry, Nina."

"I don't know what to say. I can't trust you," I say.

"I can understand that," my mom says. "I wouldn't trust me either. I think I didn't realize what I was doing to you until this very moment. Rather, I did, but I didn't know how to turn it off. It's like I got into this horrible habit with you, unsure how to handle you and what you went through. I knew it wasn't your fault, and yet..." She shakes her head, wipes her eyes. "Fuck," she breathes, and I'm momentarily shocked by her profanity. My mother never swears. "I'm just like her, aren't I?"

"I don't know," I say, because I don't.

She looks around at the place then, her expression one of discomfort. "Polka Dots, huh?"

I know she's trying to escape what she did to me by changing the subject, but I'm starting to realize I didn't know everything about my grandmother. The way my mother raised me, it came from what she knew. The fact that it was Nanna Dot who taught this to her...

I'm having a hard time reconciling it. The grandmother I knew was loving and compassionate. She listened to me, and brought me back to feeling human after what those guys did to me. But she was also horrible to my mother and Aunt Lil, who in turn, were horrible to Jordy and me.

In this, I can find a seed of compassion for my mom, knowing that she's experienced what I have. Maybe she didn't know any better.

Maybe Nanna Dot chose to compensate for her past mothering by being the exact guardian I needed in a time when I had no one.

"I figured since I bought this with Nanna Dot's money," I say, then wince as I realize how that sounds. "I mean, it shouldn't have been all mine. That was a really crappy thing for your mom to do to you and Aunt Lil."

"It's why she did it," my mom muses. She shakes her head, a small, sad smile on her face. "She wrote my sister and me out of the will. That was a message. But she put a period on it by naming only one of our daughters as heir. I think she figured we'd hate each other just as much as we hated her."

"Did you?" I ask.

"At first, but...."

"But the blame was put on me, giving you all a common enemy." I sigh, still so angry, but also just tired. "That was pretty shitty."

My mom nods in agreement. "I'll ask your forgiveness, but I'll understand if you don't give it."

I think of Jordy then, who's harboring a grudge against me, and has every right to. Yet, I'm hoping time will soften her heart and help us one day rekindle the trust and closeness we once had.

"I need more than words, Mom. I need action. I need a relationship with you. I need you to get to know me again, and I want to get to know you. So I'm willing to try."

She folds me in her arms again, and this time, I know it's all her. How lucky we are to get this chance to start over, because she never got that with her mother. Even though we have such a long way to go, I can't help but believe we'll get there—that the potential is there.

"I love you, Bug," she says, kissing the top of my head.

"I know," I say. I love her too. I'm just not ready to say it yet.

Chapter Thirty-Five

Nina

A week later, I'm at Insomniacs again, nervously tapping my feet and checking my phone every thirty seconds. It seems this place is becoming quite the setting for strained conversations, as I watch the door for Jordy's arrival.

She'd texted me back a few days ago, no doubt at my mom's prompting. I haven't talked to my mom since she showed up at Polka Dot's, though she's sent me links to articles about clothing store pop-ups and fashion ideas. It's her way of connecting, I realize. But I have nothing to base my assumption on Jordy breaking her silence except that the timing is coincidental.

Jordy finally does show up, finding me after a quick sweep of the shop. She doesn't smile, even when her eyes land on the drink I've set in her place. An almond milk latte, no sugar. Her favorite.

"I'm not sure why I'm even here," she says as she sits. Her voice is mechanic and cold, her posture like a cement wall. There are slight circles under her eyes, and I feel a sting of that familiar shame knowing I'm the one who did that. "I suppose I should thank you for the money you sent."

"It was the least I could do," I say, my eyes on the table.

"No, the least you could have done was stay away from my fiancé," she hisses.

"I'm so sorry." I keep my eyes down. I know there is nothing I can say that will fix any of this, and yet, I'm grateful she even came, even if it's just to tell me how awful I am.

She sighs, and the space between us fills with awkward silence. I wait it out, knowing it's not my place to speak.

"I think what hurts me the most is that this was all happening while we lived under the same roof. I shared something private with you, and the whole time, you were sleeping with Brayden. You both played me for a fool. I trusted both of you, and both of you were laughing at me."

"We were not laughing at you," I say, but she cuts me off with a glare.

"The fact that I had no idea," she says, shaking her head. "I can't believe I didn't see it." She laughs. "Then I send you two off to that stupid conference. I fucking hate that conference, and I actually felt bad that I roped you into going. Little did I know, I was giving the two of you a free pass to fuck around on me."

"Jordy, I'm sorry."

"Are you though? Or are you just sorry you lost both of us?"

"I'm sorry for hurting you," I say firmly. "You're everything to me, and I didn't treat you that way at all. I let my own nee... I let my own wants become more important than our friendship, and for that, I am so ashamed. To know I betrayed you this horribly, I can't even live with myself. I know there's nothing I can say or do to make you forgive me, but I will try every day, regardless. I will do anything. I'll give you my house, let you decorate it any way you want. I'll buy a billboard with my face on it, telling all of Sunset Bay what I did."

"Nina, come on."

"I will never talk with Brayden again," I continue. "I've already blocked his number, and I won't contact him. If you are able to work things out with him, I will be your hugest supporter. Even if you leave him in your dust, I still won't talk with him."

"Do you love him?"

I should say no. Instead, I pause, my mouth open, and the word right there but not coming out.

"Nina, do you love Brayden?" she repeats. Tears spring to my eyes, because of course I love him. I am dying without him. I miss him so bad, I can barely sleep. I'm just existing without him, not knowing what he's doing or where he's at or how I can keep going like this. Because this is torture, and I deserve every second of it.

"I'll give him up forever," I finally whisper.

Jordy sighs, looks up at the ceiling. She leans back in her chair, crossing her legs as she regards me.

"We'd known each other about a month when I found out I was pregnant," Jordy says. "I don't know if Brayden told you any of this, but we were strangers who were thrown together by this sudden development. I wasn't planning on having kids, but there I was, suddenly faced with having a baby with someone I hardly knew. He doesn't know it, but I overheard his father lecturing him on doing right by me. We were in the hospital, right after his dad's heart attack. We'd just learned his dad would never walk again from the fall from that horse, and Bray didn't know if his dad was going to die or not. We'd just found out about the baby, and his dad told him to marry me. So Brayden asked for my hand, because at that point, he'd do anything his dad asked him to do. You see, that's Brayden. He lives his life saving everyone else. Ever since he lost his sister, he's been making amends for it by saving the world. He did it with me by putting a ring on my finger, and then sticking to that promise after we lost our daughter. At least that was his intention, because that ring also became a noose."

She looks at her bare finger now, a sad smile on her lips. "Neither one of us wanted to get married," she finally admits. "I think we *wanted* to want that, but who drags their engagement on for five years except those who are avoiding their vows?" She looks at me, and this time it's with less contempt. "I think I knew our relationship was on the rocks when you two went to that conference, but only because I was glad he was away. We barely spent time together, and yet the greater distance between us gave me relief. It's why I reserved the venue and set a date. I felt like I could maybe make myself want to marry him if I just moved forward." She looks away, her hand resting on her cheek. "He broke up with me the night you two came back," she says. "It caught me off guard, especially when he told me he'd cheated on me. It was so unlike him, but also, I realized it was the first time I'd seen him do something for himself. Granted, I wouldn't have chosen an affair as his thing. But it was the first time he took a stand against my plans and my way of moving us in the direction I wanted to go. And what did I do? I made him pretend we were still together, like an absolute maniac."

"You had reasons," I say.

"Yeah, great reason. I couldn't let go because it was a blow to my ego." She flexes her hands on the table, huffing a laugh.

"Maybe," I say. "Or maybe because your mom would have made you feel worse for something that wasn't your fault."

She looks at me then, and a moment of appreciation crosses her expression. It's just a moment, but it happens. "Maybe," she agrees. "But it was mostly for me." She takes a deep breath, then lets it out. "I never should have said yes when Brayden proposed. I didn't know him, and I definitely did not love him. I also knew he was asking for all the wrong reasons. When we lost the baby, I gave him a chance to break things off, even though I'd overheard him telling his father he'd stay with me. I gave him the chance, asking if he still wanted to marry me. But in that moment, I also felt this desperation that we went through all that loss for nothing. So, even though I didn't love him and I pretty much knew he didn't love me, I wanted to hold on to him, just to prove that it happened for a reason." She runs her hand through her hair, letting out a rush of air. "We grew to love each other, or maybe we were just comfortable. But it wasn't enough to make a marriage." She looks at me, then grimaces. "I should be more pissed than I am. I should hate you forever and just write you off completely. Both of you. I should wish you both dead. But the thing is, I don't."

She wraps her hands around her coffee, biting her lip. I remain silent, barely breathing at this admission.

"There are things I wanted in life," she continues. "Before I met Brayden, I had plans. When Brayden and I got engaged, those plans died, or maybe they were just put on pause. When Brayden broke things off with me, I was sad, but there was also a bit of relief. I hung on to him because that's what I knew. But a small part of me saw the opportunity to go after those dreams I had before we met."

She studies me then, tilting her head and narrowing her eyes—but not with anger. It's more curious. "He loves you," she says, and I let out an involuntary gasp at the words, feeling like she's taken a needle and punctured the huge ball of stress that's been resting on my heart. "He also told me you broke things off with him because of me. But the thing is, I can't stop you from being with the man you love. If I did that, it's no better than…" She breaks off, shakes her head. "I won't stand in the way of you two finding happiness with each other. I've already done this long enough with Brayden, and I won't do it to you. If you love him, you need to tell him."

"I can't," I say, even though every bone is ready to do just that.

"If there's even a chance of you forgiving me, I won't ruin it for a man."

"This isn't just a man," Jordy says, a soft smile on her face. "This is Brayden Winters, a man who will bring you the moon if you just ask him to, who will spend his life making you happy, who is good and generous and would have made a great husband if he were actually in love with me." Her forehead crinkles, her eyes bordering on warm as she regards me. "But he's in love with you, and he will be all those things for you if you'll have him."

"What about us, though? Because you are the person who means most to me in this world. I can't lose you."

"You haven't lost me," she says. "But I need time to think things over and to heal, and you should too. We both have a lot to overcome when it comes to family, and I think all of us could learn a little bit about loyalty."

She's right, of course, and I suddenly feel so much lighter. There's hope for us. I know there is.

"Can I at least give you the house?" I ask. She laughs.

"No, I don't want Nanna's house," she says. "Besides, it would just go to waste while I'm traveling. It's time I got started on those plans."

"You're leaving? Where are you going?"

"To Europe," she says. "Italy, Barcelona, France. I thought I'd see the world for a bit before I settle down. By the way, I received some strange paperwork in the mail. Something about being a silent partner in Polka Dot's?"

"Don't get too excited," I say. "The store isn't even off the ground yet, and I'm still not sure it will make any money. But I've made you, my mom, and Aunt Lil equal partners with me, all of us getting 25% of the proceeds. It's kind of my way of making amends for Nanna Dot not including any of you in the will." I tell her briefly what my mom told me. What I don't tell her is that I'm also in the process of splitting the rest of Nanna's money between the four of us, setting up an investment fund in each of our names to do with as we please.

As for the house, if Jordy won't take it, I'll sell it. As much as I love my Nanna Dot, it's time for all of us to move on.

The next day, I wash and blow dry my hair, taking extra care with the platinum locks. I consider dyeing it again, but the platinum is growing on me. I do my makeup, then spritz on a light layer of lilac perfume. I put on a pair of jeans and my walking shoes, along with a t-shirt and sweatshirt. Nothing fancy because I have a long walk ahead of me.

I get in my car, that old Cadillac that still smells like my grandmother from time to time. I realize maybe it's time to find something new, something more me. Am I more of a sports car kind of girl? Or maybe a truck? All I know is that I'm ready to take life by the reins and keep riding.

I drive until I reach a dirt road next to a large swath of land that separates me from the ocean. Leaving the car, I navigate through the narrow pathway until I reach the sand. I'm not much of an athlete, but I still break into a light jog, feeling the energy flow through me as if it's a gift. I get winded, but keep going, motivated to reach the end of the beach. I can see it now, bobbing up and down as I run, getting closer with each step.

It's ages when I finally get there, and I collapse in the sand. There are the remnants of a past fire, maybe days old. The sky is deep blue, with scattered puffs of clouds. A pelican dives into the water, and the crashing waves are a balm to my soul.

My phone is in my shaky hands as I take a picture, then open up my texts. I send it and start typing.

I'm ready to talk. Meet me here.

Chapter Thirty-Six

Brayden

Nina: I'm ready to talk. Meet me here.

I've barely read Nina's text, or seen the picture of the crashing waves, before I jump up.

"What's going on?" my mom asks, sitting next to my dad at the table across from where I was, our lunch spread out between us. I look to both of them, then to Hazel, who'd been sitting next to me.

"I have to go," I say, hardly believing what's happening.

"What is it? Is it one of the guys?" Hazel asks. "Is it…" She pauses, then mouths, "Nina?" I nod, and her grin tells me everything I need to know.

"I'm going to get my girl," I say, yanking my boots on before running from the room. In my wake, I hear Hazel's excited whisper, Nina's name on her breath.

Sara is waiting for me in the stable, her eyes watching for me almost as if she knows. Next to her, Meredith knickers, poking her own head out to see what the commotion is.

"Not this time, Mere," I say. "But soon. You're going to get a lot of rides in, I promise."

I saddle Sara quickly, then fit one boot in the stirrup before swinging my leg over. I nudge her hind, and she's off. Can she hear the song of my soul, calling out for Nina? Can she feel my heart beating as she runs towards the woman I love?

We reach the trail, and Sara navigates it like a pro. Soon we're on the beach, flying down the sand as the waves crash next to us. My hat flies off my head, but I don't care. All I see is the end of the beach and a small figure standing against the solid rock cliff that looms above her. We keep going, me kicking Sara to run faster and faster, until we're finally there, and I slow her to a halt. She's barely stopped before I jump off and tie her up, then I land on Nina with a crash. I know there's so much to say. I can't even think that she might want differently, and am relieved when her mouth crushes against mine, our arms grasping each other, my body engulfing her as if I can bring her inside me just to get closer.

"I love you," I whisper in between kisses.

"I love you too," she murmurs back, her lips never leaving mine. Her face is wet from tears. Mine or hers, I don't know. All I know is I can breathe again now that this woman is in my arms, and I am never letting her go.

We finally catch our breath, sinking onto the sand. It's taking everything in me to not rip her clothes off and take her right here. But I restrain myself. I can't seem to let go of her hand, though, and my other hand can't leave the firm grip it has on her thigh. She's not going anywhere, but I still hold on to her as if she might fall through the earth. I can't lose her.

I look at the stretch of beach I just rode down, and I realize she doesn't have a horse. It dawns on me the lengths she went through to get here.

"It only took an hour or so," she says, though her cheeks are still pink. It took me fifteen minutes to get here, so I know she's still catching her breath.

"I have water in the saddle," I say, grateful I'd thought to add it at last minute. She nods, and I snag it for her. But then I'm right back to holding her, even as she drinks. "I don't ever want to know what it's like to lose you again," I say.

"Me either," she whispers. "Jordy came to see me yesterday, and while she's still mad, I guess you could say she gave us her blessing."

I shake my head. That woman is full of surprises. "I hope one day we can all be friends again."

"I want that more than anything," she says. I look down at her. "Anything?"

"Well..." She slips on a sly smile. "I guess I can think of a few things I want more."

"How about my ring on your finger."

Her smile falters slightly, but her eyes are shining.

"I won't ask you yet," I continue. "But you're the one I want to marry. I want to spend every morning waking up to you and every night making love. My life is yours, if you'll have me."

She tilts her head. "How about you try on how it feels to *not* be engaged for a while."

I laugh, a low rumble deep in my chest as I pull her closer. I smell her hair, mixed in with the ocean air, as we both watch the waves roll in and out. I can feel every breath she takes and the rhythm of her heart as she trusts her full weight against me. I wrap my arms around her, resting my head on her shoulder, closing my eyes as I memorize this moment. It hardly feels real, and yet, it also seems like I never existed before I met her.

Nina. Her name runs through my veins.

"So, while you were ignoring my calls," I say, and she laughs, nudging me, "what have you been doing?"

She tells me about the new shop she's created, and how she's letting it help her split the inheritance money. She also tells me about the investment funds she's in the process of creating, making things far more equal. Even split four ways, all of them will be very wealthy thanks to her Nanna Dot's smart handling of money and investments.

"And I've decided to sell the house. I thought I'd find something a little more modest that's suitable for one person, instead of this huge monstrosity that is just a graveyard for all of Nanna's stuff."

"Or I have a better idea," I say. "Sell the house and move in with me."

"Into your parents' home? No thank you."

"No, we have a house on the property that just needs a little fixing up. But it's livable. We could move in there and fix it up together, making it both of ours."

She tilts her head, her eyes narrowed even as she smiles. "There's no way your parents will go for that. They wouldn't even let Jordy live there."

"They won't say no," I tell her, because I know it's true. "But if they do, I'll convince them to agree."

There's excitement in her eyes, but she gives me a noncommittal "maybe."

Yeah, we'll see about that.

We ride back to the ranch, Nina sitting in front of me. I walk Sara just to make it last longer, reveling in how it feels to have Nina's ass pressed up against my cock. Hey, I love this woman, but her ass is easily my favorite physical part of hers. I will celebrate that ass every day she lets me.

My parents are on the porch when we ride through the gates, and Hazel is sitting on the steps. I'm no fool, I know they're waiting for us. I wave, and Nina lifts her hand shyly. I know she's feeling ashamed, knowing that just a few weeks ago, Jordy was here. But surely she sees the grin on my mom's face, and even the softened expression my dad is offering.

"Mom, Dad, Hazel, I'd like you to meet my…" I pause, twisting my body so that I'm looking at Nina. "Can I call you my girlfriend?" She bites back a laugh, then nods. "I'd like you to meet my girlfriend, Nina Chance."

"Well, pleasure to have you," my dad says in his gruff voice. My mom looks at him with surprise, then pride. She gets up as Nina climbs off the horse, and I follow, then she throws her arms around my girl.

"We couldn't be happier," she says, and I note the tear caught in her throat. She pulls away, keeping her hands on Nina's shoulders. "Now that you're here, I hope you're around to stay. My son has been an absolute pain in the ass while you've been gone."

"Mom," I warn.

"It's true, Bear," Hazel says, joining my mom. "You've been a huge downer." I push her shoulder lightly, and she exaggerates a stumble backwards. Then, with a grin, she leans toward Nina for a hug. "I'm so glad it's you," she whispers.

"Hazel, what do you say you, me, and Dad go out for ice cream," my mom asks. Hazel is turning eighteen in a few weeks, and yet I see the gap-toothed five-year-old she used to be when she jumps up, clapping her hands.

"I'll go get my coat!" she yells, running back for the house.

We wait until they're gone before we head into the house. I hold Nina's hand, her skin soft against the roughness of my own. Everything about her is delicate, so absolutely perfect, and I have to keep looking at her to make sure she's real.

"What?" she laughs when she catches me staring again.

"I just can't get over that you're here. Just a few hours ago, I believed I'd never see you again. But now, here you are, and I can't stop looking at you." I close the space between us, tilting her head back with my hands in her hair as I touch my lips to hers. "I love you so much."

"I love you," she says. "I can't believe I actually thought I could live without you. I am never letting you go."

"Then move in with me," I say. "Don't think about what you should do, or what others will think, because I know that's what's rolling around in your pretty little head. Just be with me, every day. Stay here on the ranch. You can work here if you want, or spend all your time at the shop, or I don't even care what, I'll support you. I just want you here every night and every morning, and every other minute you'll give to me."

"Okay," she whispers. I kiss her again, this time a little deeper. She offers a slight moan in the back of her throat, which goes straight to my head, making me feel spun.

"I think we're going to have to christen this moment," I murmur.

"In our new home?" she asks, looking up at me. I laugh, then shake my head no.

"In due time. I may have oversold it a bit. We should probably put a little work into it before we take the plunge."

"Well, we'll just have to jump on that if you want me to move in so bad."

"I can get it livable by next week," I promise, knowing I'll be working on it day in and day out to make that happen. But it's worth it. "In the meantime, we have an empty house, and I have an empty bed just waiting to meet you."

"Oh really," she laughs. I take her hand and lead her up the stairs. My family's photos line the walls, ones I used to avoid looking at because Amber is in so many of them. But lately, I've made it a practice to study them, to see those twin smiles from all those years ago. I'm coming to peace with what happened, and even the realization that it wasn't my fault. Not in the way I've been carrying it.

Life is full of ups and downs, celebrations and tragedies, love and loss. I've had my fair share of all of them, most humans have. But my role is not to be some martyr, saving others at my expense. My role is to move through the hard times to get to the good, and to honor the things I've experienced and the people I've loved along the way.

We get to my room, and Nina turns once she reaches the bed. She offers a shy smile, as I lean against the doorway and watch her. With slow, careful fingers, she lifts her t-shirt, showing off the lacy bra underneath, making me suck in a hard rush of air. She unbuttons her jeans, slides them down her gorgeous hips, leaning over to offer me a full view of her cleavage. She stands again, clad in nothing but her matching panties and bra, waiting to see what I do next.

There's no question. I close the bedroom door and lock it, just in case we're in here longer than it takes to finish an ice cream. I tear off my shirt, and her eyes land on my chest, then my abs.

"Fuck, I've missed you," she says, dropping to her knees to help me with my belt. I tug her back to standing, then gently push so that she falls on the bed.

"You'll have plenty of time for that later," I promise her. "Right now, I just need to feel your body under mine while I'm buried in you."

"Then hurry up, Winters."

I don't need to be told twice. My belt comes off, then my jeans, then everything else until I'm covering her body, nothing between us. She grips my cock, her tiny hand so strong as she slides up and down, nearly bringing me to completion before we've even started.

"Easy there, Sugar," I say. "It's been a while, and I'm afraid this might be quicker than usual, especially if you keep stroking me like that."

She gives a few more tugs, a wicked grin on her face as I groan, then grip her wrist. "Enough," I growl, but there's a grin on my face. I reach around her, unclasping her bra and sliding it down until her beautiful breasts are in full view. Holy fuck, she has such perfect breasts. I can't help but take one nipple between my lips, my hand cupping the other one as she squirms below me. Her skin is so sweet, so very tender, like my favorite dessert. I could inhale her, she's so delicious.

My hand finds the hem of her panties, and I slide them down her hips, pausing as my mouth grazes her luscious mound. She spreads for me, and I dip my tongue into her juices, lapping up that sweet nectar, savoring every taste of her.

"Don't make me come," she begs, tugging at my hair. "I want you to, but like you, I need you inside me. Please."

I don't make her beg anymore. I crawl over her body, then nudge my cock at her entrance. Before I enter, I look at just how beautiful we are together. Her glistening sex, swollen and pink, ready for me to penetrate. Then I do, sliding in, both of us breathing out a simultaneous sigh of relief. It's like coming home, and I move slow to savor every moment of it. I hold her body close, kissing her gently as she rocks against my groin. Knowing I'll soon have her every night has me nearing climax, and I have to cool my jets to regain control.

"Hold on," I say, stilling above her. She wiggles her hips, and I growl in reproach.

"Bray, we can do it again. Please, just fuck me."

I look at her, the way her hair falls around her like snow. Her swollen, rosy lips. The flush in her cheeks. The slight smattering of freckles that are barely noticeable across her nose. The love radiating from her eyes. I get this woman forever.

I slam into her, and she arches against me, meeting me pound for pound. I hope to God my family stays away, because neither one of us are quiet as we release every ounce of tension we've experienced all this time apart. I feel her clench around me, and I hold on as hard as I can until I feel her pulse, her head tilted back, her cries soft and helpless as I climax with her.

Once we've stilled, our bodies slick with sweat and juices, I lie next to her, tracing lazy circles on her belly. I marvel at her skin, how soft she feels. My finger travels up her side, then to her breast, and the way she arches at my touch has my cock responding. We offer no words, just quiet marveling as my hands explore her, and she explores me right back. I want to memorize her every curve, every sound she makes, the taste of her. I cup her face, my lips pressing against hers softly. She responds with the gentlest flick of her tongue, and I swear, it's like we never even fucked, because soon I'm inside her again, where I could live every day of my life.

I make a vow to move us into that house—come hell or high water—by the weekend.

Chapter Thirty-Seven

Jordy

Three months later.

At this moment, I am sitting at a little café, listening to a young girl speak in Italian to her mother, but only catching every other word. She's so passionate about whatever they're speaking about that I am completely engrossed, even if I pretend it's the book in front of me that has my attention.

I think they're talking about the gelato. At least, that's what *I'm* passionate about. I spoon a bit into my mouth, closing my eyes as if I'm experiencing the perfect orgasm. Let me tell you, it's better than any orgasm I've ever had. So good that this is my third gelato today.

You know that book where the divorcee eats her way through Italy on her self-exploration retreat around the world? This is me now, eating my way through Italy, and loving every second of it.

If my mother could see me now, she'd blow a gasket. Especially when she finds out I've gone up a size to accommodate my food adventure. My God is it worth it.

It's been almost two months since I left the states. I started in Spain, exploring the Gothic Quarter, seeing Barcelona from a cable car, and losing my inhibitions while dancing the night away in darkly lit nightclubs. Now I'm here in Italy, where I've slept in late every morning, perused numerous art galleries, enjoyed lazy afternoons floating in a gondola, and indulged in eating. So much eating.

My mom would also be horrified at how utterly uncultured I am most days. I've also watched American movies in the theater and visited touristy dive bars, just to feel a bit of America while I'm away. All normal stuff I never really enjoyed at home, and I love it.

Maybe, like that book, I'll find love in one of these places—or maybe I won't. It's definitely not my main objective. For the first time in my life, I'm living life by my rules, with no one to tell me I can't.

I think about Brayden now and then. Sometimes I'm sad, but mostly I'm fine. I realize that wasn't the life for us. I couldn't take him away from the ranch, and I was a fool to think I could, or even should. Just like he couldn't take me away from the city. I'm already looking at real estate ads, thinking of buying a New York loft when I'm ready to come back. It's time to make my life my own, and I'm so ready for it.

I think about Nina too, maybe because we've started texting again. Nothing earth shattering. It started when she sent me photos from family dinners she now has with my parents and hers. It's weird to see them all together, but their smiles look genuine, which makes me happy. She's also sent me photos of her new house on the ranch, the one she and Brayden moved into.

This one stings a little, especially since I was never allowed to live there, even though I'd expressed interest. It's all history, but I can't help hoping the house burns down. Maybe just a little fire, nothing dangerous or anything.

I send her photos of me living my best life eating all the foods, and she tells me how jealous she is. That makes me happy.

Right now, in this perfect little café moment, I shoot a video of the bustling street in front of me, with the bell like voice of the little girl as the background sound. I move the camera to my gelato, then lift a spoonful to my mouth, closing my eyes with the camera trained on my face. I smile for the camera, then I send it to her, adding the following message:

Jordy: Glad you're not here.

Three little dots appear below my text, followed by a laughing emoji. Three more dots, and then her message pops through.

Nina: Italy looks good on you, cousin.

I smile at the text, almost like she's right here with me, and in this moment, I miss her terribly. Beyond the whole Brayden thing and all the lies and misunderstandings, I miss the times when it was just the two of us at Nanna Dot's house, cuddled under our blanket while we watched *Practical Magic*.

I make the bold move, touching her name and then hold my phone against my ear.

"Ciao, Bella," she says in awful Italian.

"Nanna Dot would cringe at your accent," I say. "*È bello sentire la tua voce,*" I say in perfect Italian, one of the few phrases I remember from those Italian lessons I took years ago.

"I have no idea what you said," Nina laughs.

"I said, it's good to hear your voice." I smile, closing my eyes. "And it is."

"Oh Jordy, it's good to hear yours too. How's Italy today?"

"Delicious," I say, then spoon another bite of melting gelato into my mouth. "I just called to say hello, and tell you I miss you."

"I miss you too," she says. "When are you coming home?"

"In another month," I say. "France is next, and I think I'll come back to the States after that. But you'll have to fly to New York to see me."

"I'll even fly to France, if you want me to," she laughs. I laugh too. It's tempting, but no. This trip is mine, and I'll finish it that way. "I love you, cousin," she says.

I breath in sigh, realizing how far we've come, knowing we still have a ways to go. But I see us getting there.

"I love you too," I tell her.

Chapter Thirty-Eight

Brayden

One year later.

The orchestra has already started up, seated under the largest oak tree on the ranch. Facing them are about a dozen rows of chairs, each filled by our family and friends, and I am in the back, taking it all in before I walk down the covered path that leads to my future.

"Are you ready for this?" Jake asks beside me. He's wearing a cowboy hat, just like I am, just like all the groomsmen are. He's also wearing a grey suit, the most dressed up I've ever seen him look. I give him a thumbs up. I've never been more ready.

I haven't seen Nina yet. She stayed at her parents' house last night, our first night apart since we moved into our modest cabin, which we lovingly refer to as the Winters Suite. I missed her in my bed last night, and I can't wait to unwrap her tonight before we leave for our honeymoon tomorrow.

She insisted on Italy, and plans to eat her way through the country.

Along with her parents, Nina spent the evening with her maid of honor—her cousin. It's funny to think that Jordy will be in my wedding after all, just not in the way we originally planned. She's living in New York now, but she and Nina have talked almost every day since she came back from her travels. I even talk to her sometimes. It's interesting to get to know her as a friend. She's told me on numerous occasions that if I hurt Nina, she'll hunt me down and cut off my balls. I believe her. But I'd die before hurting Nina.

Forrest and River skirt around us, each holding the arm of a beautiful woman—my mom and Nina's mom. My mother pauses next to me and kisses me on the cheek.

"I'm so proud of you, son," she murmurs. "You got the girl, and she's just so special. Thank you for bringing her into our family."

"I love you, Mom," I say, kissing her back before Forrest leads her to her seat in the front row. I can feel the tears stinging my eyes, and I know there's going to be a lot of that today. It's not every day you get to marry your best friend.

Poppy squeezes my hand before it's her turn to walk. "You make my daughter so happy," she tells me with a smile. "Thank you for all the ways you've loved her."

I squeeze her hand back. This past year has been one of healing, and Nina and her mom have made huge strides in their relationship. It's still not perfect, but it's so much better than it was. I'd say it even borders on normal.

River leads Poppy down the path, and then I hear the shift of music. It's my turn. I'm not nervous at all, but my heart is racing, nonetheless. In just a few minutes, I'll stand in front of the love of my life and make her vows I'll keep forever. Soon, she will be Mrs. Antonina Dorotea Winters, and I have never heard a lovelier name.

I walk down the path, taking my time to look at everyone who's supporting us today. There are all the workers from the ranch, from the stable boys to our horse groomer to our housekeeper. I spy a few people who have stayed on the ranch as guests, including the Jones family and their young son. He's playing his Nintendo Switch, but I'll overlook that. Weddings aren't the most exciting things for kids.

Jordy's parents are in the second row, right behind Poppy and Steve. Lil is wearing a fascinator, just like her sister. I realize I owe Nina five dollars thanks to her bet that they would.

I reach the huge oak tree, and there's my dad in his wheelchair. I stand near him and place a hand on his shoulder.

"Thank you for doing this," I say. He pats my hand. He's also in a suit and cowboy hat, but where I'm wearing a striped grey tie to match my suit, he's wearing a bolo tie with a metal medallion in the center. He looks sharp.

"Thank you for asking me," he says. "I love Nina. She's been an incredible part of this family. It's my honor to marry you two."

Thanks to the good old Golden State, anyone can perform a wedding ceremony. However, as soon as I asked my dad to officiate, he quickly went online and became an ordained minister. He's even made us call him Minister Pete the past few weeks, much to our amusement. My dad is a praying man, but he'd drop dead before setting foot in a church. To him, nature is his church, which makes this ceremony on our ranch all the more sacred.

Jordy is next, escorted by my best man Jake. She's radiant, even if I only have eyes for Nina. There's something about her now that wasn't there when we were together. A true happiness. Absolute freedom. She winks at me, then takes her place on the other side of my dad while Jake stands next to me.

Nina's friend Maren follows, escorted by Levi. It's hard to miss the huge rock on her finger, which she has been wearing since Mac proposed last month. She told him she was never getting married but would make an exception for him. Her only stipulation is to wait until her tour is over next year, since she's headlining her own sold-out concerts across the United States.

Claire is after that, holding the arm of River, and man is she glowing. Her small protruding belly might have something to do with that, which looks lovely in the pale pink dress Nina had her bridesmaids wear.

My sister comes next, walking arm in arm with Forrest. With her copper hair and freckles, I'm blown away at how beautiful Hazel looks in her pink bridesmaids dress. For a moment, I imagine what it would be like if Amber were here to see this. How the girls would be together. Seeing Hazel grow up into the woman she's becoming, I get a glimpse of who Amber would have been, but also a reminder that she's forever seven years old and will never see a day like this.

The last of my wedding party to come down the aisle is Nate, and he holds something small in front of him. As he gets closer, tears sting my eyes. He's carrying a photo of Amber and Hazel hugging each other, and when he reaches the front, I can see he's visibly affected by this important task. I forget my place and move forward to hug him, the tears spilling down my cheeks, even as I try my hardest to hold it together. Fuck man. This is hard. But I'm so glad they thought of this.

Nate rests the photo on the chair in the front row right next to my mother, then takes his place at the end of the line.

Finn is next, though I can tell by the look on his face that he believes he's too old for the job of ring bearer. He stomps down the aisle, thrusts the pillow at me, then makes a beeline for his dad instead of standing next to Nate like we'd told him to. The audience loves it.

Last is Ariel, the two-year-old daughter of our housekeeper, Rosa. She's wearing a doll-like white dress and holding an Easter basket full of petals. Last night at the rehearsal dinner, she cried until Rosa finally took her home. To my relief, she toddles down the aisle,

368 — CRISSI LANGWELL

dropping a petal at a time. At this rate, we're going to be here until next week.

"Date prisa mija," Rosa says from her seat. Ariel looks at her mother, and then at everyone watching her, and I watch in slo-mo as her mouth form an O and a silent cry forms into air. But then the shriek follows. Rosa scoops her up, takes handfuls of petals, and tosses them while scurrying down the aisle. She crosses in front of us and keeps going until she reaches a safe distance to soothe her screaming child.

Everything is perfect, especially as the music shifts again.

Nina and I had gone over every romantic song there was out there, but together we could not come up with something for her to walk down the aisle to. I finally asked her to trust me to pick a song, and she let me.

Maren takes her place next to the orchestra as they shift songs, going from something unrecognizable to something I've listened to dozens of times. When I sat and listened to this song again a few weeks ago, I knew it was everything I felt about Nina, and I knew it had to be Maren to bring this song to life.

"Something in your smile, speaks to me," Maren starts, beginning the song by Tony Bennett. I know it's my favorite, not hers, but it just incapsulates so perfectly all the ways I feel about her. I hear an audible sigh from the audience at the sound of Maren's whiskey voice taking on the old crooner's lyrics, the cool, dark tones of her singing. It's this voice that now owns the Top 100. You can't turn on the radio without hearing Maren Huerta belting out the latest rock ballad.

But now she's here, singing at her best friend's wedding. I keep my eyes trained on the back of the audience until finally a vision in white appears a few yards down the way. Nina is all I see, from her hot pink hair to the form fitting ballgown she's wearing, to the pink high-tops that peek out from under her skirt. Her face is beaming, her eyes locked on mine as she stands holding her father's arm, the photographer clicking away. Then she's moving, so slowly I want to run to her, pick her up and get us married. But I wait, savoring the beauty of my bride, not sure how I convinced her to be mine.

When we first came back together, she told me we couldn't be engaged yet. After all, I had just come off an engagement, and needed time and distance from that relationship before asking her to marry me. But I knew she was mine from the day I first saw her. There was no denying how I felt about her.

So I waited a week, then asked her. She said no.

I waited another week, then asked her. Again, she said no.

We did this several more times. Sometimes I waited a week. Sometimes a day. Every time, she let me know it was too early and to be patient.

Patience has never been my virtue, but finally, I listened. I waited months, saying nothing about wanting to marry her, all the while holding that engagement ring in my pocket just in case the moment ever arose. Apparently I waited too long, because one night we were at home having dinner, Cherokee at my feet waiting for food to drop. It was such a normal night, not one thing special about it. But she asked me if I was ever going to ask her to marry me again.

That ring was upstairs in my dresser drawer, but you better believe I ran up those stairs, two at a time, to grab it before flying in front of her, landing on one knee. I'd had this whole speech set up and kept thinking up romantic places I could pop the question. But in that moment, on our concrete floor, the rain pounding on our windowpanes while we ate a spaghetti dinner, I knelt in front of her and simply asked her to marry me.

And she said yes.

That was three months ago, and we threw this whole wedding together in record time.

Now she's standing before me, her father kissing her cheek before releasing her to me. Steve shakes my hand, holding on to it for a moment.

"Welcome to the family, Son," he says. I nod my head, because at this moment, I have no words, and I can't keep my eyes off Nina.

Up close, she's even more beautiful. I'd told her to pick whatever dress she wanted; I'd pay for it. She reminded me that she has her own money and could buy her own dress, and this is the dress she chose. It's covered in lace, tapered to her waistline then billowing out in tulle. Her hair is in soft curls, covered by her veil. In her hands is a beautiful bouquet of daisies, which I recognize as Amber and Hazel's favorite. I'm touched by the sentiment, but it's Nina's face I can't look away from. This is the face I get to see every day for the rest of my life. I'll get to see it change as she ages, and I'll always think she's beautiful. This is the face of the woman I love, and I've never seen anyone so stunning.

"I love you," I whisper.

"I love you," she whispers back. Then she plucks a daisy from her bouquet and hands it to me before taking one for herself. "We have one more thing to do before we get married." She hands Jordy her bouquet, then takes my hand and leads me to that chair up front with my sister's photo. She nods to it, and I understand what she wants. Carefully I place my flower next to the photo, and Nina does the same.

"Thank you for being here," I say to that chair, then look up to the sky. I don't know if she's actually here, but for a moment, I feel her. A breeze blows through the trees, caressing my face, then disappears as quickly as it came.

My father leads the ceremony with meaningful words about love and marriage and what it means to be in a partnership. When I'm not looking at Nina, I look at my dad, who moves his eyes to my mother often as he talks about love.

We get to the vows, and this is the part where I do get nervous. Nina and I chose to write our own vows, and I'm not the best at making public speeches. But I do know how much I love Nina, so I tried not to think of other people as I just wrote down what I felt.

But now that we're here, my nerves are getting the better of me.

"Breathe," she reminds me in a whisper, and I realize how tense my face must look. I smile at her, then take out the piece of paper from my pocket. It's just a formality, though, because I know my vows by heart.

"Ours is an unlikely love story," I begin. "It starts with the most beautiful girl in the world who finds herself in a dangerous situation. Enter a wannabe hero who comes to save the day. Since then, we've been on a crazy journey together. We've made mistakes, burned some bridges, then rebuilt everything with the help of our families. We've grown together, learning what it means to be a daughter, a son, and a cousin, what it means to be part of a family. We've cried a lot. Laughed a lot. Fallen down only to get back up again. But in all this time I've loved you, I've realized I'm not really the hero. You are, as you've saved me every day you've been in my life. It's because of you I've learned what it means to be a true partner, who knows how to give and take, to win and lose, and to understand that true communication means not agreeing with everything you say, but listens before everything else.

"So on this day, when I stand before God and all our friends and family, I make these promises to you.

"Antonina Dorotea Chance, I promise to be slow to speak and quick to listen, to hear you completely when you have something to say.

"I promise to tell you the truth, even if it's hard, and even if we don't agree.

"I promise to build this life *with* you, not just for you, because we are equal partners, and this is our life together.

"I promise to reserve Meredith only for you, since she was your horse all those years ago, and she's still your horse now."

Nina laughs, wiping away tears as they fill her eyes.

"I promise to bring you coffee in bed every time I wake up before you, and I promise to accept coffee in bed anytime you wake up before me."

Everyone laughs this time, as Nina bites her smile.

"I promise you will never need to ask me to do any chores because this is both of our home, and both our responsibility.

"The same goes for our future children. You will never need to ask me to care for them, because they are *ours*.

"I promise to be the best father I can be to our children.

"I promise to be the best husband I can be to you.

"I promise to never forget to romance you, to remind you in little ways how much I love you.

"I promise to continue dating you, even when we're old and grey and our children are making families of their own.

"Most of all, I promise to love you every day, in every way, until the day I die. But even then, I will go on loving you into eternity. You are the woman who called to my soul, and all I could do was answer, and now we get to create this beautiful life together."

Nina frantically dabs at her eyes, looking at me with furrowed brows. "Damnit, Winters, do you know how long it took to do this makeup?" She smiles as she whispers it. I blow at her face, and she jerks back in surprise and gives a confused laugh. "What the hell?"

"It works for babies," I say. "Makes them forget what they were doing. I thought it would help you stop crying."

"You're an ass," she laughs.

She collects herself, then addresses the crowd. "I have no idea how to top that, but I guess this isn't a competition. Here I go."

She brings out her own piece of paper, but this one looks old and weathered, as if she's been holding this for years.

"Many of you know my cousin Jordy. We've been close since we were young, and our favorite movie of all time is *Practical Magic*. There was this one night we watched the movie, and Jordy thought it would be a great idea to come up with our own lists for the man of our dreams."

"Oh my God, the list," Jordy laughs behind her. "I thought you lost it!"

Nina turns around, shooting Jordy a grin. "Not exactly," she says, then she continues.

"The thing is, I had just experienced something that convinced me I would never fall in love. So, just like the lead character, I came up with things that were so specific, there was no way any guy would match up. I'd like to read that list for you now."

Nina unfolds the paper, and I nervously watch her, not sure what to expect.

"He will make me feel safe," she reads, then looks at me. She doesn't lower her gaze back to the list as she shares the rest.

"He will call me Sugar. He'll like country music, and he'll have a good singing voice. He cares for animals." She smiles at me, then cups my face. "He has deep dimples, and he listens with his eyes and his ears. He has ties to San Francisco where my grandmother met my grandfather." She smiles softly, while my jaw drops. Then she moves her hands to my hair, tugging on my curls. "He will have curls I can wind my fingers through." Then she looks at everyone in the crowd. "He'll like Tony Bennett, just like my grandmother did." She looks at me then. "Just like the song you chose for me to walk down the aisle." She smiles and takes my hand. "My love for you started with this list before I even knew you. When I met you, I recognized you immediately, but I couldn't tell you, because it's all so crazy, right? Except, it isn't. Every day I'm with you, I'm introduced to a new kind of magic that can only exist within the safety of loving you. Because my love started with that list, but every day I've learned so many more things to love about you. Still, I can't help feeling like that list is a sign that our love was written in the stars."

I am speechless at this. At the list, at everything she said, at how obvious fate had a hand in our meeting.

"You really wrote that list when you were young?"

"She really did," Jordy pipes in. She looks at Nina. "Oh my God. It was Brayden this whole time."

The realization takes my breath away. It's a sign. I have believed Nina was the one since that very first day. But hearing her list, something she came up with years before she met me? It just solidified the meaning of our union.

"I love you so much," I say.

"I'm not finished," Nina returns with a grin. "I still have vows, you know."

I remain quiet, but I'm bursting with so much love for this woman, I can barely contain myself.

"Brayden James Winters, I don't have a long list of promises to give you. All I can promise is that, in everything I do, from the most mundane of chores, to any arguments we may have, to the good and bad times, the hard and easy times, and every other time in between, I promise to do it all with love for you in my heart. I will remain grateful that you chose me, and I chose you to love in this life, and I will never take that for granted. I promise to stay by your side, to support you and accept your support, and to love you through all your strengths and faults, and accept your love in all of mine. I promise to love you loyally and fiercely—as long as I shall live."

"Sweetheart," I breathe, taking her hands in mine. I don't even bother wiping away the tears. There's more where those came from.

My dad clears his throat, and Nina and I shoot watery grins at each other.

"Before we get to the good part, I thought I'd find an Italian prayer to honor Nina's heritage, and this one fits the bill," my father says. He clears his throat, then continues.

"Brayden and Nina,

"Now you will feel no rain,

"For each of you will be the shelter to the other.

"Now you will feel no cold,

"For each of you will be the warmth to the other.

"Now there is no more loneliness for you,

"Because now you are no longer lonely.

"Now you are two bodies,

"Yet there is only one life set before you.

"Go therefore into your dwelling place,

"To enter into the days of your togetherness.

"That your days may be good and beautiful and long upon this earth."

My father folds the book in front of him, then looks at me.

"It's time," he says softly.

"Thank fuck," I say, and he laughs.

My father runs us through the ring ceremony, and I am there but not there, barely listening as I place the ring on Nina's finger, and she does the same. I look in her eyes the whole time, realizing that this is it. I offer her a small, secret smile, and she returns it. I almost feel like a kid who's getting away with something big, not sure if anyone's going to catch on that I don't deserve this woman. Still, she said yes.

"I do," I answer automatically, my eyes locked on Nina's.

"I do," she says a few moments later, her eyes once again filling with tears.

"Therefore, it is my privilege as a minister and by the authority given to me by the State of California, I now pronounce you husband and wife. Brayden, you may kiss your bride."

I hold Nina's hand in mine and lean my face down to hers. Her lips are soft, parting slightly as we share our first kiss as a married couple. I deepen it, not caring about anyone else in this room, wrapping my arms around her and losing myself. My father clears his throat, and I laugh against Nina's mouth while she does the same. Reluctantly, I break away.

"Ladies and gentlemen," my father booms out, "it is my privilege to introduce to you for the first time, my son and new daughter, Mr. and Mrs. Winters."

The wedding reception is a blur of happy faces, good food, and a carefully curated music playlist Nina put together. The trees are lit up with tiny fairy lights, and numerous heaters keep the place warm so we can remain outdoors. I'm ready for all of it to end, though, and to take my wife to bed. I can tell by her face she's exhausted, and it's possible we might wait until the honeymoon to consummate our marriage. I don't mind. We have a lifetime together.

"Great wedding," a voice says behind me, and I smile. I turn to Jordy, and she's holding a glass of champagne for me. I take it and clink glasses with her before taking a sip. "Nina is positively glowing," she says, turning toward my wife, who is gabbing away with Maren and Claire.

"She is," I say, nodding.

"No. I mean, she's *glowing*." Jordy nods in her direction. "Don't think I haven't noticed she hasn't had a drop of champagne. When it comes to bubbles, Nina is not the type to pass it up. So…" She gives me a pointed look.

"I'm not supposed to say anything to you," I hiss, but I can't help the proud smile that breaks through. We found out just two weeks ago that she was expecting. Apparently she'd missed a pill, and it was just enough of a lapse for that little bugger to squeak through.

Even though it's early, we already have names—Juniper if she's a girl and Ocean if he's a boy. "If you want to know anything, just ask her."

"I'll wait until she tells me," Jordy says, then winks. "Congratulations, Dad. You're going to make an amazing father."

I reach out and squeeze her hand. But there's no sadness on her face. Just a happy smile.

"What about you? What's going on in the Big Apple? Anything exciting?" I glance at the table where she was sitting, where a man with dark hair and eyes only for Jordy sits, waiting for her to return. She glances over at him, offers a little wave. Then turns back to me.

"Several someones," she says, flipping her hand dismissively. I raise an eyebrow, and she laughs. "Come on, I can't settle down now. Besides, Paulo knows this is all for fun. He returns to Italy next week, and I suspect I'll never hear from him again. But while he's here…" She winks. "Besides, I'm too busy building Flourish to have time for romance. Business is great. Every time I show clients the photos from Nina's store, they book me in an instant."

"She practically lives at Polka Dots," I say. "So the fact that you could take her vision and make it something even grander than she expected, it's just amazing. You should see her there. She's in her element, and you should be proud of what you did."

It's actually a huge gift that Jordy even decided to do this. She'd already moved to New York, but she still flew in every week to help Nina design the store of her dreams. Now Polka Dots is one of Sunset Bay's cornerstone clothing boutiques, and it became the start of a lucrative design business for Jordy.

"Well, it's not completely altruistic," she says. "I do own a quarter of that store."

The evening starts winding down, and I cross the patio to find my bride with that kid who can't get off his electronics. But he does for Nina, and the two of them are engrossed in a conversation about who is the best bender in *Avatar: The Last Airbender*.

"I mean, Katara can blood bend. Imagine that kind of power," Nina says.

"Yeah, but air? Aang can freaking fly. Plus, he's the last of his kind. I think that deserves extra points."

"Mrs. Winters, I hate to interrupt this important conversation, but we have a toast to make before we call it a night."

"We're not finished," she says to the boy, who grins at her and waves his arms like he's flying.

"Oh yes you are, or we're never getting to bed tonight."

"Mr. Winters, is someone getting impatient?" Nina grins up at me, and I can't help but kiss her smile.

"When it comes to you and getting you alone, always."

We reach our table, and I tap my knife lightly against the glass. The talking around us quiets to silence, and I wrap my arm around Nina's waist as I face our family and friends.

"My wife and I would like to thank all of you for joining us as we celebrate our love for each other. We'd like to end this night with a special toast to all of you who are here with us. This past year, Nina and I have both come to understand the importance of family, and what it really means to be a part of these connections, whether by blood or by friendship. Tonight, you all are our family, and we are so grateful for each and every one of you." I raise my glass, as does Nina, and everyone does the same.

"Before we drink, I want to add to that," Nina says, "tonight is a celebration of our love. But it's the love of our parents that brought us here, and their parents before that. Tonight I'd like to add a toast that not only celebrates family, but the love that connects all of us to each other."

"Here here!" my father calls out, and we drink.

"I have a toast," Jordy calls out, and again everyone is quiet. Nina and I turn to Jordy, and she holds her glass in front of her.

"In our collective lifetime, I've learned that not everything we deem important is meant for us, and not everything that's meant for us feels important." She looks down at her glass, pausing before continuing. "I've learned that sticking to a set path is not always the right way, but forgiveness always is. *Always*." She smiles at both of us. "We've had a hell of a year, haven't we?" I nod, and I feel Nina nodding too. She wipes at her eyes, and I squeeze her waist. "But in the end, knowing it led me to friendship with both of you, and being able to witness your love story without any kind of resentment…" She waves her hand. "Sorry, I'm not talking about that. But you know what I mean. I'm just so happy for the both of you, and grateful to be in your lives. I love you, Nina and Brayden."

"We love you," Nina says in a shaky voice.

Everyone drinks again, and I look at my wife.

"If we don't make our escape now, we might be stuck here all night."

"I got you," Steve says, my father sitting next to him. Nina's dad turns to the crowd and lets out a whistle.

"Everyone say goodnight, the happy couple is leaving the ranch!" Steve yells.

"He does know we're just going up the road, right?" Nina hisses.

"Shhh, or they might follow us." We both wave as everyone cheers us on. We get into Nina's car, a Lexus ES she bought brand new earlier this year when she traded in the Cadillac. Tied to it are beer cans that I recognize as the ones my crew drinks in our off hours.

"Don't worry, boss, we'll make sure everything is taken care of while you're gone," Jake says, clapping me on the shoulders. The other guys are there, and I grab them all into a group hug. "That's what I'm afraid of," I say, but laugh. With my dad here, there's no way they'll get into too much trouble. Besides, I trust these guys with my life, let alone my ranch.

"Get out of here," Jake says, nodding at Nina who's waiting in the passenger seat.

"I'm trying, but you keep yapping."

I get in the car and close the door. It is blissfully quiet in the car as we drive away, save for the gravel under the wheels. I take Nina's hand, resting it on her thigh.

"How are you feeling?" I ask. It's the first chance we've had to really talk tonight.

"I'm tired, but good." She yawns, leaning her head against the window. Her hand covers her still flat belly. I add my hand to the top of hers, caressing her soft skin, holding our child with her.

"But tired," I say when she yawns again. We reach our home, and there's Cherokee, waiting for us on the porch. He gallops down the steps, meeting us as we exit the car. He follows as we enter the house. I set up the coffee, changing the alarm for a few hours early since we have a flight to catch. Then I guide my tired wife up the stairs and into our room. I can tell she's absolutely drained. I wasn't around Jordy much in her pregnancy, something I regretted often, but couldn't change due to circumstances. This time around, I'm studying everything and doing whatever I can to make Nina more comfortable. I'd read that the first trimester can often feel like the hardest because it takes so much energy to grow a baby.

Tonight, I help Nina undress. I unlace the corset of her dress, with all the millions of layers that are both sexy and tedious at the same time. But sex is the furthest thing from my mind as I finish removing my wife's clothes. I help her to bed, and then when I'm undressed, I turn off the lights and wrap myself around her. She kisses me, then pats my hand.

"I'm sorry," she apologizes, but I shush her.

"Sugar, holding you on our wedding night is both an honor and privilege. Now go to sleep so tomorrow can come quicker."

I feel the rumble of her laugh, but soon she falls into heavy breathing. On the floor, Cherokee is lightly snoring. My hand rests on Nina's belly while my face is nestled in her hair. It's how we've slept almost every night we've lived together, so in a way, nothing has changed. Except, everything has changed. Nina is now my wife and the mother of my child—and I'm the luckiest man in the world.

This is the thought I keep as I drift off to sleep, starting my new life as the husband of Nina Winters.

SAVIOR COMPLEX FAMILY TREE

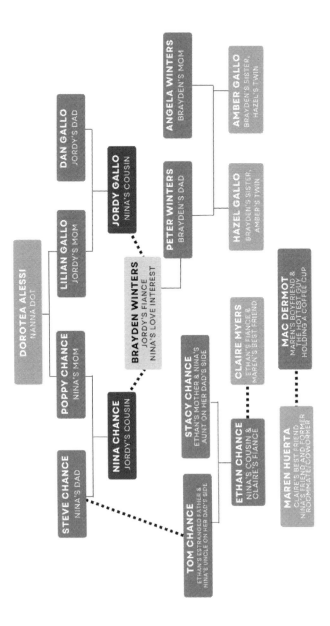

DOROTEA ALESSI
NANNA DOT

STEVE CHANCE
NINA'S DAD

POPPY CHANCE
NINA'S MOM

LILIAN GALLO
JORDY'S MOM

DAN GALLO
JORDY'S DAD

JORDY GALLO
NINA'S COUSIN

NINA CHANCE
JORDY'S COUSIN

BRAYDEN WINTERS
JORDY'S FIANCE
NINA'S LOVE INTEREST

ANGELA WINTERS
BRAYDEN'S MOM

PETER WINTERS
BRAYDEN'S DAD

AMBER GALLO
BRAYDEN'S SISTER,
HAZEL'S TWIN

HAZEL GALLO
BRAYDEN'S SISTER,
AMBER'S TWIN

STACY CHANCE
ETHAN'S MOTHER & NINA'S
AUNT ON HER DAD'S SIDE

TOM CHANCE
ETHAN'S ESTRANGED FATHER &
NINA'S UNCLE ON HER DAD'S SIDE

ETHAN CHANCE
NINA'S COUSIN &
CLAIRE'S FIANCE

CLAIRE MYERS
ETHAN'S FIANCE &
MAREN'S BEST FRIEND

MAREN HUERTA
CLAIRE'S BEST FRIEND,
NINA'S FRIEND AND FORMER
ROOMMATE/COWORKER

MAC DERMOT
MAREN'S BOYFRIEND &
THE HOTTEST GUY
HOLDING A COFFEE CUP

Savior Complex Character List

MATRIARCH
- ◊ Dorotea Alessi (Nina & Jordy's grandmother, Poppy & Lil's mother)

CHANCE FAMILY
- ◊ Nina Chance (Jordy's cousin)
- ◊ Steve & Poppy Chance (Nina's parents, Jordy's maternal aunt & uncle)

GALLO FAMILY
- ◊ Jordy Gallo (Nina's cousin)
- ◊ Dan & Lilian Gallo (Jordy's parents, Nina's maternal aunt & uncle)

WINTERS FAMILY
- ◊ Brayden Winters
- ◊ Peter & Angela Winters (Brayden's parents
- ◊ Hazel & Amber Winters (Brayden's sisters)

FRIENDS
- ◊ Maren Huerta (Nina's former co-worker and roommate, starred in Naked Coffee Guy)
- ◊ Mac Dermot (Maren's boyfriend, starred in Naked Coffee Guy)
- ◊ Claire Myers (Maren's best friend, starred in Masquerade Mistake)
- ◊ Ethan Chance (Nina's cousin & Claire's fiancé, starred in Masquerade Mistake)

Author's Note and Acknowledgements

When I first started writing the Sunset Bay series, Nina was an unknown character to me. I knew Claire and Maren, and their stories were already taking shape in my mind in those early planning days.

Nina came out of nowhere, the bitchy side character who was allergic to her perceived perfection of Claire, and drawn to the rebellious and independent nature of her coworker Maren.

But towards the end of writing the second book in this series, I started getting nudges from this small-time character that she, too, deserved her own story. And as I started writing it, I was surprised by the amount of heart that went into a character I'd originally seen as cold and unfeeling.

Oh man, do I love Nina.

One of the things I wanted to share through Nina was the struggle she experiences with food and body issues, because I share this too—and I believe many women can relate. For Nina, it was her mother who placed that negative voice in her head, tying her worth to the size of her body. But for many women, myself included, it's society and all the messages we download and personalize from all corners. And it's not just body size, but skin color and texture, age, body hair, facial features… It also is about the food we eat, the quantities, and the secret behaviors we might develop because of our feelings of shame and embarrassment.

Through Nina, I wanted to offer a voice of healing in this arena, my version of a hug to every other woman like me who has felt the need to hide because she doesn't fit society's view of beautiful.

Guess what? Nina is beautiful. I am beautiful. And I think you're beautiful, too.

I hope you loved this story. But if you also resonated with Nina's inner journey, I hope you felt my hug to you.

Also, I was sooooo nervous about writing this as a love triangle with actual cheating. I know it's not everyone's favorite trope, and even gives me the ick. But hopefully I pulled this off respectfully, since there are really no bad guys in this novel, just very human characters. If you're reading this far, I hope that means you agree!

There are several people I need to thank for helping Savior Complex become a book. First and foremost is my cherished editor, Sarah Villanueva. I always feel so lucky I get to work with her, and love how she's as invested in my characters as much as I am. Thank you, Sarah, for always making my words sing!

My good friend Helga Breyfogle and my friend and daughter Summer McLerran, who don't mince words as my first readers. Thank you for investing in the success of my books by always telling me the truth. I appreciate you!

To my kids for all your support: Summer McLerran, Lucas Dillon, and Andrew Langwell. I am so proud of the amazing adults you've grown to be!

To Shawn, my favorite and most handsome book boyfriend husband. Thank you for all your love and encouragement as I churn out another book baby. I love you bigger than the sky, even if our cat chooses you over me.

And finally, to YOU. Thank you so much for reading my books and letting me know when they resonate with you. I love writing, but it would mean nothing if you weren't reading my work. Thank you for your support!

By the way, one of the best ways you can help any author you love is to leave reviews on their books. If you loved Savior Complex, I hope you will take a few minutes and share what you loved about it at your favorite book platform page. I appreciate your help in spreading the word about my books!

Crissi Langwell

Books by Crissi Langwell

ROMANCE

Masquerade Mistake ~ Sunset Bay 1

Naked Coffee Guy ~ Sunset Bay 2

Savior Complex ~ Sunset Bay 3

For the Birds

Numbered

Come Here, Cupcake

OTHER BOOKS BY CRISSI LANGWELL

Loving the Wind: The Story of Tiger Lily & Peter Pan

The Road to Hope ~ Hope Series 1

Hope at the Crossroads ~ Hope Series 2

Hope for the Broken Girl ~ Hope Series 3

A Symphony of Cicadas ~ Forever After 1

Forever Thirteen ~ Forever After 2

www.crissilangwell.com

Sign up for Crissi Langwell's romance newsletter:
mailchi.mp/crissilangwell/romancereads

About Crissi Langwell

Crissi Langwell writes stories that come from the heart, from romantic love stories to magical fairytales that happen worlds away. She pulls her inspiration from the ocean and breathes freely among redwoods. She lives in Northern California with her husband and their blended family of three young adult kids, and a spoiled and sassy cat.

Find her at crissilangwell.com.

Made in the USA
Columbia, SC
30 June 2024

f04034d1-b614-42db-baa5-95573355eff1R01